MADAM POTUS

Madam President of the United States

HANNAH STEVENS

To Dark
Hope you enjoy
Hannah
Steve

iUniverse, Inc.
New York   Bloomington

iUniverse books may be ordered through booksellers or by contacting:

iUniverse
1663 Liberty Drive
Bloomington, IN 47403
www.iuniverse.com
1-800-Authors (1-800-288-4677)

ISBN: 978-0-595-51903-3 (sc)
ISBN: 978-0-595-62081-4 (ebook)

Printed in the United States of America

iUniverse rev: 08/24/09

If you ever injected truth into politics you would have no politics.

Will Rogers

Chapter 1

The Road to France

They had driven from Seville that fateful day, Carol at the wheel, in search of a safe haven from the reaches of government agencies that were trying to track them down, capture them and bring them back to the United States. Andrew, Carol's only son, feared he would be jailed for obstructing justice or some other obscure charge and thrown into prison for an indeterminate length of time. Even rescuing his own mother from the nursing home could be construed as interfering with the government and, conceivably, they could lock him up forever. And Carol, the First Lady in exile, knew her husband's administration would not want her to surface again, unrestrained, to tell her story of how she had been taken from her bed in the middle of the night, drugged and held against her will, all because she was divorcing her husband during the election year for his second term.

They had run away to Mexico, only to be discovered in the mountains near Guadalajara, and then escaped again to a small fishing village on the southern coast of Spain, to be pursued once more by agents of the United States government. Carol and Andrew were on the run again and they were determined not to be found.

As they wound northward through small towns and villages in this picturesque country of Spain, Carol wondered if she would ever see her mother, father and friends again. Would she ever pet her beloved dogs, Opal and Buffy, and would she ever again see the sun setting behind the coral of the Mountain Sky ranch in Colorado. Would they ever be able return home?

The narrow, black ribbon of a road punctuated with small towns and villages every fifty miles or so, led them to Toledo, Spain's capitol city until the 16ᵗʰ century and the home of El Greco. They found a small hotel, stayed the night and the following morning arose early to tour the magnificent Moorish buildings, Jewish synagogues and splendid Gothic Renaissance cathedrals of this great city where religions of the world have collided for centuries.

Then across the Castilian plain and on to Madrid, present capitol of Spain, where Christians and Arabs clashed until it was conquered by Alonso VI in the 11ᵗʰ century. They spent three days wandering through baroque and neoclassical structures of the 17ᵗʰ and 18ᵗʰ centuries, the Palacio (Royal Palace) and the Plaza Mayor (main square). Both Carol and Andrew began to have a better understanding of the history of Christianity and Muslim religions and more insight into the current conflict of these cultures. They learned that early Muslim Arab culture, which began on the Arabian Peninsula with Muhammad's first recitations of the Qur'an in the 7th century, was very advanced in mathematics and science. They had developed the concept of zero, discovered how bacteria were spread among humans and developed an operation for cataract surgery. Realizing that in recent times other cultures had surpassed them, as a religion and a culture they were attempting to find their place on this planet.

Leaving Madrid and Moorish history behind them, they continued on, driving a winding road over the Pyrenees Mountains and into France.

Andrew pulled over on the side of the road where there was a junction and asked, "Where to, Mom?"

"What are the choices?"

"North to Paris or south to the French Riviera for a little fun in the sun."

"Paris."

"Are you sure? Seeing some bikini clad ladies would be a sight for me. And they don't even wear tops, I hear."

"I think you have a one track mind, Andy. No, Paris it is and then we can head south and see the rest of the country. Do you realize how long I have waited to see Paris?"

"No, how long?" Andrew asked with repartee.

"Thirty years at least. I want to see the Louvre. I want to go to a French restaurant and experience the wonderful French cuisine I've heard so much about. And I want to sit at a sidewalk cafe, drink French wine and watch the people walk by," Carol said, for the moment forgetting they were fugitives.

"I've been overruled. You shall have all of that and more."

Andrew took out the map and studied it for a while. "It looks like if we drive north to Bordeaux, we can catch a freeway that goes all the way into Paris."

"On to Bordeaux then."

The highway again was only two lanes and there was quite a bit of traffic, especially around the small towns. As they passed through Roquefort where cheese of the same name is made, Carol turned to Andrew. "We have to come back through here again and spend some time."

"We could stop now."

"No, I want to get to Paris and then we can do some exploring."

It was early evening when they reached the city of Bordeaux and started searching for a place to stay the night. They found a visitor's bureau still open and the older woman behind the counter directed them to a small three star hotel off the main avenue. After bringing their bags in, they walked down the stairs to tour the city before the sun set.

"This is the wine country of Europe," Carol said.

"This is the wine country of the world."

"You are right about that. We need to find a good restaurant and sample some of the local wines."

As they turned the corner, they saw a small cafe, with tables in the front and they walked in and looked at the menu. After being seated, Carol ordered a dish of white fish with asparagus and new potatoes simply prepared, with a Sauterne wine from the region and Andrew a two ounce filet of beef smothered in red wine with fried potatoes and a salad.

"This is wonderful," Carol exclaimed as she sipped her wine.

"It is, I agree," Andrew said between bites of steak.

"Are you thinking about your father?"

"Not that much. I'm more concerned about what will happen to us," Andrew said as he fidgeted with his napkin.

"I know. Do you think we'll be able to go back?"

"We have to go back. You have to divorce Dad and get on with your life."

"I know I do. I just have to wait for the right time."

Chapter 2

James's Second Term

Six months into his second term and President James Walters was already in trouble with his numbers plummeting in the polls. But the public was unaware, as it was seldom mentioned on the network news or in any of the newspapers inside the US. Whereas they had used the polls to their advantage during the election campaign, they now ignored them and the news agencies were so flooded with other news items fed to them by the Whitehouse staff and the Pentagon, that people rarely heard the results of these polls. Only those surfing the NET, and getting other sources of news like BBC, the Guardian, the Economist, were even remotely attuned to what was really happening inside the beltway.

And, as often happens in second term presidencies, his cabinet was changing with over half of them leaving; some to work in the private sector as lobbyists and others retiring or going back to state and local government jobs. Josh Dean, Secretary of State, was the first to announce his resignation. Josh had never fully supported the war in Iraq and felt that he had compromised his position in supporting the administration, talking up the Weapons of Mass Destruction and the imminent danger to the United States, when later it was revealed what the inspectors had told them all along and what Saddam had said was true, there were no weapons and Iraq posed no danger to the United States or to its neighbors. Josh could no longer continue the lies and James and Jason, the vice president, wanted him out, although they did not publicly say this. In February James elevated Tom Wiley, his national security advisor in his first term, to secretary of state and replaced him with Wilson Adams, a former CEO of Spectrum, Inc., and an apologist for US defense policies in the Middle East and throughout the world. Susan Rogers, long time friend and James's advisor from Colorado when James was a state senator, was brought in to replace Terry Fleming as chief strategist and Mark Richards replaced Stanley Thompson as James's press secretary. James was circling the wagons and surrounding himself with only those loyalists who would support him and his administration. No dissenters allowed.

The Senate and the House maintained status quo with Dick Hobart continuing as Democratic senate minority leader and Jack Turner the majority leader. The House and Senate actually picked up three and two Patriot party members, respectively. The Patriot's Party, James's party, the right wing spin-off of the Republican Party in the early nineties, was on the move diminishing the number and power of Democrats and moderate Republicans. And far right Republicans often supported the Patriots on most issues, giving them the majority power in both houses of congress.

Other cabinet members resigning, included the Secretary of Interior Nora Lundstrom, the Secretary of Agriculture Harry Capstone and Secretary of Education, Janice Northrop, all claiming to have little or no clout with funding drastically cut for these agencies, now being funneled to the war effort in Iraq and Afghanistan.

Jason Martin remained as James's vice president and he had been summoned, along with Secretary of Defense Charles Robertson, to the Oval Office by James to talk about the on going violence in Iraq.

The two men gathered, sitting in the opulent silk brocaded chairs, eyeing the president who was seated across from them behind his massive desk.

"Who are these insurgents?" James asked.

"We don't really know. Some of them are Saddam's former military troops who are fighting for the return of power to the Baathists. We think there are also al Qaeda members coming into the country to stir up trouble among the Sunnis. With the Shiite gaining majority control in the January election, the other factions are now vying for power."

"How is the construction of the bases coming, Chuck?" James always called him by his nickname.

"We have thirteen fully built to date and one more to go. Should be complete in another month," Charles grinned as he spoke.

"Good, good. As long as we're making progress in that area. And the oil fields. Are they secure?" James turned to Jason.

"We've had a couple of pipelines blown up last month, but we're putting more troops on that detail and with more Iraqi police coming on line to work and patrol the cities, we can concentrate our troops on protecting the oil and the construction of the bases."

"We need to get some kind of infrastructure for the Iraqis. I'm hearing that they still don't have twenty-four-hour electricity, and the sewage plants aren't fully operational yet. Don't you think they would see their lives improving if these services were in place?" James interjected.

"True. Yes, that is probably true. But we just don't have the manpower to make it happen. Our priority is to get the oil fields operational and to do that we need our troops protecting the contractors seven by twenty-four. And that's the bottom line," Charles said.

"I want a daily briefing on this, Chuck. Let's meet again tomorrow and see where we're at. That's all for now."

Charles nodded his head in agreement and headed for the door, while James motioned for Jason to stay behind.

"Have any word on Carol?" James asked.

"No. We think they, Carol and your son, are headed for France. But we haven't tracked them down yet. We will. We always find the perpetrator."

"You're making them out to be criminals."

"They are criminals. They've resisted arrest twice now and they are fugitives from the law."

"I'm really unhappy with the way this has been treated. We didn't need to kidnap my wife. I think we should just let them go at this point. They are in no position to do us any harm. We won the election so let's just stop pursuing them."

"No, James, we can't afford to take a chance. If Carol and your son came back to the States and went public with their side of the story, it would be all over for us. You would most likely be impeached and the same could happen to me. No, we'll continue to hunt them. That way they'll think we're still hot on their trail and hopefully stay in hiding until you're out of office. We don't care what happens after that."

"Look, Jason, this is so wrong. Carol and Andrew are my family and I will not tolerate any mistreatment of them. I'll go public if you do."

"I don't think so. We're all in this together and if you make any moves to squeal, we'll have to take other measures."

"Just what do you mean by that?" James eyes widened.

"I think you know what I mean. We have too much invested in this; there is too much money on the table. Just get those thoughts out of your mind. How about if we find you a lady friend to take your mind off this. I know some really sharp women and they would be discreet."

"So I've heard. No, forget it. I have no time for such nonsense. I just want to know that my family won't be mistreated."

"You seem to forget that Carol is divorcing you. She meant to harm you and now you want to protect the enemy?"

"I don't think Carol was aware of the ramifications of her actions. And my son is just protecting her."

"We'll go easy on them but we're still going to monitor their movements."

And Jason left James to wonder how much he could trust Jason or anyone else for that matter. His wife had left him and now he was alone in this battle for power. Who could he trust? Who were his friends?

Chapter 3

On to Paris

Carol could tell by the road signs and the traffic on the freeway that they were nearing Paris. Fields of hay and grass dotted with sheep were giving way to apartment buildings and small homes and cottages with backyard gardens. How different this was from where they had traveled in Mexico and Spain where the surrounding villages were more rural in nature. Even Paris in the suburbs was more cosmopolitan. She saw a sign pointing east to Chartres. "Andy, we have to go there." And another sign saying Versailles, 10 KLM. "Versailles, I've always wanted to see that," Carol exclaimed.

"Looks like we'll be in Paris for awhile." Andrew smiled as he maneuvered through the small trucks and Renaults rushing all in one direction, to Paris.

It was late morning on this spring day in March. They had spent the night in Tours as they had gotten a late start from Bordeaux the day before, lingering over a leisurely breakfast. Early signs of spring were everywhere, with trees sporting new green leaves and the ornamentals and fruit trees wearing white, pink and peach petals, showing the world that life begins anew this time every year.

"I think we should try to find a hotel as close to the center of town as possible. That way we can take the train anywhere in the city."

"I've heard that the left bank is older and that's where the artists and intellectuals hang out. I'd like to find a small hotel somewhere in that area."

"That would work. And then we'll see what we can walk to and where we will need public transportation." Carol was so excited to finally see her City of Lights.

Andrew slowed to read and try to make sense of the road signs. "You know, I'll have to find a job if we're here for very long. I transferred the rest of my trust money before we left, but that won't last forever."

"Maybe I could find something too," Carol said looking at Andrew, shading her face with her hand as the morning sun flooded into her window. What a handsome young man he has grown to be she thought. Tall, with dark curly hair, he resembled his father with strong, high cheek bones and a prominent nose. And, because he worked out and participated in outdoor sports, skiing, hiking and running, he had the muscular body of an athlete. But Carol was prejudiced; Andrew was her little boy grown into a man now.

"I don't think you should. The less public exposure you have the better. They don't know me as well but they might recognize you."

"We look so different now. My hair is almost totally gray and I'm wearing it long, not in the short bobbed haircut that I had before. And you with the beard and a pony tail no less. How could they recognize us?"

"You'd be surprised."

Andrew somehow followed the signs into central Paris and they came to the West Bank of the River Seine. He found a parking place along the river and pulled out the map and the hotel guide they had purchased in Bordeaux. There were artists painting and vendors selling souvenirs and jewelry along the path by the river. Spring was in evidence here also, with couples strolling along side the river, kissing and caressing one another. It made him feel very alone.

"I've picked out a couple of small hotels and I'm going to call on my cell phone to see if they have a vacancy." Andrew got out his French for Dummies book so that he could try to converse in the native language. He punched in the first number and asked if they had a room and was told no. The second call brought the same results. Carol was becoming concerned. Then on the third call he was told that they had one double room with single beds and if they came right over they could rent it by the week. After getting directions, they got back into the car and tried to find the Hotel de Nesle at 7 r. du Nesle. And confusing it was. The streets of Paris run in every which way like a maze in a cornfield. There are circles going nowhere and streets dead-ending and running into other streets. They got lost two more times and had to call for directions again and again before finally driving up a little narrow street and seeing the sign hanging above the door. Carol heaved a sigh of relief as they got out of the car and approached the desk. Andrew signed in for the room as John and Helen Michaels to hopefully throw any agents that might be looking for them, off the trail.

The desk manager, a young woman in her late twenties, with dark hair pulled tightly in a ponytail, escorted them up the stairs to the fourth floor to their room. Carol inspected the accommodations. The two beds with pink chenille bedspreads, took up most of the bedroom with white washed walls and a picture of the Eiffel Tower on one wall. There was no closet, but a provincial looking armoire sat on the wall away from the window. Of course, no telephone and no TV, but there was a small bathroom with a postage stamp sized shower, no less. Yes, this would do and for only eighty euro a night or 560 a week, including a continental breakfast. More than adequate.

Carol walked over to the window and pulled open the shutters. It was not a view of the Eiffel Tower, nor was it a view of Montmartre, but merely an every day Paris street scene and Carol was delighted. She gazed down on a small cafe on the corner where people were already drinking wine and smoking cigarettes. She could see a market several doors down with bins of fresh vegetables in front and a boulangerie next to the market. An old man in an oversized jacket and baggy pants was selling multihued bouquets de fluers from his flower cart and he was handing out fresh daisies to the children. And there were dogs everywhere; running with children, being led on leashes and one was answering the call of nature right in the middle of the sidewalk as people stepped over it, not seeming to mind. This is not New York, she thought.

Andrew came back into the room lugging their bags.

"I should be helping you."

"Always the guilty mom, never doing enough. No, you just enjoy. I have the muscles anyway."

Andrew opened up the bags and started hanging clothes in the armoire and Carol continued to gaze out the window.

"Do you think they're still looking for us?" Carol asked.

Andrew stopped what he was doing and thought for a moment. "Yes, as long as Dad's in office, they'll be looking for us. We can never let down our guard."

"But the election is over and he won, even if it was by the smallest margin ever."

"Doesn't matter. If we ever told the story of how you were kidnapped and held against your will, the public would be outraged."

"I don't think so," said Carol looking at her son. "It seems that the American people are not easily outraged these days. The administration has lied to them about weapons in Iraq and then told them they were bringing democracy to the Iraqis and they bought it, no problem. The American people are lied to every day by this government and they do nothing. I just bet that if we surfaced back in the States, they would find a way to spin it and the people would again believe them."

"You could be right. But the administration wouldn't want the trouble we could make. And Dad could be impeached. There are already enough reasons to impeach him and one more might be more than he could take."

Carol sat on the bed closest to the window. "Andy, do you think your dad had a hand in my kidnapping?"

"Mom, I don't know. Don't ask me that. I don't want to think about it."

Andrew walked over to the window, standing behind his mother and looked over the roof tops

"Well, we're in Paris and I'm not going to worry every minute that these goons will find us again," said Carol. "I'm going to enjoy."

"That's a good way of looking at it. But keep your eyes and ears open and watch everyone around you like a deer being hunted in the forest."

Carol thought that was good advice and she would take it. Even though she was in the city she had dreamed of seeing since childhood, and yet she knew this was no vacation, this was serious business and at some point in time she would have to face the reality of it. But for now, wonderful sights were waiting for her.

"Where to now, Madam?" Andrew asked Carol, breaking her reverie, as they finished unpacking. They had the afternoon to explore.

"Let's find out when we can get into the Louvre. And then I think we should pack a lunch and head for the Arc de Triomphe and a stroll down the Champs Elysees and have a picnic at the Tuilleries. And then tomorrow we shall see Notre-Dame in the morning and the Eiffel Tower in the Afternoon."

"Woa, wait a minute. There's no hurry. We can take our time. We have all the time in the world."

"Oh, Andy, I'm just so excited to be here and see all of the places and things that I have been reading about for years."

Andrew and Carol walked down the narrow staircase to the desk on the first floor and asked about tickets to the Louvre. The desk clerk, this time a balding man in his late forties named Arnaud, who also owned the small hotel, was very helpful. He mentioned that the young woman who had checked them in was his daughter, Janelle. This was a family owned hotel and Carol liked that. He gave them more maps of the city, schedules and maps of the Paris Metro, told them where they could rent bicycles and where the best restaurants were for the budget minded.

Armed with all of this information, Carol and Andrew walked across the street to the market and bought fromage, fresh fruit and a bottle of blanc de blanc wine and then on to the boulangerie for a fresh baguette of bread. The entrance to the Metro was only a block away and they easily found the route to the Arc de Triomphe. When they reached the grand monument, Carol was awestruck.

"You know the Arc was planned by Napoleon to celebrate his military successes," Carol said as she turned to Andrew to see his reaction.

"Yes, I took a course in French history at CU. He considered himself the heir to the Roman Emperors. He was actually building it to honor his new bride, Marie-Louise. But it wasn't even finished until twenty years after his death."

"Andy, I'm impressed with your knowledge of French history."

Andrew blushed as they climbed the spiral staircase to the top of the monument, stopping in the museum before going out to view the five avenues spinning out from the arc like spokes on a wheel. Carol could see another Paris in the distance, a modern Paris with office buildings piercing the skyline. When Andrew was finally able to pull her away, they descended to the ground level and Carol glanced up at the monument once more and then looked at the street filled with cars circling in every direction.

"How are we ever going to get across this street," Carol gasped.

"Here, take my hand and when I see an opening in the traffic we'll run for it," said Andrew. Carol was breathless as they dodged through the oncoming cars and motor bikes, miraculously reaching the other side of the street unharmed, they joined the throngs of people for the tradition of French flaneur or boulevard strolling. And after the picnic lunch in the gardens of the Tuilleries, which turned out also to be dinner, they headed back to the hotel thoroughly exhausted. Sleep came easy that first night in Paris, even though the sounds of the street drifted through the open window from below.

It seemed like only a couple of hours before the sun shone through the window. Carol stretched and yawned and recalled some of her strange dream she had while sleeping. In her dream she was walking along the River Seine and a young artist with dark black curly hair and a bushy mustache came up beside her, put his arms around her and started kissing her. At first she thought it was very pleasant and she kissed him back, but then she remembered she was still married and she turned and saw James running towards them with a gun, pointing it at them. Carol grabbed the artist's hand and they ran together with James in pursuit, who was then joined by four men in black suits carrying assault weapons. She woke up, sweating, got up to get a glass of water and then went back to sleep.

Andrew was in the bathroom trimming his beard. "Mom, I'm going to take some time today to see if I can find work. I thought I'd go to the Sorbonne. Students are always looking for part time jobs."

"In that case I think I shall find a little cafe and drink coffee, read the paper and watch the people."

Andrew walked the six blocks from his hotel to the Sorbonne and into one of the historic buildings looking for the Office of Administration. When he finally found it, he saw a bulletin board with job listings all in French. He fished his French primmer from his backpack and tried to make sense of the listings. Just as he was deciphering some of the words on the board, a young woman walked over to him.

"Are you looking for a job?" she asked in perfect English, albeit with a slight accent.

"Well, yes. I am." Andrew stammered.

"Maybe I can help you."

"Who are you?" Andrew was skeptical and didn't like talking to strangers even if they were young and beautiful.

"My name is Simone and my father is a professor at the University. I saw you looking at the board here and I thought maybe I could help. And you are...."

Sounded reasonable enough. They were on the campus and why would she lie to him? He decided he had to start trusting people and besides, maybe she would be his friend. Or even more than his friend. His mind was racing. "Oh, ah, my name is John. John Michaels," Andrew stammered, using his pseudo name.

"My dad knows some lawyers in the city and they sometimes have courier jobs, running divorce papers and summons around town. Do you have a car?"

"I do. And that sounds like pretty good work. What does it pay?"

"Thirty euro an hour."

"That's good money, but I don't know Paris."

"I can help you."

"Where do I sign up?"

"Let's go to the Petit Cafe down the street and I will fill you in," Simone said.

They walked together out of the office and down the street to the cafe. As they reached their table, Andrew pulled out a chair for Simone and motioned her to sit. He sat across from her. He looked at her extraordinary deep blue eyes underneath dark brown eyebrows that nearly met in the center of her forehead. Her olive skin was flawless and her lips were thin but expressive. She wore very little makeup, only a hint of lip rouge. He found himself staring at her as she pulled back her long dark brown hair from her face with graceful, slender hands. They ordered two espressos.

"Are you Parisian?" Andrew asked. "You speak the queen's English.

"Yes, I have lived here all my life, but my mother is American."

"And you are a student?"

15

"I was until this spring. I graduated and now I am looking for work too."

"What kind of work are you looking for?"

"Accounting." Simone took a pack of cigarettes from her purse and offered one to Andrew and when he declined she lit one for herself and inhaled deeply. "My major was economics and accounting. I hope to find something soon, but it is difficult for people like me in Paris these days. And my dad wants me to fly from the nest as you say in America."

"Why is it so difficult?" Andrew asked.

"People with my background. You wouldn't understand," Simone said dismissively.

"Why do you want to help me?" Andrew asked, still somewhat skeptical. "I thought the French hated Americans."

The waiter brought their coffee and asked if they wanted anything else.

"We don't hate Americans. We hate your American president. Although we were unhappy when your people were boycotting French products last year. Our wine industry really took a hit. "

Andrew tried his best not to react, but he was sure she saw him grimace when she said that.

"Here is the address of the agency that will give you work. It's not far from here."

"Will I see you again?"

"Yes, if you want to," Simone said without hesitation.

"How about dinner tonight?"

"No, I have plans."

Andrew was disappointed but he thought Simone probably had a date for tonight and she must have many men interested in her. She was very beautiful and exotic.

They arose to leave and Simone was walking away from Andrew. "Hey, where can I call you? What's your last name?" he shouted after her.

Simone turned to walk back to him. Andrew noticed the nipples of her small breasts under her top. She pulled a tablet out of her handbag and wrote down her name and phone number. "I would go over to the

Courier office today. They might have something for you," she said as she walked off and disappeared into the crowd.

"I will," Andrew said as he gazed after her.

Chapter 4

The Town Hall Meeting

James had an aggressive agenda for the second term of his presidency and one of the items was to rescue, as he put it, Social Security. It had been known for some time now with more baby boomers retiring, with fewer workers paying into the program that the current federal pension plan, put in place by Franklin Delano Roosevelt during the great depression of the thirties, would, at some time in the future become insolvent. FDR could not have predicted this would happen, and that people would be living longer into their seventies and eighties. Just when that time would be was up for debate. Some were saying that the trust fund, managed by the Department of Treasury, would be paying out more benefits than it was taking in by 2012 and it hadn't helped that more than one administration had raided the funds periodically. But in reality, measures were put in place by Alan Greenspan and Ronald Reagan that would keep the fund going way beyond into 2042 or 2052. And there could be some truth in that another contributing factor was that the quality of jobs in the United States was rapidly declining with high paying manufacturing, technical and engineering jobs going off shore. Americans were being laid off at a high rate and had to compensate by working in the service sectors, nursing and health care.

James administration had devised a plan that they thought would be appealing to people who like to "take responsibility" for their own money. The new plan called for the creation of private investment accounts, aimed primarily at younger workers, in addition to the current government trust account, and these accounts would be invested in stock market mutual funds.

There were some who thought this could be a viable plan and workers would be able to realize a larger pension from the market that in good years can appreciate by ten percent or more, but many more realized that the market is not always on the up tick and in down years, people could lose everything and then the elderly would be on the street so to speak. Social Security is the sacred cow of social programs for Americans and they were concerned that this new system would further undermine the program. So, James and Jason decided to take the show on the road and travel to sixty cities in sixty days and present Private Account Pensions, or PAP, to the people.

Jason was the instigator of this program and he particularly wanted to sell this to the younger people of the country, telling them that those who were twenty years old today could pay into Social Security all of their working life, but would likely never collect a dime as things stood today. "When we hold these meetings across the country, we will reiterate our case for private accounts over and over again and drive this home to the people. And before you know, it will be accepted. And I see a need to have a very controlled climate for these town hall meetings," Jason continued in the closed door meeting with James and Susan Rogers, James's chief strategist. "I don't want to have to worry about dissenters talking against our plan. That would defeat the whole purpose of selling this program."

"But that's the purpose of a town hall meeting, to have a discussion," James said. "And not only that, but you are preaching to the choir. What good does that do?"

"No, the Vice President is right. We'll screen everybody and make sure they are supportive of our plan. We'll have them sign a pledge. And then let the media know our itinerary so they can give us national coverage on network news. Yes, James, we're preaching to the choir, but the choir will cheer us on and the press will spread the word to everyone else. And those who are watching the news will never know," Susan said.

"I don't like the idea. But I can see where it will be safer. I won't have to worry about somebody shooting me," James said. "Where do you think we should start?"

"Cincinnati will be the first city and then work our way down into the Carolinas, Georgia and Florida. I'll get my people working on this right way," said Susan.

"And another point here, we can use this opportunity to raise more funds for the Patriots and mid term elections. A super campaign trip paid for by US taxpayers again," said Jason. "We can't lose on this one."

The plans were made, press releases sent out to all of the news agencies and James boarded Airforce One with his entourage, including Susan and his new press secretary, Mark Richards. He also invited Warren Kennedy, secretary of the treasury, along to help explain to the people just exactly how Social Security worked now and how it would work when PAP was in place. They arrived on a Monday morning the first week of March and were whisked from the airport directly to the Cincinnati Convention Center on Elm Street. James looked out the window of his black armored Lincoln limousine and saw empty streets. There were no cars to be seen, with the exception of patrol cars and motorcycle cops, and there were no people lining the sides of the street to cheer him on. They must not know I'm coming, he thought. If they knew they would surely be here.

People of all ages, 150 of them, some with children, had been screened and had signed pledges saying they were Patriots and that they supported the president's PAP for Social Security. They were now being ushered into the main auditorium at the Convention Center. The majority of them were white, affluent, upper middle class. These were people who were likely knowledgeable in how to invest in the stock market. Not everyone is and in fact many of these people would probably never need to depend on Social Security for their retirement. They had trust funds, pensions, money from bonuses and would have enough money from earnings set aside for a comfortable life. Some in off shore accounts away from the reaches of the IRS.

The presidential motorcade drove up to the convention center and stopped in the passenger unloading area. The Secret Service got out of their cars first and walked to the president's car, opening the door for him. James stepped out and immediately three Secret Service men surrounded him as they walked in unison into the convention center and into the auditorium. Again there were no people outside the center. The area had been swept with the exception of one man across the street who carried a huge sign saying NO BLOOD FOR OIL, DEFENSE COMPANIES WIN and yelling at James saying "Stop the illegal wars". Within seconds five policemen were on top of the man and they cuffed him and dragged him off. James was too far away to hear or see the fracas.

James entered the auditorium to a standing ovation. The crowd waved banners that said JAMES WALTERS, THE PRESIDENT FOR THE PEOPLE. There was music and the cameras were rolling, scanning the audience catching the exuberant smiles on all of the faces. From all appearances, this was a very popular president.

James strolled to the center of the stage, smiled and raised his arms above his head in a victory salute. It seemed much like a mini Patriots convention.

"Thank you for coming," James said. "I know how busy you all are with your work and your families."

He paused and the audience settled into their seats to hear to him speak. A baby in the back of the room cried out and the mother hushed him and popped a pacifier into his mouth and the auditorium was again quiet.

"And that is what I want to talk to you about today. Your family's security for the future. After working hard for all of your lives you are entitled to a decent retirement. With Social Security in the state that it's in, it will be bankrupt in twenty years. If you were born after 1950, there will be nothing for you."

Boos came from every corner of the large room.

"But if we put our Private Account Pension plan in place, you will have more money than you would have with the Social Security pension fund now in place."

The crowd cheered and the cameras caught the excitement.

"Investing in the market will bring a better return than our current system,"

James continued.

Then, unexpectedly a man started running down the middle aisle from the back of the room shouting, "Stop the illegal war" and "No blood for oil". And this time James heard him loud and clear and he frowned as two guards ran after the man and caught him. They wrestled with him, handcuffed him and led him out of the auditorium screaming, "Stop killing our soldiers for oil", "No bid defense contracts are illegal".

The audience was visibly shaken but James went on with his speech as if nothing had happened.

"And you will own your accounts. You can even pass them on to your heirs. With the present system, you lose the money when you die."

The audience clapped again seeming to quickly forget the disturbance.

"And isn't that what America is all about. Ownership. Not the government dictating to you how you invest your money. You will have control."

After another twenty minutes of speaking, attempting to drive home his points he opened the meeting to questions from the audience. Some were asked to stand and give testimonials for investing in the market. One person stood and asked, "What if the market goes bust? Where will that leave me?"

James paced and then answered carefully, "The market is strong. You are investing in America and America is strong. We have the largest GDP in the world and the chances for it to fail are minimal to say the least."

And when the same man stood up to argue against James, the microphone was taken away from him and given to another person.

The PAP Town Hall meeting lasted for one hour and thirty minutes and at the end of the meeting James left the hall and was escorted back to his limousine, again surrounded by Secret Service, and back to Airforce One and on to the next city.

When they got into the air, James called all of his people into his executive suite.

"Well, how do you think we did?" he asked.

"I think it went well."

"But who in the hell let those dissenters in?" Jason exclaimed.

"We screened everyone very carefully. They signed pledges."

"You were not thorough enough. No more of this. If we have to give a lie detector test to everyone before they are allowed in," said Jason.

"It was embarrassing and it looked bad for the news," said James who was by now accustomed to the vetted town hall meetings.

"We'll take care of it," Jason said.

"The guy could have had a gun."

"Don't worry. That won't happen again," Jason said.

And Airforce One skimmed the clouds, heading south for another meeting in Charleston later that same day.

Chapter 5

Carol Loves Paris

Andrew bounded up the narrow staircase to their room on the fourth floor. Out of breath, he turned the key in the knob and opened the door. Carol was sitting in a wicker chair by the window gazing at the happenings in the street below. She turned to Andrew and smiled. "How was your day?" she asked.

"Wonderful."

"You met a girl."

"How did you know?" And when Carol only raised her eyebrows and didn't answer, Andrew turned to his mother and said with a smile, "You are so perceptive."

"You have that look."

"I met a woman and I found part time work. I found this agency that hires couriers to deliver documents and packages around the city. It pays thirty euro an hour and I can pick and choose when I want to work. It's perfect."

"And the woman?" Carol was skeptical.

"Her name is Simone. She has lived in Paris her whole life and her father is a professor at the Sorbonne. That's where I met her. I was looking at the job listings on a bulletin board outside the administrator's office and she came over to ask if I was looking for work and one thing led to another. We had coffee and she told me about the courier jobs."

"But how are you going to deliver packages in Paris when you barely know the city?" Carol asked thinking that Andrew seemed like a little boy again who needed protection.

"Simone said she would help me."

"Oh, I'm sure she will."

Andrew shook his head at her. "So I went over to the office. It's near the university. And they signed me up and I have my first job this afternoon. And when I get back we'll go to dinner. Pick a restaurant."

"Andy, you are usually the careful one. I think you should check this out more carefully and check her out. What is her last name?"

"I have her phone number. She only gave me her first name. But I will. You are right about that. Kind of got caught up in the moment."

"Kind of got caught up by a pretty lady, I suspect."

Andrew looked a little sheepish. He knew his mother was right. He did need to check her out.

"Why aren't you taking Simone out to dinner tonight?"

"She has a date."

"Oh, so I'm second best now," Carol laughed. "What time is your job?"

"I have to leave right now. It's at three o'clock. I should be back by six. Put on your best dress. I am taking you out in style."

"That'll be easy, I only have one dress."

"Well, we'll have to do some shopping in Paris then." Andrew was silent for a few moments. "How was your day?" asked Andrew.

"It was great. I went to the cafe on the corner and had coffee and a brioche and watched the people for a while. Then I walked down to the river and talked with an artist and he did a portrait of me in pastels. Look over there on the dresser. It looks quite like me."

Andrew looked at the impressionistic likeness of his mother. "It's beautiful, Mom. We'll have to frame it. Tomorrow we'll play the tourist some more. We have tickets for the Louvre for Thursday and that'll take all I day I would imagine. And we may even want to go back."

"I agree with that. One day is not going to do it."

"I've got to go now. Be back soon, so your job is to find a restaurant."

It would be at least three hours before Andrew returned, and so Carol thought she would go for another walk and maybe visit some shops. But first she thought she had better make a reservation for dinner. She looked in their guidebook. For some reason it seemed few offered French cuisine. She saw Mediterranean, Indian, Arabian and finally found one that sounded good to her.

She called. "*Allo, Chez Janou,*" a deep male voice answered.

"*Parlez vous anglais?*" She asked.

"*Non.*"

She took that to be no and quickly reached for her French Phrasebook.

"*Reservation, s'il vous plait?*"

"*Quelle heure?*"

"Eight o'clock for *dos*, I mean *deux* ," Carol said, using Spanish and then realizing.

"*Bien entendu,*" the answer came back.

"*Merci,*" said Carol. I guess that means yes she thought.

She then grabbed her hat and purse, locked the room and walked down the stairs. She greeted Jannelle at the front desk, "*Bonjour*" and Jannelle greeted her back, "*Bonjour, Madam*".

I think I am going to like France, she thought, and I love Paris. They always say in the United States that the French are not friendly, but she now knew that was not true. She walked out onto the street and turned towards the river, intending to cross and find some shops. She looked behind her and saw a strange man and it looked like he was following her. But two blocks later he had turned down a side street and was gone. She then wondered, would she and Andrew have to live like this forever?

Three hours later, with very sore feet, Carol trudged up the stairs to their room and found Andrew asleep on his bed. She tried to be very quiet but he woke up and yawned and stretched.

"I'm sorry to wake you. How was your first courier job?"

"It was okay. I had some trouble finding the address. It was way over in the west side of town. One thing I didn't take into account was the cost of gas. It's expensive in France. But they paid me and they said they would have more work for me."

"That's good. I made the reservation for dinner at eight o'clock so you can rest awhile longer if you choose."

And he did close his eyes for another half hour, while Carol put on her one dress, her green two-piece linen Andrew had bought for her before rescuing her from the nursing home. She had bought other clothes when they were in Huelva, Spain, but had left most of those behind when they were hastily escaping from the agents.

Andrew then got up and showered and dressed and they caught a cab to the restaurant.

The maitre de seated them at a small table for two near a water fountain as soon as they arrived. There were large murals of Parisian scenes on the walls, the Eiffel Tower, Notre Dame and the room was very dark with most of the light given off by a flickering candle in the center of the white linen covered table.

A male waiter approached, dressed in black pants and a white shirt, handed Carol and Andrew menus and said something in French. Carol looked at the French words on the menu and asked if he spoke English and he said he did a little. They ordered a red wine from the Bordeaux region. Andrew ordered steak smothered in mushrooms while Carol ordered a fish dish with a delectable butter and wine sauce. The waiter brought the wine and poured a glass for each of them.

"This is a very fine wine," Carol said after a time.

"It is special." And then Andrew looked at his mother and asked, "Are you glad you did what you did?"

"What do you mean?"

"You know. That you started the divorce proceedings with Dad."

"Yes and no."

"What's that supposed to mean?"

"Well, I had to do it. Your father and I were strangers. I didn't know who he was anymore and I could no longer support the policies he was proposing and most importantly the Iraq war. I thought it was wrong then and I still do today. And, as it turns out I was right. Iraq wasn't a threat to our country, they had no weapons. Iraq had been weakened from the sanctions imposed on them by the UN for the past twelve years."

"And no because?"

"I wasn't prepared for the way the administration would deal with this. If you had told me they would take me away in the middle of the night and hold me against my will, I would have thought you were out of your mind. I'm still having nightmares. Sometimes I wake up in the middle of the night, sweating all over, thinking they are coming for me again."

"I didn't think they would go that far either."

"And I'm sorry I've disrupted your life so much. I'm sorry for Allison. I hope I can make it up to you."

"Yeah, I know. When they killed Allison, and I think they did, I lost all faith in our government. They didn't have to do that. She wasn't a threat to anyone. And I loved her so much."

"But this just shows how devious these people are. They're extreme. And that's why we must do what we are doing."

"And what is that? Running away? Is that going to solve this mess?" Andrew asked in anger.

"So, are you sorry you rescued me?" Carol said to him softly.

"No. Not one bit. I couldn't leave you there knowing they might harm you. But I have very mixed feelings for where we are now."

The waiter brought out a first course of cold cucumber soup with a fresh loaf of herb bread and a cheese spread.

"I can understand that. It has to be frustrating to feel as though this is never going to end and we might have to be on the run forever... ," Carol said as she was sipping her soup. "But I think if we lay low for a time, things will change and we'll be able to go back and pick up our lives again. And there is part of me that doesn't want to go back. I love it here. I can't wait to see the rest of France," Carol continued.

"Just what do you think is going to change?" asked Andrew.

"I'm hearing that James, your father's ratings are falling fast. Just as I thought, as the body bags come home, the support for the war dwindles. You know, they could even impeach him."

"With the House, the Senate and the White House controlled by the Patriots? Won't happen."

"Mid terms are coming up. If these people in the House and Senate think they might lose their job, they might stand up to James."

"Well, that's true. I guess we'll have to wait and see."

"That's what I am saying. Let's enjoy the time we have together and our time in this wonderful country."

Andrew raised his wine glass. "Here's to France and all of the beautiful French women."

Carol laughed. "Well, here's to France and the wonderful French men then. Although I haven't met any as yet."

"Mom, you are a married woman."

"Yes, don't I know that? But an estranged married woman."

They both laughed together. And after enjoying the meal they decided to walk back to the hotel and it was late by the time they got there. When they were back in their room they changed into nightclothes and crawled into the small beds.

"We are going to be okay, honey," said Carol.

"I know, I know…..."

And maybe it was that last thought or maybe the wine, but they slept well that night.

*   *   *

The morning light filtered through the window shutters. Andrew threw aside his cover and got out of bed while Carol turned away trying to get a few more minutes of sleep.

"What is the plan for today?" Andrew asked.

"You're up early. Got a date or something?" Carol asked sleepily.

"I have to check in with the agency and then I am free for the day."

"I asked if you had a date."

"Not yet, but I hope to by the end of the day."

"Andrew, remember what I said." Carol's voice had an edge to it.

"Yes, I will check her out, Mother. I don't know why you're suddenly so suspicious. She's a Parisian and she's a student. Well, a former student. And her father's a professor."

"I know how you can be blinded by women," Carol said. "You've been drilling it into me about how we have to be careful……"

Andrew didn't answer but pulled on his pants and walked into the bathroom. When he came out he asked again, "Where are we going today?"

"Well, I thought we would see the Catacombs."

"I'm not up for that. It's too gruesome. All those skulls and bones. How about the Eiffel Tower. I think that would be really fun. We could go to the top of the tower and get some great pictures of Paris and then after that take another stroll down the Champs Eylsee."

"That sounds good. Then let's go and see Notre Dame," said Carol.

And Andrew agreed. He made a quick call to his agency and was told there would be no work for him today. He then called Simone and asked if she was free this evening and luck was with him. He made the date for eight o'clock and said he would meet her at the Chez Janou, the same restaurant where he and his mother had dined last evening.

They decided to visit Notre Dame first as it was more expedient to do so. And they decided to walk, as it was not far from their hotel. As they approached the front of the great Gothic cathedral completed in 1212, people were lining up for tours. When they entered they could feel the ghosts of the past looking down on them with the multitude of stories of human sacrifice and misery but also of triumph of the human spirit continuing to live today. Portals of light streamed through the inner sanctuary like rays from heaven with the huge supporting columns showing the architectural advances of the time.

"Every piece of stone is hand carved. Imagine if our buildings were built like this today," said Andrew as he read one of the historical markers.

"Nothing can compare to this beauty. It will last forever," murmured Carol. "The stained glass windows are other worldly. But I guess that's what the artists were trying to portray."

After spending several hours exploring the cathedral they hailed a taxi to take them to the Eiffel Tower. Upon reaching the tower they spent some time walking the grounds of the 100-year plus industrial structure and then went inside, took the stairs to the second floor and then rode the elevator to the top. When they walked out onto the observation deck, they could see all of Paris before them and it was breathtaking. The sky was a deep cerulean blue with puffy white clouds dancing across the horizon and Carol looked up and expected to see cherubs at any moment.

"Oh, Andrew. I am so glad we're here. Even under these circumstances. This is better than I could have imagined."

Andrew put his arm around his mother and just held her for a few minutes forgetting the argument they had had earlier. They stood there for quite some time, each in their thoughts. Carol thinking of the rich history of Paris and what an influence it had on the world for hundreds of years, this famously cosmopolitan city whose inhabitants continue to be notorious for their haute couture. And Andrew about his date tonight with Simone.

After a time they took the elevator back down to the ground floor and then started to walk to the Champs Elysee. The grand, mile long boulevard with shops, cafes and bars was like a carnival, with people strolling and shopping. Many were gathered at the sidewalk cafes, eating and drinking, laughing and talking and most of all watching other people. They found one of these cafes and after the maitre de showed them to a table they both ordered salad nicoise and iced tea.

"So is this why you love Paris, Mom?" Andrew asked. "People watching?"

"One of the reasons. I know most of these people are probably tourists from other countries, but you can tell a lot about a country and its culture by just watching the people."

"How is that?"

"Look at their clothes. Are they wearing the latest fashion or not? That will tell you whether they are affluent. And then look at the faces and how they interact with one another. Well, case in point. Go to any large city in the US and watch people on the street. What do you see?"

"People rushing around, going to work," said Andrew.

"And do they look happy?"

"Not really, but you have to remember that this is a place where people are on holiday. And as far as the clothes are concerned, we're in an upscale part of Paris. I'm sure Paris has its share of slums and poor people."

"I know, but even if you go down into the business district here in Paris, I would bet that people do not look as stressed as people in the US. Andrew, I was reading in the New York Times the other day that our country has the highest rate of mental illness of the developed countries. The article said that one in four adults in the US is mentally ill, enough so that they cannot carry on with working and daily activities."

"I don't know, that sounds really high to me. Where did hear that?"

"I read it on the Internet."

"You can't believe everything you read on the Internet. You're really down on the US today, Mom." Andrew thought about this for a few moments and then said, "It's true that Europeans work fewer hours and I guess they have longer vacations."

"I love our country. America has the most innovative, hard working people and it is so vast with so many natural wonders, the mountains with glaciers, beautiful rivers and canyons. I could go on and on, but I just think our country is headed in the wrong direction. The corporations own our government and they are making slaves of us and it should be the other way around. They should be there to serve the people. As it is now they are there to serve the elite. Most of these countries provide education, health care and a pension plan. In America, you can work hard all of your life and end up in poverty."

"Europeans pay high taxes," Andrew said. "And we have a pension plan in the US. It's called Social Security."

"Not if your dad and his cohorts have their way. They want to get rid of it. If private accounts are approved, that will only further weaken the program and then they will phase it out altogether. They are trying to get rid of all of the domestic social programs. They call it taking personal responsibility. "

"So are you a socialist?"

"I am a social progressive," said Carol. "You see, the so-called conservatives believe in survival of the fittest. They think that people should just have to work hard to get ahead, otherwise people would not have the incentive to work at all. But our system is flawed and a person in the US can work hard all of his or her life and then be wiped out financially by a catastrophic illness if they don't have health insurance and sometimes even if they do. And now the average person has a harder time filing for bankruptcy after congress passed the new bankruptcy law."

"Yeah, I see what you're getting at."

"A college education is becoming more expensive reducing the upward mobility of minorities and the poor."

"There are still grants and scholarships," Andrew noted.

"Yes, but the government has cut back on the funding for Pell grants. Fewer disadvantaged kids will have the chance at a college education."

They both continued to eat and watch the colorful parade of multinational people walk by.

"And another thing, your dad's administration cut funding for head start. Do you realize what that does for poor kids? Head start was giving those kids a boost up so they could grow up and lead productive lives. And he cuts the funding."

Carol took a bite of her salad and continued, "And when you think about it, the wealthy have that leg up already."

"Mom, why don't you run for office when you get back?"

"Not a chance. I'm not a politician."

"But that's what America needs. I think we have too many so-called politicians now in Washington and all they know how to do is play politics. We need someone like you who will work for the good of the people. You know, doing the People's Work as they say on the Hill."

"I'd be eaten alive in Washington the way it is today. Politics are mean and ugly."

Andrew gave no argument to that and they finished eating and whiled away the rest of the afternoon hours talking and observing people until it was time to go back to the hotel. Andrew called a taxi and Carol gritted her teeth as the cab driver twisted and turned through the rush hour traffic. Back at the hotel Andrew showered and trimmed his beard, putting on a clean light blue shirt and khaki pants in preparation for his date with Simone.

"I guess I'm on my own for dinner tonight, huh?" Carol looked a little dejected.

"I'll go out and get you a sandwich."

"No, I'm not that hungry. And if I do get hungry later, I can get a bowl of soup at that cafe down the street."

"You're sure now."

Andrew left his mom reading by the window as the shadows lengthened and twilight approached. He felt a little guilty, but then he had spent the whole day with her and this was his time. He drove to the restaurant and walked inside expecting to see Simone waiting for him but she hadn't arrived yet. He sat down at the bar and ordered a scotch on the rocks. There was another couple sitting at the end of the bar, holding hands and kissing. Andrew sipped his drink. He looked at his watch. It was eight fifteen. He would give her a few more minutes and then have the waiter take him to his table. Maybe she isn't going to show up, he thought. Eight thirty came and went and then...

"I'm sorry I'm late," Simone eased up on the bar stool beside him and kissed him on the cheek. "My parents were having a party and I just couldn't tear myself away."

"No problem," Andrew turned and kissed her back feeling relief that she had arrived.

"Would you like a drink?"

"I'll have an iced tea."

Andrew asked the bartender for the iced tea and then signaled the maitre de that they would like to be seated. They were then taken to a table near where he and his mother had been the night before and Andrew thought about her being back at the hotel alone. But it was a fleeting thought as he gazed across the table at this great beauty, her long dark lashes quivering over her deep blue green eyes. She was wearing a pink silk top with a deep V-neck and a long black knit skirt with a slit nearly up to her thigh. Her pearl drop earrings caught the light of the single candle on the table and danced like animated characters when she talked.

"I really hate it when people are late," she said.

"Not to worry. I'm in a holiday mood." Andrew was ordering a bottle of wine. "Will you share this with me?"

"No, I don't drink alcohol," Simone murmured.

Andrew raised his brows. He hadn't known that many women, especially in college, who didn't drink. But he could accept this. He decided to order a glass of wine for himself.

"How was your first job yesterday?"

"It was okay. I got lost but I guess that was to be expected."

"Paris is a complex city, but soon you will get to know the different areas. They will only send you to certain sections of the city where the commerce is."

"You seem to know all about this kind of work. Have you done it yourself?"

"No, but I have lots of friends who have."

"And the gasoline. It is expensive here. One and a half euros a liter, almost ten dollars a gallon, that really takes a bite out of my earnings."

"You Americans, you are so spoiled. That's what we have to pay here all the time. Ask them to reimburse you for the petrol. I think they will."

"Tell me about your family. Are your parents long time Parisians like you?"

"No, they came here shortly before I was born."

"From another part of France?"

"No, my father is from Iraq and as I mentioned before, my mother is American. He was teaching at the University of Baghdad when he met my mother who was working in the country as a journalist. They fell in love and married and because our culture is not open to this kind of marriage, they thought it best to move to a country where there was more tolerance."

"A journalist in Iraq? Not the best place to be especially for a female."

"She was writing a story for Time magazine about the oil industry in the Middle East," Simone said as she pulled a pack of cigarettes from her purse and lit one, inhaling deeply. Simone sipped her iced tea all the while staring at Andrew. "And your family? Why are you in Paris?"

"We're here on holiday," Andrew lied. "My mother is divorcing my dad. The divorce was not going well, he is fighting it and she was in a real funky mood and talked me into bringing her to Paris. She's always wanted to see this city."

"Are you still in school?"

"I took a year off. I'll go back when we return to the States." And then Andrew looked at Simone and said, "You must really hate Americans."

"No. I think we had this conversation before. I say again it is your president and his administration that we hate, not Americans."

They ordered dinner and spoke little during the meal. Simone did not seem distant however, but Andrew was concerned, remembering what his mother had said to him. Then he thought that since her mother was American, she should be trustworthy. Or was he just trying to justify this friendship because he was so very attracted to Simone.

After dinner Andrew and Simone got into his car.

"Where too?" Andrew asked.

"Look, I can catch a cab. I am still living with my parents. I'm looking for an apartment though."

"I'll drive you."

And he drove her back to her parent's house, parking next to the driveway and turning off the motor. Simone moved over closer to Andrew and he pulled her into him. He kissed her deeply and she responded.

"When will I see you again?" Andrew asked.

"Tomorrow if you like."

"I like. I'll call you."

He kissed her again feeling his heart pounding and the heat in his groin. Simone pulled away and opened the car door and stepped out. Just as she was turning to leave she bent down and blew a kiss through the window on the passenger's side.

Chapter 6

Carol on Her Own

Carol was in bed and had finally fallen into a restless sleep when she heard Andrew come in after his date with Simone. She awoke to hear him washing in the bathroom and then heard him slip into the twin bed beside hers without turning on the light. She decided to wait until the morning to talk with him. She had been thinking about the future, worrying about being found again and captured. What would they do to her this time she wondered? They couldn't allow her to have her freedom and tell her story; it would ruin everything for James and his administration. Was the man she saw the other day near the River Seine following her? And now Andrew. Who was this girl he had met? Why would she befriend him and be so helpful to him unless she wanted something from him.

She heard the street sweepers below the window as she turned in her bed to see her son sleeping peacefully in the bed next to hers. He looked like the little boy she had shielded and comforted as a child. She remembered the time he had fallen out of the apple tree while stealing a neighbor's apples. He had hobbled a quarter mile with his leg lacerated and bleeding. He was only eight years old. She cleaned the wound and put merthiolate on it and it stung like a torch scorching his skin as she put gauze dressing on the wound. He cried and she held him in her arms and told him he would be all right. But whenever he was hurt in any way, she felt it in her own gut as if she were the injured one. And now he was a grown man and she was afraid he could be hurt again and she could no longer protect him

Carol saw Andrew's eyes flutter. She waited until Andrew looked to be fully awake. "How was your date?" she asked.

"It was really wonderful. Simone is a lovely woman."

"Are you going to see her again?"

Andrew turned in his bed and then turned back again, throwing off the covers, got out of bed. "Yes, I am. Today as a matter of fact," Andrew said curtly.

"And did you find out more about her?"

"I told you, she's French. Lived in Paris all her life." Andrew, frowning, went to the window and pulled back the shutters to see what Paris looked like early in the morning. He had decided not to tell his mother anything more as he knew she would be concerned. "She's just an ordinary, no not ordinary, extraordinary French girl and I like her a lot. She's smart and pretty and fun to be with. What more do you need to know? Geesh, I feel like I'm in high school again."

Carol decided to drop it. Obviously Andrew wasn't going tell her anything and there wasn't much she could do about it. "So what's your schedule for today?" she asked trying to change the subject.

"I'm afraid you're on your own for today. I have a job this morning and Simone and I are renting bicycles to ride around the city and then we're having a picnic this afternoon." Andrew was feeling bad now for his brusqueness with his mother. He had been taught by his father to always be respectful of her and for the most part he had been. He also felt bad that he wouldn't be spending the day with her. "I'll be back for dinner."

"I thought we were going to the Louvre today."

Now he felt twice as guilty. He had completely forgotten that they had planned this day for the Louvre. He was so wrapped up in Simone. "Tomorrow. We'll go tomorrow, I promise. Is there something else you could go and see today?"

"Sure. I think I'll see the Sacre-Coeur today and since you weren't interested in seeing the Catacombs, I will go there as well."

Andrew hurriedly dressed and was gone within fifteen minutes and that left Carol to take a leisurely shower. She pulled on her khaki slacks and the light blue polo with the Eiffel Tower embroidered on the front that she had bought several days earlier, and headed down stairs to find a roll, some juice and coffee. She asked Janelle at the front desk how to use the Metro, Paris' underground subway system, and was given a map showing all of the routes. After walking two blocks, she took a mental note of where she was so that she could get back again. As always these days, she turned to look behind her for any strangers, men or women, who might be following or watching her. Finding the entrance to the Metro, she walked down the stairs, stepped up to the ticket window and asked for a weekly pass. The ticket person mumbled something in French to her when she asked how to get to Montmartre. Not all French people are friendly, thought Carol. She then, looking at the map Janelle had given her, located the train that would take her north in the city to the Sacre-Coeur. Boarding the train and finding a seat, she again thought how civilized and organized this city was even though it is was a very ancient one. Within twenty minutes she arrived at the location where she was to get off the train and she walked another two blocks to the cathedral in the Montmartre area, one of the most picturesque districts in Paris. The white domes of the Byzantine style basilica, completed in 1919, loomed in front of Carol as she took in the entire splendor of the ornate building. In reading the history she found that the French had begun building the church with contributions from the people after the defeat of France by the Prussians in 1873. She stepped inside and was in awe of the beautiful mosaics, the most striking being the depiction of Christ on the ceiling and the mural of the Passion found at the back of the alter. Even though Carol was not Catholic, she could feel the reverence of the years of people worshipping here. She then climbed to the domed tower where she could see the panorama of Paris before her. The day was clear; there was a light breeze to take away any air pollution. She wished Andrew could be with her.

Going back down the stairs of the tower, she had to follow the crowds of tourists. The high season was beginning and Paris and the streets were filled with people everywhere of every kind and color. Carol thought how nice it was to be anonymous once again, where she could be alone in a crowd without Secret Service agents following her every move and no one hounding her trying to get close to her for an autograph. She was just another tourist.

Carol walked down the street again and came upon the Espace Montmarte Salvadore Dali gallery and she went inside. What a find. There were 330 of Dali's original works on display including the famous

Don Quixote he had painted in 1956. She spent the next two hours viewing the art of this very talented and bizarre man.

*   *   *

Andrew followed Simone, peddling as hard as he could to keep up with her. Every so often Simone would turn her head to see if Andrew was with her and then turn back and pick up speed with her dark brown hair flowing in the wind like a mare's tail. Riding a bicycle in Paris traffic was like maneuvering bumper cars at the state fair. They rode by the Pantheon then on to the Latin Quarter and from there to the place de la Bastille where on July 14 in 1789, a mob of Parisians attacked the Bastille and sparked the French Revolution. Here they stopped for a short rest and a drink of water. From the Bastille they followed the Rue de Rivoli and on to the Jardin des Tulleries, the statue studded gardens designed by Louis XIV's gardener. There had once been a palace here connected to the Louvre, however it was burned to the ground in 1871 and never rebuilt.

"Over there, under that tree. Does that look like a good place," said Simone pointing to a grassy area under a large oak tree.

"Perfect. Let's grab it before someone else does."

Simone spread out the blanket she had brought and on top of that a blue and white checkered tablecloth. She took out a bottle of wine and handed that to Andrew. "I brought this just for you. I know how you like wine."

"That was very thoughtful of you, but what are you drinking?"

"I have apple juice." Simone handed Andrew a pita sandwich filled with tuna salad and a container of potato salad.

"Did you make these?" Andrew asked.

"Yes, I did."

"And you can cook too."

"Just what is that supposed to mean?" Simone teasingly asked.

"Well, you are smart and very pretty and you can cook. Multi talented."

"I thought you would like the potato salad. Isn't that what Americans always have on a picnic?"

"Yes, how sweet of you to think of that."

They ate until they were full and then they lay down on the blanket and did what thousands of Parisians do on a spring day in the park. They kissed and giggled and kissed some more. Andrew looked longingly at Simone and wondered how he was going to get her alone in bed. She lived with her parents and he shared a room with his mother. He could send his mother out to see a movie or some other site in Paris and then bring Simone to his room. But that would be deceitful and was not who Andrew was.

"John," Simone said looking into Andrew's eyes calling him by his alias, "You must see the Cote D Azur. I am going to Antibes this weekend and I would be pleased if you would join me."

My prayers have been answered, Andrew thought. "I'd love that," Andrew answered. "I have always wanted to see the French Riviera. Just you and me?" Andrew wanted to qualify.

"Yes, my cousin has a villa there and she is going to Rome for the weekend so it wouldn't cost very much. I can cook for us most of the time."

"You've got a date. And you don't have to cook."

The road from Paris to Marseille, all on freeway, is about 500 miles and under normal circumstances would take about eight hours. But Andrew and Simone were setting a record. They left Paris at eight o'clock that morning and were just reaching the outskirts of Marseille, the gateway to the Riviera, at 2:30 that afternoon.

"I thought they only drove like this on the Autobahn," Andrew leaned over to Simone, raising his voice to be heard above the wind whipping them in the dark blue Peugeot convertible. Simone had asked when they started if he wanted the top down and he thought why not, they were on holiday weekend.

"Am I frightening you?" Simone asked as she steered the small car around another truck in the far left lane, her long brown hair flying in the wind under her hat.

"No. Not at all," Andrew lied. He gripped the door handle once more. "I'd just like to see some of the countryside and when we're going 100 miles an hour, it's kind of impossible. You have to realize, I… I've never been here before."

"I'm only going 150 kilometers an hour. That's slow for me. I asked if you wanted to drive."

"I thought I'd let you drive since it's your car and you know the roads."

"It's Daddy's car. But, yes, I've taken this road many times. So just sit back and enjoy."

Andrew wanted to ask her to slow down, but he also didn't want to seem like a wimp, so he kept quiet the rest of the trip while gripping the side of his seat with his hands.

He had told his mother about the invitation the night before and, as he had expected, she was not pleased that he was going on this trip. He hadn't asked if he could go, he told her. She would be fine. He had lined up a group tour of Versailles and he thought that would keep her busy for at least a day and then he would be back and she would get over it.

They had spent the day before going to the Louvre, which they both enjoyed immensely, seeing many of the historic and beautiful paintings and sculpture of the Renaissance and Impressionistic periods. The most thrilling, of course was the Mona Lisa and it was everything they thought it would be. And so that evening he broke the news to her.

And now he and Simone were close to the places in France he had heard so much about and had always wanted to see. Nice, Cannes, where the famous film festival was held every year, St. Tropez, the playground of the rich, and Monaco, all with the woman of his dreams.

After Marseille, they passed through the city of Tonlon and then on to Cannes where they turned off the main highway onto the winding two-lane cliff road that would take them to Antibes. Andrew looked out at the immense expanse of the Mediterranean Sea, where the ever-present sun, still in command of the sky, reflected off the waves dancing and shimmering. And then, just as he was enjoying the beauty of the moment, his stomach took a turn, and the nausea overwhelmed him. He put his head over the window to get more fresh air, but nothing seemed to make him feel better.

"Are you okay? You look a little green?"

"Yeah, I think I'm going to be sick. Pull over. Now!"

"There isn't anyplace to pull over."

Andrew leaned over the car door and vomited. How embarrassing he thought. "I'm sorry. I've never had this happen before," he lied.

He didn't want her to know that he sometimes suffered from motion sickness.

"No harm done. Sorry I couldn't pull over for you. Do you feel better?"

"A little. How much further?" Andrew asked as he rinsed his mouth with the bottled water they carried and spat it out the window.

"We're almost there."

"I….I'll feel better once we get there."

Thirty minutes later they pulled up in front of a white washed three-story building with a red tile roof that looked like it had been built 200 years ago. There were two large windows in front with a balcony that looked out to the sea. Andrew, feeling a little better now that they had stopped, dragged himself out of the car and waited for Simone to open the trunk so he could carry their overnight bags to the apartment. He had to redeem himself somehow.

They climbed the first flight of stairs. "What floor is your cousin's apartment on?"

"The third floor. Are you tired? I can carry the bags."

"No. I've got it," Andrew huffed. He would do this even though his stomach was still churning.

They finally reached the third floor and walked down the whitewashed hallway. There was an open door at the end and the ocean breeze washed over them. Andrew was finally feeling better. Simone took the key from her small brown leather purse, opened the white painted door and they walked into the large room that was the living room, the bedroom and the kitchen. The furnishings were sparse; a day bed, an art deco floor lamp and a large wicker chest that served both as storage and a coffee table. There was a very small bathroom off the kitchen area. Even though the apartment was small, it appeared to be large, with a high vaulted ceiling, light colored walls painted a south sea pastel green and French doors opening onto the dining area on the balcony, with the magnificent view.

Andrew dropped the bags and turned to Simone. "Hold on just a minute. I'll be right back," he murmured. He searched his bag for this toothbrush and finding it headed for the tiny bathroom.

When he returned, he saw Simone on the balcony and he joined her. Taking her in his arms, he kissed her. Without words, Andrew led her back into the great room. Simone reached in the back of her dress and unzipped her blue cotton shift and let it fall to the floor revealing her slight figure with small breasts under her string bikini underwear. Andrew removed his pants and then his shirt and they lay down on the day bed together intertwining their bodies. Andrew removed Simone's bra and her panties and they lay naked together. At that moment Simone reached for her bag and pulled out a condom and helped Andrew put it on and as the ocean breeze gently caressed their bodies, they made love together.

They were silent afterward, each not wanting to spoil the moment. Then Simone arose from the day bed and turned to Andrew and said, "You must be hungry. Do you realize we haven't eaten all day?"

"Yes, I was aware of that. But I knew you wanted to get here."

"And so did you, by the looks of you," Simone teased and then winked.

*   *   *

Carol took the elevator back to her room after a long day with the tour of Versailles. She opened the door, walked in and lay down on the bed. She was very tired. She had loved seeing the very beautiful, opulent palace, but she hated the crowds and disliked being on a tour with so many people. Some of them were American and she thought one of them, an older woman, recognized her because the woman kept staring at her. But Carol tried to pay no mind and also stayed away from her as much as possible. And now here she was, alone in Paris, her son off with a woman she knew nothing about. But then she thought, it was good, and that he should have friends and some enjoyment. But now what to do? The dinner hour was fast approaching and she did not want to eat another deli sandwich from the corner store. She closed her eyes and fell into a light sleep. In twenty minutes, opening her eyes, she saw the colors of twilight washing across the room. She removed her slacks and shirt and showered and put on her green linen dress. She left off the jacket and put on a silk scarf she had bought at one of the boutiques on the Champs Elysees two days ago. She felt better. Taking the elevator down to the main lobby she stopped at the desk where Arnaud was working tonight.

"*Bonsoir Madame*. How can I help you?"

"Arnaud, I am on my own for dinner. Can you recommend a restaurant where a single lady can have dinner without being conspicuous?"

"*Oui Madame.* What is your pleasure? Where writers dine or artists?"

"Writers. Intellectuals."

"I have just the spot. Cafe de Flore on Saint-Germain. It is very, what you say in America, popular. I know the headwaiter there and I will call ahead for you. Would you like a cab? It is not far from here."

"*Oui*, Arnaud, *merci.*"

Carol arrived at the cafe twenty minutes later and went inside and asked for Marcel, the headwaiter. A very tall, heavy man with a red face appeared, wearing a white shirt, black pants and a white apron and in a hurried voice he mumbled something in French of which Carol only heard "Madame".

"Arnaud from the Hotel de Nesle said you would have a table for me? My name, Helen," Carol mumbled, somewhat intimidated, using her alias name they had used to check into the hotel.

"*Oui, Madame* Helen. I have the perfect table for you." And he whirled around, saying, "Follow me."

He took her to a small table for two and seating her he gave her a menu.

"Let me know if I can be of help to you. A friend of Arnaud's is a friend of mine."

"*Merci,* thank you." Carol was relieved that he did speak English.

She looked around the room seeing many couples, one or two families, no single people like herself. She thought of Andrew. But then she thought that she could not always depend on him to be there. He needed a life of his own. Then as she opened her menu a single older gentlemen was shown to a table not far from hers.

A tall thin waiter appeared. "*Parlez-vous anglais?*" Carol asked.

"*Oui*, yes. My name is Maubert, Marcel sent me to help you. Call me Bert. I am one of the few *anglais* speaking waters here. What can I get for you? Champagne? Are you celebrating? No?"

"No. What is Foie Gras?"

"Yes. It is the liver of the very well fed Moulard duck."

"You mean an obese duck?"

"They encourage the duck to eat well."

"You mean they force feed it?"

"Ducks love to eat, so not really. Would you like to try some?"

"I don't think so. I think I'll try the pate with truffles and the salmon in wine sauce, a salad and a glass of white wine."

"*Merci*, Madame."

Carol eyed the older man. He was dressed in gray flannel slacks and a blue dress shirt. His hair, what there was of it, was gray around his ears and he had a slight paunch belly. He must be at least sixty years old, just the kind of man I don't like, she thought as she pictured James's muscular body. His eyes looked up and met with hers and she looked away. The waiter brought her glass of wine and she took a sip. Then the pate arrived. She tried not to look at him, but out of the corner of her eye she caught him looking at her again.

"Would you like another glass of wine with dinner, Madame?"

She hadn't noticed that she had finished the first one. "Yes, I would."

She thought she would be daring. After all she wouldn't be driving. She saw him looking at her again. And then he started walking towards her table.

"I don't mean to be rude, but you are alone and I am alone. May I join you for dinner?"

How brazen, she thought. Then she reconsidered. Why not? What harm is there?

"Sure. Pull up a seat," she said, amazed at what she had just said.

The man asked the waiter to bring his wine over to her table and he sat down across from her.

"Do Parisians often ask to have dinner with strangers?" Carol asked.

"I am not Parisian."

"Oh, where are you from then? You are French aren't you?"

"*Oui*. I am French. I live near Bordeaux, off the Bay of Biscay. And you?"

"I'm from the United States."

"I couldn't tell," he joked. "But let me introduce myself. My name is Claude Montague. And you are.....?"

"Helen. Helen Michaels."

"Helen. I love the name Helen, the daughter of Zeus and Leda."

Carol smiled and Claude continued talking. "Why is a beautiful woman like you dining alone on a Saturday night in Paris?"

"My son is having dinner with a friend tonight and I didn't want to be a fifth wheel, if you know what I mean." Carol did not want him to know that her son was out of town and he most likely was having dinner with Simone, so she wasn't really lying.

"And what brings you to Paris?"

So many questions. Did she have to answer? "I've always wanted to see Paris and my son was taking a break from school and so we thought it was the perfect time to take this trip."

Claude could see her discomfort. "I hope you are enjoying this beautiful city. It is my favorite of all cites in the world."

"Now it is my turn. What brings you to Paris?"

"I am here on business. I have a little vineyard in the Bordeaux area and I needed to meet with my distributors. I hate traveling alone and I hate eating alone. That is why I asked to join you. I will leave if you want."

"No. Stay. I'm sorry. I have been doing the tourist thing today and I'm tired. I want you to stay."

Claude raised his bushy salt and pepper eyebrows over steel blue eyes and smiled. The waiter brought both of their meals and they started eating.

"Why didn't you order the Foie Gras?" he asked. "You cannot come to Paris without having it just once."

"It sounds like they abuse the ducks. I won't eat veal because they pen the baby lambs up until they kill them and I think that is cruel. I don't eat ham because pigs are very intelligent and they must know they are going to die."

"One of those," he laughed and then she laughed with him. The comfort meter had risen.

Carol asked how long he would be in Paris and he said another week. They continued eating and the meal was ending. Claude ordered Champagne with cheese and fruit, and they toasted Paris as the most beautiful city.

"May I see you again?" Claude asked. "Wait, maybe you are married. Are you?"

"Not really," Carol answered.

"And what does not really mean? Either you are or you are not."

A man who likes absolute, Carol thought. "I am divorcing."

"Ah, I understand now. Had to get away from the husband to think things over."

"No, I've thought it over. I just have to get it done now and there are some obstacles."

The waiter brought two bills and Claude picked up both of them even though Carol protested. Then he asked if he could take her back to her hotel and she accepted. When they arrived at the hotel he walked inside with her.

"Madam Helen, I would like to take you to dinner tomorrow evening at the premier restaurant in all of Paris, Maxim."

"Claude, you are so kind. I don't know. My son might not approve."

"I will ask him then when he returns from his date."

"Actually he's in the south of France for the weekend."

"I will ask him when he gets back."

"All right, I accept."

"I will fetch you at seven."

Claude kissed Carol on the cheek and turned to leave.

What have I gotten myself into, Carol thought as she took the elevator to her room? Accepting dates from strange men in a strange city in a strange country. But somehow she was beginning to like him.

Chapter 7

G8 Summit Paris

Air Force One climbed through the black thunder clouds and into the sky from Andrews Air force base in Virginia, en route to Paris for the annual G8 Conference on this stormy April afternoon. James looked out the window of his Oval Office in the sky and saw lightning dancing on the wing, but soon they were above the clouds and the sun was shining down on cotton candy clouds. The summer storms were early and more dramatic this year.

The G8 is currently a group of eight countries including the United States, Germany, France, Italy, Canada, Japan, Russia, and the United Kingdom. The European Union is included also and is represented by the President of the European Commission and by the leader who is the president of the European Council at the time of the Summit. The first conference was held in 1975 when French President Giscard d'Estaing invited leaders of Germany, Japan, the United Kingdom, Italy and the United States to a gathering at the chateau Rambouillet, near Paris, to discuss world issues in a frank and informal way. There were no military people, just the leaders in a relaxed and private setting.

The discussions typically revolve around economic, political, social and military issues at the global level. This first conference was so successful that it is still being held today with additional countries being invited into the group, increasing the number from the original six to eight.

Over the years every summit has been different. In 1996 it was the HPC, Highly Indebted Poor Countries initiative, 1997 saw an end to the cold war with Russia being invited to join the group and the 1998 summit, the first G8 summit, adopted the first "heads only" policy, separating the Heads of State and Government from that of their Foreign and Finance ministers. During this summit they would be discussing the troubled countries in Africa, Uganda, Sudan, Ethiopia and the Congo, the war in the Middle East and global warming.

James had not wanted to participate with the deteriorating relations they now had with the European nations due to the war in Iraq. But his advisors told him it would be a way to mend fences and hopefully repair the image of United States in the world.

He had gathered his loyal advisors and cabinet members, Secretary of State Tom Wiley and his Security Advisor Wilson Adams, among them, to discuss the upcoming conference. Mark Richards, his press secretary and Susan Rogers were part of the group also, as they were more or less appendages to James wherever he went.

Settling into his brown leather executive chair, James reviewed the agenda for the meeting as the others filed into the President's office in the sky and greeted him one by one.

"Good morning, Mr. President," said Tom as he eased himself into his chair and poured himself a drink of water from the carafe on the table. "We should be landing in Paris about 1:00 a.m. our time. That'll give us plenty of time to discuss the issues and get our ducks in a row. Prime Minister Hawkins is going to bring up global warming and he is supporting measures to curb it, leaving us to decide where we stand on this issue. "

"Are we even going to be a part of the discussion on global warming?" Susan said as she sat at the table next to James. "I think we should stay out of it altogether. They all know our position on this."

"No, we need to engage. If I tell them that I acknowledge climate change, say that I now believe global warming exists, we can throw them a bone without committing to participating in any government policies to set higher emissions standards," James said as he looked around the table at everyone. "It might then be perceived that we intend to do something about it in the future. But I do not want to slap limitations on industry now and I don't want to hamper corporate growth and the building of new power plants at this time."

"We can say that our scientists have established the fact that it is occurring but that they found it to be happening more slowly than was first perceived," said Susan.

"Brilliant. If we have the scientists verifying this, then who can dispute that?" said James.

"It was a strategic move on our part to contract this group to do the study. We had full control over the results and now we have the scientific studies tailored to fit our agenda," said Tom.

"I agree. Now as for the aid to African nations, we need to get on board with this. We can cut what we gave last year and still look philanthropic. Most won't even know what the number was last year," James said.

"Why cut it? Why create more controversy?" asked Tom.

"We need the money for Iraq," James murmured.

"Speaking of Iraq, we have issues to discuss there," Susan interjected.

"We haven't finished talking about Africa yet. The point I want to make here is, when we give this aid, food and debt relief, we need to make sure that they are instilling our policies of not allowing abortions and limiting birth control. This was our policy last year and we will continue on with it," said Tom.

"Isn't it pointless to give food aid if these people are breeding themselves further into poverty?" asked James. "And the use of condoms will prevent aids which is killing hundreds of thousands of people in many African nations. There are 6.5 million people infected in South Africa alone. Many of them pregnant women who will give birth to babies with aids."

"This is our concession to the religious right. We need to do this. I doubt we will be successful in overturning Roe V. Wade this year and we have to give them something. They donated millions to get us elected again," said Susan.

"What will the American people say to this?" James turned to Susan and tapped his pen on the table. "Won't they be outraged when they learn there are strings attached to the food and aid we are giving Africans?"

"Outraged? I doubt it. There's another missing child in Florida. Michael Jackson is being sued by the parents of the kid he allegedly molested. American people aren't paying attention to Africa. They could care less about Africa," Susan exclaimed. "But they are starting to pay attention to WMD's or lack thereof in Iraq. Do you understand,

Mr. President, that we are headed for a crisis? The administration will have to explain just exactly why we went to war. Not to mention the possibility of war crimes."

Tom took another long drink of water. "Do you really think so? Or will this blow over like everything else has? The public has a short attention span."

"True. But the bombings in Iraq are escalating. There are ten or more suicide bombers a day now. Can't even drive the seven miles to the airport from the Green Zone in Baghdad without an armed escort and fear of a roadside bomb. Foreign fighters are streaming into the country from Syria, Iran and Jordan. Al Qaeda has set up shop. And the press is reporting this every day. Granted it's on the back page, but it's all over the Internet," said James. "I think we've got some explaining to do."

"Yeah, but those Internet folks, they're a small percentage of the population and they are not our base," Susan said.

"I'm worried about mid term elections. If the moderate Republicans and the Democrats win more seats, we could be in for a shit load of trouble," said James with a scowl on his forehead.

"I've been hearing the impeachment word lately," said Mark who had been silent up until now.

"Impeach? No. They couldn't do that. They wouldn't even try to impeach. We have a majority in all of the branches of government. They wouldn't have a chance," James implored.

"The Democrats are getting an independent council to investigate. There are those memos from Chester Hawkins," said Susan referring to Britain's Prime Minister. "I'm worried and you should be too."

"Britain is a close ally. They will stand behind us. We need to get Chester over here for a meeting and that will quash these rumors," said James. "Let him speak directly to the American people, tell them how Democracy in Iraq is going to make everyone safer."

Air Force One slipped through the sky, high above the turmoil of the world below with the sun setting in the west on troubled waters in the Atlantic. James and his advisors talked on for another three hours and then broke for dinner. He then retired to his private quarters to rest while the others went back to their assigned areas on the airplane.

Susan cornered Tom. "I don't think the President is aware of what we are up against. The tide is turning; more people are against the war. Have you seen the polls lately?"

"We'll keep him in the dark. He doesn't need to know this. He can't do anything about it anyway."

"Can we do that? He reads the newspaper doesn't he? I don't know if that's such a good idea."

"Of course we can. He's so isolated now. We're vetting all the crowds and town halls that he's speaking to. He'll never know and in the meantime we need to push back on the independent council. And most importantly not let this information make the front-page news. Mark's area of expertise is to manage the news coming out of the White House."

It seemed like hours later, James awakened to the slight thud as Air Force One touched down at Aeroport Charles de Gaulle in the small town of Roissy, northwest of Paris. The meeting was to be held the next day at a 200-year-old chateau in the country outside of Chantilly. James was not looking forward to this gathering. All of the heads of state of the countries, with the exception of the United Kingdom, had spoken out against his administration mainly due to the Iraq war. Britain of course was his staunchest ally, but even the majority of the British people, seventy percent, were against the war and against his government. The French were especially vocal in their dislike of American foreign policy and James feared they would be demonstrating and he hated any kind of dissent, and this being a foreign country, he had less control. In the United States, the Secret Service always swept the streets of any demonstrators, corralling them in small fenced areas where the press couldn't get to them and they couldn't be heard. This worked very well and he had seen few demonstrations since he had been in office. He hoped that his Secret Service were successful in getting the French police to cooperate. But the G8 was known for anti globalization activists and this year the anti war activists could join in as well. And in France, the government feared the people, unlike the United States where the people feared their government.

Chapter 8

Carol and Claude

"You are not going out with this stranger are you?" Andrew yelled at his mother. Andrew had just returned from his trip to the south of France to find his mother wearing a new silk dress she had bought that day from a small boutique on the Champs Elyse, carefully combing her hair and splashing cologne behind her ears. When he asked where she was going all dressed up, she told him about meeting Claude and that he was taking her to dinner at Maxim's.

"I am. He's a fine person. He owns a winery in the Bordeaux region. He looks to be very honest and has impeccable manners."

"How do you know that? He could be working for the CIA for all you know."

"How do you know that Simone isn't working for some agency, spying on us?"

"Simone is different. She's genuine and honest."

"Claude is genuine and honest too."

"Is he married?"

"I don't know." Carol chided herself for not asking that question. She had been overwhelmed that he had joined her for dinner that evening and then asked her to go out with him. "He was alone and it really doesn't matter anyway. We are just going to be friends and after all I am still legally married."

"I still don't like it. When is he coming for you?"

"Any minute now."

She looked at her watch. "He must be here now. I have to go," said Carol as she grabbed a little black evening bag and straightened her hair again.

"I'm going down there to meet him."

"You are treating your mother like a teenager?" Carol looked Andrew straight on. "And I haven't even met Simone yet."

"You will. I'll bring her by tomorrow and we can have lunch."

They walked out of the room together and got on the rickety cage of an elevator riding to the first floor. Carol walked out of the elevator first and saw Claude standing near the front desk dressed in dark navy slacks, a gray blazer, and a light blue shirt with a cravat at his neck, holding one red rose. He looked very debonair.

"Claude, I'd like you to meet my son, John," Carol said using Andrew's alias.

"I am pleased to meet you, John," Claude said as he shook Andrew's hand. "Don't worry, I will bring your mother home safe and sound and on time." He then turned to Carol and handed her the rose and kissed her on the cheek.

Andrew chuckled at Claude's statement. After seeing Claude, he too thought that he looked like an honest, French businessman and it would be all right for his mother to go out with him. And he had to admit, he was taking a chance with Simone given her family background?

Claude and Carol said goodbye and walked out to the front of the hotel where there was a sleek, black limousine waiting. They climbed into the back seat and Claude took Carol's hand and smiled, as Carol smelled the sweet fragrance of the rose. They arrived at Maxim's fifteen minutes later. Claude exited the limousine and came around to Carol's side, opened the door and took her hand as she climbed out. Claude noticed Carol's slim legs as her royal blue silk wrap around dress parted. They entered the very busy restaurant and Claude announced their arrival to the maitre de. They were immediately shown to a small table in an intimate corner of the restaurant. The haughty maitre de seated them, laying their white linen napkins on their laps, handing them a large and important looking menu.

"*Champaign, Monsieur?*"

"*Oui,*" Claude said. "*Je voudrais escargot, s'il vous plait.*"

"I have never had escargot," Carol said. "I'm just a simple girl from out west."

"You're anything but simple, my dear. I think you will like escargot." Claude surveyed the menu. "Can I order for you?"

"I would be pleased. My French leaves much to be desired."

"*Fruits de mer, boeuf or perhaps agneau*, lamb?"

"I seldom eat meat and certainly not lamb. I prefer fish, halibut or salmon and a Chablis would be fine."

The waiter brought the chilled bottle of Champaign and poured the two flutes for them and then Claude ordered.

"Something I should have asked you before. Are you married, Claude?"

"No. My wife Jocelyn died three years ago in an auto accident and I have been alone since that time. I haven't pursued a friendship as I was too stricken with grief for the first two years and then I have been very busy running the winery."

"I am sorry. That must have been a very difficult time for you. Do you have children?"

"No, we were never successful in having our own. Years ago we had started an adoption process, but we were moving and couldn't go through with it. I am looking for a wife though and I shall find one," Claude announced as he sipped his Champaign. "And tell me more about yourself, Helen. You are divorcing. What are your plans for the future? Will you get a job, go back to school?"

"I'm going to law school when I get back to the States. I've been a teacher and I thoroughly enjoyed the children but now I want to make a real difference and I think good knowledge of the law is helpful."

"Teaching is such a noble profession. Imagine inspiring children to learn and shaping young minds. The children of the world are our future."

"I couldn't agree with you more, but it has become so politicized, especially in our country. The public school system is under siege with the current administration trying to weaken it. There is a federal program of testing to disqualify failing schools and close them. The children from the closed schools are then taken out of their neighborhoods to another school where classes are even larger and ultimately these schools will fail as well over time."

"I can't picture you as a lawyer," Claude said changing the subject. You are too soft and feminine."

"Don't let my demeanor fool you. I am tough. I was thinking environmental law."

"I take it you are not in agreement with your government concerning environmental issues either."

"That is an understatement."

"We here in France are perplexed as to how you can support your president and the war in Iraq. You know when 9-11 happened, our country was solidly behind the United States. Our intelligence agency, which is one of the best in the world, was sharing information in trying to help your country. And look what happened. We were ridiculed for not supporting the Iraq war."

"I know. I am embarrassed for my country," Carol said as she attempted to pull a huge snail out of its shell. "You know the French have very different food fetishes," Carol said as she tried to move on to another topic.

"Good food and good wine are the soul of France. Our *fromage* is the best, Roquefort, Camembert, *se magnifique*. Fresh breads, the best."

"I have noticed. And the markets have the freshest fruits and vegetables," Carol said as she mastered the escargot.

The waiter brought the second course, a creamy cold onion soup and then the rest of the meal, more wine and a wonderful crème brulet for desert. They talked about growing grapes and Carol told Claude about running a cattle ranch in the west and then she looked at her watch and it was eleven o'clock.

"I have so enjoyed. This is a beautiful restaurant."

"Maxim's is the place to see and be seen. The wealthiest people in the world come here."

"Does that impress you?"

"No. I am not impressed by wealth, but Maxims should be on everyone's list when they visit Paris and that is why I brought you here."

As they left the restaurant, the limousine appeared and the driver got out and opened the door for them.

"It is late and I must get back to the hotel. Andrew, uh....John will be wondering where I am."

"Do you turn into a scullery maid at midnight?" Claude teased.

"I might. And this limousine will turn into a pumpkin. Does this belong to you?"

"No. I just rented it for the evening. This was a very special occasion," Claude said as he sat next to Carol in the car and took her hand in his. "But let me take you to one more place before you go home. It won't take long, I promise."

The driver pulled out into traffic and turned toward the river Seine. Carol looked out the window as they parked and saw the cathedral Notre Dame, with the lights playing on the flying buttresses and gargoyles. They got out of the car and started walking on a path near the river. Another couple strolled by, then stopped and kissed.

"I know who you are."

Carol looked at Claude, startled by his words. "I don't know what you mean."

"You're Carol Walters, the first lady on the lam. You looked familiar when I first met you and then I looked at your picture in an old Newsweek magazine. And when you called your son Andrew a while ago.... I knew."

"I'm not on the lam. I... I ...."

"You don't have to explain. I am on your side. I think.... I mean I won't rat on you. Well, you know what I mean. I want to be your friend."

Carol heaved a sigh of relief. She hated lying and being incognito. "I am glad you know, but is it that obvious? Am I that transparent, I mean, do you think others recognize me?"

"No, I don't think so. I am very interested in politics and have read much about you and your husband. And you do look very different now than when you were at the White House. Your hair is longer and it is turning gray. You just don't look the same. If I hadn't met you the way I did, I would not have guessed who you really are."

"Are you trying to tell me that I look older?"

"Looking older is not a bad thing. The French love older women. They are experienced in love and life."

"Oh, I see."

"And you don't have to talk about it if you don't want to. I respect your privacy," Claude took Carol's hand again as he faced her and looked into her eyes.

"Thank you. I need a friend right now."

"I understand."

Claude pulled Carol closer to him and tried to kiss her, but Carol turned away.

Chapter 9

Carol's Surprise

Carol took the elevator to the fourth floor and walked down the dark hallway to their room, number 410. She fumbled for the old brass key and looked back down the hallway to see if anyone had followed her. Finally she opened the door, went inside turning on the light, quickly closing the door behind her. Andrew's bed was empty. He must be spending the night with Simone, Carol thought. She was too tired to worry about it. She took off her dress and put on the big t-shirt that she wore for sleeping, went into the bathroom, washed her face, brushed her teeth and put on her night cream. Looking in the mirror, she saw the lines by her eyes, there was extra skin now under her chin and her hair was turning gray, with still some dark strands throughout. The last year had taken its toll and she had aged, she felt considerably. But it didn't matter. She was here, a free person, free to pursue her dreams on her own terms. She was happy in herself; she didn't need a man to achieve her goals in life. In fact, a man might drag her down.

Crawling into the small single bed by the window, she pulled the sheet and the light blue cotton blanket up to her chin, turned on her side and curled into the position that she always maintained when she slept. She remembered that she started sleeping that way when she was carrying Andrew; her belly had gotten so large that she had to pull one of her legs up in front, while lying on one side. She thought about that time so long ago. Life was so much less complicated then. James was an attentive father-to-be and brought her treats of ice cream with chocolate sauce and peanut butter cookies. When it was time to go to the hospital, he had helped her to the car and then had forgotten the car keys and her suitcase that she had carefully packed with nightgowns and the baby's new clothes. She remembered sitting there, the pains coming closer together, while he went back into the house. It was snowing and she was so worried about the ten-mile drive from the ranch to the hospital in Fort Collins. Finally he came back and started the car for the drive into town. She would never forget that long night in the labor room, James standing vigilant by her side as each wave of pain washed over her with more intensity every time and then her water broke and she felt the urge to push. They wheeled her to the delivery room and James put on a surgical gown, following the doctor and the nurses. He came by her side once more, holding her hand, squeezing it, smiling with bliss when baby Andrew entered the world screaming, his little red body covered with white birthing film. They laid him on her stomach and when she looked at his tiny hands and feet and saw his eyes open, her joy was like nothing she had ever felt before. Here was this beautiful baby boy that she and James had created together and her body had nurtured for nine months.

If only she could go back to those days. But she couldn't. She could only go forward.

Carol thought about Claude. He was a nice person. How would he figure in her life if at all? She drifted off to sleep with the sounds of people on the street below. Paris was like Las Vegas; people never slept.

Carol's cell phone rang. She opened her eyes and looked at the small black digital travel clock on the nightstand beside her bed. It was 8:15. Had she really slept this long? She was usually up by 5:30. The phone kept ringing. Must be Andrew calling. Maybe he wants to meet for breakfast and introduce me to Simone, she thought. Carol picked up the cell.

"Hello."

"Hello, is that you Carol?"

The voice was unmistakable.

"James, is that you?"

"Yes, Carol, I'm here in Paris for the G8. Thought I'd give you a shout and see how you're doing."

Carol couldn't believe what she was hearing. Her hand shook as she changed the phone over to her other ear.

"How did you know where I was?"

"We've got the detail on you. Can't just let you be out there all by yourself; it's too dangerous."

"How dare you call me?" Carol said indignantly. "How dare you, after what you let them do to me. I don't want to talk to you ever again."

"Whoa, hold on. Just listen to me for a minute and then I promise I won't bother you again."

Carol waited. She thought about hanging up, but something inside her said that she wanted to hear what he had to say.

"First, I want you to know that I didn't order your ....your capture. It was completely out of my hands. Just like most everything else is. Other people are running this show. They call the shots."

There was silence.

"And I have to worry for my life every day. So many people hate me. They would kill me if they had a chance," James continued.

Carol didn't know what to say to this.

"It's gotten ugly in Washington, you know. I'm glad you don't have to be there. But I miss you terribly."

"I gave you a chance to step down. You took this path and now you have to follow it."

"I know. I'm almost sorry I didn't. Step down, that is."

"Almost? That's a laugh. Giving up your family for power and you're almost sorry?"

"Carol, I know you won't believe this, but I do love you."

"You could have really loved me a year ago, but you didn't. Do you know what I've been through? Drugged and held hostage in that nursing home. I felt like I was in prison. Oh, I know, you didn't want your precious constituents to know. You were more concerned about winning the election than you were about your family. Well, it worked and you won and now you say you're unhappy. I don't feel one bit sorry for you."

"Well, I made a mistake."

Was she hearing this right? He said he made a mistake? James hadn't ever said that since becoming president. This was the old James. The one she used to love.

"I am under siege. Even the Republicans are asking that we pull out of Iraq. And the Democrats are attacking saying the war was started under false pretenses. Josh is questioning my authority, as are some of the other cabinet members. It's a sorry mess."

"And you're slipping in the polls. Well, what do you want me to do about it?" Carol asked sarcastically. "Come back to you and give it the woman's touch. Not on your life. I'll be coming back to the States, but not back to you."

"No, I'm not asking you to come back. I just wanted you to know that I really love you. That's all. Remember that. And I wish I had never been elected president at all. It is a job that…" James paused. "I don't know why anyone would want it. Do you know what I am saying?"

"I can't feel sorry for you James. You got what you wanted and so you'll just have to deal with it."

There was a pause. Carol could hear his breathing.

"Are you okay, though?" James asked.

"Yes, I am okay. And keep your goons away from me."

"I just wanted to hear that you were all right. I'll hang up now. If you ever want to call me, you can."

"I won't, you can count on that. Goodbye James."

Carol sat on the bed and the tears rolled down her cheeks and onto her bare legs. She put her face in her hands and cried and cried some more. And then she stopped and wiped her tears with her night shirt, wondering why she was crying. The life they once had can never be had again. Being with James in Washington was not a partnership. He was the president and she was the first lady, the unelected, unpaid official hostess with no voice in the White House. That was unacceptable to her as were the policies coming out of James administration and so she took measures into her own hands to solve it. She filed for divorce. And now she had to move on to a better life and it would have to be without James.

She heard the key turning in the door and Andrew walked into the room with a small overnight bag. He looked at his mother.

"What's wrong? You've been crying. Did Claude hurt you? If I get my hands on him…."

"No, Andrew, it wasn't Claude. Your father called."

"Dad? Called here? How did he know ….."

"I don't really know, but he said they're watching us. Andrew, we have to get out of here and go somewhere where they can't find us. I don't trust them. They could just swoop in and try to take us into custody at any time."

"I agree, but where can we go?"

"Maybe if we go to a smaller town. Or we could go to Italy."

"What did he say?"

"He said he was sorry and that he wished he wasn't the president. I guess things are getting messy for him. He said the decision to abduct me was not his idea, and that others are calling the shots. He said that he has little control anymore over what happens in his administration."

"I don't know if I believe all that. He's going along with everything and carrying through with the war," said Andrew as he sat down beside his mother on the bed and put his arms around her. Carol put her head on Andrew's wide shoulder. "I'm sorry Mom. I should have been here with you. I spent the night with Simone. She has a new apartment. She's down stairs now and I thought you'd like to meet her. We could go for some coffee or something."

"No, not now. I'd like to meet her, but I'm just not up for it. I think I'll just stay here this morning and read and then go for a walk later."

Andrew left his mother alone. He was as dismayed as she was that his father had called. They would have to move now that they were being watched again. Whoever or whatever was watching them was like a Cyclops, all seeing, all knowing with tentacles reaching everywhere. Could they ever get away from them?

Chapter 10

Simone's Apartment

Andrew stepped out of the elevator and saw Simone sitting in an over stuffed, red chair by the window in the lobby of the hotel. She was wearing black Capri pants and a white tank top, reading Time magazine, her long brown hair falling over the magazine all but covering her face. She looked up as Andrew approached.

"Is your mother joining us?"

"No, she's not feeling well. She said that she wanted to rest. She sends her regards and said she would love to meet you, but another time would be better," Andrew stammered, trying to sound diplomatic.

"I am sorry to hear that, I was looking forward to meeting her. But no matter."

Simone rose from the chair and Andrew stepped close to her and kissed her on the cheek. "Where to now?" he asked.

"I have an idea. I have a new apartment and very little furniture."

"You can say that again."

"What?" Simone looked perplexed.

"It's an America saying. It means that I strongly agree with what you're saying," said Andrew. "You have a bed and that's all."

"It's the most important piece of furniture to have."

"Couldn't agree with you more," murmured Andrew as he thought about sleeping with Simone last night on that very bed, on the floor of her apartment, enveloping her body, caressing her. What a beautiful night it was.

"Well, what I was going to say was that we should go shopping and buy furniture for my apartment. Since you'll be spending time there too, I would like you to help me pick out the furniture and accessories you like."

Simone's words gave Andrew a warm fuzzy feeling. He was in complete agreement, but did he want to go shopping? Sleeping with Simone in her apartment was one thing but buying furniture? "I don't know. I'm not an interior designer. Maybe you should get your mother to help you. Women know more about these things. I'll like anything you pick out. I'm easy."

"I know you're easy, but come along. It'll be fun."

And they started off with Au Bon Marche on the left bank. Andrew marveled at the size of the store that seemed to go on forever and have almost anything a person could want: clothing, sporting goods, house wares and linens and even a grocery store. He and Simone picked out dishes and flat ware. The designs were minimalist and utilitarian, simple white dishes with a Swedish design flat ware and linens in natural shades of camel and white in keeping with the house wares. Simone said that she would introduce color in accent pieces, paintings and throw pillows and other accessories. Andrew felt like he was the groom and they were getting ready to be married and he wasn't unhappy at the thought. After the large department store, they visited IKEA and purchased a couch with a removable slipcover in an off white color, an armchair of the same color and a small dining table with two chairs. All told, adding everything up, Andrew figured Simone had spent four or five thousand dollars easily and Simone put it all on her credit card.

"How will you pay for all of this?" Andrew asked.

"Don't worry about it. I have the money. Dad gave me an allowance to get started on. I think he really wants me out on my own."

It was late in the afternoon by the time they reached her fourth floor apartment in the Monte Mart area. Simone poured a glass of wine for Andrew and juice for herself and they opened the doors to the small balcony that overlooked the rooftops of Paris, a scene right out of Mary Poppins, only in Paris, not London.

"It has been a good day and I like all the things we bought. I can't wait for them to be delivered. Thanks for coming along."

"It was fun. I enjoyed it. But I enjoy any time that I have with you."

They both looked out over the rooftops watching the birds coming home to roost for the night. Andrew could smell the aroma of pot roast cooking in one of the other apartments and it made him homesick.

"Do you ever go to Baghdad to visit? You must still have grandparents, aunts and uncles and cousins there."

"No, it's too dangerous since the war began. We used to go when I was little."

"Do your parents hear from your relatives?"

"Yes, all the time. They call every week and tell us what is happening, especially my dad's brother, Jabar. It's pretty gruesome you know, the suicide bombers and roadside bombs and the Marines breaking down the doors of suspected freedom fighters and shooting people for no reason. We would like for them to leave but they won't hear of it." Simone looked down for a time. "I am very worried for my family."

Andrew put his arm around her. "But the government is coming together. They'll be free to decide their own destiny. When Saddam was in power, he was a tyrant and the people were powerless."

"Yes, that is true, Saddam was a tyrant. He used Stalinist techniques to rule. In fact he had his security people train in Eastern Europe. If one member of a family opposed his regime, he would get rid of the whole family with the idea that if one is against him, they all will be."

Simone stopped talking. Her eyes became focused on the sky above with the last light of the day fading.

"So, you agree with the Americans coming in and getting rid of him?"

"Saddam came from a very poor family in a village near Tikrit. As a boy he stole so that his family could eat. And to answer your question, no, I don't. Saddam held the country together with a secular government. Women were educated. And they could go out at night without a male escort. They can't do that now. They held jobs. There are few jobs in Iraq except security jobs and you know what that's about."

"But we are rebuilding the country and it will be better than it was before."

"You do know Saddam had the backing of the US government during the Iran Iraq war, don't you? In fact the Americans, your country, helped to bring him to power with the overthrow of General Kassem whom they thought was pro communist. In studying American foreign policy, this seems to happen quite often. Meddling in the politics of small countries, getting rid of the dictator, installing another pro American, worse than the one before and then if he doesn't go along with them, they get rid of him. It happened in Panama, Chile. And now in Iraq. Saddam wasn't co-operating with the US. Iraq has oil and the US needs oil. But as far as rebuilding the country, why did they have to bomb it in the first place? Thousands of antiquities were lost, stolen or destroyed right after the fall of Baghdad. They can never be replaced. There is very little electricity now, clean water is a luxury item, garbage and sewage everywhere. And the security is so poor that the contractors can't work."

"You really get worked up about this don't you," Andrew said. "I shouldn't have brought it up."

"Yes you should bring it up. You and all Americans need to know what it is like to live in a war zone. You need to picture your own family having to choose between sleeping inside at night and sweltering in 100 degree heat without air conditioning or sleeping on the roof, risking death. You know they are families just like American families. The parents want to hold jobs to provide for their children. They want their children to go to school and grow up to be productive and happy just like in America. They didn't ask the American Military to come in a blow their country apart."

"Yeah, I see what you mean. If people could think about how much we are all alike, we would be better for it."

"Exactly. But there are things about the Americans attacking Iraq that we will never know."

Andrew thought for a minute. "What do you mean by that?"

"Well, we will never really know why America attacked Iraq. I mean the real reason. Was it Saddam killing his people, I don't think so. Was it WMD's. I think the Walters administration knew they weren't there. Was it for oil? Possibly. And to position themselves in the Middle East so they would have more control of the region."

"I am sorry for your people. I hope we can make it right for them some day."

"And look what the war is doing to your country. Americans are divided, billions of dollars being spent on war. Your soldiers are dying. Your president's credibility is in question."

"How so?"

"Well, the administration lied to go to war. Saddam had gotten rid of his weapons long ago. And he wasn't a threat to anyone. He was just trying to keep his country together."

"All of what you say is true. I can't disagree with you."

Andrew pulled Simone into him.

"I'm tired, John. I need to go to bed early and get a full nights sleep."

Andrew still couldn't get used to being called by his alias. "Yeah, I'd better go. I don't want to leave Mom alone tonight."

*   *   *

"What are you doing, Mother?" Andrew asked as he walked into their hotel room later that night.

"I am packing. Can't you see that?" Carol retorted sarcastically.

"Yes, I see that, but where are you going? Are you angry because I'm late getting back from Simone's place?"

"No, I'm not angry. I am leaving early in the morning for Bordeaux. Claude has invited us to come and stay with him for a while. He says we'll be safer there than we are here in Paris."

"I thought we were a team. Why didn't you wait to talk to me before you committed to going?"

"You didn't consult with me before getting involved with Simone. And I wouldn't expect you to."

Andrew shook his head in disgust. "That's different." Andrew started to pace the room. "You hardly know this man. How can you trust him?"

"You're right, I hardly know him, but I think I'm a good judge of character and he seems honest and I'm willing to take the risk to be out from under the eyes of the FBI or CIA or whoever is following us. They're watching us constantly. Do you realize that they could just sweep in and arrest us at any time at their whim?"

Carol folded her dress and put it into her bag and then went into the bathroom to collect her cosmetics. "Claude has a cottage we can stay in and have privacy. He said he would teach us all about growing grapes and making wine. Doesn't that sound fascinating? And we can see another part of France. I am so excited."

"I'm not going with you."

"What're you going to do? Are you staying behind in the hotel? You'd better get an apartment, it'll be cheaper," Carol said, resigned to the fact that she could no longer control her son's life.

Andrew sat down on his bed. "I think I'll bunk in with Simone. We just bought a bunch of furniture and stuff for her apartment today and I don't think she would mind having me move in with her."

"And how well do you know *her*? And can *you* trust *her*?"

"Touché. But I feel that Simone is trustworthy just like you do with Claude. And I don't want to leave Paris. This is where it's happening and to go to Bordeaux would be really boring for me. I'd literally die on the vine in Bordeaux, no pun intended."

"Very funny. Well, I am going and you can stay here if you want. I can't tell you what to do. Come and visit and bring Simone. And call me often. We need to have that communication going between us."

"I agree," said Andrew as he took off his shirt and pants and crawled into bed. His mother was going to do what she liked as she had shown in the past. He couldn't stop her even though he had misgivings about her leaving him and Paris. He did not like the idea of her being so far away from him where he couldn't protect her. But he had to have trust.

Chapter 11

The Iraq War

"Twenty-one US soldiers killed when their assault vehicle was blown up by a roadside bomb on Wednesday." James sat in the Oval office and read the headline in the Washington Post. He had returned from Paris two days before and was catching up on paper work that had piled up while he was gone. Looking at the headline again, he was dismayed that this was on the front page. His media group tried to manage news so that all Iraq news, especially if it was bad, would be put towards the back pages of newspapers. Although he knew this would be all over the Internet. They had not been able to control the Internet, as it was not yet in the grips of the large media giants and corporations. But soon this would change. There was a bill in Congress to regulate the Internet. On page 2,058 at the very bottom in small print, there was a clause stating that if the nation was at war and if the article reported on issues that were incendiary to the war, they could be censored for national security. It made sense to him.

He read on. "The attack on Wednesday which targeted the lightly armored assault vehicle, calls attention to the fact that the US is dealing with a highly adaptable, ever changing enemy using deadlier techniques and explosives in an attempt to carry out even more spectacular terrorist strikes."

This war was indeed becoming the mess that everyone had warned about and James success as president depended on winning. But could they ever win when they were fighting in the middle of a civil war? And just what was winning?

James recalled reading about the history of Iraq. The world's first civilization was developed in Sumner, what is now southeast Iraq, in

3500 BC. And in 539 BC the Persians conquered Mesopotamia and then Alexander the Great took control of the area in 331 BC. Iraq had been an area of fertile land with two major rivers, the Tigris and the Euphrates. Crops grew abundantly in the fertile soil and civilization flourished long before Egypt, Greece and Rome were established. Baghdad was founded in 750 AD after the Arab Muslims conquered the Sassanids and it grew to a million people becoming a center of trade and culture. But then in 1258 the Arab Empire was destroyed when the Ottomans gained control of the region. By the 1700's the Ottoman's power in Mesopotamia began to decline. The United Kingdom became involved, wanting to protect trade routes with India in the 1800's. Having an interest in its oil reserves in 1920, the League of Nations gave them a mandate to rule over Mesopotamia and in 1921 they set up a new government choosing an Arab, King Faisal I, as ruler and renaming the region Iraq. The United Kingdom signed a treaty with Iraq in 1930, promising to provide military protection and eventual independence if Iraq would allow the British to maintain air bases in the country and in 1932 Iraq became an independent nation.

After World War II started the Iraqi government sought to form an alliance with Germany, Italy and Japan wanting to get rid of the British influence in their land and after five years of conflict with the British, they finally gained full control over their country forming the Arab League. Iraq then signed agreements with foreign companies where Iraq would receive fifty percent of the profits of oil drilled there. Conflict continued though, well into the 1960's with the Kurds asking for autonomy and the Shiites and the Baathists vying for power, until 1970 when Al-Bakr overthrew then current leader, Abdul Arif and took power, giving the Kurds self-rule and positions in government. The Baath party was reestablished and all oil production was taken over by the government.

James then remembered when Saddam Hussein came to power with the help of the US government in 1979 and the invasion of Iran in 1980, which lasted for eight years. 150,000 Iraqi soldiers died in that war and the Iraq economy was severely damaged. And then in 1990, Iraq invaded Kuwait after accusing them of violating oil production set by the Organization of the Petroleum Exporting Countries, OPEC, and causing the price of oil to drop. The United Nations called for

Iraq to withdraw and the UN Security Council approved the use of force to remove Iraqi troops if they did not leave by January 15, 1991. Iraq did not comply and thirty-nine countries formed a coalition and began bombing Iraq, defeating the Iraqi army in the Persian Gulf War. By April 11, 1991 Iraq agreed to a formal ceasefire and the war was formally over. As a part of the cease-fire agreement, Iraq was supposed to destroy all of its biological and chemical weapons and the facilities to produce those weapons. And this is one of the reasons United States gave in the lead up to the current war with Iraq. They maintained that Saddam had not destroyed those weapons, weapons given to him by the United States in the first place during the Iraq Iran war.

James thought about how it was almost a curse to be a small country in our present day society and have a resource like oil that everyone needs and wants. If the country is too small to defend itself, a goliath will take it over along with its valuable resource like the United States was doing with Iraq. But there were other reasons for the US to be invading Iraq. The country was geopolitically situated in the center of the Middle Eastern countries and if the US forces could maintain control there, they could control the whole region and the very valuable oil resources. In addition, Iraq was threatening to start trading oil in Euros, which would have a devastating effect on the dollar and subsequently the US economy. And a side benefit of the conflict would be the boon to defense companies with contracts to rebuild the country after bombing it. But, as sometimes happens, the efforts to control Iraq after the initial invasion, had gone awry. And James was in a quandary as to what to do. If they pulled the troops out altogether as many of the American people and the Iraqis were asking, the country would likely disintegrate and if that happened, the oil would be lost altogether. If they didn't pull out, the conflicts would continue with the insurgents and many more US soldiers and Iraqis would be losing their lives. As it stood now, over four million Iraqis had left the country fearing for their lives. And the monetary cost was becoming more of a liability for the United States. How many times could he go before congress and ask for another eighty, ninety billion dollars to fund a war that we were apparently losing.

The other problem was that Iraq was becoming the new training ground for al Qaeda and terrorists. They were flowing in from neighboring countries with borders that were impossible to guard and they were learning how to blow up busses and trains and then going out into the world and using this knowledge. There were more terrorist attacks in 2004 than any year since 1985 and because they didn't want the American people to know these statistics, they decided to eliminate a nineteen-year-old international terrorism report called Patterns of Global Terrorism. This way the American public would not be alarmed.

James rose from his desk to attend a cabinet meeting he had called especially to deal with the escalating Iraq crisis. When he entered the room all of the cabinet members were present and rose to greet him as he took his seat in the middle of the table.

"I have called this special meeting to discuss our strategy in Iraq. You are all aware that the violence in Iraq is escalating. We now have contractors pulling out of the country because it is just too violent and dangerous to work there. And we are also losing some of our coalition forces this fall. Japan is pulling out, Australia and even Great Britain, our staunchest ally. With more of our troops dying, and the media reporting these deaths, the American people are turning against the war and against our leadership. We need to find a strategy to counteract this and we need it now. I have called you all here to talk about this and to help me find a solution," James said as he started the meeting.

"I don't think we should do anything. This will blow over. As the Marines train more of the Iraqis to police the country, coalition casualties should go down," said Jason the vice president.

"I agree with you, Jason. But we could set a tentative date to pull out. And then if that doesn't work out.... well you know what I mean. That way the Iraqis will think we are leaving and take on more responsibility, quite likely the insurgency will drop and the American public will then see that we have a strategy to bring the troops home. That will appease them for the time being," said Secretary of Defense Charles Roberts.

Tom Wiley, James new secretary of state was taking all of this in and making notes. "We can't leave Iraq," he said. "If we do, all hell will break loose. Do you all realize that the Iraqi Shiite is forming an alliance with Iran? If the majority Shiite become the dominant party and take over the Iraqi government, Iraq will revert to a fundamentalist Muslim country. And we don't want this to happen."

"And what about the bases that we built in the last two years?" asked Chuck Roberts. "Are we just going to abandon them? We've spent billions in building these bases and we need to get ROI."

James took a long drink of water from the white crystal glass in front of him. "No we can't just pull out, but to allow the insurgents to keep on killing our troops is going to be a loser for us." James paused again to see if he could read the facial expressions on the faces of his cabinet. He couldn't. "I like Chuck's idea of setting a tentative date."

"But if we do that and then renege, our word won't be worth anything anymore," said Tom.

"I don't think it is anyway these days," said Jason. "But that doesn't matter. What matters is getting through mid terms with as much support as possible and then it will all be moot." Jason fidgeted with his pen. "We should set the date for next spring some time, say April. Mid terms will be in full swing by that time."

"But if we say we're going to pull out and then we don't, how will we explain this to the American public, the voters?" James asked.

"I think we should have Iraq hold elections at the same time that we are having ours. Then we can use the excuse that we decided to stay to help with elections. The country is not stable, who could quibble with us on that point?" said Jason.

"And the American people have a short attention span. Within a month they will be back with their sports teams and TV series and forget that we ever said we would pull out."

"I like that idea, Jason. I think we should run with it. I'll call Mark Richards and have him issue a press release this afternoon. And likely this topic will come up in the daily press conference tomorrow. We need to prepare a statement for Mark."

They all seemed quite satisfied with the new strategy and talked for another hour on other issues; the economy, the price of oil and cost of gas at the pump and terrorism abroad. James then went back to the Oval office alone and sat down again at his desk. His mind was racing. If they couldn't maintain the majority in Congress, he might as well resign. He would be a lame duck president and more than that, he feared impeachment.

Chapter 12

Carol Goes to Bordeaux

Claude drove through the outskirts of Paris, getting onto highway A10 that would take them all the way to Bordeaux, some 700 miles south of Paris on the East Coast of France. From the comfort of Claude's dark blue Volvo with soft, camel colored leather seats, Carol saw the other side of Paris with apartment buildings lining streets where the working class and the unemployed lived in sometimes squalid, crowded conditions. People with the ethnic diversity of the United Nations, coming into France from every poor country, hoping to find work where they had been unable to in their own country; from Africa, Spain and Italy, blacks and Muslims, some Asians hoping to better themselves only to find that they were again in a pool of piranhas, eat or be eaten, living as second class citizens. She had seen similar conditions in Mexico City and in Madrid. How many of these people go to bed at night without supper, she wondered. But living conditions in Paris were probably better than those in many places in the world.

They had departed from the hotel at 6:00 a.m. that morning as it would be a twelve-hour drive from Paris to Bordeaux and Claude wanted to get an early start. As a precautionary measure Claude parked in the alley of the hotel just in case someone would be watching and he told her to wear dark clothing and cover her face with a scarf, Muslim style, when she walked from the hotel to the car. Andrew came down to the lobby to talk to Claude and Carol cried as she held onto Andrew and kissed him goodbye. She began to have second thoughts about going with Claude. She had known him for less than a week and she was going to his home with him? Far away from her son who had been her protector these past few months in exile. But she had invited

Andrew to come with her and he refused. And after all, Andrew could take care of himself, couldn't he? She had turned to walk away and Claude gave Andrew a handshake and told him that he didn't have to worry about his mother. She would be well taken care of and looked after and that he should visit soon.

And now they were driving through French farm country with rolling hills and white fenced pastures where black and white cows while chewing their cud, whisked flies away with their tails. Oh, to be a cow, she thought. Eat and make love and eat some more. It seemed like the ideal life, but cows had other problems.

"Are you enjoying your time in France?" Claude asked, breaking the silence and trying to make small talk.

"Yes, I love your country. I would like to live here."

"You could do that you know. There are many expatriates from the States living in France."

"It is a beautiful country and so rich in history."

They drove on until reaching the first large city, Orleans.

"Speaking of history, this is where Joan of Arc was martyred in the mid 1400's", Claude said.

"Yes, I've read about that."

"The city was badly damaged by World War II, but has since been rebuilt."

"Wars! What do they solve?" Carol asked.

"This war was necessary I'm afraid to say. Hitler wanted to take all of Europe and more and he had to be stopped."

"I agree with that. But how was he able to get as far as he did. People must have supported him to allow him to become so powerful."

"This seems to happen periodically throughout history. Napoleon was another one of those power hungry leaders that wanted to rule the world. Some say President Walters is imperialistic. With his go it alone policies in Iraq, opting out of the World Court of Law and the ABM treaty."

"Yes, you could be right about that. All I know is that I couldn't go along with the administrations policies, domestic or foreign."

"And that's why you're divorcing him?" Claude asked hesitatingly. He paused and looked at the road for a few minutes and before Carol answered he said, "Excuse me, I don't mean to pry. You don't have to answer that if you don't want to."

"It's okay. I can talk about it. But there isn't much to say really. I went forward with the divorce and James and his people tried to stop me. So here I am running away from everything."

"You aren't running away, you just had to get to a safe place where they couldn't harm you. I understand your husband's administration not wanting people to know about the divorce, though. He likely would have lost the election."

"That is true. You know I asked him to step down and he wouldn't. And when I talked with him on Wednesday he said he was sorry and almost wished he had." Carol looked out the window at the pastoral farm scene they were passing through. "I think he's in way over his head."

"Would you go back to him if he did step down?"

"I don't think so. Our marriage is broken. He should have done more to protect me and he didn't. I can't forgive him for that."

"When he took that oath of office, he promised to put his country first. You know that don't you."

"I don't think he is putting the country first. The road they are following is really bad for our people and our country."

They passed near Blois, another larger city. The countryside had not changed, still farm country with rivers, small lakes and ponds here and there. Carol missed seeing mountains, but there were no mountains in this part of France.

"I think we'll stop in Tours for some lunch. How does that sound to you?"

Claude was very considerate and polite. She wondered if he was always like this or was there a dark side to him. She hoped she wouldn't find out.

"Yes, I would like that."

They found a small cafe, mid town and ordered soup with bread and cheese.

"I think what I love most about France is the food."

"Yes, we are known for our food and wines. Just wait until you taste some of my fine wine. You will love it I know.

"And what is the history of this city?"

"How much time do you have? But to be brief, this is the Loire Valley and Tours was where Charles Martel defeated the Moors, halting the Muslim advance in Europe in 742."

"I can't even think back that far."

"I know. America is such a new country, with the exception of the Native American Indian."

"Any building 200 years old is considered old in our country,"

"I think America is just now beginning to grow up, like a troublesome teen on the verge of becoming an adult."

Carol had to agree with that.

After lunch they got back on the freeway and traveled south and east. They passed through the smaller town of Poitiers. As they came closer to the Atlantic Ocean, the vegetation became verdant with moisture constantly bathing the coastline.

"This must be the perfect place to grow grapes for wine," Carol said.

"It is. We produce the finest wines in the world here. But I will have to say that California is giving us some competition."

It was seven in the evening when they pulled up to the ornate wrought iron gate of the Montague Vineyard. The early evening air was heavy with the fog coming in from the coast and smelled of the earth and the plants that were abundant everywhere. It was a fresh, pleasant smell, so different from the dusty smells of the ranch back home and she liked it.

"I called ahead and had my housekeeper prepare *la petite maison* for you," Claude said as he hit a button on the dashboard of his car, opening the gate. "I'll take you there first as you must be tired. It is a long drive from Paris."

He then drove up a long, narrow road flanked on both sides by small trees that Carol supposed to be the vines of the grape. As she turned her head and looked out the window, Carol caught a glimpse of a magnificent chateaux that looked like a small castle. Claude drove a little further and stopped in front of a small English looking cottage, whitewashed with a thatched roof, windows with dark green shutters and a very inviting front door. He got out of the car, opened Carol's door and helped her out.

"Welcome to Chateaux Montague. I hope you have a pleasant stay here."

"I'm sure I will. This is beautiful."

Claude opened the door of the cottage and turned on the lights. They walked into the living room area that was furnished with a cabbage rose print sofa and a big old easy chair upholstered in forest green velvet. There was a small fireplace in the center of the room with a painting of what Carol thought was the Loire Valley done in the style of the impressionists. Claude went to get her bag and when he returned he took them into one of the two bedrooms and set it on the luggage rack at the end of the bed. Then he turned to Carol, who had followed him into the room, and put his big arms around her, enveloping her.

"Welcome to your home away from home. If there is anything that I can do to make your visit more enjoyable, let me know. I am here to please."

Carol hugged him back. And then he left her there.

After looking around the cottage, seeing the small dining area with French Country style dining table and chairs and the kitchen with white cabinets and an old gas stove, Carol went back into the bedroom to unpack.

He really is a nice man, she thought. And then she picked up the telephone and called the hotel to see if Andrew was still there and Janelle answered at the front desk and told her that Andrew had checked out that afternoon. Carol said *"merci"* and hung up the phone. But she was worried. She had no way of reaching Andrew. Claude had given him his phone number and so Andrew could call them at the chateaux but she didn't know Simone's number. No matter, she thought. Andrew would call soon, she was sure. And she put on her nightshirt and got into the very soft down bed, pulled up the down comforter and fell asleep in minutes.

Chapter 13

Washington is Watching

"What do you mean, you lost her?" James yelled over the phone to Secret Service Director Nick Bowerman from his bedroom in the White House private quarters. "You were supposed to be watching her at all times. She couldn't just slip away that easily. What happened?"

"She was in her hotel room last night. We saw her go into the hotel after dinner. And we didn't see her leave in the morning. We've had our detail with a video cam directed on her room from an office building across the street since she got there. Then about 3:30 p.m. we saw Andrew walk out of the hotel without her. So we got curious and called the hotel and they told us they had checked out. Separately. I don't know how it happened."

"Well, goddam it, you find her," James exclaimed.

"Look, Mr. President, she's not going to do any harm from where she is. The way we see it, she's just trying to stay out of the way right now. Unless she would come back to the States," said Nick. "And we have better things to do. Our full effort is on you these days and it isn't an easy task. We caught this guy trying to sneak onto the White House grounds last week carrying a Glock. He told us he was intending to kill you because you killed his cousin in Iraq. Sure, he was a kook, but they're all over the place."

"Looks like she and Andrew have split up. What about this new girlfriend? Have you seen her recently?" James asked ignoring Nick's last statement.

"She's been dragging furniture and boxes into her apartment. That's about all. But there is something strange going on there too. We've seen some guys going into her apartment building that look like they are straight from Saudi. Don't know what that's all about."

"Do you think they're going to see her?" James asked.

"We don't really know. We saw her with two of them in a cafe a couple of days ago, so there must be a connection."

"We need to get the CIA involved in this. If his girlfriend is palling around with Saudis, they could be planning something and it could involve Andrew."

"I'll call over there today. I agree, it doesn't look good. But we did find out that his girlfriend, Simone is her name, is part Iraqi. Her old man is from Baghdad and her mother is American."

"This really concerns me now. You have to keep on top of it and I want you to find Carol. We need to know where she is so that if and when she comes back to the States we'll know about it. And then let the other agencies handle the Andrew thing."

"Yes, Mr. President. We will."

"And report back to me tomorrow. In fact I want a daily status report from you. Do you understand?"

"Yes, Mr. President."

James slammed down the phone. "Damn," he said under his breath. He had enough to deal with without this. She could slip into the country and restart the divorce proceedings and some wild ass reporter could pick up on it and blow their cover. So far, the public had more or less forgotten about Carol, his wife, the first lady gone missing. It was almost as if they didn't care. But he was sure that wasn't it. There was a lot for people to sort through these days. The war, sky rocketing gas prices, people losing jobs and homes. And then the Social Security and Medicare problems and the list goes on. He was sure they hadn't forgotten about her, they just had more pressing matters. But if Carol made the headlines again, people would start asking questions and there might be an inquiry and Congress could appoint a special council to investigate. Those who were working against him could use this to indict him and the public cry for impeachment could become very loud indeed. He shivered thinking about it. He felt like he was on a high wire between two buildings in Manhattan, looking into an abyss and he could fall in at any moment. If someone cut the wire, down he would go, splat on the street below. He shivered thinking about it.

The phone rang, breaking his reverie.

"Hello, James here."

"James, hi, this is Jason."

"Damn it, I know who you are. What do you want? It's late."

"Little testy now aren't you?"

"I just got off the phone with Nick over in Secret Service. They've lost Carol again. If she comes back and starts trouble, we could be in for some difficult times."

"We have more to worry about than that. We talked with the Iraqi president this morning and he said that they will not be finishing the new constitution before the deadline next Saturday."

"And so. What difference does it make if they don't?"

"It will look like another failure on our part to bring democracy to Iraq. We've missed deadlines on the elections over there three times. If this keeps happening, our credibility will be in question. And, you know we are hoping that having the constitution in place will deflate the support for the insurgency."

"What's holding it up?"

"They've worked a good portion of it, but they can't get past the questions of federalism and the role of Islam in the government."

"What are you talking about?"

"The different factions are trying to split the country into separate federated states with a weaker central government in Baghdad. And these would be comprised of the Shiite Muslims in the south, the Sunni Arabs in and around Baghdad and the Kurds in the north."

"And just why is that a problem?"

"The Sunnis are agreeing with the self rule for the Kurdish region in the north, but they fear that full federalism could break up the country making it weaker. Giving the Shiite an autonomous government in central and southern Iraq would give them control of the largest oil fields. And of course there is the issue of how the Islamic influence will play out in all of this."

"There's not much more that we can do, is there?"

"We may need to step in and put some pressure on the Sunnis to accept the new constitution. Of course if we do interfere at this point, we could be castigated for trying to influence them and our critics would label the new Iraqi government a puppet government of the

United States. But if this continues the way it's going, the whole thing could fall apart in October."

"How so?" James asked as he lay back down on his bed.

"The Sunni clerics are urging their followers to register and vote in the October 15 constitutional referendum and to vote against the charter if it contains federalism."

"But with the Shiite and the Kurds in agreement, they would have the majority, overruling the Sunnis. I've also been hearing rumors that the Shiites are aligning with Iran. This could be disastrous for our intervention into the area," said James.

"It's almost like the Shiite and the Kurds are ganging up on the Sunnis in retribution for years of abuse when Saddam was in control. They even want to change the name of the country to the Iraqi Federal Republic and the Sunnis are having none of this." Jason was quiet for a moment. "I just wanted you to have a heads up before this all hits the headlines tomorrow. You will be asked questions about it tomorrow so you had better prepare some statements and let Mark know also."

"Thanks, Jason. I appreciate the warning. I'll talk to you tomorrow. Looks like we will have to call a meeting tomorrow with Tom and Chuck, maybe even get Don Struthers involved if it's necessary to develop a military strategy."

"I don't know if we want to get General Struthers involved, but I'll talk to you tomorrow and we can decide then."

James hung up the phone. He had that empty feeling that took over his body much of the time these days, the feeling that he was losing control. Control over this runaway government, the Iraq war and control over his own life. But he didn't know at this point what he could do about it. He missed Carol.

Chapter 14

Domestic Bliss

Andrew and Simone had been living together only a week, but they were beginning to act like an old married couple. They both worked now and shared household tasks, the cooking, cleaning and laundry. Simone had found a job as a junior accountant with one of the large accounting firms in Paris and she was gone most of the day and Andrew continued to pick up courier jobs allowing him to be able to meet half of the financial obligations with the apartment. In the evening they would both come back to the apartment located in the sixteenth arrondissement on a small street off Ave Victor Hugo. It was an older area of Paris, but they were all old as Paris is one of the oldest cities in the world.

Most evenings they would bring home fresh food from the market, Andrew would pour himself a glass of wine and for Simone juice or iced tea and they would sit on their balcony and watch the sun set over Paris roof tops, talking about the day's activities. Then they would cook and sit at the small dining table to enjoy their meal together. After dinner they would often walk to the park or maybe go to a cafe for coffee, joining the multitude of other Parisians out for the evening; then it was back to the apartment for bedtime.

Andrew had tried calling his mother several times since she left for Bordeaux and was not able to reach anyone. He was concerned but he felt more comfortable with his mother in Bordeaux, out from under the radar of the prying and potentially dangerous US agents. He now wondered if they were monitoring him and he thought they probably were. But there wasn't much he could do about it. He wasn't doing anything wrong. Certainly they could try to arrest him, but if that made headlines in Paris, Americans would hear about it and start to ask questions. So he just went about his business and tried to forget about Secret Service and FBI and everything American, immersing himself in French culture, picking up more of the language every day as one does when living in a foreign land.

He and Simone spent most of their non-working time together, but occasionally Simone would go out alone. She told him she was going out with girl friends, but he somehow felt she was lying to him. One evening she stayed out very late, after midnight, and he was worried. Andrew was in bed when she turned the key in the apartment door and tiptoed across the living room into the kitchen. He was going to pretend to be asleep, but then he got up and walked out into the kitchen wearing only his boxer shorts.

"Where have you been? I was worried about you."

Simone was standing at the window drinking a glass of milk. She was wearing black silk slacks with a low cut royal blue silk top.

"Out with friends."

"What friends?"

"Girlfriends. Look, we're not married. I don't have to answer to you. I can go out with whomever I please."

"I saw you talking with two Arab looking guys yesterday. What was that all about?"

"Are you spying on me? Because if you are...."

"No, I'm not spying. I was looking out the window last night as you were coming home and I saw you crossing the street and these two men were just there like they were waiting for you. And then you were talking to them. Are they friends of yours?"

"Look, John, we have a large Muslim community here and you knew that I was Muslim didn't you?"

"The thought crossed my mind with your dad coming from Iraq," Andrew said thinking what he had been afraid to ask.

"They're friends from school. I know many Arab looking men. That's who I am."

"But what are you doing with them. I've heard that Muslim women are not even allowed to talk to males unless they are with their fathers or brothers or they're marrying them. And you smoke cigarettes. Isn't that against Islamic faith? "

"I don't practice the fundamentalist faith. I am living in France and we do things differently just like I am sure the Muslims in America do. If I were fundamentalist I wouldn't have even approached you that day at the Sorbonne. And I certainly would not be cohabitating with you."

"What sect, ah, just what kind of a Muslim are you?" Andrew stumbled over his words.

"Sunni. You know the same as Saddam's Baathist's were, are still today. Our people make up about thirteen per cent of the Iraq population."

Andrew paced the small kitchen and then walked into the dining area and opened the doors to the balcony to breathe some fresh air. Simone followed.

"John, don't worry so much," Simone held Andrew's shoulders and looked into his eyes and smiled. "One of them is in my father's class. They are fine. It seems that Americans are so homophobic about anyone who looks like an Arab these days."

"I guess you're right. I'm sorry. Why don't you invite them up to the apartment some time? We could all have a drink together."

"I will do that. Now, *chérie*, let's go to bed."

Simone led Andrew back to the bedroom and sat him down on the bed while she took her clothes off. He felt like he was being patronized, but he was enjoying it.

They turned out the light and made love. Afterward, Simone turned to Andrew.

"You know John, sometimes I think you are not being totally honest with me. Is that true?"

Andrew looked up at the dark ceiling and thought for a minute or two. Should he tell her? Could he trust her? He wasn't certain. But he sure hated living a lie.

"You are right. I have not been totally honest with you."

Simone sat up and turned on the light, pulling the pastel sheet up over her small breasts. "You can trust me. I promise you can."

"Let's start with my name. It's not John. It's Andrew."

"I like the name Andrew. Is there more?"

"There is but I'm not so sure that I should tell you."

"Take your time. If you don't want to tell me now, you can later." And with that Simone turned off the light and snuggled down next to

Andrew. "But now I am really intrigued. Are you a CIA operative? A spy maybe?"

Andrew laughed. "Hardly. Living with my mother in a hotel room? I don't think so."

"You are a beautiful man Andrew and I love being with you."

Andrew purred and, together they drifted off to sleep, arms and legs entwined.

*　　*　　*

Carol opened her eyes to the bright sun peeping through the shutters and it reminded her of home on the ranch so far away from France. She thought it must be late in the morning. She had slept well, thinking she was finally safe and away from any agents who might be trailing her. She remembered that they had not had dinner last night as they had enjoyed a late lunch in Tours and she was hungry.

Not that she was starving these past weeks. Food had been too plentiful and highly caloric since she had been in France and she knew she was partaking more than she should by the way her clothes were fitting lately. As a teenager and a young wife and mother, Carol had always been super thin, wearing a size four or six and food was a secondary item for her; she could take it or leave it. But lately, eating had become a passion, the rich sauces and meats and even the wonderful pastries and deserts she had seldom eaten before coming to France were tempting her at every meal and she could see the beginning of a roll on her stomach when she looked in the mirror. She could just barely get into her clothes anymore.

The telephone by the bed rang and she picked up the receiver.

"Hello, Madame. This is room service. I hope I didn't wake you."

"Claude, you aren't room service," Carol giggled.

"I am this morning. How about I bring breakfast to you. I have blueberry muffins, scrambled eggs, fresh squeezed juice and hot coffee."

"That sounds like a very delightful American breakfast."

"It is. I want to you to feel at home. Put on something suitable and I will be there in a few minutes."

What a sweet man, she thought. What if she fell in love with him? Then she thought she couldn't do that. She was still a married woman.

But it was an intriguing idea. She had always heard about how gallant French men were, but she had also heard that they cheated on their wives and she would not go for that. But American men did too. Fortunately James had never been unfaithful to her, that she knew of.

Carol raced to find a pair of slacks and a knit top, and then went into the bathroom to wash her face, brush her teeth, comb her hair and put on some lip gloss. There was a slight knock at the front door. Searching for a pair of shoes, she ran to the door and asked who was there and Claude answered, "Room service, Madam." Opening the door, there was Claude holding this oversized tray of food covered with white linen napkins.

"At your service, Madam. May I come in?"

"Oh, Claude, you are so wonderful. But I am afraid I look travel worn."

Claude walked through the door and into the dining area, placing the tray on the table. He opened the shutters and the windows and the sunlight and fresh country air flowed into the room. He went to the kitchen and gathered up plates and silver ware and set the table, then pulling out a chair, he motioned for Carol to sit.

"You are beautiful in the morning."

He then sat in the chair opposite hers and started passing the eggs and muffins, pouring the juice and coffee.

"You slept well, I trust."

"Like I haven't slept in days. It must be the fresh country air."

Claude took her hand between bites of food. "I am glad you're here."

"Thank you. I am too."

They continued to eat and Carol looked out the window and she could see the rows of grape vines.

"They are everywhere."

"What is everywhere?"

"The grapevines."

"Yes, we have to utilize every square meter of land."

Carol looked then at Claude. "You speak English so well. How is that?"

"I was raised in the United States."

"Your parents moved there?"

"No. My parents were at Auschwitz but before the Nazis took them away, they sent me to England to live with an aunt and she couldn't take care of me so after a couple of years she sent me to live in New York with my father's sister. I was five years old by then."

"Did your parents survive?"

"No, they figure they must have been killed in 1945, just before the war ended. I didn't really ever know them of course, but I have seen photographs. It's strange though, even as I was very young when I was separated from them, I remembered my mother's face. She had very dark hair, rolled up around her face and she had a warm smile. I must have been about two years old."

"I am so sorry. But did your aunt and uncle treat you well?"

"Oh, yes, very well. They were very strict. But I know they loved me. They had two children of their own, my cousins, Gwendolyn and Chad and we fought like most siblings much of the time, but if anyone on the playground attacked one of us, we were there to protect. We were family."

"And then how did you happen to come back to France?"

"Well, that's a long story. My Uncle Fred and Aunt Ruth had money. He was a jeweler and owned a jewelry store on Long Island where they had this big old house. He sent me to college, New York University to learn to be a civil engineer. He said that engineers would never be out of work as there was always something being constructed and you had to have someone design it before it could be built. I graduated in 1960. I then married Jocelyn. Her father was in the same business as my father and we had known each other as children."

Carol sipped her coffee while listening intently to Claude's story.

"I was hired by the City of New York as a civil engineer. I had interned with them the summer before my senior year in college and they liked my work, so they hired me. I was very pleased. We bought a little house on Long Island to be close to the family and I commuted into the city every day for fifteen years. And then one day, in 1975 I believe, uncle Fred told me about some land the family had owned in the Bordeaux region of France. The Nazis had taken it over during the war, but then when they were defeated, it was turned over to a distant relative in France and he died and willed it to Uncle Fred who then asked if I would like to go to France and start a vineyard? The old chateau was on the property, although in disrepair as was this cottage which was used by the hired help."

"You must have been thrilled."

"Well, yes I was, but I knew nothing about growing grapes or making wine. I was only about thirty-five years old and we were just about to adopt our first child."

"Yes, you told me about that."

"Being adventuresome, we decided this might lead to a very fine life. New York was kind of getting to me, although I loved my work. We would be living in the country and working the land and that appealed to me. So I took a crash course in wine making at the university and we packed up and moved to France. We thought we could then adopt when we got settled but it didn't work out that way."

"And so does this all belong to Uncle Fred then?"

"No, he told me that if I built a successful winery, in ten years it would all be mine and so he deeded it to me in 1985."

"You have a generous family."

"I think this land belonged to Uncle Fred and my father, so it most likely would have been handed down to me at some point in time. And I have worked for it. Jocelyn and I both worked very hard to get Montague Vineyards profitable. She handled the accounting part, the business end of it and marketing, and I took care of the growing and the making of the wine. We had a partnership."

"I had that partnership with James when we were running the ranch. I took care of the accounting and he handled the livestock although I was out there in snowstorms feeding cattle a couple of times."

"Oh, I forgot to tell you, Andrew called. He wanted to know if we had gotten here safely and I told him that we arrived in good time yesterday. He's very concerned about you."

"I'm so glad. I didn't know where to reach him since he had checked out of the hotel."

"I invited him to come and visit and he said he would bring Simone next week."

Carol spent the next few days touring the winery, learning all about growing grapes and the art of making wine. To her surprise, it was a relatively simple process, albeit delicate, in the timing of picking the grapes at the height of their maturity when the sugar content was just right. Then, the crushing, no longer done by people stomping on them in huge vats with bare feet, but by efficient crushing machines that separate the skins, the seeds and stems from the juice which was then put into large oak barrels for fermenting. This ancient process intrigued her.

She and Claude spent the next few days touring the area. They spent time in Bordeaux, a city of 100,000 people in the heart of the wine country and then they drove through the ancient Dordogne valley, visiting the hilltop castles. They spent another day driving to Roquefort-sur-Soulzon in the south of France, touring the cheese factories where the famous cheese named after the region, is made. Claude told her that this was the favorite cheese of Charlemagne and Carol learned that the blue veins of mold in the cheese came from the penicillin found in the soil in the local caves. She also learned that traditionally the cheese makers extracted it by leaving bread in the caves for six to eight weeks until the bread was covered with the mold, then adding it to the ewe's milk when they made the cheese and aging the cheese for four months in those same caves. That was the old way but nowadays the mold is produced in laboratories.

The days were flying by and Andrew and Simone were soon to arrive, and Carol was excited about this. She missed Andrew terribly having not been away from him for any length of time during their exile. She prepared the other bedroom in her cottage for them, making sure the sheets and towels were fresh. She went to the market and bought food, fresh fruits and vegetables, bread and eggs for breakfast. Claude had given her a car to use any time she wanted to go into the nearby village or into the city. She was grateful as this made her feel less dependant on him.

The day of Andrew's arrival came. Carol put on her best dress and carefully combed her hair and applied her makeup. She was nervous about meeting Simone. What if she didn't like her? And maybe Simone would not like her. But she soon put this out of her mind. After all, Andrew was not marrying this girl. At least not that she knew of.

Carol went to the window, pulled the lace curtains aside to see if they had arrived and then went back to tidying up the cottage. Finally she heard a car drive up in the driveway in front of the cottage. She looked out the window again and saw the Peugeot convertible with

Simone in the driver's seat. She opened the front door and ran out to greet them. Andrew had barely gotten out of the car when his mother ran up to him and engulfed him in her arms, hugging him with tears streaming down her cheeks.

"I've been so worried about you."

"I know. I'm fine. And I have been worried about you. But you look great."

Motioning for Simone to come over and meet his mother Andrew said, "Mom, I would like you to meet Simone. She is a very special lady."

Carol extended her hand in friendship. "I am pleased to meet you, Simone," she said. "Andrew has told me much about you."

Simone took her hand and warmly shook it. "He's told me about you as well. I am pleased to meet the mother of such a fine son."

The three of them went into the cottage and Carol called Claude who then invited them all for lunch at the chateau.

After freshening up from their drive, Andrew and Simone joined Carol and they walked to the chateau. They walked up the long driveway lined with more grape vines, dispersed with a few oak trees spread out in between to bring shade to the walkway. As they approached the oversized double carved oak doorway, Carol rang the bell that had the sound of a church bell in an ancient monastery. Claude opened the door and the introductions continued. Claude, being a warm person embraced Simone and welcomed her to his home. Claude is a true French man, Carol thought. He then took them to a veranda overlooking the valley and more grape vines on the back of the house where a large round white table clothed table had been prepared with food and wine.

After they took their seats Claude passed a bottle of Montague Bordeaux wine around and another of Chablis Blanc. They exchanged pleasantries and Claude asked Simone about her family and when she told them that her father was from Iraq, Carol's eyes widened. She said nothing at that moment, but Andrew saw her concern. After lunch Claude said he would take them on a tour of the winery. It wasn't until they came back to the cottage that Carol was able to talk to Andrew alone with the ruse that she had some legal documents concerning the divorce that she wanted Andrew to look at and advise her on. Simone said she wanted to take an afternoon walk and left the cottage to Carol and Andrew.

"Let's go out to the garden in back," Carol said.

They walked out to a small flower garden with roses blooming in a profusion of color. Carol sat at the small wrought iron table on the patio and Andrew took the other chair.

"What's up?" Andrew asked.

"I am really concerned."

"I could tell that you were at lunch."

"Her family is from Iraq?"

"Just her dad. Her mother's American."

"Yes. I heard that. But there could be some sympathy there for the war in Iraq."

"I don't think so. She said most of her friends hate the American president, not Americans."

"Are you forgetting who you are?"

"No. But I haven't told her who I am."

"Are you that naive? She knows who you are, don't kid yourself. Oh, Andrew I don't want to lose you. You are all I have."

Andrew looked down at the table. He was thinking how overprotective his mother had been of him most of his life. This was most likely because he had an infant brother who died when Andrew was two years old, making him the only child and he could understand that. But his mother sometimes went overboard, not wanting him to ski because he could get caught in an avalanche and she didn't want him to play football because it was too dangerous, which he didn't want to do anyway. She was always telling him to be careful. It seemed as though she felt that death was around every corner. But then he thought about the Arab friends he had seen Simone with. Possibly Simone did know who he was. His mother could be right. Maybe he should leave Simone.

"I don't want you to go back with Simone. Stay here. You don't even have to stay in this cottage. Claude has another small house that a caretaker was using. You could live there. I am afraid for you."

"No, Mother, I'm going back with her. But I'll think about it. I might come back in a week or so."

Chapter 15

Andrew's Folly

Three days after they had arrived in Bordeaux, Simone and Andrew drove back to Paris. They left very early in the morning on Monday. When Carol put her arms around Andrew to say goodbye, tears welled up in her eyes, but she did not want to let on that she was crying. She hugged Simone, but could think of nothing to say to her. As the Peugeot pulled out of the driveway, Carol had that sinking feeling that she might not see her son again. But, no, she thought, I cannot think that way. I need to keep positive thoughts. Simone, she thought, is a nice person. And if Andrew came back in week, everything would be fine.

Claude was there and he walked back into the cottage with her and they sat together on the cabbage print sofa in the living room.

"I know how you are feeling," he said.

"I don't think you can ever know how I'm feeling," Carol said with such emotion that Claude was caught off guard. Tears were streaming down her face now and falling into her lap.

"What do you mean by that?" Claude asked, very concerned.

"I don't think you could ever know what a mother feels for her children."

"That might be true. I've not ever had any."

"I'm not talking about you. I am talking about men in general. Don't take this personally. Let me tell you a story. When Andrew was a young child, about eight years old, he was in little league. I went to every game to support him. He didn't do well because he's dyslexic. One time he had a hit and ran to third base instead of first. Everyone laughed and he was so embarrassed."

Carol put her hand to her chin in a thoughtful way. "Well one day, a fastball hit one of the other boys in the stomach so hard that the boy doubled over and fell to the ground crying out in pain. Now, this was not my child, mind you, but I felt the pain for that child as if he had been my own. It's a mother's curse I guess."

Claude was at a loss for words.

"Andrew is my only son, my only child. If anything happened to him, I don't know if I could go on." Carol thought about how she had tried not to be an overprotective parent, but whenever she thought there could be calamity awaiting Andrew she was sickened by it and even though, however hard she tried not to let Andrew know this, he was aware of the burden he carried of being the only child of an anxious mother.

Claude was quiet.

"I'm not directing this at you." Carol looked at Claude for a few moments. "You do understand that. I think you are a very caring man and you would have been a fine parent."

Claude put his arm around Carol and tried to comfort her. "Everything will work out. Andrew told me he would come back to Montague. I too think that is best. And you are right, I will never know what it is like to be a mother, carrying a child for nine months, and then caring for and nurturing that child until adulthood. Men can never have the experience of having a baby. But what I was trying to say was that I understand your concerns for Andrew."

Carol was appreciative that he told her this. She felt silly now for her outburst. It seemed that lately her emotions were controlling her more and more. Was it that her life had been turned upside down, being far away from home for such a long time, on the run from an invisible enemy? Or could it be menopause? She was certainly the right age. She vowed that she would try to have more control from now on. She was uncomfortable revealing so much of herself to a virtual stranger. Although Claude was no longer a stranger; he was almost family now.

*   *   *

Simone drove all the way from Bordeaux and she drove fast. They kept the top on the car and she played CD's, one after another.

"You sure are deep in thought," Andrew said as they were approaching the outskirts of Paris and the last CD had finished.

"Your mother is a beautiful lady. You must love her very much."

"I do. But there is more going on in that beautiful head of yours than thoughts about my mother."

"I don't think she liked me."

"That's not true, she told me that she liked you very much," he lied, trying to make Simone feel better.

"I felt her ....ah, um distrust, for lack of a better word."

"I don't think so. It sometimes takes time for my mother to warm up to people," Andrew tried to explain away his mother's aloofness with Simone. They didn't talk for the rest of the trip.

Finally reaching the apartment, Simone let Andrew off in front as she parked the car in the garage underneath the building. When she walked into the apartment, Andrew was chugging a beer and pulling out some chips from the cupboard.

"Want to go out to dinner?"

"I'm not hungry," Simone said. She went into the bedroom and changed into blue flannel pajamas and a pink chenille bathrobe, put on some slippers and then walked back out to the great room with a bestseller mystery, intending to settle into the big easy chair and read for a while. "I have to go to work early tomorrow. But you can go out if you like."

"When are we going to have your friends over?" Andrew inquired.

"I don't know. When would you like to?"

"Tomorrow night?"

"I don't think so. Maybe next week."

"I don't think I'll be here next week."

"Why not? Where are you going?"

"I'm not sure yet." Andrew didn't want to tell Simone that he was planning to join his mother, although he thought she might be able to figure that out.

"Why are you leaving?"

"Look Simone, I really like you, but, well.... it's time for me to move on."

"Simple as that?"

"Pretty much."

"Your mother influencing you?"

"No. Not really," he lied again. Andrew did not want to talk about his mother with Simone.

"I thought we had something."

"I don't think there were ever any expectations, were there?"

"No, but I was starting to really care for you."

"We'll always be friends. I appreciate your helping me get work and we've had a good time together. It's just time for me to go."

Andrew went into the bedroom and took off his pants and shirt and climbed into bed while Simone continued to read her mystery late into the night.

Carol read the headline on the front page of the New York Times as she was walking into the small food market on Friday after Andrew and Simone had left.

"FIRST SON ABDUCTED."

She picked up the paper and continued reading. "First son of President James Walters has been abducted and is being held in an undisclosed location, sources said late Thursday evening. Andrew Walters, who has been traveling with his mother in Europe for the past several months, has been reported missing by a friend of his in Paris. Further word has come from Al Jazeera that a faction of al Qaeda is holding him captive, but no further information is available. The Arab news source reported that they have a tape to be released at a later time after they verify the validity of the video."

Carol crumbled to her knees and put her head in her hands and wept. The store clerk came over and asked what was wrong in French and could he help her. She didn't fully understand what the clerk was saying but said no and rose to her feet, ran out of the market and drove back to Claude's house in a blur. Driving up to the front of the chateau, she got out of the car and ran in the front door forgetting to knock. Claude was there and he caught her in his arms.

"Darling, I know. I heard."

"They've got him. I was afraid this would happen. My god, what are we going to do?" Carol buried her head in Claude's shirt and sobbed.

"He's still alive. We'll get him back."

*   *   *

The headlines screamed with the news worldwide; "US PRESIDENT'S SON CAPTIVE IN IRAQ". "Andrew James Walters reportedly held captive in Iraq in an undisclosed location. Al Qaeda claiming responsibility. Photo shows president's son, wearing an orange jump suit, shackled to a chair."

James looked at the headlines in the Washington Post. He buried his head in hands and wept. What have I done, he thought. None of this should have happened. But then if Carol hadn't left me, Andrew would be safe at college right now. No, it wasn't my fault; it was Carol who caused this calamity. Now we have to work to find him and bring him home safely.

The phone rang and James answered.

"Oh, Jason, it's you. Yes, I know. I saw the headlines. Are you sure it's Andrew?"

"Yes, we're sure. I saw the photo. There is no mistaking, it is your son."

"How could this happen? I thought we were keeping a close watch on him."

"I don't know. We have a ransom note of sorts. I'll bring it over. Adams is coming with me. We're going to have figure out a strategy."

"Strategy? The only strategy is to do whatever it takes to get my son home alive. Do you hear that? I'm calling the CIA and special forces and getting them involved."

James slammed the phone down and then picked it up again and punched the numbers for the Secret Service.

"Nick. James here. So what happened? I thought you were watching Andrew?"

"We were. We were watching night and day. But he went to this little bar down the street from his girlfriend's apartment and never came out. They must have been watching too and rousted him out the back door or something. I just don't know. Logistically Paris is a difficult city to tail anyone, all those back alleys and little streets that go nowhere."

James turned on the TV to CNN. There, before his eyes was a video of his son sitting in a folding chair, wearing the orange jump suit now so familiar to everyone as the uniform of captive prisoners of Muslim fundamentalists. Two men flanked him wearing black long sleeved shirts, black pants and ski masks, each holding an assault rifle to Andrew's head. Andrew appeared to be calm, sitting very still but then his hands were cuffed, as were his legs.

"What about Carol?"

"The good news is that we found her. Andrew led us to her. She's living with this guy down in Bordeaux."

"Living with a man?" James heart sank again. How can she do this to me, he thought? His world was falling apart a chunk at a time. His son, now his wife. But Carol had left him long ago. He just hadn't faced it. And what did he have without them?

"Keep a tail on her. We're going to see what we can do about Andrew." I hope we're not too late"

Andrew woke lying on a cot in a small room that reeked of urine and he was about to add to the odor. He had to urinate and had called for his captors, but no one responded. He couldn't even get up off the cot as he was tied down with chains on his legs and ropes securing his arms to the side of the cot. He felt the warmth of his urine flood his clothing and then pool in the cot. He wondered if the United States treated prisoners this way. Recently he had heard that they had committed acts worse than this against the prisoners in Abu Ghraib. If we mistreat our prisoners, we could expect US prisoners to be mistreated as well and this puts all of our soldiers at risk, he thought.

He heard footsteps coming down the hallway. Two men entered the room and said words in a language he didn't understand. They uncuffed and untied him from the cot and started stripping his clothes off and then marched him out of the room and down the hall, naked. His body ached, he was bruised on his shoulder, his ribs were broken, his jaw was sore and he had lost his front teeth. But he had put up a good fight. He vaguely remembered the happenings of that night that seemed so long ago, but in reality was only two or three days ago.

He and Simone had been arguing over his leaving and he decided he needed to get out of the apartment for a couple of hours and had walked down the street to a neighborhood bistro. He sat at the bar and was ordering a beer when two Middle Eastern looking men, sat down beside him. After his beer arrived, they took his hands, shoving a pointed object into his ribs and told him in English to walk out the back door with them and if he made a sound they would kill him. The three of them walked to the back of the bistro in tandem, out the back door into an alley. As soon as the door had closed, Andrew jabbed his elbow into one of the men's stomach and then kicked the other in the groin, each one falling to the ground in pain. But they soon recovered and as Andrew was fleeing the alley they overcame him, pulled him to the ground, beating him on his body and his face. Andrew passed out.

The guards walked him into a shower and gave him some soap and turned on the water. Andrew let the cold water flow over his battered, dirty body. At least he was alive. And they would come to rescue him, he thought. They wouldn't just let him rot in this place, wherever it was.

After his shower they gave him clean clothes, another orange jump suit and took him to a cleaner, windowless room with a cot, a toilet and washbasin. They didn't secure him to the cot and after they left and locked the door with one small window with bars, Andrew got up and started to pace. Back and forth, back and forth, thinking, wondering what his fate would be. Was he going to die? Would they behead him like they had done to others? Minutes later, the door opened and a guard appeared with a tray of food and set it on the floor beside the cot and then left. Andrew examined the food. He was hungry. He hadn't eaten since they brought him here. He sat down and picked up the tray and put it on the bed. There was bread and what appeared to be a bowl of soup. He bit off a piece of the bread; it was stale but still edible. He picked up the bowl of soup and stirred the spoon around in the greenish white liquid. There were chunks of meat floating in the liquid. He took a spoonful and ate. It wasn't bad, bland but it would keep him alive. He had to keep up his strength.

*　*　*

They filed into the Oval Office and selected chairs around the room eyeing James sitting in his chair behind his desk. And James stared back at them. "Well, gentlemen, what's the bad news?"

Jason was the first to speak. "They are asking us to pull completely out of Iraq. They say if we don't that Andrew is as good as dead."

"I would say that we need to do that and do it now," said James.

"We can't. If we pull out now, more innocent people will be killed there. The country is not stabilized and the Iraqi soldiers and police are not strong enough to handle it. And more insurgents are streaming into Iraq every day to fight the Jihad against the Americans," Jason said.

"I don't care about who else is going to be killed in Iraq. I want my son home now. And whatever we have to do to achieve that will be done."

Charles Robertson, Secretary of Defense had joined them. He looked directly at James and spoke matter of factly. "Mr. President, with all due respect, you don't have a choice. The decision is not yours to make. We have a war going on there now and we have to finish that war."

"Look, Iraq is never going to be stabilized and especially as long as we're there. If we pull out now, and let them sort it out, the Iraqi people will no longer be able to blame the US for the unrest. They can create their own destiny, their own government whether it is a democracy or dictatorship. It is their right to do that," James implored. "And we wouldn't be losing anymore of our soldiers. This is the right thing to do and I am going to push for it."

"But we can't take a chance. We can't let the oil fall into the wrong hands," Jason said. "And we can't take the chance that they would trade their oil in euros. That would be devastating for the dollar. And the plans to build the Iraq to Israel Haifa pipeline would be scuttled. You know that, Mr. President. That was one of our visions and it would be lost."

"I agree with Jason," Tom said. "We're all very sorry that your son had to be pulled into this, but you can't let personal matters interfere with matters of government. We'll see what we can do to negotiate Andrew's release, but pulling out of Iraq is not an option at this point."

James got up from his desk and walked over to the large window behind him. Tears were starting to run down his cheeks. "What are the chances?"

"I have no idea. Those people are not easy to deal with. The hostage situations before this have not ended well, as you know," said Tom.

"What if he was your son," James said to the group of them. "What would you do?"

"I think I would go over there and get him out myself," said Chuck. "But that's not possible for you. If you put one foot in Iraq today, you would be killed in minutes."

Tom walked over to James and put his hands on his shoulders. "We can feel your pain. But we can't give in to the terrorists. We have people and agents over there that can work a deal, money, weapons, whatever else they want. We'll do our best to get your son out of there. And that's all we can do."

Chapter 16

Carol Takes Measures

Carol punched in the number that James had given her when he last talked with her when he was in France. It rang and rang and there was no answer. Where was he? She had to talk with him. What time is it in Washington? If it is ten in the morning in France it must be midnight in Washington with nine hours difference. He certainly wouldn't be in his office at this time. She decided to call the number of the private quarters of the White House. She punched in the number and waited, and waited and finally he answered.

"Carol, is that you," James answered in a sleepy voice, noticing Carol's cell phone number in the caller ID window.

"How can you even sleep at a time like this?"

"I've got to keep my strength up and stay alert and to do that I have to sleep," James said, fully awake now. He sat up in the large super king size bed that he and Carol used to share not long ago, turned on the light and took a drink of water from the glass on the end table beside the bed. With the one light on, the room was dark, with eerie shadows in the corners, making objects take on monster images. "How are you holding up Carol? I'm so sorry about this. But we're on top of it and we'll get him out."

Carol had gone back to the cottage to make the call to James, wanting the privacy to say what she had to say to him.

"You're on top of it?" Carol bit her lip. "You're on top of it," she repeated.

"Yes. I called the CIA in on this and they have contacts with these terrorists. They can make a deal."

There was a long, heavy silence, like the calm before the cyclone. Then Carol spoke. "Why didn't you step down from the presidency when I asked you to?"

"Are you blaming me for this?" James asked incredulously.

"If you had resigned, this would never have happened. I wouldn't have left you, the government, your government would not have kidnapped me, and Andrew and I would not have had to escape from your thugs. I asked you to choose. Do you remember that?"

"I..." James cleared his throat, "ah, I remember it well. But I had a duty to the American people. I took an oath of office to protect the American people and I had to honor that oath."

"And you think by attacking Iraq, a country that was never a threat to the US, you were protecting the American people? James, you're delusional. You've been buying all of those lies your advisors fed you. You have actually made America less safe. You and your cohorts have depleted the US treasury. And al Qaeda has a new training ground and they are getting stronger every day."

"But we haven't had on attack on American soil since we went after Saddam," James said, now getting up from the bed and pacing the floor.

"It is true. We have not had an attack on US soil," Carol parroted. "And if we did would we be able to handle it? Most of our troops and National Guard are in Iraq. And from what I hear these days, our borders and seaports are wide open. But maybe they don't have to come to America to attack us anymore. We sent our troops to them. And I was reading just yesterday on the Internet that terrorism has increased worldwide since you took office."

"You can't put this off on me. If you hadn't decided to divorce me, you would still be here in Washington and Andrew would be at school in Colorado. You have only yourself to blame for this."

James struck a chord. Was she to blame? It is true that if she hadn't filed for divorce the status quo would have prevailed and Andrew would likely not be in the hands of the terrorists.

"Do you realize that you are the first First Lady to divorce her husband? Do you realize that?"

"Always standing on convention aren't you, James. I'm sure that many first ladies had thought about it. Being married to the president is no easy task. In fact I read somewhere that Pat Nixon wanted to divorce Richard and he paid her not to go ahead with it."

There was a silence on the other end.

"What are you doing to get him out?"

"I have the best and brightest working on this. We do have contacts as I said before, with Hamas and some with al Qaeda and the Saudis. We will try to work a deal with them; there must be something that they want from us. It could be very costly, but we will pay whatever it takes." James sat down again on the bed his head hanging low. "Are you coming back to the States? I hear you're living with a Frenchman. Is that true?"

"I'm not living with him, I am a guest here at his vineyard. He's just a friend and he's a very fine person. And as for coming back to the States, I haven't thought that far ahead yet. I may be more effective here in France. I'm going to try to contact his girlfriend and see if she knows anything at all about this."

"This girlfriend, could she be working with the terrorists?"

"I don't know. She is part Iraqi. Her father is from Baghdad."

"She must have been in on it. Why would you ever let Andrew get involved with someone like this?"

"Andrew's an adult. I don't tell him who he can associate with. And there is a huge Muslim population here in Paris. But Simone, on her behalf, is an educated young woman and her father is a professor at the Sorbonne."

"But, if she's part Iraqi......"

"I know what you're thinking and I agree with you on this. She could be involved."

"Well, keep in touch and I'll continue to work this from my end. We'll get him out, I promise."

"I don't know why I'm skeptical of your promises, but we have to get Andrew back. Our lives will be worthless if we don't."

Carol put the phone back in its cradle and walked back into the living room and sat down on the couch. The sun was high in the sky now and it was a bright and beautiful day at the vineyard, but Carol wasn't noticing. For her it was the blackest day of her life.

She couldn't let up. She had to find a way to bring Andrew back. Her first thoughts were of Simone. Was Simone involved in Andrew's abduction? The only way to find out would be to go to Paris and confront her. She would leave today. As she was gathering her thoughts about how she was going to get to Paris, she heard a knock on the door. She got up from the couch and looked out the window and saw Claude standing in front of her door with a very concerned look on his face.

"Claude, come in," Carol said as she opened the door. I was just talking with Andrew's father."

"I figured as much. He must be beside himself with worry,"

"I suppose he is. He seems to think it'll be a cakewalk to get him back. He says they have contacts over there."

"What're you going to do now?"

"I'm going to Paris to talk with Simone for starters. I can't just sit here and wait for something to happen."

"What about the US agents? Aren't you afraid they might take you in?" Claude wondered out loud.

"That's a chance I'll have to take. Andrew's life is more important than anything," said Carol.

"I'm going with you. I'll charter an airplane and we can be in Paris by early evening. You let me take care of everything. Just pack your bag and be ready to go in an hour."

"Claude. What would I do without you? I am so grateful"

"Let's bring that son of yours home safely."

*   *   *

James awoke many times in the early morning hours after talking with Carol. She was right. He was to blame. He should never have taken on the presidency in the first place. It was the job from hell and he wasn't making a difference in the world, only causing more harm to thousands, no, hundreds of thousands of people. Why had he allowed the Patriot Party talk him into it? And now he could conceivably lose his only son. Carol was right, if that happened his life would be worth nothing.

He looked at the clock radio beside his bed. It was 6:00 a.m.; time to get up and fight another day. The phone beside his bed rang, startling him. Who would be calling at this time of the morning? Had they found Andrew? Or worse, was Andrew dead?

"Hello, James here."

"Mr. President, we are calling a meeting this morning with the vice president, the national security advisor and the secretary of state. You may want to have your advisor there with you," said Steven Mendez, his attorney general.

"Steve, what's this all about? You sound so formal."

"We'll be meeting in the Roosevelt room at 8:00 a.m. Will you be there, Mr. President?"

"We can meet in my office."

"No, it has been decided that we not meet in the Oval Office."

"Yes…" James paused. "I'll be there" James hung up the phone. He reached for his robe and went to the bathroom to brush his teeth. What are they planning, he wondered? And why the Roosevelt room? This sounded ominous but he would wait and see. He walked back out into his bedroom and called his special advisor, Susan, and told her about the meeting.

"Oh, they're just posturing. I wouldn't worry about it," she said when he called.

He dressed in his gray slacks, a blue shirt and black blazer and walked out of the bedroom and into the kitchen area where the maid was preparing his coffee.

"I don't have time for breakfast, Marta. Just some coffee this morning."

"Oh, Mr. President. I heard about your son. Is he okay?"

"We're working on it. I hope we can free him," James said using as few words as possible. He disliked it when the help got involved in his personal life. Carol, the egalitarian, had encouraged this and he was never happy about that.

He went to his office first and read the daily briefings. Two roadside bombs had killed more Iraqi Soldiers and one American. No mention of Andrew at all. He searched through the Pentagon report and then reports from the FBI and the CIA. Again nothing about his son. He picked up the phone and dialed the number for the Secret Service. Nick Hopkins answered.

"Any word yet?" James asked.

"No. We haven't heard anything. Saw the video though. That sure enough is Andrew."

"Yeah, I know. Well, let me know as soon as you have any word on who's responsible for this. Are you still keeping a watch on that girlfriend of his?"

"Yes, we are. She just goes to work and visits her parent's home. We haven't seen her with any of the Arab types lately."

"Maybe I should go over there and see what I can dig up," said James.

"I wouldn't advise that sir. That would be a logistical nightmare for us in keeping you safe. And if someone were to take you out, what would that solve?"

"I guess you're right. I think I'll call Central Intelligence and see if they have any leads. It is just damned difficult staying here and not being able to take action myself," James said feeling so powerless.

"I can imagine, sir, but that's what you have to do."

James hung the phone up and then called the CIA and talked with them for twenty minutes trying to get some satisfaction that they were doing all they could to find Andrew and get him released. The fact that they didn't even know where he was being held was disconcerting, for if they had this knowledge they would be able to send in Special Forces.

James looked at his Rolex watch, given to him by Carol on the night of his first inauguration. It was fifteen minutes to eight. He got up from his desk and started to walk out of the Oval office. Looking at the bust of George Washington, he said out loud, "I doubt you ever had to go through what I am going through right now. I know now what soldier's parents feel when they lose a son or daughter." And he walked out the door and across the hall to the Roosevelt room, the room that FDR called his fish room. He felt like a fish at the moment, about to be hooked and sent to the cannery.

"Come in, Mr. President and have a seat," said Jason who was seated with the others at the oblong table.

"I'm going to get right to the point. We're gathered here this morning to make a request of you, Mr. President, in the name of the safety and security of the nation. I know you'll find this to be a radical solution, but we think it is necessary in view of the fact that your decision making is colored by your personal feelings for your son and therefore you are not able to make impartial decisions for this country," said Steven after the president was comfortably seated.

"Because of this," Steven continued, "We think it is in the best interest of the nation that you step down from the office of the President of the United States. If in fact Andrew is found and brought home safely, you could then resume your term, but in the interim, Jason will take over the responsibilities of your office."

James blinked and looked around the table at the faces and the expressions that were set like totems. "Do I have a say in this?"

"Yes and no," said Steven.

"And what does that mean?"

"Constitutionally you could resist, but if you do we will take it to congress and ask that you be impeached," Jason said.

"And on what grounds would you impeach?" James asked, disbelieving what he was hearing.

"On the grounds of National Security. That you are no longer able to clearly separate the protection of your family's safety from the safety of the country," Steven shot back.

"That's no reason to impeach," James implored.

"We can make a case that your decision making process is flawed and if you continue as president you could affect the national security of this country," Steven said.

"Fuck you guys. Now you're turning against me. Well, you always wanted my job, Jason."

Jason raised his eye brows but remained silent.

"That's not what this is all about. You're a security risk to this country. You cannot make rational decisions about the defense of this country any longer. It's time for you to step down, Mr. President," said Steven emphatically. "We have a document for you to sign and I think it is in your best interest to sign it now."

James held the very lengthy document in his hands and started to read the legalese line by line.

"You think I'm just going to roll over for you like a cocker spaniel in heat. Well, I'm not. I'm taking this document with me and I'll get back to you." And he walked out of the room, document in hand with Susan following not far behind.

Jason looked around the room at the others and shrugged. He knew it was a done deal.

Chapter 17

Carol Searches for Andrew

The Dassault Falcon 20 jet touched down at Orly International Airport at 6:35 p.m. and taxied to the gate especially built for private jets. Carol and Claude, after gathering their luggage, walked down the steps of the aircraft and onto the tarmac. Dark clouds hung low in the sky, announcing a summer storm in the making. Claude turned around and thanked the pilot for the smooth flight and then picked up his and Carol's luggage and headed to the terminal to rent a car. When they reached the car rental kiosk, Carol excused herself to find the ladies room and freshen up after the flight. She thought about how fortunate she had been to find a friend like Claude to help her at a time like this. When she returned, Claude was there with the luggage in the rental car ready to take her to the hotel.

"I must pay you for this," said Carol as she climbed into the blue Renault.

"Not on your life. I am here to help you and I don't want money."

"But I feel like I'm taking advantage of you. You've been so kind to me."

"I want to be your friend and I don't want to be paid for that."

The rush hour traffic was heavy with workers hurrying to homes and families. Fortunately Claude knew his way around Paris and in no time they were parked in front of the Hotel St. Germain des-pres at 36 rue Bonaparte. He got out of the car, opened Carol's door and helped her out, smiling and holding her hand tenderly. He then took the luggage from the trunk and they both walked into the lobby.

"Bonsior, Una Chambre pour Claude Montagne, sil vous plait." Claude signed the register, was given the electronic key and the bell

captain motioned for a bellboy to pick up their bags as they got on the elevator that took them to the fifth floor. They walked down the rich floral carpeted hallway with crystal sconces lighting the way and came to the last room at the end. The bell captain opened the door and Carol stepped into the room with two queen-sized beds.

"Claude, I would prefer my own room. I just assumed when you were making the arrangements that you would order separate rooms."

"There are two beds and I won't bother you.

"No, Claude, I need to have my own room."

"I'll get you another room then if you would like. I just thought it would be nice if I we could be together."

"I'll go down to the lobby and get another room for myself and I'll pay for it."

Claude looked dejected as Carol took her luggage and walked out of the room. As Carol was walking down the hall to the elevator, she was wondering what Claude had in mind. But then she knew and she was not ready for that yet. After all she was not even divorced. Hadn't she made that clear to Claude? When she reached the desk she asked the clerk if he spoke English and he said that he did and she asked for a single room with one queen sized bed and he found one for her on the third floor. It wouldn't be close to Claude, but maybe that was better. The bellboy came back and carried her luggage to elevator and they went to room 305. The room wasn't as spacious as Claude's, but it was certainly comfortable. The phone rang as soon as she had tipped the bellboy.

"Carol, are you hungry? I've ordered food. Would you care to join me?"

Carol thought again, what is he up to? It would be better to go out to eat but it was getting late and she was exhausted. Then it occurred to her that she would have more control if the food were sent to her room.

"Have the order sent to my room and come on down. I'm in room 305, but you already know that."

Carol called the number that she had for Simone, but an answering machine with a male voice told her to leave a message and Carol wondered if Simone already had a new live in so soon after Andrew. And then she thought it could be one of those phone company generated messages. Carol started to unpack the few things that she had thrown together in a hurry. Hopefully they wouldn't be here for very long. Her objective was to meet with Simone. She didn't want to merely talk on the phone, she thought that a face-to-face meeting is always more effective. That way she might be able to see if Simone were telling the truth.

There was a knock on the door and Carol asked who was there and Claude answered. She opened the door and invited him in. He had changed into a pair of slacks with a deep red silk smoking jacket over a blue sports shirt. He looked very debonair with his dark brown hair graying at the temples and his blue eyes smiled at Carol.

"Come in. Have a seat over there," Carol said pointing at the small table and chairs by the window.

"The food should be here soon. I hope you don't mind that I ordered for you."

"No, not at all. I like most everything, except okra."

"What is okra?"

"It's a southern dish served in the deep south of the US. It's a vegetable ... kind of green and slimy."

"We'll never have okra, then," said Claude as he put his arms around Carol and kissed her on the cheek.

Another knock on the door and this time it was room service. Carol opened the door and told him to put the tray on the table and Claude signed the tab. Carol took the covers off the food and found a tureen of soup with a woodsy aroma and a Caesar salad made with the hearts of Romaine lettuce.

"This soup smells so good. It's mushroom, isn't it?"

"Forest mushroom soup made with all wild mushrooms found in our forests. I think you'll like it. And I ordered a Beaujolais wine from my vineyard."

They sat down at the table and started eating, Carol taking in the subtle flavors of the soup and enjoying the wine.

"So what is on the agenda for tomorrow?" Claude asked.

"I have a call in to Simone, but she wasn't at home. I'm hoping she'll call me back tonight. That was another reason why I wanted to be here in my room."

"Another reason. And what is the first reason? I think you are fearful that I am trying to seduce you. Could that be true?"

"We have to have an understanding. Claude. I like you very much, but right now I would like for us to be friends and if later after my divorce something else happens, that would be wonderful because I think you are a very special person. But for now, I can't think of getting involved."

"Are you religious?"

"More spiritual than religious I would say, although I was raised Christian. Are you?"

"Catholic, but I've developed my own beliefs as an adult."

"As have I. And my value system says that it is not time for us to have sex." There, she brought it out in the open. But that was Carol, speaking the truth when sometimes it hurt.

"I understand …. I think." Claude gave Carol a longing look. "Carol you are a beautiful woman, inside and out and I'm starting to fall in love with you."

"Well don't. Not yet."

"Are you thinking of going back to your husband?"

"No. Never."

"I have another question for you. Knowing what you know now, would you have started divorce proceedings against him?"

Carol sipped her soup and thought for a few minutes. What a poignant question and she wasn't sure how to answer now that Andrew was in danger. Would she choose to possibly sacrifice her son's life for her own principled ideas about war and how James was leading the country astray?

"That is a difficult question. I think I would but I would be more careful. I should have moved out of the ranch immediately and not told anyone where I was. I wasn't prepared for the administration to take such drastic measures. And of course Andrew was there for me as he always is. And I have to be there for him now."

They talked and ate and drank more wine for another hour or so and then Carol told Claude that it was time for him to leave. She was very tired, the wine making her even sleepier and tomorrow would be another demanding day. He held her in his arms and told her again how deeply he cared for her and then he left.

Carol was preparing for bed when the phone rang.

"Simone, I've been trying to reach you. I am calling about Andrew."

"Yes, of course. Mrs. Walters, I am so sorry. I didn't have any idea this could happen to Andrew."

"Meet with me tomorrow and let's put our heads together and see what we can do to get him back."

"Sure. I work all day but I could meet you at five. Where do you want to meet?"

"Come to the hotel. We can go to the bar and talk there. I'll see you at five then."

Carol prepared for bed and gratefully crawled in under the covers after a harrowing day. But the thoughts of the day would not vanish so quickly. Simone most likely knew who she was all along. She called her Mrs. Walters. And was Simone really sorry about Andrew or had she been involved in his capture? She hoped she could find out the truth and hoped most of all that she could find Andrew.

.

Chapter 18

James Makes a Decision

For the next week, James was in denial of what was being asked of him by the vice president and the attorney general. He went about his routine as normal during the day, calling meetings and directing the generals on military matters in Iraq. He was trying to shuffle the problem under his desk, hoping it would go away. He read the document every night before he went to bed and shook his head in disbelief that they could do this to him. It was not until he tried to call a cabinet meeting for the next Monday morning to again discuss the Iraq war that he realized that it wasn't going away. He had contacted the cabinet members and they all accepted, but when he called Jason, he was told to make the decision or else.

"James, we cannot have this cabinet meeting until you sign the agreement and if you don't, we'll go to congress and then the media will pick it up and we'll then see what happens," Jason said over the phone. "You can do that. You can fight us. But you will eventually loose. Save yourself the trouble."

"You wouldn't do this. It would tear the country apart," James said.

"We would have to take that chance," Jason came back.

James was beleaguered, not only with the many problems of the office of the presidency, but now with problem of his son in some far away place, possibly being tortured or even worse, being killed and he couldn't bring himself to face it.

"I'm not resigning," James said as he looked across his historic, old mahogany desk used by many presidents before him.

"You don't have a choice," Doris Johnson, James personal legal counsel shot back. A black woman with short, black straightened hair and wide eyes, in her late fifties, Doris had been with James since his senatorial term in Colorado. This morning she wore a somber black two-piece dress that minimized her ample body.

"I do have a choice. They can't force me to step down." James got up from his chair and walked around to the front of the desk. "I am the president and they just can't do this to me."

"You're right. You are the president. But if you don't comply, they can send this to the House and ask that you be impeached," said Susan, James chief strategist.

"On what grounds? I've done nothing wrong. I haven't broken any laws. They have nothing on me that they could use to impeach."

"The war. They could say that you lied to congress to start the Iraq war," said Susan.

"I didn't lie. I was using the intelligence given to me by the CIA. Everyone knew that Saddam had weapons. At least he did at one time. He used them against his own people."

"You should have let the UN inspectors finish their job. Pulling them out before they were finished looked bad," Doris said insistently.

"That wasn't my choice. If it had been up to me I would have let them continue."

"And you went against the United Nations resolution," Doris continued.

"We tried to get their buy in, but we had to act. As you all recall, we had troops waiting on the border and Saddam was preparing for us. We had to act."

Doris looked under her glasses at James and then got up from her chair and walked over to his desk where James had again taken his seat. "Those will be the accusations. And you may or may not win, but you will lose with the public and be even more weakened as a president than you are now. The public opinion polls on the war have shifted since 9/11. Most people now think we should not have gone to war in Iraq, especially since the death toll is rising along with the deficit. James, I would advise you to go along with them on this. And then when Andrew is returned, you can regain your presidency."

"I would agree with Doris. The people will understand and empathize with you, whereas if you were to go through an impeachment battle, you might lose and you would lose hugely in the public opinion arena," said Susan who had joined them for this critical meeting.

"James," Doris said, calling him by his given name where most called him Mr. President, "we know how you must feel about this. Not knowing what will happen to your son and now being embattled in the White House, but it will all be for the better. You have the best people on the case and they will find your son and bring him home."

James turned his chair and looked out the window behind his desk. It was raining, a steady drizzle from gray skies. "I can only hope. This is the worst day of my life. And that bastard Jason has been after my job since day one. But I see what you're saying and you're right as usual. I am not a quitter and this goes against my grain, but your points are well taken. I will step down." He dropped his head as he said the words.

"Now let's go over the document very carefully to see if there are any gotchas," said Doris. "And then we can send this over to the attorney general."

"This shows me who my friends are in Washington. I would have thought there would be more of my cabinet behind me."

"You are right, you don't have friends in Washington; no one does," said Susan. "You always have to walk looking over your shoulder to see who is going to throw the first knife."

James eyes fell onto the document. "I think you're right. Maybe this is all for the best. Maybe it's time for me to leave this place."

*   *   *

Carol settled into the chair at the bar and ordered a 7-up from the bartender. This was not a social visit and she felt that it was inappropriate to be drinking alcohol. She looked at her watch; it was five past five. The bartender brought her drink and she sipped from the glass, wondering what Simone would have to say. She glanced towards the door and saw Simone walking in, dressed in Jeans with sequins, a bright turquoise cami top with a matching scarf draped around her neck in true French fashion.

"I am sorry to be late," she said as she slipped onto the seat next to her. "I am being hounded by the press these days. I tried to ditch them and it took me awhile longer to get here."

"You aren't that late. What would you like to drink?"

"I'll have a Coke."

Carol motioned to the bartender and ordered the drink for her and then turned to Simone. "When did you last see Andrew?"

"He left that last night, just to go out for some fresh air or go to a bar or something. I don't really know. He was angry. We had had a fight. He told me he was leaving and I didn't want him to go and...."

"Why was he leaving you? I thought the two of you were getting along well together. He seemed to be in love with you," Carol said, not wanting Simone to know that she had asked Andrew join her at Claude's vineyard.

"Do you think so? We appeared to be getting along until we went to Bordeaux and then when we returned, Andrew was acting different." Simone lit a cigarette. "He wouldn't have left if he loved me, now would he, Mrs. Walters?"

There was a long silence. Carol looked down at the table and fiddled with her cocktail napkin.

"He was worried. He told me he saw you with some friends that he was concerned about. And you have not been totally honest with us. You knew all along whom we were."

"Not at first. Not until I saw his photo in one of the tabloids. And that was after he had moved in with me. But look who is talking about being honest. Andrew lied to me about who he was."

"There was a reason for him doing that. He was protecting me, us from being found by the Americans who were trying to capture us."

Simone didn't answer to Carol's last comment. "And as for my friends, they are just school friends. Oh, and they just happen to be Muslim. But there are thousands of Muslims in Paris."

"Did you tell your friends about Andrew?"

"I may have, I don't remember."

Simone sipped on her drink. Another silence.

"Look, Simone, your first allegiance has to be to Iraq. You don't even know the United States and its people. You've never been there, you can't possibly understand what our people are like, and your mother being American doesn't change that."

"My allegiance is to France. This is my home country, where I was born and have lived all my life. Iraq means nothing to me, although I do understand the plight of the Iraqi people. To be attacked without any provocation.... well, that's criminal in my mind."

"I'll agree with you on that point. But what I'm wondering is did they, al Qaeda or whoever is responsible for taking Andrew use you to get to him? Did you call them and tell them where he would be at a certain time so they could carry out this horrific act?"

"No, I swear to you I didn't do that. You have to believe me." Tears were starting to stream down Simone's cheeks but she turned away from Carol and wiped her nose and face with a bar napkin.

Carol looked away for a moment gathering her thoughts. "Well, then help me. Go to your friends. They must know someone who knows someone who can help find Andrew."

"I will. You will see. I will help get him back. I love Andrew and I wouldn't do anything to hurt him for the world."

Carol wasn't so sure. How could she know if she could trust Simone? Carol rose from her chair and thanked Simone for coming to meet her and then she left the bar and walked through the lobby of the hotel to go to the elevator. Several guests were congregating around the front desk asking about restaurants. She would eat in again tonight. She was in no mood to go out and be among people. She didn't even want to be with Claude tonight but she didn't know how she could avoid that. Maybe if she told him she was ill; a migraine or something.

Upon reaching her room and opening the door, the phone was ringing.

"Carol, I have news for you that you will be very interested in. I'm coming right down to see you," Claude said almost breathlessly.

And before Carol could protest, he had hung up the phone and he would be there in minutes. She went into the bathroom to freshen up and heard the knock on the door.

Carol opened the door without even inquiring who was there.

Claude strode into the room. "He has resigned."

"Who, James?"

"Yes, I heard it on BBC News just minutes ago."

Carol couldn't believe what she was hearing. James resign? She didn't think he would ever do that. They must have forced him out. And how did this change things with Andrew? Would it make it any easier now to get Andrew back? And what did Andrew's captors, the militants want from the US government?

Carol took Claude's hand and led him to the small loveseat in the corner of the room by the window. "Claude, I have to go back home. I know that now. I think I can influence them more if I am there."

"What did Simone have to say?"

"She says she doesn't know anything."

"And do you believe her?"

"I'm not sure. But I do know that it is time to go back and face my demons and work to get Andrew back home safely. That's all I care about."

"Is it safe for you to go back there? You never know what this administration is going to do."

"The election is over. Yes, they'll have to explain my absence to the public, but they will find a way to spin, they always do."

Claude took Carol in his arms and held her and then he kissed her. "Carol, I love you dearly and I don't want anything to happen to you."

"Don't worry, I'll be fine. They wouldn't dare do anything to me now. The public wouldn't stand for it."

"But what about us. Do we have anything? Do you care for me at all?"

"Yes, Claude I do. But I have to take care of things first before I can really give my heart to you. You understand that don't you?"

"I'm trying to understand. I just don't want to lose you."

"I have to get my divorce from James. I have to get Andrew back and then I can think about being with someone. I think I love you Claude, but I'm not sure of anything right now."

Chapter 19

Carol Returns Home

What would she find when she returned to the States, Carol thought as she sat in the terminal at London Heathrow Airport? How would the administration explain her sudden disappearance, her exile to Mexico, Spain and France when she suddenly shows up after being missing for months? Should she tell the truth? Or should she avoid the press and say nothing about the abominable treatment by the administration? At first she thought, she would speak out. The people had to know the truth about their government and its thirst for power. The fact that they would sacrifice her, to prevent the opposition from winning is something the American people had to know. But what if they didn't believe her? The administration could again paint her as being a loony who needed to be hospitalized and some people might believe that. She knew she had many battles ahead of her. The divorce, finding Andrew and finding her path in life again after this horrendous five years of acting in the subservient role of First Lady while her husband lost his identity and became consumed with power and then the horrific events that followed.

The flight from Paris to London had been uneventful. Carol had arrived at Charles De Gaul Airport early, grabbing a croissant and a cup of coffee at one of the small restaurants in the terminal. When she went to check in and was walking through the security gate, an alarm went off and a female security officer pulled her aside to search her luggage and then patted her down, scanning her body with the wand. She had that eerie feeling that someone was going to try to capture her again. But she didn't think that would be happening as she had called James before she left and asked him to broker a deal with the administration.

She told him to tell the administration that she wouldn't talk to the press about her abduction if they would leave her alone and no longer threaten her and she hoped they would agree to this. But what if they hadn't gotten the message yet? Security soon let her pass, but she felt violated and would never get used to being searched like a criminal. How useless she thought, to physically check innocent people, and still she had heard how many weapons, knives and guns slipped through the system. What a waste of time and money.

When it was time to board, Carol selected a window seat and settled in for the short flight to London. As the Boeing 747 left the ground, she looked out the window seeing the French farmland below and here and there quaint little villages dotting the landscape. She was sad to leave France as she thought she had not seen nearly enough of the country, but she vowed to return. And she had another reason to come back, Claude.

Arriving at Heathrow, Carol had three hours before her departure on British Airways to Chicago. Strolling through the airport after checking in for her flight, she marveled at the numerous shops. One could buy almost anything from perfume to liquor, jewelry, clothing, chocolate, coffee and tea. There was a large area in the center devoted to Harrods and Carol browsed through the women's clothing, handbags and luggage. She looked at the exquisitely designed fine china; Wedgwood, Royal Doulton, Villeroy & Boch. She eyed the sparkling Waterford crystal all outrageously expensive and wondered how anyone could afford such luxuries in this time. Then wandering into a shop selling tea and coffee, she bought some Earl Grey tea, a large chocolate bar and some English teacakes all the while wishing she had more time to see London. That would have to be another day.

After spending the rest of the morning stuffing herself with a full English breakfast as she didn't know what the food situation would be for the rest of the day, she settled into the boarding area to read for awhile and then finally the agent called her flight and she boarded. Again she had chosen a window seat but this time the flight would be full whereas the flight from Paris had been half empty. She had declined Claude's offer for first class tickets thinking that she had better get used to economy class as that was her station in life once more and it wasn't a problem for her. There is a price to pay for riding on Air Force One and she no longer wanted to pay it.

After settling into her seat with her traveler's kit of headset, socks and toothbrush, a young man, obviously from India, took the seat next to her. Carol politely greeted him; after all she would be spending the next ten hours with him as a seatmate. When asked where he was from, he said Mumbai.

"And are you living in the States now?" Carol asked.

"Yes, I am. I work in Minneapolis as a computer programmer," the young man replied.

"Are you working on a green card?" Carol couldn't help asking, thinking how many people were in the United States illegally from foreign countries.

"No, I am on an H-1B Visa."

"Oh," said Carol with no more response. So here was one of the foreigners taking good jobs away from Americans. She had little conversation with him for the rest of the flight, not because she resented him, but because she had difficulty communicating with him.

The flight attendant brought wine for everyone and then a hot casserole meal. Carol had thought she might read, but she searched the movie channels and found an old classic she had always loved, Alfred Hitchcock's North by Northwest. Cary Grant was as handsome as ever and she laughed at how he wore a suit everywhere. How outdated that was, but then all the men in the movie were wearing suits and hats. And Eva Marie Saint was the cool, beautiful blond double agent, but still submissive to men. Times had changed and for the better, she thought. Or had they?

Carol dozed for a short time and then, upon waking nudged the young sleeping Indian next to her to let her out to walk for a few minutes and go to the rest room at the rear of the plane. Several people nodded to her as she passed and, as always, she wondered if they recognized her. She tried to blend in, wearing jeans and a jeans jacket. Certainly a former first lady would not be wearing such clothes. But, no, they just appeared to be friendly she then thought. She took her seat again and watched the progress of the flight on the GPS screen showing the route passing over the tip of Greenland and heading for Hudson Bay. They would soon be in Chicago.

*   *   *

The day before, James, seated at his desk in the Oval Office, had gone on national television and, with regret announced his resignation of the presidency. In his speech to the people he said that this wasn't his choice, but that he would be doing the country a disservice by continuing on in view of the fact that his foreign policy decisions, especially those concerning Iraq, could likely be influenced by his desire to save his son. He went on to say that he had tried to do his best for the country during his time in office in these difficult times and now the future lay in the capable hands of the new president, Jason Martin. He did not talk about ever returning.

James opened his Samsonite suitcase and started packing his clothes in preparation for his leaving the White House. His maid, Marta had offered to do it for him, but he told her that he wanted to do this himself. Five years in the White House and what did he have to show for it? Five Armani suits, two sets of running sweats and headaches and heartburn. Had it been worth it? He'd loved the power and the intrigue, but he had wanted to accomplish so much more. Contrary to what Carol thought, he had wanted to do well for America and he felt that he hadn't achieved anything of value. He had come to office with an idealistic view that if he were president he could make a difference with education, jobs, with health care, the environment. He was not really a conservative. But in reality, he was never the powerful one. It was the lobbyists for the corporations that he owed because they in fact picked up the tab for him to be elected the first time and were there again for the second term. He owed them and he didn't know how to get around that. It was the lobbyists for the defense and oil companies that drove the march to war. He hadn't really wanted to go to war, but he again owed these interest groups for donating to his campaign and there were powerful forces in Congress, people who had financial ties to the defense companies that campaigned for the war. He had tried to tell Carol that when she was leaving him. And now that he thought about this, what he did and what the congress had done was horrendous. They had started a war with another country that was of no threat to the American people. They had killed thousands of people, mostly Iraqis, and raped the US treasury putting the United States at risk in an out of control deficit. And now they had to cut domestic and social programs. A spending bill had been sent to congress that would cut school lunches for poor children and food stamps, Medicare and loans for college students. This was not the direction he wanted for his country. But he was out of power now and leaving, as if he had ever been in power. He would find another way to help to make America whole again.

"Marine One is waiting for you sir," a young aid popped his head into his bedroom.

"I'll be right there," James said. He dreaded this moment. He couldn't cry although he felt like it. And unlike Richard Nixon who had had his wife and family with him, he was alone. He would have to walk this walk alone.

Striding out on the South Lawn he saw the helicopter waiting for him, and crowds of reporters. He took a deep breath and stepped out onto the walkway. Cameras snapped and video cams were rolling, but everyone was quiet. No one spoke as he made that long walk through the crowd to the waiting helicopter. They seemed to all know and understand his pain. He reached the steps of the aircraft, stepped up and then turned to the crowd.

"Until we meet again. I wish this country and it's people the very best. We Americans are a good people and now we have to show the world. It is not the biggest gun that counts, but the caring and compassion. Farewell for now."

James turned and walked onto the helicopter for the short ride to Andrews Air Force base where Air Force One was waiting for his last flight back to the ranch in Colorado.

Chapter 20

The Road to Baghdad

The Royal Jordanian Airways Boeing 737 landed at Baghdad International Airport, formerly called Saddam International Airport, at 8:00 p.m. Iraq time. Simone's flight from Amman, Jordan, had been uneventful up until the last fifteen minutes of the flight, when the aircraft, maintaining a high altitude, had swooped in for the landing, attempting to avoid being shot down. As she walked down the steps of the aircraft, glad to be on solid ground, she looked for her uncle, Jabar in the crowd behind the chain link fence surrounding the area. It was getting dark and she had difficulty seeing with so many people pressing against the guards at the fence. Simone, against the wishes of her father, had arranged to travel to Iraq to try to find Andrew. And she had to keep her trip secret from the press and the special agents that were following her every day. The CIA had tried to take her into custody, to interrogate her, but French officials stepped in and would not allow this on French soil and with Simone's promise to not flee the country they backed off. So even though she knew this trip would be difficult and dangerous, she was willing to take her chances. She had grown to love Andrew in the short time that she had known him and now she felt somewhat responsible for his disappearance.

"Simone, Simone, I am over here," her uncle shouted to her in broken English.

She looked in the direction of the voice calling her name and then ran to him, with her black veil almost falling off her head. They embraced and then looked at one another.

"It has been such a long time since I have seen you. Is Thana with you?" asked Simone referring to her aunt, Jabar's wife.

"No, no. It is too dangerous," said Jabar. "The trip is too dangerous. I am glad to see you, but you should not have come. Baghdad is such a dangerous place these days," Jabar repeated. "Well, you will see."

Jabar picked up Simone's bag and together, they walked out of the nearly empty terminal to the parking lot and got into Jabar's white 1995 Chevy sedan. Jabar turned out of the airport for the sixteen-kilometer drive to Baghdad, roughly ten miles. Simone had only been to Iraq once when she was a very little girl and she had remembered how beautiful she thought the city was with its striking Persian minarets and date palms lining the streets. The capitol city of Iraq with an estimated 6.5 million people, Baghdad is located on the Tigris River and is the largest city in Iraq. Simone recalled from reading the history of the region that the city dated back to the eighth century and was once the center of the Muslim world.

Looking out the window of the car, even though it was dark, she could see that the landscape had changed. It looked as though it had been burned over by a devastating fire with wrecked trucks and cars laying by the side of the road, it was a no man's land. And then she saw two, three, she didn't know how many, American soldiers come out of nowhere, brandishing M16 assault rifles, waving them to stop.

"What is this? What do they want?" asked Simone, her stress level rising.

"This is a checkpoint. We have to stop here and let them look at your papers. They are all in order aren't they?"

"Yes, I have my passport and a visa. I got it from the American embassy."

"Be very careful. Many Iraqis have been killed here. The Americans are very quick to shoot."

The soldiers approached the car, one on either side, and peered inside. Simone looked up at the young face of the Marine, who looked as frightened as she was at this moment.

"We need your papers," one of them asked. Simone handed over her passport and visa as Jabar told them he was a resident of Baghdad.

"Why are you coming to Iraq?" the soldier questioned Simone.

"I am coming to visit my uncle. He is having an important birthday and I am here to help him celebrate," Simone lied.

"Where are your mother and father?"

Simone became agitated. Why were they asking these questions? She had her papers. It was none of their business. But the country was at war. They have to be careful, she thought.

"My mother and father are in Paris. Father couldn't come and so I am here representing the family."

The soldiers, still carrying her papers, walked to the side of the road and two more soldiers joined them. She could see their faces in the headlights as they looked at the documents and talked between them but she could not hear what they were saying. She only hoped they would not associate her with Andrew for if that happened she knew they would not let her into Iraq. She then thought how this checkpoint was like a primitive customs entry system for the country.

The soldiers sauntered back to the car. They gave Simone back her papers warning her that Iraq was at war and that she should check in with the American Embassy in Baghdad as soon as possible. Failure to do so would mean that she would be asked to leave the country. Simone agreed and the soldiers waved them on.

"Is it like this for everyone here?" asked Simone as she saw more wreckage along side the road.

"Worse than this. We were fortunate. They have shot families here that they thought were threatening them," Jabar said as he rolled up his window and checked to see if his door was locked. "They could have taken us into custody, but the US government is concerned about the image of US soldiers and how they are treating Iraq civilians, so I would guess they are lightening up a bit. You've heard about all of the prison abuse haven't you?"

"I have. Is it true that they are torturing prisoners?"

"It is. There are many imprisoned that don't belong there. They were rounded up early in the war and thought to be Saddam loyalists and now they are being held indefinitely, without due process, no access to council," said Jabar, who was himself a lawyer. "They were businessmen and family men just like me, but because they are Sunnis, they were suspected of having ties with Saddam."

There was silence as they approached the city that was darkened with the exception of a light in a building here and there and in spite of the darkness Simone could see that much of Baghdad was in rubble. And the stench was overpowering; garbage and sewage, the city reeked of dreadful odors. She was very sad, as she had fond memories of her early visits here with her cousins.

"Is all of the city like this?" she asked.

"No, some parts have been barely touched, but as you can see we don't have any of the services like we used to have. We only have electricity for maybe four hours a day and there is no garbage pickup." Jabar drove on, trying to avoid the potholes. "Now I have a question for you, Simone. Why are you here? Your father neglected to tell me and I know it is not to celebrate my birthday as that doesn't happen for six months from now."

"I'll tell you later."

"No, you had better tell me now. When we get back to the house we will have little time alone and I don't want Thana involved in whatever you are doing."

"You knew that I had a new male friend."

"No, I didn't. When your father and I talk we don't discuss such things. We only talk about the war."

"Well, I met Andrew at the Sorbonne and helped him get a job. He's from America. Then we started going out together and when I got my apartment, he moved in with me. I really care for him."

"And what does that have to do with your coming to Iraq?"

"He was abducted a week ago."

"You were dating the American president's son?"

"Yes. I didn't know he was the son of the president until I saw his picture in one of the American magazines. He told me his name was John when I met him. And he never did tell me the truth. And then one night he went out for some fresh air and he never came back. So I called the police and told them he was missing and that I thought this was the American president's son and then I saw the headlines the next morning. His mother thinks that I had a part in his abduction."

"Simone, I am afraid for your safety. In fact I am afraid for all of our safety. I think you should go back to Paris immediately."

"No, I won't. I won't go back. Not until I find Andrew."

"We're going to have to find a safe place for you. You can't stay at my house."

Simone was quiet. She hadn't thought she would be endangering her uncle's family. Well, if she had to stay somewhere else, she would do that. She wouldn't want to put her uncle's family in jeopardy.

She turned her face to her uncle Jabar as they were pulling into the yard of his house on the north side of Baghdad. "Tell me, Uncle Jabar, what was it like the night they bombed Baghdad?"

"It was the most frightening night of my life. We didn't know if we would live to see the morning. The sky lit up with flares and the bombs were everywhere, boom, boom, boom. We gathered in the kitchen and huddled together and prayed to Allah to spare us. I found out later they were targeting Saddam's palace but they did hit some houses and many people were killed that night. And then the next few days were even worse. We didn't have any electricity and we couldn't go out of our homes because of the looting and lawlessness. I hope never to see anything like that again in my lifetime."

"Did you know that it was being televised in America as if it were some movie or something? I didn't watch, but Andrew told me about it."

"No, I didn't know that. But Simone, I don't want you to talk about this in front of your aunt. She gets too upset."

Simone agreed and they both went inside the house to meet the family, Thana and her two children, Mohammed and Fadhila, Simone's cousins. A bomb exploded somewhere in the city, lighting up the sky for seconds, silhouetting buildings against the skyline. Simone jumped.

"You had better get used to that. It happens many times a day," said Jabar.

* * *

Carol awoke as the plane touched down at Denver International Airport East of Denver. She had never been so tired. She looked at her watch and it was 6:00 a.m. Paris time. She had been traveling for twenty-four hours. No wonder she was tired. And it was only 8:00 p.m. Denver time. As the plane stopped at the gate, Carol got out of her seat and reached above for her luggage, struggling to retrieve it. A tall man across the aisle from her asked if he could help and she gladly allowed him to do so. And Carol was grateful that he then continued to carry her bag until they reached customs. Waiting in line, several people noticed her and the customs agent did a double take as he looked at her and then looked at her pseudo name on her passport and said nothing. As she walked through the ramp and into the terminal she looked for her lawyer, Marshal Dale, in the crowds of people lining the walkway. She had called him before leaving Paris and asked him to pick her up at the airport. He spotted her just as she saw him.

"Welcome back to America Carol, now that you're a woman of the world. How was your flight?"

"Uneventful. Good to see you Marshal. You haven't changed a bit. Still that same, smart looking guy."

They hugged and Marshal reached for her bag and together they walked through the terminal to the parking garage.

"And how is your family? Your wife, Louise?"

"They're fine. Louise and I are divorced you know."

"No, how would I know that? I'm sorry Marshal. I know how much your family meant to you."

"It was a long time coming. We didn't have anything in common anymore and Louise met someone at our country club. The guy is twenty years her junior and she left me and took nothing from the marriage and married this guy."

"You must have been devastated."

"No, I wasn't. I was happy for her. Except this guy doesn't have a lot of money, so I don't know how long that's going to last. Louise is high maintenance"

Marshal looked for his gold Eldorado Cadillac and finally saw it two aisles over. When they reached the car, he opened the door for Carol and then put her luggage on the back seat and got into the car himself.

"So, is the divorce still on?" Marshal asked as he started the motor.

"Absolutely. That's one reason why I came back to Denver."

"Much has happened in the last few weeks. I was so sorry to hear about Andrew. Do you think they can get him back?"

"I hope and pray they can. He is my whole life."

"And your estranged is no longer president. That will make it easier for your divorce."

"Do you think so? I don't think this is going to be easy any way you look at it."

Carol looked out the window at the streets as they were coming into Denver. How different this looked from France, so clean and new. But there were similarities too. The houses may have looked different on the outside but families lived inside and she thought how they most certainly had some of the same problems French families had. Only France wasn't at war. And French families didn't have to be concerned with sending their young men and women to a far off land, with the possibility that they might not come home alive.

"Did you find an apartment for me?" Carol had asked Marshal to do that for her.

"Yes, I did. It's not far from my office. One of those new high rise apartments. A bit pricey, but we can afford it."

"We? What is this we business?"

"Until you get your money free and clear, you may need some help and this place is very secure. You are going to need that to keep the press away from you."

"No, Marshal, I don't want that kind of help. I have money."

They wound through the streets of downtown Denver until finally Marshal drove into an underground garage and found a parking place. They then got out of the car and walked into the lobby of the building where there was a guard station. The guard asked for identification and Marshal introduced her as Mary Davis, using another name to insure anonymity. The guard checked his roster for the name and then waved them on. As they got on the elevator, Marshal explained that he used the alias for security reasons. Riding to the fifteenth floor, they stepped off the elevator and into the hallway. Standing before a door marked with the number 1501, Marshal opened it with an electronic key and motioned Carol inside.

"Welcome to your new home Mrs. Walters."

Carol walked in and was in awe. The spacious living room was furnished with a white leather sectional and a contemporary glass coffee table with arc lamps on either side. An oil painting in the style of Mark Rothko filled the wall behind and there was a vase of two-dozen red roses on the coffee table. The wall of windows across from the couch looked out over the city of Denver with lights flickering from the tall buildings and the traffic below.

"Marshal, this is beautiful, but it is too much. I'll stay here for tonight, but I need to have something smaller and less expensive than this." Carol didn't mention the roses.

"You may change your mind in the morning. You can see the mountains of the eastern slope from these windows in the daytime."

"Thank you, Marshal, I appreciate your help. We'll see in the morning, like you say," said Carol wanting Marshal to leave. "I'm really tired now and I need to get some sleep, so I'll talk to you tomorrow."

Marshal shrugged his six foot shoulders and gave Carol another hug, wished her a good nights sleep and left. Carol then dragged her bag into the opulent bedroom with a super sized king bed covered with a rose colored silk duvet. Even this bed is too much, she thought. She had been used to the small beds in Paris and this one was huge in comparison. Taking her nightgown out and putting it on, she thought it was good to be home, but she missed Paris and she missed Claude. And most of all she missed Andrew and wondered what lay ahead of her.

Chapter 21

Carol's Quest

Marshal was right, the view was magnificent. Carol looked out the massive floor to ceiling windows at the panorama of mountain range in the distance, frosted with a light dusting of snow like powdered sugar on gingerbread. She then went into the kitchen, all shiny with new stainless steel appliances, and walls painted an eggshell white with a light sand colored Italian tile floor. Opening the two-door Sub Zero refrigerator, she found fresh squeezed juice, eggs and cheese, fresh fruits and vegetables. Marshal had thought of everything. Carol found a loaf of bread, poured some juice and sipped on that while she ground the coffee to brew a fresh pot. She made toast, poured on some orange marmalade that she found in the cupboard and took her small breakfast into the great room and sat at the teak dining room table gazing out over the mountains. She read the card attached to the roses; "To Carol, Welcome Home, Love Marshal" it said. Love Marshal, she thought. Is he smitten with me, she wondered? He's divorced now so she wouldn't be a bit surprised. Men, she thought, they just had to have a woman around and they'll grab the first one available, anyone will do. But then she wasn't just any woman.

She turned on the plasma TV on the wall opposite the expansive windows. She wanted to hear the news, to know what was happening in the country and the world. Even though most network news was lightweight fluff news she thought she might get an idea of the political climate of the country and how the economy was doing. She switched to CNBC News. They were showing footage of Marines patrolling the streets of Falujah and then Dave, the anchor person said they had a film clip of Andrew being held by al Qaeda and there before her eyes was a video showing Andrew in an orange jumpsuit sitting, chained to a chair with two armed thugs dressed in black, their faces covered with black head masks, holding machine guns to his head. Oh, my god, she couldn't watch. But she had to. A voice in the video was saying something in Arabic that was being translated by another deep male voice in the background. A translator was deciphering, saying they wanted all the American troops to leave Iraq and if that didn't happen in one month, they would behead their hostage without hesitation. Well, we have some time, she thought, but her heart was in her stomach as she thought about what Andrew was going through. Were they torturing him? She had to find a way to get him out of there, even if she had to go there herself. The phone rang and she jumped.

"Hello. Oh, Marshal, it's you. Have you seen the news? They're parading Andrew for all to see. I'm so sick.... I can't watch this. We have to get him out."

"Yes, Carol, I saw. I know and I will try to help you."

"I have to call Washington to see if I can find out if they have any news of Andrew."

"Carol, have dinner with me tonight. I made a reservation at Townley's steak house for eight o'clock."

"I don't know, I can't think about going out."

"It'll do you good. There's nothing you can do about this tonight."

"Well, I guess you're right about that. Okay," Carol relented. He was right, there was nothing to be done tonight, but would she be able to do anything at all to get Andrew back home safely? She had just hung up the phone, when it rang again.

"Carol, James here. Welcome back to civilization. Your trip went well I trust."

"I am amazed at how you can track my every move, James. And civilization, I do think that Europe is many times more civilized than this country. They don't go around attacking smaller countries for no reason."

"I need to see you. I want to talk about Andrew," James said, letting the last comment pass by him.

"Have you seen the video on the news? I'm beside myself. What are we going to do?"

"I don't know but meet with me today and maybe we can figure out something."

"I can't today, but maybe tomorrow. Where are you living, James?"

"I'm back at the ranch but I'm coming into town tomorrow. How about lunch? Can I pick you up?"

"No, I'll meet you. There's a Pasta Palace right down the street from my apartment, I'll meet you there at eleven thirty tomorrow."

It infuriated Carol that he seemed to always know where she was and what she was doing, like he was spying on her. She wondered if he still had the Secret Service protecting him. No doubt he did, there were many people in this country who would like to see him dead.

And then she thought about Claude. She missed him. She missed his rock solid support and his hugs and kisses. She wondered if anything would ever come of their relationship. But that was up to her, as Claude was willing. She had no doubt that he loved her very much and all she would have to do is say the word and he would be with her. But she had to get the divorce done. And she had to get Andrew back home safe and alive. She could do nothing else until those two things were accomplished and then she could get on with her life.

The dinner with Marshal that evening was boring. All he could talk about was his ex wife and how she had betrayed him. Evidently she had been carrying on this affair for a couple of years and he had known nothing about it. And he was shocked that she would just run out on him. Not that he had been faithful to Louise. He admitted to having an affair with one of his secretaries, but he always came back to Louise. She had probably known about his affairs and was just getting back at him and then she saw that Marshal was a boring person, totally wrapped up in his own world of law, and she fell in love. That's how those things happen. But Marshal was an exceptional lawyer and she wanted him on her side so she said nothing and just listened. When he took her back to the apartment, he tried to kiss her on the lips and she turned her face to the side, his kiss landing on her cheek.

"I really care for you Carol," Marshal said.

"Whoa, it's too soon to even think of anything like this. I'm not even divorced yet and you haven't been single that long and I need you as a lawyer and friend, not a lover right now," Carol said, trying to be forthright with him, but not wanting to turn him off completely. Now she knew what it was like to have your boss hitting on you. If you brush him aside you could lose your job, if you don't you could still be fired.

Carol turned and opened her door and said good night and thank you for the dinner. She said she would invite him in but the jet lag was kicking in and she needed her sleep, and he didn't persist.

The next day she made some calls to Washington, but no one would talk to her and she wasn't surprised. After all James was out now. They had moved on with Jason as the new president and he had selected Charles Robertson, his secretary of defense for his vice president, replacing him with Ronald King, a retired four star general.

Carol looked at her watch; it was ten thirty. She dressed in a dark brown pants suit with a turquoise shell and pulled on her western boots that she had bought in Paris. After pulling her long gray streaked hair back into a ponytail, she put on some lip-gloss and mascara and she was ready to go. She walked out of the apartment and got onto the elevator, still not used to the newness of everything compared to Paris. She greeted the guard as she passed and walked out into the bright August sunlight. It was warm, but not unbearably so as Denver, the mile high city was seldom hot in the summer like Phoenix or Las Vegas. The streets, wide and open unlike the narrow streets of Paris, were filled with people rushing to appointments or lunch. She also noticed how large Americans were compared to the French. Not just big, but obese. She had seen very few fat people in France. But of course they would have little chance to get fat, they were always walking everywhere and to get onto and off the metro often times meant climbing many stairs. She then remembered climbing the hundreds of stairs ascending the Sacre Coeur and how out of breath she had been when she reached the top. Most people rode the tram, but she wanted to walk, to get the feel of the area. And it was worth it. The view of Paris from the Basilica was as breathtaking as the walk.

Carol crossed the street and noticed one more difference; the sidewalks were spotless, unlike the narrow sidewalks of Paris where you had to pick your way through brown spots and streams coming off most every lamp post from the many dogs in the city. But Carol loved dogs so she hadn't minded. She approached the Pizza Palace and walked inside. There very few people at this hour and the overhead television screens were blaring with re-runs of preseason football. It was quite dark, but she couldn't miss James sitting in a back booth and her heart skipped a beat. He looked good, a little grayer maybe, more lines in his face, but he appeared to have come through his ordeal relatively unscathed.

"You don't waste any time do you," she said as she slid into the booth opposite James.

"What do you mean by that?"

"I haven't been in the country three days and you're calling me."

"Well, if you're going to have an attitude, maybe we shouldn't even talk."

"I don't know what we have to talk about anyway."

James ignored her last remark. "I ordered for us, I hope you don't mind. A large pizza, half sausage, half vege and a pitcher of beer." Exactly what they used to order when they were dating.

"You look good," Carol finally said.

"So do you. Europe seems to agree with you."

"I'm having jet lag big time, and I'm worried sick about Andrew."

"I know, I know. I am too. I'm in constant contact with the CIA and I promise you we are doing everything we can to get him back."

"Not enough. They're threatening to kill him. Do you understand that?" Carol yelled and then looked around the room to see if anyone had heard her.

"I do, Carol and I'm sorry."

"Being sorry is not going to bring him home," she said, her voice softer now.

James took her hands in his and pleaded with his eyes. "Come back home, Carol. Come back to the ranch and we can start over. We can have the partnership and love that we had before all of this happened."

"But everything has changed, James. You're not the same person anymore."

"Yes I am. I just got off track for a while, but I can get back on again. I got caught up in the power thing and it was bad, real bad. I forgot what my real values were. You were right about everything and I was wrong."

"You had your chance before the election, but you chose to go on. It's too late now. Andrew is gone and our lives will never be the same. We can't go back."

"I am going to get Andrew back. That's why I resigned. I'm going to Iraq and I am going to meet with the leaders of al Qaeda and I will pay them whatever they want to bring our son back home safely."

"I don't think they want money, James. They want American troops out of their country. They want the killing to stop. And you can't do anything about that now because you are no longer president."

"You are really pessimistic about this. You have to keep thinking that he will come home alive. And then it will happen."

"Look how many people they've beheaded. And now they have the prize, the son of the president that started the war in their country."

James was silent. He looked down at the table and rolled his napkin and then unrolled it again.

"This is our son, James. This is our only son." Carol started crying, but then the waiter brought the pizza and the pitcher of beer and she took out a tissue and held it to her nose, stifling the tears.

"I know Carol, I know. I love him as much as you. I am working on this every day and I have talked to the Saudis and they have connections, so we are making progress.

James took a piece of pizza and put it on his plate and offered Carol some. He poured the beer and started eating. Carol took a couple of bites and drank some of the beer but she was no longer hungry.

"James, I'm not coming back to you. Not now, not ever. Marshal is getting the divorce on track and hopefully you won't fight it."

"No, I won't, if you're sure that's what you want. You can have everything. Take the ranch, all of the money. My life is worth nothing without you."

"I only want what is rightfully mine and nothing more."

"What are your plans, Carol? Are you going to marry that French guy?"

"No, I'm going to law school and I don't know after that. One day at a time."

They ate in silence and then Carol got up to leave. She gave James a hug and walked out the door. She was sad. Sad that Andrew was still missing. Sad that their lives couldn't be put back together like it was in the early days of their marriage.

Chapter 22

Simone Searches for Andrew

Jabar had told Simone that she could not go out alone, day or night. Women in Baghdad, and other parts of Iraq for that matter, he told her, had to have a male escort, a father, husband or brother to accompany them on the street. It wasn't safe for anyone in Iraq, especially women. But Simone was not one to follow rules and she needed to get to the mosque to make the contact for her search for Andrew. She donned all black clothes, a long black peasant skirt that just hit her ankles and a long sleeved, loose fitting black cotton knit top. She threw a black scarf on her head and draped it around her neck, covering her hair. Simone was trying to blend in.

Her uncle had gone to work and her aunt and cousins were at the market buying what little food was available in Baghdad. That left her alone to carry out her plan. Walking out into the bright sunlight, Simone shielded her eyes from the glare. The August heat was oppressive and her black clothing only made it worse, absorbing the heat and causing her to perspire. Picking her way down the street, she headed in the direction of where the mosque might be according to what her uncle had told her. There was garbage everywhere, birds and rats were picking at the refuse. Four young boys ran by her, crossed the street and then disappeared and a Humvee drove by with two American soldiers.

Walking two blocks and turning the corner she saw the mosque at the end of the street, carefully choosing her way through the potholes on the once paved road. It must be about noon, she thought. And, unlike a normal city, there were very few people out walking on the streets. But then Baghdad was not a normal city, still under siege from the so-called insurgents and from the America troops trying to contain them.

Like as not people were afraid to venture out unless it was absolutely necessary, to get food, go to prayer, or go to work if they were fortunate enough to still have a job.

She reached the door of the mosque and entered the large open area covered by many multi-colored Persian rugs and was greeted by an older man with a gray beard, wearing a dishdash, a long white tunic like robe and a shimagh covering his head. He told her to take off her shoes and go to a special area for women. She removed her shoes but she did not want to be segregated from the men. She was looking for a man named Amahl Hakim, an acquaintance of one of her Muslim friends in Paris. She asked the man if he had heard of him and he shook his head. Simone then followed orders and headed for the women's area when a young man ran to her side.

"Why are you looking for Amahl?" he asked in Arabic.

"Do you speak English?" she asked. He shook his head up and down and she took that as a yes. "I was told that he could help me find my friend. I was told that he knows everything that is going on in Baghdad and Iraq."

"That is true," he said in very broken English. "If you come to this house tonight at eight o'clock, you might find Amahl, he said handing her a piece of paper with an address written in pencil."

She could barely understand him, but she looked at the piece of paper and she could decipher what was written. "I will try to be there," she said. But how would she do that? Perhaps she could talk her cousin Mohammed into taking her out tonight. She continued on into the mosque and tried to look like she belonged, kneeling to the floor with the others, bowing when they bowed and mumbling she didn't know what. Simone had seldom been in a church, and certainly not a mosque, so this was all very new to her. When she finished, she walked back out into the bright, ever-present sun, hurried back down the street sweating profusely under her heavy dark clothing. When she reached her uncle's house, she opened the door, walked into the coolness of the house and was greeted by Jabar.

"Simone, where have you been? I was very worried about you."

"Uncle, I just went to the mosque. No one else was home so I thought it would be all right. It's not very far from here."

"Remember I told you not to go out alone. And you have disobeyed my orders. If you are to remain here, you will have to follow the rules," Jabar said in a threatening manor.

Later that afternoon Simone approached Mohammed and told him about the meeting she wanted to attend and he was skeptical at first, but then after she told him they would be meeting some of the elite Sunni underground militia in Baghdad, he agreed. Simone didn't really know that, but to Mohammed, who was eighteen and adventurous this would sound very exciting.

After dinner that night, Mohammed told his father he was taking Simone to the coffee house that evening to meet some friends and asked if he could use his father's car. Jabar said yes, but told him to be very careful and be on the lookout for any trouble that might be brewing and they were to be home by ten o'clock. Mohammed agreed.

Simone put on her black clothes she had worn earlier that day. They got into the car and she gave Mohammed the address.

"Do you know where this is?" asked Simone.

"Approximately. We might have to ask directions."

"This escort thing for women really sucks, you know."

"I'm with you Simmy," said Mohammed, calling her by her childhood nickname. "Women should be free to go about as they please, just like men."

Mohammed drove down into the heart of Baghdad and turned onto a narrow street with no streetlights. "Father said you were living with the son of the American president. Awesome."

"Yes, he's an awesome guy. And that's why I'm here. You know that he's been abducted, don't you?"

"Of course, everybody knows about that, it's been on TV almost every night. You don't really think you can find him do you? The people who have him are pretty ruthless and you could never deal with them."

"I think you're right, but I could find someone else who might help me." Simone took a cigarette out of her purse and lit it.

"That might be difficult to do also, as Muslim men cannot associate with women. Not even Muslim women. And I wouldn't smoke when you go into this place."

"What is this shit? How can women live like this?"

"You are living in a free, secular, democratic society in France. I hope Iraq will be like that one day, but it will take a long time I think. And I don't think it will happen with the Americans here," said Mohammed.

"Moh, you're going to have to come to Paris and hang out with me when this is all over."

"I would like that."

They turned down another street and Simone took note of the street names so she could find this place on her own. She knew now she wouldn't be able to stay with her uncle, although it would be the safest place. She couldn't see having to ask for an escort every time she went out. She knew that her uncle was just trying to protect her, but she would not be able to accomplish her goals this way.

They turned again, this time into a dark narrow alley where cars were parked along the walls of the buildings.

"This is it," said Mohammed.

"How did you find this so easily?"

"I grew up in Baghdad and I used to ride my bike all over this town."

They parked and got out of the car and walked down the alley to a door, lit with one bare light bulb above it. Simone had been watching people going into the doorway.

"Should we knock or just go in?" Simone said, her voice wavering.

"We are going to open the door and walk in like we belong."

Mohammed went first with Simone following. A tall, black bearded man with a black keffiyeh covering his head and a flowing robe stopped them and asked in Arabic why they were there. Simone gave him the name of the man she had met at the mosque and they were allowed to pass.

There were small groups of people, all men, talking and gesturing with one another and they stared at Simone as she walked past them. Simone pulled her veil higher on her face. Minutes later one of the men approached, saying his name was Abdul and asked where they were from. He told them that women were not usually allowed at these meetings and they should not stay long. Mohammed asked if he knew Amahl and he looked at him quizzically for a moment and then said that everyone knew Amahl but he was not here tonight. And then he turned to Simone, his eyes looking intensely at hers, and said that Amahl would be there tomorrow night and would they like to come back. Simone said she would and then she took Mohammed by the hand and turned away from Abdul.

"This is creepy. I wonder why, at first Abdul told us that women were not allowed at these meetings, but then invited us to come here again tomorrow?"

"I don't know, but I think we should leave now," said Mohammed as he was looking around the room at the men who were by now staring at Simone.

They went back through the groups of men, out the door and down the alley to the car, looking sideways as they walked. As they were driving back to Mohammed's house, Simone asked if he would like to stop for a drink or a cup of coffee and he agreed. They found a small coffee shop not far from where the meeting had been. It was a warm Iraqi evening so they decided to sit outside.

"This is our national pastime in Paris, you know."

"What are you talking about?" Mohammed asked.

"Sidewalk cafes. They are everywhere and people spend hours noshing and watching people parade by."

"In Iraq we have suicide bombs with our sidewalk cafes," Mohammed said cynically.

"Do you think it's going to get better in Iraq when the new government is in place?"

"I doubt it. Iraq has never really been one country, it is made up of many tribes and they haven't gotten along in thousands of years, why would they now."

"Was it better when Saddam was in power?"

"Yes and no. He wasn't a good guy, but then good guys don't often win do they. Look at the United States. They had that good guy Carter for president and everybody said bad things about him. And from what I read about him, he was honest and he wanted to get solar power to get America off oil and he brokered the peace deal between Israel and Egypt."

"Been studying American history, have you."

"After the Americans invaded, I wanted to know more about them."

They drank their coffee and watched the few cars going by.

"You know the American soldiers didn't know anything about us when they first came here. You would think they would give them some history of our people and its culture before they invade a country."

"I don't think this war, if that's what you want to call it, was very well thought out. I think the Americans had an agenda and it wasn't for the good of the Iraqis," said Simone.

They talked for a while longer and then left as it was getting late and there was a ten thirty curfew and they had promised Jabar, Mohammed's father, that they would be back by ten.

"I am coming to Paris. You can count on that, Simmy. Maybe I will come there to live."

"Oh, Mohammed, I know I asked you to come and I would love to have you visit, but as far as living there, I don't think Paris is a very good place for Muslims right now."

They drove back through the rubble and pock marked streets. Another bomb went off not too far away and Simone was sure she was hearing gunfire. She was thinking about how difficult it was for women in this patriarchic society.

"Mohammed, I have an idea. When we go to the meeting tomorrow night, I will dress like a man."

"You are crazy and I didn't say I would go tomorrow night."

"You've got to help. Otherwise I won't be able to do any of this?"

"Look, Simmy, you are so much not like a man. You could never pull it off."

"Not so. I have very small breasts. And I am tall. I may not be muscular, but if I'm wearing baggy clothes they'll never know."

"And what about your voice? You could never sound like a man. And your beard, how do fake a beard."

"Try me," said Simone, lowering the pitch of her voice. "I will be your younger brother. I haven't grown a beard yet. And I'll cover my face anyway."

"I'll think about it. Sounds really far out to me." And they drove home arriving just minutes before ten o'clock.

The next morning, Simone wanted to go for a walk after breakfast, but she had to again wait for her cousin, Mohammed to go with her.

As they were walking along the street, Simone talked about her idea of dressing like a man and Mohammed was still against the idea and told her that he hadn't agreed to take her to the meeting that night.

"You're scared. I know it," said Simone, taunting Mohammed.

"I am not. I took you last night. I barged right in. Did I look like I was scared?"

"Then take me tonight. Just one more meeting. I won't ask you again."

"But what if this Amahl guy isn't there? What will you do then?"

"He'll be there. I feel it in my blood."

"Well, just one more time."

"Bring some of your clothes along and a wrap for my head and I'll dress in the car on the way to the meeting. We don't want your father to see what I'm doing. I am sure he wouldn't like it."

Simone was so excited she could hardly wait for the day to be over and trying to stay occupied was not easy. She asked her aunt Thana if she could help with the housework or the laundry. They went to the market at noon and bought kebabs and fruit from a vendor for lunch and then did shopping for the evening meal. This was a daily ritual, as Thana could not depend on their refrigerator with the intermittent electrical blackouts. Thana bought lamb chops, fresh string beans and a pineapple for desert. Simone offered to pay for the food, but Thana refused saying that Jabar would not accept money from his brother's daughter.

Arriving back at home, Simone helped Thana prepare the evening meal and it was finally time for dinner. Midway through the meal, Mohammed announced that they were going out again this evening.

"Simone, you are bringing bad habits to your cousin. Do you go out every night in Paris?" Jabar asked half teasing.

""No, I don't. But it is so interesting in the coffee houses in Baghdad. I see a part of the city that I would not otherwise be able to see."

After desert, they excused themselves from the table. Mohammed secretly stuffed some of his clothes into a bag and they stole off into the night. Simone asked Mohammed to stop a kilometer away from the house and she started to strip off her clothes.

"What are you doing? You can't just take your clothes off here in the middle of Baghdad. You'll be arrested."

"Keep an eye out for the police, will you. This won't take long," as she took off her shirt and her jeans and then her bra. She grabbed the white shirt from the bag and quickly put it on. "Didn't you bring some of your shorts, or underwear? She asked struggling with the pants and the belt.

"No, who's going to see your underwear?" Mohammed asked as he shielded his eyes from seeing her half naked body.

"What if they capture me and strip me."

"By that time they'll know you're a girl."

"Woman. I am not a girl," snapped Simone.

Mohammed kept looking all around. "Hurry, I see a Humvee coming down the street. They could shoot us, you know."

Simone put on Mohammed's striped vest and then tucked her hair underneath the head wrap fashioned like a turban and turned to Mohammed. "How do I look?"

"You look like Simone to me."

"Come on, that's because you know me. If you didn't know me, would you say I looked like a guy?"

"I guess so," Mohammed said unenthusiastically as he began driving again, retracing the route from last night. When they arrived at the alley entrance, there were no parking spaces to be had close by and they had to go back and park several blocks away and walk back to the sinister door with the bare light bulb above. There appeared to be more people here tonight and Simone hoped that meant Amahl would be here also. They opened the door and the same bearded man from the night before stopped them. He remembered Mohammed, but asked who was with him and Mohammed told him it was his brother, Sahar and he let them pass. Security is not too tight, thought Simone.

The atmosphere was very different. Instead of men gathering in groups and talking, there were folding chairs placed in front of a small stage like area where a podium had been placed indicating there would be a speaker. And no one stared at her as they took a seat in the back of the room, not wanting to attract attention. And then Abdul saw them and came and sat beside Mohammed.

"I see you made it to the meeting," said Abdul in Arabic. "Who is your friend?"

"This is my brother, Sahar," said Mohammed. Simone briefly acknowledged Abdul, and then turned her head away, hoping he wouldn't recognize her.

"It is good you didn't bring that woman with you," said Abdul.

Mohammed shook his head in agreement and then asked, "Is there a speaker tonight?"

"Yes, the one you are looking for, Amahl, he is speaking tonight. That is why there are so many more members here."

Minutes later, Amahl walked out onto the stage wearing white baggy pants and an oversized white tunic shirt with a black keffiyah on his head. He started speaking in Arabic and he spoke so fast that Simone could not understand what he was saying.

"Tell me what he's saying," she said to Mohammed.

"He's just talking about the progress they are making with attacking the US troops and the new weapons they are getting from Iran and Syria."

"Do you think these guys are Andrew's captors?" Simone whispered in Mohammed's ear, hoping Abdul, who was engrossed in the speech, would not hear.

"It's hard to say. I doubt it though. These men are leftovers of the Sunni Baathist army. You know what I mean, Saddam's Republican guard," he whispered back to her.

"If they are Sunnis, what are they doing dealing with Iran and Syria?" Simone asked.

"I don't know. But it could be that in time of an emergency, and this would be that time, all Arabs and Muslims tend to come together."

"I hope I can talk to Amahl. According to my friend in Paris, he knows everything that happens in Iraq and he might know where Andrew is."

Amahl talked for another hour and Simone was losing interest as she understood little of what he was saying. Then he abruptly concluded his talk by raising his hands above his head and shouted something, Simone didn't know what, and everyone around them raised their arms and shouted the same word. Probably victory, thought Simone. Then everyone got up from their chairs and pressed in on Amahl as he walked down from the stage. But Amahl seemed to take it in his stride and he talked to each one, patting them on the back like a politician. Mohammed and Simone stood in one corner watching all of this.

"Want to go now?" asked Mohammed.

"Without talking to Amahl? That is why we are here."

They waited and they waited. Amahl talked to the men, one by one. And then miraculously he made his way to the corner where they were standing.

"And did you agree with what I was saying tonight?" Amahl asked Mohammed in Arabic. "I don't believe I have met you or your friend here."

Mohammed introduced himself and bowed, as is Iraqi custom and then introduced his "brother".

"And you, Sahar, did you like what I said tonight?"

Simone didn't understand what he had said. "I am looking for someone and I was told you might know where he is," Simone blurted out in as low a voice as she could muster as Mohammed looked at her long and hard.

"And who might that be?" Amahl answered back in English.

"I was told that you might know who is holding the president's son, Andrew Walters."

"I might. And why would you want this information?"

"I want to communicate with him," Simone said.

"That would be impossible. But we can't talk here. Let's leave and find a quieter place where there are fewer eyes and ears. Come, follow me."

And Amahl walked towards the door with two other men following and Simone and Mohammed bringing up the rear. Once outside, Amahl motioned them to get into a panel truck parked close to the door.

"No, we'll follow in our car," said Mohammed not wanting to be captive by Amahl and his cohorts.

"I am afraid not. You will have to ride with us or not come along at all. We are going to a secret place few know about. We will bring you back here a little later."

Mohammed looked at Simone thinking how silly she looked in his clothes. Simone signaled yes, to Mohammed that she wanted to go. He took her aside.

"Are you really going to trust these guys?" he asked.

"Yes, it's the only way I can find out about Andrew."

"They could take us hostage."

"That's the chance we have to take. Look, if you want to go back home, I'll go without you."

Mohammed thought for a minute or so, and then decided he couldn't let her go alone, his father would be furious if something happened to Simone and since Simone was determined to go with them he would just have to follow along. He hoped they would be true to their word.

Chapter 23

Carol Gets Help

By now the public knew that Carol was back in the States and they knew about the divorce. The administration made the announcement shortly after her arrival from Europe. It seemed strange to her that people appeared to accept the administration's explanation that she had run away from the nursing home where her mental health was in question, gone to Europe with her son for therapy and now she was back, good as new and that was that. And, in addition, the administration lied, saying that James was divorcing Carol for running off and leaving him. Carol wanted to set things straight, but she was bound by her promise not to talk to the press or anyone else in exchange for amnesty from the Secret Service and the FBI to not follow her or keep records on her. She, of course didn't believe that they were fully keeping their promise, but she would keep hers for the moment.

Marshal was calling almost every day, asking her to dinner and the theater and cocktail parties which she truly hated. She occasionally accepted his invitations; she treated him with respect as he was a good friend and she still needed him for the divorce and he was helping her to get into law school. But she was keeping him at arms length. Carol had to give him credit for working out a fine settlement for her; one half of the ranch, James was to buy her out and one half of their financial investments and bank accounts, which amounted to over five million dollars. Not a huge sum in today's money, but enough so that she could go back to school and live a reasonable life while doing so. She had decided to temporarily stay in the apartment that Marshal had rented for her as it was very secure and she admitted to herself that she had become accustomed to the luxury and she loved the view.

As soon as the divorce was final she vowed to herself to find a smaller, less expensive, less ostentatious apartment. Carol wasn't one to spend money unwisely. And she looked forward to the day when she would graduate from law school and get her first job. That would be two years of long days and nights of studying and hard work.

But Carol's first priority was getting Andrew back and she spent every day working on it. She kept calling Washington, and finally was able to talk with Senator John Morten, head of the Armed Services Committee who told her that they were doing all they could to bring him home. They had offered a large sum of money to no avail and they were sending a group of senators to Iraq to try to negotiate his release. But they still would not bow to the demands of his captors to end the US occupation in Iraq, saying that to pull the troops out now would put the Iraqi civilian population at risk. And Carol feared that he would be killed. Another tape had been released showing Andrew sitting on a stool, blindfolded, the armed terrorists standing by his side pointing weapons at his head. Another was behind him holding a machete like knife over his head as if they were going to behead him at any moment. Carol could not bear to watch these videos, knowing these extremists were often true to their word and they would likely bring that knife down on Andrew and he would be taken from her forever.

She had asked Senator Morten if she could go to Iraq, but he advised against that. He said it was just too dangerous and they were doing everything they could right now and she should let them handle it. Carol wasn't buying that. She knew she must do more, but what.

Then, one afternoon after she had finished another fruitless call to Washington, she had an idea. There was a significant anti war movement in the country, spread across many different groups. Many of these people were, like her, against the war from the very beginning, knowing that what the administration told them just wasn't true. That Saddam had very little power and certainly was not a threat to the United States. They were marching on Washington in September. Could she rally them to her cause, and bring pressure on Washington to bring her son home as well as the troops? They would surely be sympathetic to Andrew's plight. One of the leading activists, Debra Johansen, was herself the mother of a fallen soldier and she had been holding sit ins in front of the White House and in fact had been arrested twice for failing to stay in the prescribed zone that hid her from the press and crowds. Carol would contact her and attempt to enlist her help. It was worth a try.

Claude had called several times since she had been back in Colorado but she had been out and so one morning she thought she would give him a call. It was difficult finding the right time, with eight hours of time difference between France and Mountain Daylight time of Colorado. She dialed his number, using the phone in the bedroom, lounging back on her luxurious bed, still in her nightgown and robe. The phone rang and rang and then she heard the voice of a woman.

"*Allo*," the woman answered.

"Claude, I am calling for Claude. Is he there?" Carol asked, wondering if Claude had a new woman in his life.

"*Oui, ne quittez pas!*"

She heard someone walking towards the phone and then voices talking.

"*Allo, qui est a l'appareil?*" Claude asked.

"Claude, this is Carol. I've been trying to reach you and every time I call you're out."

"Yes, I have been doing the same. Are you all right? How was the trip? And what have you found out about Andrew?"

"I am fine. The trip was uneventful and it is good to be back. And nothing yet on Andrew. I've been talking to Washington and they're sending a group of people to Iraq, I think some senators. I'm trying to stay positive about this, but I just saw him on TV being threatened by his captors." Carol felt the tears starting to roll down her cheeks and she started to choke up.

"I know sweetheart, I saw that too. You must think the best and it will happen. They will get him out. I just know it."

Carol then told him about her idea to engage the anti war activists and help her appeal to Congress and he was very optimistic that her plan might do some good.

"Carol, I miss you terribly. When are you coming back to France?"

"Not for awhile. I've just enrolled in law school," Carol said as she took a deep breath and lay back on her pillow. "Who was the lady who answered the phone?"

"Oh, that was my new housekeeper. The other one quit a week ago and I hired Adele yesterday." Claude laughed and then said, "No, I don't have a new lady friend. I think of you every minute. I need to see you. Come to Paris, just for a weekend. I'll make the arrangements."

"Claude, that sounds very enticing. I'd love to, but I don't know....." Carol wondered if the new housekeeper was young and pretty.

"Are you divorced yet?"

"Soon. In about three weeks."

"Let's plan the trip to celebrate. You tell me the date and I will make the reservations."

"The date as of now is September fifteen."

"It is done. I will spend every minute thinking of our reunion in Paris. You will see Paris as you have never seen it."

"I don't think so. I cannot celebrate until Andrew is back," Carol said. She didn't think that getting a divorce was a cause to celebrate.

"You could come back here and talk to Simone's friends. They might know something about Andrew." Claude paused and then said, "Carol, I love you."

"Oh, Claude I love you too," Carol said, surprised that she had said the "L" word. Did she really love Claude or was she just lonely and reaching out to a friend.

"I have been waiting for you say those words," Claude said endearingly.

*   *   *

The morning sun rose again someplace in the Middle East, but Andrew could not see it from his windowless cell. Soon it would be unbearably hot, over 100 degrees and Andrew would be enduring another sweltering day in anguish. Using a small rock he had found out in the yard when he was allowed his one day a week of exercise, Andrew put another mark on the wall beneath his cot to keep track of the number of days he had been held in captivity. He counted twenty-three of these marks today. Twenty-three days with little human contact with the exception of the two times the guards had taken him from his cell to make videos, no doubt to be shown around the world. He was blindfolded and made to sit on a stool with masked gunmen beside him and this last time with another henchman behind holding a huge knife, threatening to cut off his head if the United States would not cooperate and leave Iraq immediately. It was unnerving and he never knew when the day might come when they would make his last video, the one where his head rolled.

The guard would bring one of his two meals for the day, usually dried bread and coffee and if he were lucky, a glass of lukewarm goats milk that would often be bordering on sour. He lay on a canvas cot with a thread warn, green cotton blanket. Although the cell was relatively clean with a toilet and washbasin, it was small, eight feet by five feet, with little room to move about. Andrew felt his body slowly losing strength with little exercise and the poor diet. He tried to compensate by doing pushups and sit-ups every day, but some days he did not have the strength.

Along with the lack of amenities like a fan or air conditioning, there was no electricity in his cell and when twilight came, darkness folded over him for all of the hours of the night, leaving Andrew to lie on his cot and think and wonder and worry; what would his fate be. But he would hang on no matter what, hoping that either someone would find and rescue him or the United States would negotiate his release. Some days he would be hopeful and some days in despair, but he was thankful that he was still alive. That was all he had for the moment.

Chapter 24

Out in the Desert

Riding in the back of the panel truck over Baghdad streets was like riding a wild bucking bronco and twice Simone lost her balance and fell over onto the floor, while trying to hold on to Mohammed for stability and once even he was toppled as they hit an extraordinarily large pit in the street. Against Mohammed's better judgment, they had climbed into the large white Chevy van that was dented on every fender, looking like it had been in a demolition derby. Two Arab men sat across from them staring at them from time to time in stony silence. There were no windows in the back of the van that would provide them with the knowledge of where they were being taken, in case they had to escape. But Simone was trusting and even if they had to make a dash for it, she was counting on Mohammed to know the territory and lead them back safely. They had to take the chance. This was her only opportunity to find the people who were holding Andrew. But she had to admit that she didn't have a plan. So what if they knew where Andrew was. Could she talk them into letting him go? It was a long shot, but she had to try. And then she thought that Andrew might not even be alive. But no, she would erase those thoughts from her mind. She could only think that he was alive and she would be successful in gaining his release.

The van stopped and then it pulled ahead. They must have arrived at their destination, wherever that was. She looked at her watch and it was ten o'clock, one half hour before curfew. They would surely be spending the night and she worried that her uncle would be upset when he found out they had not returned. But they would be back in the morning and then she could explain why they were gone for the night.

The two doors of the back of the van opened abruptly and she saw Amahl and one of the other men motion for them to get out of the van. As Simone moved forward and crawled out, her headgear shifted, her long black hair fell over her shoulders and Simone quickly pulled it up into her headdress, hoping no one noticed.

"This way," said Amahl as he pointed in the direction of a low, adobe brick building, surrounded by tall date palm trees and various types of vehicles, one of them an American Humvee, no doubt stolen from the military. Simone looked around to try to see where they were, but it was darker than dark, with only a small light coming from one of the miniscule windows of the building like a chiaroscuro painting. They were far from Baghdad; somewhere in the desert was all she could determine.

They walked up a sandy, dusty path led by Amahl and a tall dark Arab dressed in brown baggy pants, an oversized brown shirt and a keffiyah on his head. Two more similarly dressed Arabs followed behind them. Walking into the building, Simone adjusted her eyes to the dim light provided by one bare light bulb hanging from the low ceiling. There was very little furniture, one small wooden table in the middle of the room, a couple of rumpled, dirty couches lining the walls and several wooden chairs.

"Please sit," Amahl said as he motioned toward one of the dusty couches. They sat as they were instructed as Amahl pulled one of the chairs closer to them. Another man brought tea and offered each of them a cup.

"Now, you were saying, Sahar. You are looking for someone?"

"Yes, I am looking for the President's son, Andrew Walters. Do you have him?" Simone said meekly, trying to lower her voice.

Mohammed blinked his eyes and couldn't believe how bold Simone was. He hoped it wouldn't get them into trouble with these men, but he was concerned.

"Maybe and maybe not. Why are you interested in him? Is he a relative? Lover?"

Simone's body flinched. They knew she was a woman.

"A friend of the family. They contacted me hoping I could locate his captors and negotiate his release," said Simone.

"I don't think that is possible. The President's son is our bargaining tool to remove the American occupiers from our country so we can carry on with the business of running our own country."

"But the Americans are not going to leave, you know that," said Simone. "You might as well let him go. If you kill him they will have retribution and thousands more Iraqi people will die."

"They have killed thousands already; a few more won't matter now will it."

"Do you know where he is? Can I see him..... talk to him?"

"That is not possible. He is in a very safe place where no one can find him."

"Is he still alive? Is he well?" Simone asked.

"Yes, he is alive and he is well. We don't abuse our prisoners like Americans do," said Amahl. Of course he was lying.

All the while, Mohammed sat in silence taking all of this in, but not wanting to get involved in the highly charged exchange between Simone and Amahl. But he was listening and what he heard did not please him. He was afraid that they were now going to be held captive.

"You must let him go. It is doing you no good to hold him," Simone's voice cracked. "I will get money for your people. I can get a million American dollars in exchange for Mr. Walter's release. That is a lot of money. You could buy many weapons with a million dollars."

Amahl looked thoughtfully at Simone as Mohammed's eyes widened. "A million dollars is a drop in the bucket. The Americans have already offered twenty million and we turned that down."

Simone was disappointed and relieved at the same time. Where would she have gotten a million dollars if they had accepted her offer?

"Take the money then. Take it and run and let him go. The money is worth more to you than holding him. You can fight with that money and then, maybe, just maybe if you kill enough American soldiers, they might pull their troops out. Public opinion is going against the war in the United States. They are having an election next year and those fat men in congress don't want to lose their lucrative jobs over this war. Trust me, I know about such things."

"I will think about it. You seem to speak with experience and knowledge. How do you know all of this?" Amahl asked.

"I know the Americans. They are fickle. They were for the war after the World Trade Center was brought down, because they were told that Iraqis were involved. They then wanted their government to attack this country. But now the truth is coming out and the numbers of dead and injured are rising and Americans are not happy with their government for misleading them into war under false pretense. It is the American people who will decide."

"Are you sure about that? I have heard that American elections are rigged just like they are here in Iraq."

"Doesn't matter. Public opinion is important in America. Look, President Walters has even stepped down. This will weaken the administration and leave room for another party to take over and if that happens, they will likely want to pull the America troops out."

Mohammed was impressed with Simone's arguments and her knowledge of American politics. "I'll think about it, I truly will think about it. Now, we have to find a place for you and Mohammed to sleep tonight. It is too late for you to go back to Baghdad."

"We can go back. It's not too late," Mohammed said, uttering his first words since they had arrived.

"No, I won't hear of it. It is past curfew and it would be dangerous. You will be my guests for the night. Akabar, take them to the room near the kitchen and make them comfortable."

Akabar opened a side door and ushered Mohammed and Simone down the dark, dusty hallway, opening a door to a small windowless room at the end. He turned on a light and Simone saw two small cots with ragged blankets hugging the walls. No matter, the blankets would not be needed tonight as the temperature in the room was nearing eighty degrees and there would be no breeze. He then told them where the bathroom was and said he would be outside the door in case they needed anything in the night and then he left the room, forcefully shutting the door behind him.

"Are we guests or are we prisoners, that is the question, Simone," said Mohammed after he was sure Akabar was gone. "Why did I ever let you talk me into this?"

Simone sat on the cot and started to take off her head covering. "Don't worry. I trust these men. They are not bad people. They only want their country back."

"How do you even know that Amahl is telling the truth? He might not even know about Andrew."

"He knows. I can tell."

"You are foolish, Simone."

"Don't call me that, they might hear you."

"They know you have a disguise. They could even hear your French accent."

"Do you think so? I thought I did a good job of hiding it."

"One thing I will give you credit for, you really do know the politics. You know what is happening in Iraq and America."

"Thank you. And we have them thinking about releasing Andrew. I just know it."

They both took off as many clothes as they could without stripping down to nothing and lay down on the cots for what was going to be a very long and uncomfortable night in this hot box.

Chapter 25

The Divorce is Final

Carol called Debra Johansen to set up a meeting with her to ask if she would help to bring Andrew home. Uncannily, Debra lived in Denver making it very easy for them to meet. She asked Debra if she would meet her at the downtown Hilton Hotel on Tuesday, September 13 at ten o'clock in the morning and Debra eagerly agreed. It was Friday and Carol would have to endure another weekend of Marshal pressuring her to see him. He had asked her to dinner on Saturday and then again on Sunday. She declined both invitations. It was almost over; the divorce would be final on Thursday and she was starting law school the following week. She still wanted Marshal as a friend, but she definitely did not want to get involved with him at a deeper level. She had been up front with him and still he persisted.

Her weekend had been spent calling Washington where still no one would talk to her, writing letters to her Colorado representative in Congress, Ralph Melter, trying to persuade them to take drastic measures to free Andrew. By the time Tuesday arrived she had made fifty phone calls and written twenty letters to anyone who would listen. And so far, it appeared that few were. She hoped Debra would be able to help.

Carol, dressed in a camel colored pantsuit with a white blouse, grabbed her purse and walked out the door to meet Debra. Once on the street, several people stared at her, and one woman stopped to talk with her, telling her how sorry she was about Andrew. Carol thanked her and walked on. No more anonymity for her. She was back in the US and unless she put on a disguise, people were going to recognize her. Not a bad idea, she thought. She no longer had the Secret Service, although she had often wondered if they ever protected her. It had sometimes seemed to her that they were spying on her, following her every move..... No, she must not think such paranoid thoughts.

Carol walked into the Hilton and found the coffee shop. She saw a woman with long, straight blond hair, dressed in jeans and a t-shirt sitting in a booth in the rear of the restaurant.

"Are you Debra?" Carol asked, as she was about to sit down. "I recognize you from seeing you in the news."

"Yes, Mrs. Walters? I am so honored to meet you," said Debra as her face flushed.

"Please call me Carol."

"Yes, Carol, please join me. Would you like some coffee? I ordered breakfast. I haven't had time to eat yet this morning; so much to do. Oh, I'm gushing. I'm so excited about meeting you. You are my idol."

"Debra, thank you. I am honored to meet you. I greatly admire what you are doing," Carol said as she slid into the booth opposite Debra. "You are a very brave woman."

"Tom, my son died a year ago. It was a roadside bomb that blew up his Humvee. Two of his fellow soldiers were wounded, one lost a leg, another is blinded in both eyes," said Debra. "I had to do something. He left a young wife and a baby back home and their lives are changed forever. My grandchild, Timothy, will never know his father and Sarah, his wife is trying to cope and raise her son alone. Although, I must admit, family and friends are pitching in to help as much as possible. And what was this all for? Oil?"

"I know Debra, I know only too well. Telling you how I understand is not enough and will not make the pain go away. But I am so sorry."

"And then the wounded who are still alive..... well, more often than not, their lives are ruined forever." Tears started to roll down Debra's cheeks as she talked. "You see the homeless people on the street? Do you know that many of those men are wounded veterans, who couldn't make it? They are never the same and can't compete in the workplace with others who are whole. Do you know what I'm talking about?"

"Yes, Debra, I do. And I agree with you wholeheartedly."

"Are you going to join our movement? You would be such a help to us." Debra brushed away her tears.

"I hadn't thought about that. Yes, I guess I could do that. But the reason I wanted to meet with you is that I need to ask a favor."

"And what is that?"

"I thought... well, I was wondering if you, your group would help me get my son back from his captors in Iraq."

"How could we possibly do that? We don't have any influence with our government. In fact we are fighting against government policies."

And Carol explained to Debra that when they demonstrated, they could make banners asking not only for the troops to come home but also that Andrew be brought home alive and well.

"You could add his name to your banners. STOP THE WAR, BRING THE TROOPS HOME, BRING ANDREW HOME.... This will put more pressure on congress and the administration."

"Yes, I think we could do that. I don't know if it will help though."

"Oh, it will. Just by keeping it out in the news, creating the awareness. Otherwise, people forget, you know," said Carol. "Mid terms are coming up next fall and there are about fifty in the House and Congress who up for reelection. Their jobs are on the line. They will listen."

"Will you help us, Mrs. Walters, I mean Carol?"

"Yes. Yes, I believe in your cause. You don't even know how much I believe in your cause. Just tell me what I need to do and I'll do it."

"Oh, I am forever indebted to you. Having your name associated with us, we can do anything."

"I hope so. I'm not Superman ... er woman, you know."

"But you are... I mean, you were the first lady. People will listen to you."

They talked for another hour, planning the strategies and how Carol could get involved. They were each inspired by one another.

Thursday arrived much too soon. The days were speeding by like cars in the Indy 500. Carol knew this was the day the divorce was final, but she tried to put it out of her mind, until mid afternoon when the phone rang. She answered with much trepidation. "Carol, you're a free woman. I just thought I'd call you to let you know."

It was James. Her heart jumped. And at once she was sad. Sad that their marriage couldn't survive the tumult of the presidency.

"James, I don't know what to say."

"Meet with me this afternoon."

"No. No, I can't. Let's just leave it here."

"I have a plan to get Andrew back. I need to talk with you."

"I'm really busy...."

"We're still the parents of Andrew, you know, together. That isn't going to change. Please meet with me. Just for an hour."

"Well, okay, for an hour." How strange that James was almost begging. Not like him at all. But something in her heart said, yes she wanted to see him. She couldn't explain it, but there was just something.

"How about the same place we met last time."

"No, why don't you come up here. I don't want to go out." What was she saying? But, that was true, she really didn't want to get dressed up and go out. She had on blue jeans and a sweatshirt and she would have to change.

"All right. I'll be there in half an hour."

Carol went into her bedroom and combed her hair. She looked in the mirror and somehow she looked younger and her blue green eyes still had that sparkle.

Thirty minutes later the guard buzzed her apartment.

"Ma'am, there's a gentleman to see you. He looks like the former president, says he's your ex. Should I send him up?"

"Yes, send him. I'm expecting him."

Minutes later her doorbell rang and she opened the door and there he was, all six feet two inches of him.

"Come in. Have a seat," Carol motioned to the white leather couch and she sat beside him. They looked at each other and then they were hugging and crying together.

"I never wanted this," James said.

"It's for the best. We are different people now."

"I still love you, Carol. I will always love you. You know that don't you?"

They embraced and then they kissed. Carol arose from the couch; taking James hand, she led him into the bedroom. She pulled down the comforter and removed her sweatshirt and jeans and then started to undress James who was more than willing. They lay together on the bed, bodies entwined, kissing, embracing one another. James pulled off her pink bikini panties and entered her slowly, moving into her deeply, Carol responding arching her back. The explosion came, as together they reached the pinnacle. They stayed together, holding, caressing, kissing.

"We were always good in bed, you know," said Carol.

"Yes, we were. But we were good at other things too."

"I guess I still love you James, but I don't want you back."

"What was this all about then?"

"I just wanted to make love with you one more time."

Chapter 26

Simone and Mohammed are Captive

Simone awoke with a start, hearing an explosion somewhere in the distance. At first she was disoriented, not knowing where they were or, due to the windowless room, what time it was. She wasn't even sure what day it was. Had they been drugged? She had wanted to decline the tea offered to them last night, but she also didn't want to offend their host, Amahl.

She was terribly hot, her mouth was dry and she had to go to the bathroom. The room must be ninety degrees by now and it seemed that it was getting hotter by the minute.

Mohammed was miraculously still sleeping, but that could be the drug. She pulled her aching body off the cot and started to put on her clothes when Mohammed stirred. She then went to the door, opened it a crack and peered outside. As she suspected, the guard was sitting by the door holding an AK-47. This was definitely a problem. It now appeared that they were captive, otherwise why the guard with the gun. Had he been there all night?

She decided to walk out the door and find out if they were free to move about or not and she did just that, turning to the guard asking where the bathroom was.

"I'll take you there," he said in broken English.

"If you just tell me, I can find it on my own," Simone said fearing what his response was going to be.

"No, miss, you are not allowed to be without a guard in this complex," he said menacingly, pointing his gun at her.

"Okay, take me to the bathroom then," she said, not wanting to argue with a machine gun.

The bearded Arab, cradling the AK-47 in his arms, escorted her out of the building to a small outhouse and opened the door for her saying that he would wait until she was through. The stench was so overwhelming that she almost vomited, but she held her nose, did what she had to do and got out as soon as she could. The guard then took her back to the room where Mohammed was coming to life. He too, wanted to go to the bathroom and Simone explained the drill.

"It appears that we are captive," said Mohammed.

"I know what you're going to say, a big fat I told you so. Maybe they just don't want us snooping around. We'll ask Amahl to take us back today. I'm sure he'll do that," said Simone, although she was worried that what Mohammed said was true. What then? Would they be able to escape? They were likely in the middle of the desert. Insurgents or even the Marines could kill them. And the guard had addressed her as miss, so they knew of her disguise.

Simone looked out the door again after Mohammed returned from the bathroom.

"We need to speak with Amahl. Would you take us to him?" asked Simone.

"He is not here. He has left for the day."

"We need to get back to Baghdad. Our family will be worried about us," Mohammed then pleaded.

"Not today. Amahl has to authorize it. And I do not know when he will be back. Would you like some food? I can bring you food."

Simone's heart fell. Why had she been so trusting? It was all her fault, but then she felt that she might have done some good in talking to Amahl about Andrew. He seemed to be considering what she had said.

"Yes, and some water, please," she said, not wanting to anger the guard.

Somewhat later, maybe thirty minutes, or maybe an hour, time had no meaning, the guard opened the door without knocking and brought a tray with a carafe of water and two tin cups, some bread and dried cheese. "This is all I have to offer you. I hope it is okay for you."

"Yes, thank you," Simone said looking at the dried bread and cheese. "When will Amahl return?"

"Not today. Maybe tomorrow. Maybe next day."

The guard left and they drank the water and chewed on the bread and cheese in silence.

"Now what, Ms. Liberator," asked Mohammed?

"Well, we'll just have to escape. That's all."

"And how are we going to do that? No windows and a guard with a machine gun staked outside our door." Mohammed shook his head. "It doesn't look good."

Simone looked around the room trying to think of a way out for them.

"And even if we escape, we have no idea where we are and we're most likely in the middle of the desert with no cover. We'll be sitting ducks for target practice."

Then Simone had an idea. "What is this building made of?" she asked.

"Mud, dried clay. Most of these buildings are made that way. It is so dry in the desert and there aren't that many trees around, so it is a cheap way for people to construct buildings."

"Hide your cups if the guard comes back to take them. We can dig our way out. Pull the cot away and we can use that as cover."

"That will take forever."

"Do you have a better idea?"

"We could wait until the guard changes and just bolt out the door?"

"And be shot? I don't think so."

Simone pulled the cot away from the wall, hoping that it was an outside wall. The heat was enveloping her, sweat running down her face and under her arms. She could smell the perspiration. But this was the only way.

*   *   *

Carol heard the phone ringing on the other end. It was Saturday and she hoped Karen would be home today. She hadn't talked with her long time college friend since before she had abruptly left Colorado, many months before. She needed a friend now, a true friend and in that way she could count on Karen. It rang two more times and then Karen breathlessly answered.

"Hi, Karen, it's Carol."

"Oh my god, I've been so worried about you. I heard you were back but I didn't know how to get a hold of you. Are you okay?"

"I am fine. I'm sorry I haven't called before this. I have been fairly busy."

"No kidding, no need to apologize. A divorce, a son being held somewhere in the Middle East. I've been following on the news. What do you hear about Andrew? Will they get him back?"

"I don't know right now. We're doing everything we can. Karen, I need to talk to you. Today."

"Sure. I was just doing some gardening out back. Come on over."

"You know I don't even have a car. I guess I could borrow Marshal's. Why don't you come over to my place?"

Carol gave her the directions and then started straightening the apartment. She looked in the refrigerator to see if she could find food for lunch. She pulled out luncheon meat, cheese and some fruit. This would have to do. She didn't have time to go to the market. The guard buzzed just as she was constructing the sandwiches and she told him to send Karen upstairs.

"Wow, you're living in luxury," Karen said as she entered the living room taking in the grand view and the opulent furnishings. She hugged Carol and they looked at each other as old friends would after not seeing one another for a time.

"It's temporary. I am finding another place as soon as I get my settlement."

"And when will that be?" Karen asked as she sat on the white leather couch.

"Another couple of weeks. Come on into the kitchen. I'm fixing sandwiches."

Karen followed Carol into the kitchen and sat at the bar while Carol finished preparing the food.

"I need to know everything. From the time you left Colorado, about Europe and what has happened since you got back. Tell me everything."

And Carol told Karen about her kidnapping, about going to Mexico and then escaping to Spain and how they traveled to Paris. She told her about Claude and how much she loved him and she told Karen about Andrew meeting Simone and then tearfully about learning of Andrew's abduction. Karen listened, not wanting to interrupt and finally when Carol had finished, asked how James was taking all of this.

"Not well. You of course know that he has stepped down from the presidency. Actually, they forced him out," Carol said. She trusted Karen as she was her best friend, had been for years.

"I thought that was what happened. So, have you heard from James since the divorce?"

"I have. In fact, he was over here on Thursday, the day of the divorce and we had sex."

"You had what?"

"Sex. That's all it was. I don't know why I did that but I did. James was always good in bed and I was well......... I was horny. I guess that's what you call it."

"Are you going back to him?"

"No I'm not," said Carol emphatically. She paused and looked at Karen. "It just happened. I was sad that our marriage ended, but I don't want to be with him anymore. I have my whole life ahead of me. It just seemed right at the time. Now I don't know, but I'm not looking back."

"Hey girl, you don't have to explain to me. It's okay."

"Well, onward and upward. I'm starting law school next week. Can I count on you to tutor me if I need help?"

"You know you can. You'll be fine though. You have the smarts and the tenacity to do this. I have confidence in you."

"I'm glad someone does," said Carol.

And they spent the rest of the afternoon talking. Carol told Karen about Claude, that she thought she loved him but wasn't sure and didn't know how it would work out. She wasn't sure if she wanted to live in France however much she loved the country and Claude certainly wouldn't want to give up his wine making and move to the United States. She felt that in time she would know what was right.

Karen looked at Carol with understanding. "You know Carol, after all you've been through in the last year, you deserve to have something really good happen. Your life will turn around, it just has to."

"All I ask is to have Andrew back. Everything else is so unimportant," said Carol.

Chapter 27

Carol Starts Over

Carol started law school on Monday. She was taking fifteen credits, a fairly heavy load, but she wanted to finish ahead of the prescribed two years. She was also able, through Marshal, to get a part time job as a law clerk with a prestigious downtown law firm, Smith, Halsey and Brugeman. She didn't need the money; however, she thought the job would give her the experience she would need later on. Just being around lawyers was enough for her to learn what this attorney business was all about.

Her schedule was brutal; classes for five or more hours, three days a week, including Saturday and working at the law firm two days a week. And on Sunday she studied and wrote papers. Marshal was calling her inquiring if he could help and she declined for the moment. James would call occasionally asking to see her again, she guessed he was hoping for another meeting like the last one, but she vowed to be strong from now on. He had caught her at a weak moment, but that wouldn't happen again. And Claude called almost every day now, begging her to come to Paris. He sent flowers almost daily as well and her apartment was taking on the look of a florist shop. One night he called her late in the evening and they talked for an hour or more.

"Carol I miss you so much. I'll come over there to see you."

"No, Claude, I don't think so. I'll see if I can come at Christmas break. That's only two months away. I'm so buried in my studies and my job."

"Quit the job. I'll help you if you need money,"

"I don't need money, Claude, I need more time."

There was a silence. "Did you hear about Simone?"

"No. What about her?"

'Well, it seems that she went to Iraq, and she and her cousin are missing. The authorities think they were abducted."

"Was this in the news?"

"Yes, but only on the BBC. If you hadn't been paying attention, you would have missed it."

"Oh Claude, she went there to find Andrew. I just know it. She wouldn't have gone to Iraq otherwise. I have misjudged her."

"How so?"

"I thought at one time that she might have had something to do with Andrew's disappearance and I said as much to her. Now I feel bad."

"I don't think you should feel that way. After all, she was hanging out with some questionable characters that could have been a part of the crime."

"I know, but I as much as accused her of being an informant to her Muslim friends."

"Could be that Simone feels guilty," said Claude

"Guilty? About what?"

"That she might be indirectly responsible, by telling her friends about Andrew."

"She appears to be a very brave lady and I now have great admiration for her. She must love Andrew very much to put herself and her cousin in such danger."

"Not as much as I am in love with you, my beautiful lady. I will look forward to Christmas. I love you very much."

"I love you too, Claude." And Carol hung up the phone and looked around the apartment at the multitude of flowers. When she closed her eyes she could breathe in all of the wonderful fragrances, but she had to admit that she felt that Claude was being excessive.

When Carol found a few extra moments, she continued to call her congressman in Washington to see what was being done for Andrew. There had been no further word from his captors, no videos, no news and she had to take that as a good sign. Then, since she wasn't getting any satisfaction from Washington, she decided to write letters to Britain's Prime Minister, Chester Hawkins and the French President,

Jacques Leraund, hoping that if they got involved, they might put more pressure on Washington and possibly Chester could coerce the government, such as it was in Iraq, to find Andrew and demand that he be returned. It was worth a try.

Carol was glad to see that her activist friend Debra was helping in demonstrating with banners demanding that the troops be brought home and that Washington ask for the release of Andrew. It had been on all of the news services, TV, the Internet, radio and the major newspapers. This would create public awareness so that Andrew would not be forgotten and, hopefully persuade Congress and the administration to take action. Carol was sure something would break on this soon. In the meantime, she studied, went to class and worked. This was her whole life now.

*   *   *

Simone worked through the night, scooping out the earth under her cot and when she was tired, Mohammed took over for her. When Simone first started digging, she found the clay to be solid and hard like plaster and Mohammed had to use the knife that he always carried with him to start the hole. But once they cut through the surface the material underneath was made up of straw and dirt and fairly easy to scoop out.

They kept the cot close to the wall so that when the guard opened the door, the excavation was hidden from view. Fortunately they had been able to keep the cups, giving the guards the excuse that they needed them for drinking the water given to them twice daily. They were now going into their third day, and the heat and lack of good food was starting to weaken both of them. Simone kept asking the guard when Amahl might be coming back, genuinely wanting to know but also hoping to allay suspicion that they were attempting an escape.

"Look," said Simone, "I think by tomorrow night we might have an opening large enough for us to crawl through."

"Yes, I think you are right. And it will be good for us to go in the night. Better chance for us to hide and it will be cooler."

"We need to carry water. How can we get a container for water?"

"Hide the carafe when they bring it tomorrow. Maybe they won't ask for it. And then only drink a part of your water."

"Will there be any water in the desert?"

"Nothing drinkable. The river of course, but that is so polluted now that if you drank from it, it could be fatal," whispered Mohammed. "I don't know how far out of Baghdad we are. But I may be able to tell when we get outside. I will use the stars as our guide."

"Do you know how to do that?"

"Yes, I studied astronomy in school. I know my way around the galaxy pretty well."

"Hush, be quiet. I hear the guards coming," said Simone as she crawled under her cotton blanket and hiding the cup under the cover. She heard two or more guards talking, no arguing.

The door opened and two guards entered the room with machine guns on their hips. They each took Simone by her arms and escorted out her of the room with Mohammed protesting as they left. Taking her down the hallway, with her screaming and protesting and trying to break free, the guards opened a door to a bedroom with one large bed in the middle of the room and they threw her down on the bed as four other men entered the room. Simone looked up at them knowing what her fate would be. One of them pulled off her headdress and her long black hair fell around her shoulders, while another ripped off her shirt revealing her small white breasts and her womanhood. Two others with heavy black beards, held her arms down while another pulled off her pants and then lowered his pants and went at Simone, violently thrusting into her again and again, saying words that Simone didn't understand although she did pick up fragments of words; vile, woman disguised, cheating and bitch.... Then another took his turn with her more viciously than the first one had and then another.....the one bare light bulb above her dimmed and swayed. The smell of blood and semen nauseated her... yet another one thrust his organ into her.. Her body screamed in anguish...until Simone passed out.

When she awoke, she was in a room by herself, on a small cot. Her clothes were bloody, her jaw hurt. She felt like she had been beaten about the face and her lower body was on fire. She raised her head to see if there was any water that she could use to wash herself and there wasn't. How would she ever escape now? She let her head fall back on the cot and closed her eyes, tears falling on her blood stained face.

Mohammed waited for Simone to be brought back to their room but he didn't hold much hope for that. He sat on his cot putting his head in his hands, knowing what had happened to Simone when he heard her screams. He clenched his fists in anger. Why had he let her talk him into this? It was a huge mistake. But what to do now? Could he get to Simone and break her out with him? Or should he continue to dig the hole and escape, hoping to come back and rescue her? He decided to continue to dig, get out if he could, get help and come back to rescue Simone.

He dug the rest of the night with a vengeance. He had never before felt such rage. He would kill them if he could, even risking his own life. By early morning, Mohammed had a hole large enough to crawl through. He tore one of the blankets to make a knapsack and filled it with some food that he had hidden and the carafe of water and pulled his body through the small opening in the wall and out into the darkness. He stood and looked around for guards. The wind was whipping the date palms and sand was blowing at him from every angle. Fine, he thought, this is all I need, a sand storm. But then he thought it might provide cover for his escape. He shielded his face from the sand with his hands and quickly walked away from the building looking for the road that led out of the compound until he found the tracks of wheels in the dust. He followed the tracks for what seemed like miles but was only a mile or two until he came to the main road. I can't travel along this road, he thought, it is too dangerous. The US military might mistake him for an insurgent and kill him, or the Iraqis could think he was an enemy. And there were landmines and roadside bombs to worry about. The sandstorm seemed to be subsiding. He walked for another couple of miles until he came to a river. This must be the Tigris he thought and he decided to hide and rest here for the day and then travel by night until he reached Baghdad. His plan was to go to the US military base outside of Baghdad and elicit help from the soldiers to come back to where Simone was being held captive, and rescue her. He didn't totally trust the US soldiers, but it was his only hope.

Chapter 28

Carol Joins the Movement

Carol picked up her phone messages when she returned late one night from studying at the school law library. Among the usual messages from Claude and Marshal, she had a message from Debra. She wondered why she was calling and then she remembered that she had promised to help her. Carol had been so wrapped up in her daily activities that she had completely forgotten. The message said that she should call her as soon as possible. Well, Debra would have to wait until morning. It was much too late to be calling people.

Carol slipped a pink and blue flannel nightgown over her head, slid into her Acorn lambs wool slippers and went into the bathroom and washed her face and brushed her teeth, as was her nightly routine. She then went back into the bedroom, pulled back the comforter on the bed and climbed in under the covers, burying her head in the down pillow, burrowing down in the blankets. This was the only place where she felt no one could harm her. But that wasn't exactly true either and she recalled that other night over a year ago when they entered her bedroom at the ranch, injected her with a drug to sedate her and took her to the nursing home in Southern California. That was the most horrific night of her life. And then she started to think about Andrew and what he must be going through every day and every night. Were they torturing him? Was he getting enough food to eat and exercise to keep his body healthy? Would they ever release him alive? Could she go on living if he were killed? Too many thoughts, she just could not turn off her mind. She looked at the clock. It was one o'clock in the morning. She had to get some rest if she was going to get through another grueling day tomorrow. She would be taking her first test in Constitutional Law.

Carol finally got up and went to the bathroom and took out her sleeping pills. As was her habit, she took one pill with a glass of water and returned to her bed. In about a half an hour she drifted off to sleep with thoughts of Andrew and Claude and James and, yes, of Marshal too.

The early morning sun washed across her bed with the promise of another demanding day. Carol opened her eyes and stretched her arms above her head; her mind a little foggy with a slight hangover from the sleeping pill she had taken in the early morning hours. And then she started thinking about her life and, in a sense, how empty it was even with law school and a part time job. Claude was so far away and she wasn't sure that she wanted to marry him. I think I need to get a dog, she thought. I miss not having a living being in my bed with me and marriage is just out of the question right now. And dogs, she thought, are always happy to see you and forever faithful. Not that James was unfaithful. But look at Marshal. How many affairs had he had? She could never marry a man like that. She could never trust him. She was aware of how her thoughts were rambling. Must be the effects of the sleeping pill.

After downing a cup of very black coffee, she remembered the message from Debra. What would she tell her? Her schedule was so full right now, how could she possibly fit in another activity as much as she wanted to. She dialed the number. It was early, seven o'clock, but Debra was a busy person too and busy people are typically early risers. The phone rang and then it rang some more. Finally a sleepy voice answered.

"Debra, I'm sorry. Did I wake you?"

"I need to get up anyway. Who is this?"

"It's Carol. You called yesterday."

"Oh, Carol, thank you for calling me back. I want to invite you to speak to our local group next month. We have been inviting state and local leaders to speak to our people, you know, kind of to inspire them to keep up the good work."

"Oh, Debra, I am so bogged down with school and work and trying to get Andrew home. I don't know if I can…. I barely have time to sleep these days."

"I can understand. But do you know how this would help our cause? People really look up to you. They believe in you. It would only be for an hour or so."

"When is your meeting?"

"We meet every Thursday, but the meeting that I would like you to speak at is October 20th. Can I tell them you are coming?"

"Yes, I'll be there," Carol said reluctantly. How could she refuse? She had promised and giving a talk was such a small thing. Now, she worried about what she would talk about. Andrew; she would talk about him and the war and how it affected so many families in such an adverse way, even hers. And she had time to prepare.

* * *

Simone opened her eyes and looked around. She heard voices arguing in Arabic outside her door. And then the door burst open and Amahl entered the room with another guard. He stood there and stared at Simone for a moment and then walked over to her and put his hand on her forehead as Simone shrank back in fear.

"I am sorry this happened to you. But you see they knew you were not a man all along as did I. And they felt betrayed by that. Any woman without a veil is considered open to having sex. So you see, it was your fault. You must know that. You have an Iraqi father."

Simone sat up and looked at him in disgust. What were these people? Animals? No, they were worse than that. She started to speak, but Amahl silenced her by putting his hand on her mouth. "Do not talk. I will protect you from now on. I want you to come and live in my apartment in the rear of the compound and no one will harm you there."

Simone rose from the cot pulling her torn clothing about her, as Amahl took her hand and led her out the door with guards on either side. Were any of them her rapists last night? She didn't know; they all looked the same with bushy black beards and black beady eyes. But she did know that what was about to happen to her now was possibly worse than what had happened last night. She was about to become a slave girl to Amahl. Like a prostitute only not paid. Well, she would be paid of sorts. He would protect her from the others. He would feed her and keep her healthy so that she could perform for him. But she would not be free. She would be a prisoner. Her eyes betrayed her fear as he led her into his apartment and into a back bedroom.

"I will let you rest. Would you like to bathe?" Simone shook her head saying yes. "There is a bathroom next to my bedroom and I will draw a hot bath for you. Do not fear me. I will not harm you." And Amahl showed Simone where the bathroom was and led her inside and then left her to her privacy. Simone ran the water into the large marble tub and removed her clothes. She stepped into the bathtub, lying down immersing her body in the warm soothing water and she could feel the healing begin in the places where she was injured and battered. She ran her hands over her body to see if she was all there, if every part was still a part of her own body. And she cried again, crying for the pain of last night, a night that she would relive for the rest of her life and for the pain that she was about to endure in her enslavement.

*   *   *

The applause was thundering as Carol entered the room where the anti war activists were gathering to hear her speak. There were over five hundred people attending, crammed into the tiny auditorium of an old high school turned trade school, like sailors in a submarine. Carol was unprepared for this reception, but she gathered her equilibrium and walked out onto the stage as she was introduced by Debra.

"Ladies and gentlemen, I would like to present to you one of the bravest women in our country, our former first lady, Carol Walters."

More wild applause. Carol looked at the audience and thought about being the former first lady. Was she in fact, due to divorcing her husband, considered a disgrace? Did they think she was mentally ill as the media had portrayed her after her abduction? Obviously not, at least not to this group. She smiled and raised her hands in a motion to quiet them in order for her to speak.

"Thank you, Debra. Thank you for inviting me to speak this evening. I am honored," Carol said. She paused. "I come to you tonight with much pain in my heart. But my pain is no more than what other mothers, fathers, sisters, brothers and friends of those maimed or killed in the war are feeling. My son Andrew is still alive, we hope, and we will bring him home safely. Of that, I am confident. But there are now those who will never see their family members and friends again and it is of those that I wish to speak to you tonight. To raise a child to adulthood and to lose that child is the most devastating thing that can happen to a parent. And then to think of the many young wives and husbands who have lost spouses. And children whose mothers and fathers will never come home to them again. Their lives will never be same."

The audience was quiet as everyone pondered Carol's somber words.

"And then, we must consider all of those who live but are wounded, one way or another. I say this because there are physical wounds of losing an arm or a leg, eyesight, horrific wounds caused by RPGs and homemade bombs made by the Iraqi insurgents and there are psychological wounds carried deep down in the souls of these men and women. Some will recover and get their lives back, but many will be scarred for life and have to adjust to changes in their lives that are unimaginable by us here in this room."

Again, silence. Carol wondered if they disliked what she was saying.

"I think about the parents who raise their kids to be loving, caring people. They teach them to be honest, to work hard and never hurt another human being. And then when those same children are inducted into the armed forces, they are taught to become killing machines, particularly in the Special Forces in our country. How does a soldier reconcile with himself after he or she has riddled an Iraqi family with bullets, watching as women and children die right before their eyes? Well, the rational is they might have killed him, so he had to shoot first. This is war and this is what we must do. Well, let me tell you, we don't need to be doing this. We don't need to be scarring our soldiers for life in this way. There is another way."

The audience cheered and clapped and they didn't stop for five minutes.

"There is no good war and it should always be a last resort after all other strategies have been tried; diplomacy, talking with our so called enemies and trying to work it out in a way that does not affect hundreds of thousands of lives. We didn't need to attack Iraq. They had never attacked us and they weren't going to. Iraq was not involved in 9-11. And to do a pre-emptive strike like we did is criminal."

People were on their feet this time applauding. Carol had struck a chord.

"Now, there have been more suicides in this war than in any other war in history, both in Iraq and at home and there is a reason for this. Our soldiers are deployed time and time again and even though they are battle weary, they have to go back to the war zone to fight again. War is hell, we all know that. Fortunately most of us have never experienced it first hand and probably never will. But Debra knows. She knows that her son died in this war for oil and she doesn't want other people being injured or dying."

More applause and Carol looked over to see Debra sitting in a chair off to the side of the stage. Their eyes met and there was common ground between them.

"I say to you tonight, let's bring these brave soldiers home. And let's not stop there. Let's make sure we never have another war like this, ever again."

The audience was ecstatic.

"And we can do this. But first, we must get those in power to see our side. And that would be your congressman or representative in the Senate and the House of Representatives. Peace rallies are a good thing, raising public consciousness and keeping the movement alive with newspaper and television media coverage. But you need to call, email and write letters to your congressmen and encourage others to do the same. You need to get petitions circulated and signed. And you need to threaten those in office, yes I said threaten them with the fact that they are up for re-election next fall and you and millions of others will not be voting for them if they don't find a way to end this unnecessary war and bring our soldiers home safe to America."

More applause and the audience shaking their heads in agreement.

"I know how helpless you must feel. You probably think there is nothing that can be done; that you're wasting your time here. But let me tell you, you have power, power in your numbers and I do believe that the majority of the people in this country agree with you. Get them behind you and if those in Washington think they may lose their jobs over this, they will make it happen."

Carol stopped and looked around the audience. "It is a sad commentary that this is what will motivate congress, isn't it. And they must be parents like you and me. Wouldn't you think that these people would think of the human cost of this war? It is estimated, now they don't know for sure, that over 100,000 Iraqi civilians have been killed so far since the invasion of Iraq. That's a lot of mothers, fathers, children and family members being killed," Carol exclaimed. "So, I say to you, keep up the pressure, don't give up. What you are doing will bring results and if it saves one life it is worth it."

Carol again looked over at Debra and then said, "Thank you again for having me here. When I return to talk to you, here's hoping our soldiers and others will be home. Thank you."

Amidst roaring applause Debra walked over to Carol and shook her hand and then Carol embraced Debra and whispered in her ear, "What you are doing is very noble. Keep up the pressure and I will be there for you. You can count on me."

Debra thanked Carol again and Carol walked off the stage leaving the auditorium. She called a taxi and waited, as she had not as yet bought a car. Twenty minutes later the taxi pulled up to the auditorium and Carol gave the driver her address and settled back for the ride. As the taxi approached her building, Carol fished out the five dollars plus a tip showing on the meter, paid the driver, went into her building, nodded at the guard as she walked by him and took the elevator to her apartment. Opening the door, she noticed more messages on her machine. She decided they could wait until morning. She then went into the kitchen, opened a bottle of wine and poured herself a glass, then taking the bottle with her, went back into the living room and collapsed on the white leather couch. She couldn't stop thinking about how a few men's decisions can affect millions of others. Her husband's administration's decision to invade Iraq had killed a multitude of people and caused irreparable harm. The war was having a negative effect on America by taking resources that could have been used for domestic programs at home; health care and education to name two. She knew in her heart that she was right to divorce James.

Carol sipped her wine and looked at the newest vase of flowers from Claude on the end table. Big, beautiful, yellow Chrysanthemums. They reminded her of the yellow Chrysanthemum corsages the coeds received for college Homecoming in the fall. It was the time of year when the leaves on the trees had turned orange and yellow and red and there was a nip in the air, a sign that winter would soon be lowering its veil over the land. Those were such carefree days. But they were just children then and she hadn't even met James yet. The question now was, what could she do to end this war and bring the troops home? And what more could she do to bring Andrew home? She was determined to try and help.

*   *   *

Mohammed had spent the night walking through the desert, as far from the road as possible but still in sight of it. When vehicles came he would crouch and hide as best he could. He then found another place by the river to hide. He slept the rest of the day and then started off again as the sun went down in the west. By what must have been midnight, he wondered how far he had come and then thought at least thirty kilometers or more, but was not sure. He had rationed his water carefully but would soon run out and he didn't know where he could find more, fresh, drinkable water. He just might have to drink from the polluted river. Just as he was contemplating these thoughts he saw lights rapidly approaching in the desert behind him. Who could this be? Amahl's men coming to fetch him back? American soldiers? The Humvee pulled up beside him, stopped and two American soldiers popped out of the vehicle and told him to stop, pointing their assault rifles at him.

"Who are you and what are you doing out in the middle of the desert at this time of night?" a very young man with a blond crew cut and pimples asked.

Mohammed held his arm open to try to show that he had no weapons and then, somewhat relieved said, "I am lost. My truck broke down twenty kilometers back. I am trying to get back to Baghdad. Can you give me a lift?"

"Do you have identification?" the other one with dark hair asked as he ran his hands over Mohammed's body searching for weapons or a concealed bomb. He was big and burly and looked to be somewhat older than the man with pimples.

"No, I left it all back in my truck. I am Mohammed Hashim. My father is an attorney in Baghdad. At least he was before the war." He didn't want to mention Simone yet.

The two soldiers walked back to the truck and talked for a few minutes and then returned and asked him to get into the Humvee. Mohammed climbed into the back of the vehicle as he was instructed, feeling fortunate to have a ride back to Baghdad.

The Humvee took off with a start and the ride back was very rough as they did not take the road, instead traveling on the desert near the river. These two soldiers were evidently on some kind of a patrol looking for insurgents. They would stop for awhile and survey the area, using some device to search bombs he thought, and then move on. It was morning by the time they pulled up in front of a military base outside of Baghdad and the soldiers asked Mohammed to get out of the vehicle and they escorted him into the headquarters office where there were more soldiers sitting at desks writing on computers.

"What have we here?" a soldier with a very long face and a large nose, sitting at the front desk asked.

"We found this one roaming about out on the desert last night. Thought we'd better bring him in."

The long faced man started asking Mohammed questions and where were his papers and identification. Mohammed repeated what he had told the other soldiers.

"Can you give me a ride into Baghdad," Mohammed spoke up. "My father will be worried about me. I have been gone a couple of days now."

"Ya have, have ya," long face said. "I'm just afraid it's going to be a few more days. We'll have to hold you until we can get some id on you."

Mohammed's heart fell. Was he going to be a prisoner again? And who knows how long they would hold him.

"Take the boy to the men's area. We'll process him later," said long face.

"You can't do this. I am an Iraqi citizen. This is against the Geneva Convention," he yelled at the soldier.

"I'm afraid we can. This is war and we can hold anyone we suspect of being an insurgent," long face said with a smirk.

"I just need some water and food," said Mohammed as they were leading him down the hall to a small room with a cot and a chair.

"We'll get to it. You just make yourself comfortable, young man," long face said sarcastically as he closed the door and locked it.

Chapter 29

Inside the Beltway

President Jason Martin turned from the window in the Oval Office to face his advisors. Another crisis was brewing in Iraq with the roadside bomb attacks increasing daily, as many as thirty a day, throughout Iraq. Along with attacks on civilians in markets and mosques, sometimes killing hundreds of people, the insurgents were attacking the oil fields in the Kurkuk region in the north with a vengeance and this was where most of the oil was located. Oil production was half of what it had been when Saddam was in power and, coming from the second largest oil field in the world, the diminished Iraqi oil production was affecting the world market, driving already high prices even higher. A barrel of crude was now going for close to seventy dollars a barrel. It had been twenty five dollars a barrel before the attack on Iraq. And this was driving consumer prices sharply higher. Not only were Americans paying more at the pump, as high as four dollars a gallon, but the price of food and clothing and household goods had risen dramatically as well. The majority of the goods sold in the US were brought to market by the trucking industry and when fuel prices rise, the cost to ship goes up as well. Trucking companies and independents were passing these costs on to the customer. But there was a winner here. The oil companies were realizing record profits with a thirty two percent increase amounting to more than eight billion dollars.

Jason's main concern was how the public would view this trend with mid term elections fast approaching. If the Patriots were not able to sustain a majority in Congress, their agenda would be just that much more difficult to pass and they had more legislation yet to address. But there was another nagging problem that would not go away and that was the capture of Andrew and the impact this was having on public opinion.

"Did you see in the latest antiwar rally? That bitch Debra whatever her name, is rallying for Andrew now?" Jason said addressing his question to his political advisor, Norm Swift. In the interest of creating a seamless government, Jason had kept most of James cabinet, however he had hired a new political advisor and he replaced Mark Richards, James press secretary with his own choice, Anthony Marquette, former spokesperson for the auto industry.

"Yes, we saw that," said Norm. "I don't think it'll do much good. We're putting out press releases now on Debra's infidelity in her second marriage and soon, I don't think people will be taking her too seriously."

Jason pondered these words. "She's getting all this press coverage. And TV. Did you see her marching in front of the Whitehouse with those placards? Her and five hundred of her friends. The polls are telling us that fifty six percent of the people are against the war and when you add Andrew's abduction into this mix, you've got disaster."

"There's another incident happening in Iraq that you should know about, Mr. President," said Wilson Adams, the national security advisor, addressing the president with his formal title. Jason had explicitly requested that all cabinet members and other advisors to the president address him in this manor, more than likely to remind everyone that it was he who was president now and not James.

"And what is that Wilson?"

"Our military picked up a guy on the desert a couple of days ago, a male Iraqi about eighteen years old. We're not sure what he was doing out there. But he told them he had been kidnapped by some Baathist insurgents, he and his cousin, a female, from Paris."

"God, like we need more trouble right now. Find out who they are and what they were doing. Does the media know about this?"

"No, not yet. We're trying to keep it off the wire services," said Anthony. "Associated Press hasn't picked it up yet. But you know how that goes. It won't be long before the story breaks and then it will be all over the Internet."

"Make sure there is no torture going on here. Tell them to treat that young Iraqi like he is on holiday in Tahiti. If this gets out, it could be a mess," said Jason.

"It could get sticky, with the girl being from France. I guess her dad is a professor at the Sorbonne. He's Iraqi and her mother is American," said Norm.

Jason's eyes popped. "Do you think these two are related to Andrew's abduction?" asked Jason.

"I really don't know, Mr. President," said Norm.

"For Christ's sakes find out," Jason yelled. "That's your job. You mamby pambies sit around on your asses all day long doing nothing. Get busy."

Anthony looked at the others and saw expressions of disbelief. Was the president losing it?

"Yes sir, yes Mr. President," Anthony said. Jason then dismissed them and they filed out of the room shaking their heads wondering what tomorrow would bring. They knew that he had been under a lot of pressure lately, taking over the presidency after President Walters stepped down. But who wasn't. They were all under stress. The president was having these outbursts quite regularly lately, swearing, and belittling people in front of other cabinet members. And if anyone spoke out in dissent against him or his policies he would quickly silence them. He could not take criticism of any kind and disapproval was being dished out from everywhere. The country was in a state of discontent with the Iraq war, the economy and the administration in general, especially those who held the majority, the Patriots. Polls showed approval of Congress was at an all time low as well, twenty six percent and approval of the president at thirty two percent. Jason had not had the luxury of the usual year long honeymoon that most presidents experience when they first take office. He had to hit the road running. He hoped that if they could get through the Iraq elections and show that democracy was forming in Iraq, albeit however slow, he might have an easier time. But the oil prices did worry him. And he didn't know how he was going to solve the Andrew problem. For all he knew, Andrew might be dead by now, but he didn't want to be the one to say that.

* * *

Still captive, Simone thought as she looked around the confines of her small bedroom. At least she now had a window and she no longer had to use the outhouse. She wondered if Mohammed had succeeded in escaping. She hoped so. She also wondered if she would ever get out of this country and back to France where people were civilized. Or was she destined to die enslaved to this barbaric, Iraqi criminal? And escape was not in the cards this time.

It seemed to her that Iraq had gone from having a tyrant dictator to chaos and Shiite fundamentalist rule. Her uncle had told her that when the Americans first invaded Iraq, the people were very hopeful that they would be liberated from an evil dictator who was responsible for torturing and killing his own people. But after Saddam had been taken out of power, the country was in total chaos with looting and lawlessness and that was still true three years later. The Iraqis had hoped that the Americans would repair the utilities and infrastructure, bringing them back to at least the level of what it had been before the invasion. But that hadn't happened. She had seen the despair in the Iraqi people, who were afraid to go work if they even had a job at all and children who were fearful of going to school. Simone could see that Iraqis were now worse off than they were when Saddam was in power. But there was nothing she could do about it. She wished her uncle and his family would move to France, but France was not friendly to Muslim families of late. She heard footsteps outside her door and dreaded who that might be. The door opened and Amahl came into her room and sat down on her bed and took her hand.

"Are you comfortable? I sent food for you? Did you eat it?'

Simone said yes. The guard had brought her soup and fresh fruit and water to drink.

"I see that your friend escaped. Don't think you can do that. We are going to keep a close watch on you, my little butterfly."

Simone said not a word to Amahl but her heart sank when he said those words. Her only hope would be that Mohammed had gone to the Americans and they would find her and rescue her.

"My beautiful sweet thing, I want you to come to my room tonight. I have a surprise for you," Amahl said as he came closer to her. Simone pulled away from him, repulsed by his very presence. She knew what that surprise was and she didn't want it. This man was revolting to her and she hated every minute that she had to sit next to him.

* * *

Mohammed slept fitfully in his five by five room, that was a prison cell, as the mortar shells fell close to the base. It was unbearably hot and he was frightened and thirsty. He needed to talk to someone in command. He needed to tell them about Simone and that they should go and rescue her.

The hours slipped away. No one came. He paced back and forth like a caged lion, stopping only to listen for footsteps. He lay down on his cot and thought about being home with his family. Then he heard someone walking down the hall. It was a soldier carrying a tray of food, a ham sandwich, fruit and water. The soldier unlocked his door and put the tray down on his bed.

"I brought you some food. You must be someone special because we have orders to treat you well," the young man in uniform said.

"Sir," Mohammed spoke up, "I need to talk to someone. I have information that your people would want."

"What kind of information?"

"I cannot tell you, but take me to your commander."

"I'll pass it on."

"No, this is important. I have special information that they need now."

"Tell me what it's about then."

"It's about some insurgents."

"What about them?"

"And it's about the president's son, Andrew."

The young soldier's eyes lit up. Everyone had heard that the president's son was being held somewhere in Iraq.

"I'll get someone to talk to you. No doubt they'll want to hear what you have to say."

And he left the room, locking the door as he left. Would he tell them? Would they talk to him? It was his only chance and he hoped they would rescue Simone. He heard more steps, more people walking towards his room. The key turned in the lock and a very official American soldier entered followed by another soldier of lesser rank he thought.

"What's your name?" the officer asked.

"Mohammed Hashim," he said meekly.

"Come with us. We want to talk with you."

The two soldiers led him out of the room and down the dingy hallway, painted a drab yellow with gouges in the walls and dirt in the corners. They opened the door of a larger room that had a table and four chairs with a shaded light hanging from the ceiling and told him to sit in one of the chairs while they pulled up the other chairs close to him.

"What do you know, Mohammed?"

"Are you going to let me go free? You can't hold me here like this, it's not even legal."

"We'll decide that. Yes, we'll let you go, but tell us what you know first. How do you know about the president's son?" asked the ranking member. He was young, with a ruddy complexion and ears that looked like wings.

"We, Simone, who is my cousin, and I were being held by a group of men who are with the resistance. I think they know where Andrew is. We have to get back there and set her free. They are raping and beating her."

"How did you happen to come in contact with these people?" the ruddy faced officer said. Mohammed thought he might be a sergeant.

Mohammed told him how Simone came to Baghdad from Paris and how she had the name of a man who might know about Andrew. He told them how they went to the meeting two nights in a row and then the second night how Simone dressed as a man so as not to be noticed in the all male meeting. Then he told them about meeting Amahl, how Amahl took them to this remote place in the desert and wouldn't let them leave. And he told them how the night before they were to escape, the guards came to get Simone and they took her away and raped her.

"Why would you go with these men? Didn't you know how dangerous it would be? You're lucky to be alive," said the sergeant.

"Simone thought that Amahl knew about Andrew."

"And why was Simone concerned about the president's son. Did she know him?"

Mohammed said that she did and in fact he had lived with her in her apartment in Paris for a couple of months before he was abducted.

The two soldiers' raised their eyebrows as they heard him say this.

"Okay, now you can tell us where these insurgents are," the older ranking officer said.

"I can take you there. I think I know where the compound is. We need to go there as soon as possible. I know they are hurting her."

They looked at him and then they went outside the room and talked for a few minutes, then came back in and told him they were taking him back to his room.

"But you have to get these guys. They are dangerous and they know where Andrew is."

"Yeah, yeah, yeah. We will in good time."

They escorted him back to his room, opened the door and shoved him inside. It was starting to get dark and the shadows from the one window were long and ominous on the dirty walls of his space. Mohammed sat down on the cot. His food was still there, the sandwich stale and dry by now.

Chapter 30

Carol Thinks of Paris

Summer turned into fall in all of its glory, painting the landscape in the palette of Gauguin. Carol's life was crammed with law classes, studying and a part time job with the law firm and her efforts were paying off. She had taken four tests and done well on all of them. Her professors said that she was a natural, with a quick, discerning mind. And when she found extra time, she was out in the community giving talks on the war and the current administrations efforts to divert taxpayer dollars to the military industrial complex, taking away from critical domestic programs. The audiences were already very receptive and she thought she might be turning others around on the mindset of the war and what their government was doing.

There were no new developments as far as Andrew was concerned and absolutely no more news coming out of Iraq as to his wellbeing. It was long past the date when his captors said they would kill him. His body had not shown up in the desert yet, but there had been no new tapes verifying that he was still alive. Carol continued to pressure Washington and she did think they were doing all they could. She felt, short of going to Washington or to Iraq, there was nothing more that she could do. But she thought about Andrew every day and she worried about his welfare and wondered how he would ever get through this and would he be the same person when he returned. She had talked to mothers and family of returning veterans of this war who were not physically injured, but had nightmares and couldn't adjust back into civilian life. They had seen such horrific events when they were in Iraq and some of them had killed people, civilians, and families with women and children and they would carry these memories with them for the rest of their lives.

Claude was talking to her almost daily now about coming to Paris and he had gone ahead and bought a ticket for her on British Airways for December fifteenth. It was a one way ticket which concerned her and she was unsure as to whether she should go at all. She loved Claude, but she knew he was going to ask her to marry him and she didn't think she was ready for marriage just yet.

One week before her flight, she called her friend Karen and asked her to go to lunch. They met at a small tearoom across from the campus.

"I'm going to Paris to see Claude," Carol said as she sipped her tomato bisque soup.

"Ah, love is blooming."

"No, I don't think so. I know that Claude is in love with me, but I don't know if I really love him. And I don't want to live in France right now."

"Why are you going then?'

"Good question. I guess I just want to see how I do feel about him. He is such a wonderful person. And I feel that I owe him so much."

"Why do you feel that way?"

"He was so kind in helping me when I was in France. I lived on his estate for a month, not paying a thing for food or lodging."

"Carol, you should not feel that you owe him. I'm sure he received as much as you by having you there."

"You're right, Karen. I shouldn't think that way. I guess what I'm worried about is that I think he's going to ask me to marry him and I'm not ready."

"Then tell him that. And maybe you will be ready in a year or so."

"Yes, that's true, but he's older than me and I don't think he'll want to wait. I have too much unfinished business here in this country. With Andrew still missing, I just couldn't marry right now. And I haven't been divorced but a couple of months."

"I know you're not asking for my opinion, but I think you are wise not to marry right now. If it's meant to be, it will happen. And I agree, you can't ask him to wait for you."

They both sat and ate for awhile in silence like good friends do sometimes.

"What about James?"

"What about him?"

"Are you still in love with him?" Karen asked. "Is that why you can't think of marrying anyone else?"

"No, Karen. That's not the reason. Oh, I still love James. I'll always love him in a special way. After all, we are both the parents of a wonderful young man. But I will never go back to him. I need to move forward and into the future."

They talked about the war, about politics and about Paris. Carol told Karen how much she loved Paris, how she thought Paris to be a feminine city with its beautiful baroque 18th century architecture, flower stands and wonderful bistros. And it would be even more beautiful in the Christmas season. They left the tearoom and window shopped at the art galleries and boutiques for another hour, and then Karen drove Carol back to her apartment and wished her well on her trip.

*   *   *

Jason paced back and forth in front of his desk while Vice President Robert Cruthers sat on one of the satin couches watching him.

"This is despicable. We are now holding a young Iraqi prisoner, whose French cousin lived with the president's son. Do you realize that this could create an international incident?" Jason shouted.

"I've heard that her mother is American married to an Iraqi," Robert said. Robert, a former military general, was a portly man, balding and most likely had high blood pressure. He had known Jason for thirty years and when he'd been asked to become vice president, he was eager for the job.

"You would be right. Call the Pentagon and get him released as soon as possible. We don't want this getting out to the media."

Jason had been under tremendous pressure since taking over the presidency from James. He hadn't even had time for his mistress these days and that was bothering him no end. Not only didn't he have time for her, he was warned by his political advisor, Norm that he should stay as far away from her as possible.

"If the public got wind of your having an affair with a young Washington lawyer… well, it would be all over for you."

"Why?" Jason asked in all sincerity. "Most every president has had an affair or two. I can't think of any who haven't, except James. And he was always so good. I hate sanctimonious people."

"Just do it with your wife from now on. Unless you want to be ousted from this office."

"Let's talk about war strategy,' Jason said changing the subject. "Have you talked with the secretary of defense in the past couple of days? They are considering bringing some of the troops home and I think it would be a good idea. This war is becoming increasingly unpopular with the American people and the elections are coming up."

"Yes, I've heard that too. I agree that it would be in our best interest. Then after the election we can move ahead with our strategy in the Middle East and that will mean sending more troops back in again to try to quash the insurgency," Robert said as he reached for a glass of water.

"But that's okay after the election," Jason said.

"Will you be running for office in '08," Robert asked.

"That seems so far off."

"And James could come back as president. Wasn't that the agreement when he stepped down?"

"Yes, it was. But I don't think that's going to happen."

"You mean to say that you don't think they'll bring Andrew home?'

"Robert, I don't know. We've tried everything and haven't made any headway with finding him. And even if Andrew were brought home safely, I don't think James wants to come back. I think he's looking at alternatives right now."

"But, I ask again, are you running?"

"I'll tell you in another year. We have to get through mid terms first. Do you realize that if we lose the House or the Senate, we could be looking at war crimes for this administration?'

"No, that can't be."

"There are rumors that the Democrats want to hold hearings next summer. They are saying that we misled the American people into an illegal war."

"They could have a case there. We never did find the weapons that we said were there. But we're making Iraq and the Middle East a better place. These people are happy that we got rid of that tyrant Saddam. They had their first ever election this spring and they can now be self determining. Is that such a bad thing? I don't think so. And I think anyone would have a tough time proving that we lied on the weapons thing. Everybody knew Saddam had weapons at one time. Hell, we gave him the weapons to fight Iran in the eighties."

"I know, I know. But even if it weren't proven it would ruin the party politically. You know it would," Jason said as he sat down at his massive desk, the late afternoon sun shining in through the large window behind him.

"And the Democrats are powerless. They couldn't even muster a filibuster for the last nomination for the Supreme Court. With the exception of a few diehard liberals, sometimes I even think they are on our side."

"They don't have any power. We have the votes. We have the majority and the Republicans, what's left of them vote along with us because they like to be with the decision makers. And we're going to keep it that way. "

"I hope you're right, Jason. I've been hearing rumbling from the folks who put us in office and they are not happy with the way this country is going right now."

"It's all in the perception. If we tell them that our country is strong, like I did in my acceptance speech, they will believe it. And we have the media on our side. All we have to do is feed the press articles. They don't have the time or the money to write their own anymore. And we'll paint a rosy picture that all is well in America."

"Will they call us liars when the depression of '08 hits?"

"Be optimistic, Robert, always be optimistic. And by that time the Dems might be in office again and if the economy tanks when they are in power…. Well, it won't bode well for them."

"You've got that right. The Democrats can just clean up our mess so we don't have to," said Robert as he wistfully looked out on the South lawn of the White house.

*　*　*

Carol checked out of her Hyde Park hotel room and had the bell captain call a cab to Waterloo Station where she would be catching the Euro Star to Paris. She had flown into London two days earlier via British Airways, to spend a couple of days enjoying the British historical sites, the Tower of London, West Minister Abby, Windsor Castle and Buckingham Palace. She had watched the Changing of Guard and taken afternoon tea at Harrods and now she was on to Paris.

She arrived just in time to be checked in and board and soon the train was gliding through the eastern suburbs of London heading for the coast and the Chunnel. After two more stops to take on passengers, the train continued on to Folkestone, England where the entry into the thirty one mile tunnel begins. And in twenty minutes they were through it and into France. Carol marveled at the smoothness of the ride and how fast they had traveled from England and now into France. In another two hours they would be in the heart of Paris. Closing her eyes after watching the French countryside for awhile, she fell into a light sleep as the train carried her and the other passengers, at 145 kilometers, ninety miles an hour on into Paris. She woke just as the train made its first stop outside Paris. She started gathering her bags and wondered if Claude would be there to meet her. No matter; she could take the metro to their hotel. She knew her way around Paris.

Looking out the window as they were pulling into Gare du Nord, she saw him standing there waiting for her. He was tan and tall, and his silver gray hair was trimmed and neat; he was a good looking man. All of the feelings she had had before, came back to her. Her heart was a flutter and her hands were clammy. Getting off the train, he ran to her and took her into his arms and kissed her on the mouth.

"*Mes amour*, I have been waiting for this moment," Claude said.

Carol kissed him back. "It has been too long a time."

Claude picked up her luggage and they walked together out of the Metro station and onto the street where Claude had parked his rented black Mercedes. He put her luggage in the back and opened the door for her.

Dusk was falling and the lights of Christmas were glowing in the early evening time. Driving down Rue Richelieu, Claude headed towards the area of the Louvre where their luxury hotel was located. When they arrived, a valet took their car while Claude took Carol's luggage and they went inside the very palatial lobby, took the elevator up to the tenth floor and Claude ushered Carol into the suite of rooms he had reserved for their week together in Paris.

"Claude, this is magnificent," Carol said as she opened the French doors leading out onto a balcony overlooking the Tuileries. Claude joined her and held her hand and together they looked over the gardens adorned with sparkling Christmas lights on every tree and even on the Romanesque statues.

"There are two bedrooms if that is your choice. It would not be mine but I don't want to force myself on you."

"Oh, Claude, you are …. such a gentleman. I adore you. No, I'd like to share with you."

Claude beamed from ear to ear. "Well then, we shall have dinner in tonight and I will make love to you, my sweet as you have never been made love to before. This will be a night to remember."

Carol blushed. She was still wondering if she was ready. But then why not? The chemistry was there, she was very attracted to him. But what was holding her back? She just couldn't understand what it was that was keeping her from just falling into his arms and giving her self over to him.

The love making had exceeded Carol's expectations as she melted into Claude's body, burying her face in his hairy chest. Claude was every bit a young man in body and mind even though he was in his sixties. Must be all of that trampling in the vineyards and drinking exceptional wine, thought Carol. They had dined together in the room on lobster and champagne and had talked about their times together when Carol first came to Paris and to live on his estate. And then Claude began to talk about the future and Carol hushed him, saying that she wasn't ready to talk about that just yet. But then he had led her into the bedroom and they made love, tenderly at first and then with a passion that Carol didn't know she had. And now here they were together in an intimacy she hadn't known for years.

"Carol, you know I love you very much," Claude whispered in her ear as he kissed her nose and then her ears and then on her lips.

"I love you too, Claude. You are a truly wonderful man in every way," said Carol. And she truly felt that way about him. Yes, the chemistry was there.

Claude turned on the table lamp on his side of the bed, reached for his robe and put it on. He walked around to Carol's side of the bed and got down on his knees where Carol was curled up. He took out a little black box from his pocket and opened it revealing a stunning two carat princess cut solitaire diamond ring glittering in the midnight light.

"I want you to have this ring. Carol I am asking if you would become my wife and partner in life. I would be so honored if you would accept. We will have a beautiful life together."

Carol sat up now pulling the duvet up to cover her breasts, fully awake. Her eyes were wide open staring at the stunning diamond ring that Claude was holding in his hands. She had feared this moment.

"Oh, Claude, I love you I really do, but…."

"But what? If you really love me then you can only give me one answer and that is yes."

"I can't give you the answer you want. Not right now."

"Can you tell me why? You are free to marry aren't you? And we aren't getting any younger, you know."

"Yes, I know. I have too many loose ends right now. Andrew for one. I need to devote my time to getting him back home."

"But you could do that from France as well as from America."

"And that brings up another question. Would you be willing to move to America? I don't think I can leave right now."

Claude got up from his knees and sat beside Carol.

"You keep saying those words, right now. But, later on you might be able to? If Andrew were home safely?" Claude didn't answer Carol's question about moving to America.

"I don't know. I have to finish law school and then I don't know what my future will hold. You knew that I'm getting involved with the peace activists. My country, America is in trouble and will be needing people who can help turn it around. And if I can be a part of this movement, I would feel that all of what I have gone through will have a purpose."

Claude looked at Carol, his eyes pleading and his face fallen. "I want you to take the ring even if you don't wear it. I bought it for you and I want you to have it."

"No, Claude, I can't. And I can't even promise that I will be there for you in the future. I'd like to say so. We have something very special between us and I do love you and even more so now being with you as I have tonight."

Claude took the ring from the box and slipped it on Carol's third finger on her right hand. "This is a Christmas gift and if there is a future for us, you can move it to your left hand." And he took Carol in his arms and held her and kissed her again and Carol kissed him back, tears rolling down her cheeks.

"Well, then I would say that we have to make the most of this time we have together."

Carol looked into his eyes and said, "I'm sorry, Claude. I am really sorry."

"Don't be sorry. I am not giving up you know."

Claude took off his robe, showing his athletic body, pulled back the duvet and crawled in beside Carol and he took her in his arms again.

"You are so special, Carol and I will love you forever."

They slept entwined until the first morning light. Claude awoke first and ordered breakfast in the room, asking Carol what she would like to have and then he showered. Carol languished in bed, thinking about last night. Had she made a mistake in coming to France? She was only building Claude's expectations and she didn't want to do that. She would never lead him on. Maybe she should tell Claude to find someone else as, even if they were to marry later, it might not be for several years. She looked at the ring on her right hand. It was so beautiful. She didn't want to accept it, but she didn't want to hurt Claude's feelings either.

"We are going to Montmartre today. I want to show you the art museums and then to the Arch de Triumph tomorrow and lunch on the Champs Elysees and then to ....."

Carol got out of bed and kissed Claude on the mouth and he fell back into bed with her......

The British Airways jet left the runway, flying over the French countryside and small villages and hamlets. It had been a week of pleasure and happiness, but also of memories of Carol's first visit to Paris. When they visited each place, Carol thought about when she was there months ago fleeing from the administration. And Carol had mixed emotions about Claude. He drove her to the airport and waited with her until her flight left. As she was boarding, she turned to him and looked into his eyes and then kissed him on the lips. He kissed her back and held her for a time, not wanting to let go. "*Au revoir,*" he said.

"Yes, *Au revoir,*" Carol repeated. "Until we meet again." But she couldn't promise anything. She couldn't even promise that she would return, as much as she wanted to.

When Carol reached London she had a three-hour lay over. She shopped in the duty free shops and had lunch, then waited for her flight to Chicago. She boarded and found her seat and settled in and, as the huge jumbo jet lifted off the runway Carol felt empty. She looked again at the ring. Would she ever go back to France? Would she marry Claude and move to Bordeaux? Just the thought seemed remote to her now as she was hurtling through the air at mock speed heading back to her world, a world of chaos and angst. Oh, it would be so easy to say yes to Claude and spend the rest of her years with him in the beautiful, serene wine country of France.

Chapter 31

The Rescue Mission

Mohammed sat in his room now with little hope that he would be able to rescue Simone. He was still angry with himself for giving in to her in the first place. They should never have gone to the meeting and they certainly should never have gotten in the van with Amahl. But he felt there was nothing he could do now. He worried about Simone; how she would be treated by these loathsome men. They could even kill her as they had done to hundreds of others over the past years. But maybe death would be merciful, better than living in slavery the rest of ones life.

He had heard nothing from the Americans in a couple of days now. They seemed unconcerned about Andrew or Simone or even his welfare. But then they had other troubles to worry about. The insurgency had spiked in the last couple of weeks with one hundred attacks a day now in Baghdad. He had overheard the soldiers talking as they brought his food, that Baghdad belonged to the insurgents with the exception of the Green Zone where US military personnel lived.

He needed to do something to get their attention. That afternoon when they brought his tray of soup and bread, he told them he could take them to the insurgents' headquarters. He knew exactly where it was. Twenty minutes later, two guards came to take him to be questioned, tying his hands and leading him down the dusty hallway to a room at the end. Inside were three other men, all officers of a higher rank. They pushed him into a chair and started asking him questions.

"So you know where Amahl Hakim's lair is?" a tall, dark haired sergeant asked.

"Yes, I do," said Mohammed. "I can take you there. That is what I told you days ago and no one would listen to me."

The other soldier with a sandy haired crew cut slapped him in the face and said, "Don't be rude. We are in control here and don't you forget that.

"Cool it Matt, We don't have to slap this fellow around. He'll talk without those tactics," the sergeant said. And then he turned to Mohammed. "Do you know exactly where this place is? If I give you a map can you pinpoint it on the map?"

"Yes, I can. I walked many kilometers before your men picked me up and I know where I came from. Just give me a map and I will show you," Mohammed said, glad that the sergeant had spoken up against the other soldier.

The sergeant left the room and then returned with a large map of Iraq and laid it on the one table in the room. Mohammed squirmed in his chair. "Can you untie me? I am not going try to escape. I know how useless that would be."

The sergeant motioned for the third soldier, an overweight man with a double chin and ruddy complexion, to remove Mohammed's shackles. Mohammed rubbed his sore wrists and walked over to the map and studied it for a few minutes.

"Well, then show us," said the sergeant impatiently. "This is where the base is just south of Baghdad. How far away is this place?"

"I walked down this road for maybe five kilometers the first day and then came to the river here. Amahl's place should be right here." Mohammed pointed to a spot on the map forty kilometers south of Baghdad. "Here's Karbala and when I left the road I walked along the Tigris River and then you picked me up here," Mohammed said pointing to where he thought the Americans had captured him.

"And what does the compound look like? How many buildings and how are they configured?"

"We came in at night and I left at night but to the best of my memory, I saw two buildings, one larger clay brick type building, I would say had ten or so rooms where they slept, had meetings. Give me some paper and a pencil and I will draw it out for you."

The crew cut soldier retrieved a pad and pencil and handed them to Mohammed and he started drawing a picture of the layout of the buildings.

"Here's the road and the main building and there was a smaller building in the rear. I don't know what they used that for."

"How many men, would you say?" asked the sergeant.

"We only saw about ten, but there could be more. I think this is a headquarters for Amahl. They undoubtedly have more men elsewhere."

The sergeant took two of the men outside the room to talk while the soldier with the crew cut stayed behind to watch Mohammed. They were gone for half an hour or more and then returned with another, higher ranking soldier.

"This is Lieutenant Browski. He will be in charge of this mission. Are you willing to go with us and participate?" asked the sergeant.

"Yes, I would be happy to. Not happy but we need to get Simone out of there."

"Oh, your Simone. I almost forgot about her. Well, we'll do our best. The main objective here is to get this guy Amahl. We think he's been the cause of many of the bombings in Baghdad of late."

"And don't forget. He knows where Andrew is," said Mohammed.

"Ah, yes. Andrew. Well, if we capture this Amahl, maybe he'll just tell us where Andrew is," the lieutenant said.

*　　*　　*

Carol hadn't been home three days when she received a strange phone call. She had been fighting jet lag and was somewhat depressed after seeing Claude again and the way she had handled the situation. She now almost wished she hadn't gone even though she had a wonderful time. She had arrived home the day before New Years and had spent New Year's Eve alone. That in and of itself wasn't a bad thing except it gave her time to think about everything, about Andrew and Claude and James.

She remembered their first New Year's together after she and James were married. He had wanted to go out to a party with some friends, but she said she wanted to have him all to herself. They had only been married for a couple of months and after they returned from the honeymoon, she seldom saw James. She was still teaching school and James was running for office again. Carol had bought a rib roast at the grocery store and prepared a special dinner just for the two of them, with wine and Champagne. But James hadn't come home. She waited and waited and he hadn't even called. She wondered what could be keeping him so long. She took the roast out of the oven and covered it to try to keep it warm. And then finally at eleven o'clock he walked in the door and when she asked where he'd been, he said he was campaigning and seemed unconcerned as if nothing had happened. And that was the way it was until James finally lost the election that year. After his defeat they decided to start the ranch outside of Fort Collins with the land James dad had given them. Only then did they become true partners.

She dialed the number left on her message machine. The woman's name was Charlotte McKenzie and she had said she was calling from Washington. Could this be about Andrew? Maybe there was some news of his release. The phone rang and rang until a woman picked up the receiver on the other end.

"Is this Charlotte McKenzie?"

"Yes, who is this?" Charlotte asked.

"Carol. Carol Walters. You called and left a message on my answering machine and I am returning your call. Is this concerning Andrew? Have you had word of his release?"

"No, I'm afraid not. No, I am the Colorado State Chairman of the Democratic Party and we would like to meet with you next week."

"Meet with me? What on earth for?"

"I have a time set up on Thursday at the party headquarters in the Goldfield building near the Capitol. Come to room 501, it's on the fifth floor. Nine o'clock. There will be some other party members attending."

"Can you tell me now what it is about?"

'No, I would rather wait. I have been here in Washington for two weeks now and will be back tonight. Can you be there?"

"Yes, I will. I'll have to cancel a class, but I will come."

Carol couldn't imagine what the state chairman of the Democratic Party wanted with her. She wasn't involved in state politics. Could it have something to do with her anti war activism?

The next two days flew by and on Thursday morning, Carol put on her best winter suit, cobalt blue wool flannel and black leather pumps; very conservative. She carefully combed her hair and applied just the right amount of make-up. She called a taxi still not owning a car. She most usually traveled back and forth to school by bus and her job was only three blocks down the street from her apartment, the apartment that Marshal was still paying for, much to her consternation.

When she arrived, the snow was gusting and blowing as she walked into the building. She took the old elevator up to the fifth floor and walked down the hallway with large, important looking doorways at intervals along the way, and then Carol came to room 501 and opened the door. An attractive young, black receptionist greeted her.

"You must be Carol. You can go right in. They're waiting for you."

They, she thought. Who are they? And waiting for her? Was she late? Not by her clock. She opened the door and saw six people seated around an oversized dark walnut conference table. They all looked up when she entered.

"Yes, Carol, thank you for coming. I am Charlotte and I would like you to meet Jim Davies, Linda Levin, Sharon Johnson, Peter Dowling, Phil Jackson and Marion Shelby. They're all on the committee. Please be seated," she said as she motioned to a chair near the head of the table.

Carol shook hands with each of them and then sat where she had been told. "What is this about?"

"Carol, as you may or may not know, Senator Gerald Mattson, is not running this next term. He has family issues to deal with. His wife was diagnosed with breast cancer and he wants to spend time with her and his three children. So, we thought...."

Carol's eyes opened wide, her thoughts way ahead of them. "You're looking at me to run for the senator's seat in congress? I don't know anything about politics."

"We find that hard to believe. Your former husband was a state senator and then president. But that's beside the point," said Linda. "You have an unprecedented following of the people in this state. That alone can get you to Washington and we'll give you all the help you need."

"I agree with Linda," said Peter. "It's not what you know but who you know that counts."

"And you must have learned something when James was in office," Marion chimed in.

Carol looked from one person to another. She felt like she was being steamrolled. She had no desire to be involved in politics again at any level. She, in fact hated politics. That was one of the reasons for not going back to Washington a year and a half ago. "I can't. I have to get my son back home. I have to finish law school, that's another two years."

"Carol, this state needs you," Charlotte said. "This country needs you. And you have the best chance of anyone of winning."

"But there are some who believe the story the Patriots told about my being mentally unstable. How can we overcome that?"

"You are the most popular woman in this state right now, maybe the nation. I think the American people are on to the Patriots tactics. I don't think it will be an issue."

Carol sat dumbfounded. How could she ever do this? She remembered helping with James state senatorial campaign when they were first married and it was brutal. But then she thought, was this a way for her to help her country?

"I'll think about it. I can't give you an answer today. Let me think over the weekend."

Everyone around the table looked pleased. Carol hadn't refused entirely. And they would keep working on her until they persuaded her to accept.

Chapter 32

Carol's Decision

Carol tossed and turned all night thinking about being asked to run for the senate. She thought about the campaigning, the endless hours of shaking hands and giving stump speeches. She threw her covers to one side; she was burning up. Was it menopause or anxiety? Her doctor had told her on her last visit that she was in the midst of the change of life. But she had known that. She had been having hot flashes for many months now. Then she thought about the mudslinging and character assassination and when thrown into that scenario, she had no confidence in fighting back. She refused to stoop to the low levels that some candidates had in recent elections. But the most important question was could she make a difference in Washington? If she ran for office and won and then was ineffective as a senator, it would be a waste of everyone's time. Pulling up the covers again, she laid her head back on the pillow. The hot flash had passed.

After a time, sleep engulfed her but she had a dream that was so real she thought she was really there. She dreamt she had become a senator and after she was sworn in, she traveled to Iraq and asked the new Iraqi president where her son was. President Halab ala-Qawi responded by saying he didn't know and then the door opened and Andrew walked into the room in shackles, wearing rags, his bones showing through his skin with dark circles under his eyes. He was flanked by two armed guards, each carrying AK-47s. She grabbed Andrew and started to pull him away, but the guards pushed her from Andrew and then they shot him before her eyes. She watched as the blood streamed out of his body, life ebbing away. Andrew called to her. Mother.... Mother... help me... and he died there on the floor in front of her blood pouring out of his body. Carol awoke with a start. She held her head in her hands. Yes, she thought. She would run for the senate. This would put her in a position of power and maybe she could have some influence in bringing her son home.

Carol got out of bed; it was nine o'clock in the morning. She had never slept this late. But it was Friday and she didn't have class today. She went into the kitchen and made a fresh pot of coffee, poured a glass of orange juice and popped a piece of toast in the toaster. Turning on the small kitchen TV, she flipped the channels until she came to CNN. The newscaster talked about the possibility of civil war in Iraq, with the many tribes and religious groups vying for power. In the background, she could see smoke rising from trucks that had been firebombed and there were bodies lying in the street and blood everywhere. When would it end she wondered.

After eating the light breakfast, she went to her bedroom and put on a pair of jeans and a sweat shirt. Looking out the window she saw the snow capped peaks of the Eastern slope and clouds were hanging low with a promise of snow in Denver today. She grabbed her books and took them into the living room, turned on the gas fireplace and settled in for a morning of study for her next test in Civil Procedures. She studied for about an hour and then got up from the couch to get a cup of tea. The snow was falling now, large flakes hitting the window and then falling to the ground below. She thought about Andrew. What was he doing she wondered. Was he well?

The phone rang and she answered after a couple of rings. She had thought about letting the answering machine pick it up.

"Carol, how are you? I haven't talked with you in weeks," the male voice said. It was Marshal. "I heard you went to Paris. How was your trip?"

"Marshal, I'm fine. I just got back. I'm exhausted.

"I would like to take you to dinner tonight, or tomorrow night. Are you free?"

He set her up again. Could she lie to him? What would it hurt having dinner and she could talk to him about running for the senate.

"Yes, Marshal, I'm free. Tonight would be fine. About seven o'clock. I have some exciting news to tell you."

"I can't wait to hear. I'll pick you up at seven then."

Carol tried to get back to her studies but she couldn't concentrate. She decided to take a short nap. She lay down on the soft leather couch and pulled up the burnt orange chenille throw, covering her body, while flurries of snow swirled outside the window.

Waking at six, she hurried to get ready for her date with Marshal. She showered and put on a black wool pantsuit, with a gray sweater. Looking out the window, she saw that the snow had stopped, but it would be cold tonight, always was after a good snow storm. As she was putting on her makeup, the doorbell rang and she ran to open the door. There was Marshal, holding a bouquet of red roses.

"Come in, Marshal," Carol said as she pecked him on the cheek and took the roses. "How beautiful. Thank you. You shouldn't have."

"For a beautiful woman like you, yes, I should."

"You're a little early," Carol said as she went back to her bedroom to finish combing her hair. Marshal followed her into the bedroom making Carol feel uncomfortable. "I'll be ready in a jiffy. Why don't you go back to the living room, turn on the TV and check the weather."

"No need. We'll walk tonight. I thought we could go to the steak house two blocks over."

She finished getting ready, and then grabbed a coat and they left the apartment, taking the elevator down to the first floor.

Marshal held the door for her as she stepped out into the cold wintry night. Carol looked at the street with the new fallen snow, sparkling in the lights like a million tiny diamonds. It was so silent; there were few cars and very few people. When they reached the restaurant and went inside the maitre de greeted Marshal calling him by name and they were seated immediately in a secluded corner next to a fireplace with a roaring fire.

"You still have some clout in this town," Carol said as she looked at the menu.

"Of course. People don't forget what I've done for them."

Carol winced as Marshal ordered a bottle of French Bordeaux wine. The waiter brought the wine and poured a glass for each and took their order.

"You said you had something exciting to tell me. Have you heard something about Andrew?"

"No, I haven't. But I have some news. Did you know that Senator Mattson is not running for reelection this term?"

"Yes, I had heard. What does that have to do with you?"

"The state Democratic party has asked me to run in his place. What do you think?"

"I think you should marry me," said Marshal. "No, really, I don't know. What is your inclination?"

"You're enthusiasm is underwhelming," Carol said as she sipped her wine and paused for a time. "I have mixed feelings about it. On the one hand, if I could do some good work in Washington for the people of Colorado, I would be willing. But then, I also think about the nastiness of politics these days and especially in Washington. Do I want to get into the fray, and get down in the mud with all of these other politicians? I guess what I'm trying to say is I am not a politician and I might get run over by the big boys and girls." She sipped more wine. "And to answer the marriage question, is that all that men think are we are good for?"

"You would be entering the big game where the stakes are high, and with the Patriots wanting to stay in power, it is going to be a real nasty battle. It's all about money you know, and special interests and getting enough backing from people in power. Do you think you can do that?" Marshal looked at her straight on. "And marriage, yes I would like to marry you. You can have a career and be married too, you know. Men do that all the time."

Carol disregarded Marshal's last statement. They talked about campaign strategy and Carol asked him if he would help her and he said he would be honored. They talked on about how divided the nation was with the war and wedge issues like abortion and gay rights. Carol told him she wanted to unite the country for a common cause and she knew what that cause would be. She knew that deep down in the hearts of all Americans, there was a commonality among them. They all wanted a strong nation and they wanted to protect their families and to do that the nation would need to be fiscally responsible. And for families to be strong, they would need a good education to prepare them for jobs that are meaningful and fulfilling and allow them to provide for their families.

After dinner they slowly walked back to Carol's building, Marshal with his arm around Carol to keep her warm. They went into the building and past the guard who was dozing at his desk. So much for security, Carol thought. They took the elevator to her floor and walked down the thickly carpeted hallway to her apartment. Carol turned the key in the door and asked Marshal if he would like to come in for a brandy and his eyes lit up as he accepted.

Carol turned on the gas log fireplace, got the bottle of VSOP brandy with two brandy snifters from the sideboard and poured one for each of them as they settled down into the soft leather couch.

"Do you think I can win?" asked Carol.

"Yes, I think you can, with a lot of money and the right team. That's what it takes."

"I know it isn't going to be easy, but it is doable. The American people want something else, an alternative to this administration. They want honesty and someone who isn't tied to special interests and I am that person."

Marshal agreed. They sat for an hour or so, warming themselves with the brandy and the fireplace. Then Carol said that she needed to get some rest. She walked Marshal to the door and kissed him on the cheek. Marshal then grabbed hold of her and kissed her deeply on the mouth. "What I said was true. I would like to marry you, Carol."

"Marshal, I can't think of marriage right now. But I want you always to be my good friend."

Carol spent another sleepless night, tossing the covers, ruminating over her decision. On the one hand she thought it would be right for her but then she thought about the press chasing her and people saying slanderous things about her and her family. Her life would be put under a microscope, and although she felt she was above reproach, they would find ways to make her look bad. They might use the fact that Andrew had been living with a woman in Paris who was half Iraqi as an issue of national security.

But because she was so tired from not sleeping the night before, she finally fell into a deep, dreamless sleep.

The next day was Saturday and she studied all day and then had a light supper watching a movie on HBO, trying not to think about her decision. Waking early on Sunday, she put on her sweats and went to a nearby park for a long walk. The sun had come out and the weather was warming, melting the snow from Friday, creating a spring like day. Then she thought about calling James and asking his opinion. Even though she never called him otherwise, it wouldn't hurt to get his input. She jogged back to the apartment. Picking up the phone, she wondered to herself if she was doing the right thing. Punching in the number, she waited and waited and finally James picked up the phone.

"Hi," Carol said.

"And to what do I owe this honor?" asked James,

"I need some advice."

"And since when have you taken advice from me lately?"

"This is something really important."

And Carol told him about Senator Mattson not running and that she had been asked to run in his place and what did he think about that?

"Are you crazy? You would be setting yourself up for a miserable battle and I don't think you could win."

"Well, thanks for the vote of confidence. I talked to Marshal and he disagrees with you."

"No, I don't mean to sound so negative, but politics these days is run by corporate interests and if you don't buy into their program and go along with serving their needs, you won't be allowed at the table. It is going to be a dirty race this time around. The Patriots need to win at all costs. If they don't, they know they won't get into power again for years and they need to finish the agenda that they started, namely the war in Iraq and dominating the oil market. Are you up for that?"

Carol was taken aback by all of this. She hadn't expected such a strong reaction from James.

"Look, I am just trying to protect your interest. I care for you and I would hate to see you embroiled in this mess we have in Washington. You understand that don't you? I don't know if you realize it or not, but I am still in love with you."

Here we go again, thought Carol. If the men in her life could only see her as a person instead of a sex object or wife or whatever they were thinking.

"I have to try this," said Carol. "I think America is ready for change and I am the one to bring it to them. And if I lose the race, I will not have lost anything. I can go on to get my law degree and practice law and help people that way."

"Well, you asked my advice and I gave it to you. I didn't expect you to listen to me. You haven't in a long time now."

"I am listening and all of what you say is true, but I'm going to do it anyway."

"I thought you would. I wish you all the luck. Believe me you are going to need it."

"Thanks. I'll do just fine. Bye James."

She hung up the phone wondering if it was James who in fact pushed her to make the decision to run. Was she rebelling again or was this a conscious, well thought out decision? She wasn't sure.

It was noon on Monday and Carol had to call Charlotte to let her know. Picking up the phone, she punched the number Charlotte had given her and waited as the phone rang four times and finally Charlotte answered. And when she said she would accept Charlotte said she was thrilled.

"The next step is to register you as a candidate and start the machine rolling," said Charlotte.

Machine? What was this machine thing and what was she getting herself into? But she knew the answer to that question. "I'll come to your office tomorrow to register and then I would like to meet with everyone on the committee to plan a strategy for my campaign. Marshal Dale, my attorney, is going to be a part of my team."

"You are a wise woman, Carol. I am very optimistic that you will win this and when you go to Washington, hopefully we can change the way they are doing business there. We desperately need to change the direction of this country. We have been headed down the wrong road for many years now and I hope we can turn it around."

"You're right, this country does need to change and I hope I can be one of the people to make that happen. One thing I need to mention. I am attending law school and I aim to continue throughout the campaign and then possibly work out an arrangement with my school for some correspondence courses when I'm elected. I hope everyone will be in agreement on this."

"I like your positive attitude, Carol. I don't see a problem with that."

"I might not make it to every campaign event. I just want you to know that. Getting my law degree is my primary goal and I am not giving up on it. And if I shouldn't win, I will need to have the degree to get a job."

"You're going to win. You can count on that, Carol. I will see you tomorrow morning downtown at the Capitol building at nine o'clock."

Carol agreed and hung up the phone. She tried to study for the rest of the afternoon, but she was too excited about her new path in her life.

News travels fast on Internet time. The headline read, "FORMER FIRST LADY TO RUN FOR SENATE". It was plastered all over the Internet, the major newspapers and TV network news. The political talk shows took joy in discussing the merits and drawbacks of Carol's candidacy. Her phone rang incessantly and she wondered how some of these people had gotten her unlisted number. Numerous newspaper reporters called as well as Time magazine requesting an interview and she was invited to appear on the Sunday morning Meet the Press show and she accepted although she was dubious of the outcome as she knew how Tim Russett played devil's advocate and would ask her some very pointed questions.

Of course Carol was glad to talk with her friends, some of whom wished her well and others who were skeptical of her decision to go back into politics again and in such a big way. Her college friend Karen was one of the first to call.

"Carol, I don't believe it. You aren't going to do this are you?"

"Yes, I am. It is a way for me to help my country. Instead of just talking about it, now I can actually do something."

"But you told me two years ago that you wanted your privacy, and this is not the way."

"I know. But that wasn't the main reason I divorced James. I couldn't go along with his policies and I couldn't support him in the presidency."

And Carol went on to say that she felt the country needed to change direction before it was too late. They needed more moderates and progressives in office to mitigate the damage done by the current administration and she could help do that. She also explained to Karen that she might have a better chance of stopping the war in Iraq and hopefully bring Andrew home.

"Karen, it is the people in Washington who make and interpret the laws and in doing so impact how the American people live their lives." Carol said. "I will be coming from a position of power, however limited it will be, but I can make determinations and perhaps persuade others in Congress to follow my lead. And I will truly be representing the people. I am determined to do this."

Karen conceded that Carol was a strong person and that this country needed more representatives in congress who worked for the people.

"And another thing, I am not tied to special interests like many of the others are. We need to in fact get these people who are, out of our government and take the country back for the people. The working people in America are the backbone of this country; they are the ones who pay the majority of the taxes that keep this country going. These are the people that I will represent."

"Just stay as pure of heart as you are. I worry that when you go to Washington, you will become jaded like the rest of them. You know how it happened to James."

"I do know that James changed drastically when he became president. But that is not going to happen to me. I promise you. And if it does I will bow out."

Karen asked how law school was going and would she be able to finish. She offered help if she needed it. But Carol told her that, so far she was doing well. She might have to cut back on her classes, but she intended to keep on going until she got her degree, even with campaigning for the senate.

"I wish you well, Carol. You are one special lady and I am glad to have you as a friend. Don't forget me when you get to Washington."

"My friends are everything to me. I won't forget you. Maybe I won't even win."

Carol called her mother and her father, who were divorced and living separately. Her mother was very excited for her and spurred her on but her father, who had always been very protective of her, cautioned that she was putting herself out there; that these were dangerous times and Washington politics were dirty which she already knew. She tried to tell him that someone had to do this and it might as well be her. Yes, there was risk involved, but she was willing to take that risk if she could help turn her country around.

On Tuesday morning she took a taxi to the Capitol to register her candidacy for the senate. After that was taken care of she met with the Democratic campaign committee to talk about campaign strategy and the issues she would be running on.

"What are the two largest concerns facing this nation today?" Carol asked of those assembled around the conference table at the party headquarters. "What are the working people of America worried about?"

"The war is one of them and then after that, I would say energy," said Charlotte.

"There's so much, where to start," said Jim Davies with a long face. "Good jobs leaving the country, education, health care, the environment, global warming."

Phil twirled his pencil on his fingers. "I think people are worried about the federal deficit. They are concerned that their children, for the first time in America will not be living better lives than they are. That the debt is going to be so huge and the taxes to pay it off will fall on the middle class worker."

"Yes, all of those things and they are interrelated," Carol said. "First let's talk about energy. We need to get out of the Middle East and we need to make our cars, homes and appliances more energy efficient. And then we have to really dig in and make a concerted effort to develop clean renewable alternate fuels. This alone will clean up the air helping people to be healthier. And yes we need to work on a universal health care plan for America. There are millions who have no health care and having health care tied to employment is just not a good idea."

"So, what would you say are the two main issues Carol?" asked Peter Dowling.

"I think the war is immediate and then I think it is energy. When we solve the energy problem, we will also solve the job dilemma because this will create new, quality, high paying jobs for people. And when we have the alternative fuels, we will no longer have to deal with the Middle East."

"I agree. The war is a hot button item today. Four thousand dead soldiers, money being wasted on bringing democracy to a region that wasn't ready for it. Saddam was a bad guy, but now we're killing more Iraqis than he did," said Peter.

"I think to narrow it down to energy and health care," Carol said. "These are issues that most people are concerned about. The higher gas and heating bills are taking a chunk out of the average American wallet. And that goes for health care too. If we could come up with a plan somewhat like Canada's but streamline it so that it will be run more efficiently."

"Carol, you will have to open a headquarters," said Charlotte. "An office somewhere in the city where you can administer the campaign. We'll help you staff it with as many volunteers as possible. You will need a press secretary and public relations people and we will have to pay them. And that brings up the most important part here, the fund raising, because without that, nothing is going to happen."

Carol asked if one of them would help her find an office and they talked about the office location and campaign strategies for another two hours. It was way past three in the afternoon when Carol finally left the headquarters. She hurried home thinking about the studying that she had to do that evening for another test the next day. When she got back to her apartment, there were many messages on her machine and one of them was from Claude in France. She called him even though it would be the middle of the night there.

"Allo, qui est la?" Claude asked in a sleepy voice.

"Claude, it's Carol, I'm sorry to wake you."

"No, it's all right. You can call me any time. How are you? What am I hearing about you? You are running for the senate?"

"Yes, I meant to call you. I am. I decided that I have to do this."

"Oh, my darling Carol, I feel you are slipping away and I am sad. But I don't want to hold you back."

"I know what you must be thinking. I love you Claude, but I can't ask you to wait for me. I have a mission that I have to fulfill before I can settle down to being a wife."

"I understand." There was a long silence and then Claude asked Carol if she was happy.

"As happy as I can be at this time. You know there is one thing that will make me most happy and that is having Andrew come home."

They talked for about an hour and then Carol said she had to study and she said goodbye to Claude.

"I don't love you any less, Claude," said Carol as she hung up the phone. She wondered now if she was doing the right thing. Living with Claude on his estate would have been a pleasant life and now she was putting herself into the thick of it. Her life would be held under a microscope as never before and her privacy, which she zealously treasured, would be gone. But there is a price to pay for everything, she thought.

Chapter 33

Sex Slave

Simone followed the guard as he guided her down the hallway to another bedroom where Amahl was waiting. The guard knocked and then threw open the door and she could see Amahl, naked on the king sized bed, with rumpled muslin sheets. He was with another woman, who was gathering her clothing and readying herself to leave the room. Two women in one night, Simone thought? How bizarre.

The dark haired, dark eyed woman smiled at Simone as she walked past her and disappeared down the hallway. Amahl beckoned her to come into the room.

"My sweet thing, come here to me. Come to my bed and I will show you the surprise."

Simone was repulsed but she was trapped. What could she do? She couldn't flee as they would run after her and catch her and then beat her and maybe kill her. But she couldn't bring herself to go into this man's bed and allow him to have sex with her. Amahl called to her again.

"Don't be afraid my little, butterfly. I will not hurt you. Not as long as you do as I say. I am the monarch here and everyone in this compound obeys my rules and you will too or else you will suffer the consequences."

The consequences? A big English word for an Iraqi. Maybe she would rather suffer whatever those were rather than give herself to this wretched man. On the other hand, she thought, if there was no way out of this, how could she use it to her advantage? Could she get more information about Andrew? But then if she talked about Andrew, Amahl might become jealous and if he does know where Andrew is, he could harm him, even kill him. She inched into the room and closed her eyes as she gingerly sat on the bed. As Amahl was reaching for her she had a brilliant idea.

"Mr. Amahl, I have to confess that I have a very dread disease and you do not want to have sex with me. I have herpes. It is sexually transmitted and it is not curable, very painful and can even cause death." She lied about the last part hoping he didn't know what herpes was.

"I don't believe you, my sweet," said Amahl as he yanked her over to him on the bed he then pulled up her robe and thrust himself into her, pumping furiously until he came with a vengeance, collapsing onto her in ecstasy. The pain for Simone was unbearable. The gang rape of two days ago had ravaged and torn her and she screamed in agony when he entered her.

Amahl collapsed in a stupor on top of her, his armpits smelling of perspiration and the sweat of his body rolling off onto her. Then he awoke and said to Simone, "You liked it. You screamed like a whore in rapture."

Simone pushed him off of her and pulled her robe over her body, still throbbing with pain. "Can I go now? I am very sick and I think I am going to throw up," said Simone as she started to gag.

"No, I want you to stay the night. I want you beside me every night. You are, what the Americans say, a real turn on for me."

And then to Amahl's surprise, Simone turned from him and gagged and then threw up all over the bed.

"Look what you have done, you little tramp. The bed is a mess and I don't have any clean bed linens." he said as he called for the guard. Instantly there was a knock at the door and as the guard came into the room, Amahl told him to take Simone back to her room and then come back and clean up the vomit on the bed.

*   *   *

The pace was intensifying, if that were possible. Now, Carol was dividing her time between her already busy class schedule, a part time job, campaigning for the senate job and Andrew's cause. She decided to drop the part time job, hoping that would help and she cut her class schedule from fifteen hours to ten hours. She had no time now for socializing, but she hadn't done much of that recently anyway and she didn't miss it. Surely she could manage this schedule as heavy as it was.

She set the alarm for five a.m., slept in until five fifteen then arose and studied as she ate breakfast. Then it was off to the school law library to do research and on to her morning classes. She had purchased a small Honda Civic hatchback so she could drive herself and not have to take taxis or depend on the public transportation which at times was very slow. By noontime she would drive to her headquarters to talk to the volunteers, manage the phone banks and fund raisers and then retire to her office to coordinate appearances and write speeches. Then by five in the afternoon she might be meeting with the Chamber of Commerce or the Colorado Ranchers Association or some other group for cocktails and dinner. She never drank alcohol at these functions because she needed to keep a clear head and so her glass was always filled with ginger ale or ice water. After dinner she might be off to meet with the Teacher's Union for the evening arriving back at her apartment by eleven at the earliest. And even though she was dead tired by this time, she would force herself to put in at least another hour of studying and then fall into bed for her full five hours of sleep. Needless to say, she no longer needed sleeping pills; she fell asleep instantly as her head hit the pillow and that was a good thing.

So far, the press had been favorable to her, giving her high marks for her popularity, but the game had just begun. She appeared on two local talk shows, debating against her opponent, Larry Skelton, representing the Patriot party. Larry, sixty three years old, portly and bald, was an old time politician who knew how to twist and spin his answers, but Carol kept cool, took her time and held her own. She was scheduled to appear on Meet the Press for next Sunday's show which would be taped on Saturday afternoon in Washington DC. Carol was looking forward to going back to Washington and had called ahead to plan a meeting with President Martin to talk to him about Andrew and try to persuade him to take a more pro-active role in getting him released.

A nor'easter was hitting the eastern seaboard, dumping two feet of snow on Washington, delaying her seven a.m. flight on Saturday morning. But finally at eight they were able to take off and the flight arrived just in time for Carol to get to the studio for the taping.

Carol waited nervously in the green room with the other guests, the Pentagon's top general, Donald Struthers who was defending the war in Iraq and three top news reporters from the Washington Post, the New York Times and Newsweek magazine. Fortunately Carol would be interviewed first. They drank coffee and chatted about the weather and other inconsequential things. Ron French from the New York Times asked Carol if she had heard anything about Andrew and she sadly said no, that she was meeting with the president later that day to talk about Andrew. And then the program director came into the room and briefed everyone on their airtimes and when they should be ready to be on the set. She put a microphone on Carol's blouse and asked her to follow her out to the set to be ready for the interview. As Carol came onto the set she greeted Tim who was gathering notes in a last minute preparation for the program.

"Carol, have a seat. We'll be on in about a minute. Are you nervous?" Tim asked.

"No, not really. Lest you've forgotten, I was the first lady and I've done many interviews on television. I could use a glass of water though."

Tim smiled and asked the director to bring some water and then it was time for the taping to start. Tim made the opening statements and announced who was to be on the show and then he turned to Carol.

"And I would like to introduce our first guest, Carol Walters who is running for the Colorado senate seat this fall. But no introduction is necessary. You all know this lovely lady from when she was our gracious first lady. Welcome Carol. So you weren't satisfied to sit by the sidelines; had to get into the fray as we say."

"Well, yes you might say that. And when I am elected I will fight for the people of Colorado to make their lives better. Our country is headed in the wrong direction as you well know."

"But it was your husband who took us in this direction. Are you saying that you disagree with everything he has done for this country?"

"This is not about my husband. He did what he could and he is out now. Tim, this is about going forward, about jobs and health care for everyone. And about energy; we absolutely need to move towards alternative renewable fuel sources. Americans have the ingenuity; we are smart people. And when we invest in alternative fuels we are not only investing in America's future, we will create good high paying jobs and have a technology to export to other countries, other than guns. Another benefit will be cleaner air, healthier living for everyone and we might be able to slow global warming. And, of course, we will no longer have to deal with the Middle East."

"And the Iraq war? Are you for pulling the troops out of Iraq?"

"Yes, I am, when it is reasonable to do so. The war was a huge mistake, but we are there now, and the way I see it is that we should have a gradual reduction of manpower and increasingly turn the security of Iraq over to the Iraqi people. They need to be running their own country, deciding their own future whatever that may be, a democracy, a dictatorship. We might not like what they do. But you know Tim, it shouldn't matter because we won't need their oil. I am going to push firstly for energy conservation and then a concerted effort towards alternative fuels, solar, wind and any other ideas that our very capable engineers can come up with. Look, we developed the atomic bomb. Why can't we get off the old technology of the oil driven piston engine."

"Those are lofty goals. And does the fact that your son is being held hostage have anything to do with this?" asked Tim.

"Everything and nothing. It's not just my son who is in jeopardy in Iraq. There are 130,000 men and women who are risking their lives every day in Iraq and another 20,000 in Afghanistan. I want them all to come home safely to be with their families."

"I know this must be very hard on you. Have you heard any more about Andrew?"

"No, and there haven't been any recent tapes and that might be a good sign. In the last one they said they would kill him by Christmas if we didn't pull all our troops out of Iraq. And there has been nothing since then."

"But, Mrs. Walters, how can you have an impartial view of this with your son's life on the line here. You can't."

"Yes, I can. Just as much as any other mother or father or family member does with a son or daughter in Iraq. As much as Debra Johansen, a mother who lost a son in Iraq. We are all in this together."

"They are not impartial. They all have a stake in this," Tim said emphatically.

"Tim, I believe all Americans have a stake in this. We are all being harmed by our troops remaining in Iraq. Iraq has now become a training ground for al Qaeda. It wasn't before we attacked. Saddam didn't want al Qaeda in his country. We are less safe today than we were before we invaded Iraq and it's time to face that."

"We thank you for sharing your thoughts today Mrs. Walters. I wish you all the luck in your Senate race. And now for a break and when we come back we will be talking to General Donald Struthers and get the lowdown on what is really happening in Iraq. Thank you, Mrs. Walters."

"Thank you for having me."

As Carol was walking off the set, Tim said that she had done a great job and again wished her luck. Carol was happy with the interview. Now her ideas were out there for Colorado and the nation to think about.

Carol walked into the Oval office, and seeing Jason sitting behind the very desk where James sat when he was president gave her a start. She looked around the spacious room and all of the personal artifacts and pictures that James had were of course gone; even the rug had been changed. Instead of the gold and yellow sunburst, the new rug was blue and grey and it made the room look drab and dreary. But then the weather didn't help. It had started to snow again and the forecast was for record snowfall in Washington DC and up the Eastern Seaboard.

It was Sunday morning and Carol had spent the night at the newly renovated historic Willard Hotel, the residence of the presidents, not far from the White House. It was pricey but she hoped to leave on an afternoon flight, weather permitting. When she had called Jason to confirm her appointment, he was less than cordial and tried to make excuses for not seeing her, but she persisted and he finally relented. Carol was not that keen on seeing Jason either, she had never really liked him, but she had to try to get some action from him on getting Andrew home. And she thought that starting at the top would be the best way. But then, she thought, Jason didn't want Andrew to be released. If that happened, James could come back and reclaim his rightful place as president. Although, James told her he would not come back to Washington; at least not for awhile.

"Jason, so good to see you again," Carol lied as she held out her hand in greeting.

"Good to see you too, Mrs. Walters. I saw you this morning on Meet the Press. You looked a little tired."

Same old Jason, Carol thought, always playing politics. "I watched the show this morning too and I thought it went very well," said Carol. She did not want to talk politics however, because she knew whose side he was on and it wasn't her side. She was here to talk about Andrew.

"We do think he's been taken out of the country, possibly Syria."

"Why can't they find him? The richest nation in the world and the best intelligence, do they not want to find him? I don't understand."

"I know you don't understand. Iraq is very different in that we don't really know whom we can trust over there. We get a lead and follow up on it and it turns out to be an ambush for our guys. This has happened a couple of times. The CIA and Special Forces are working full time on this."

"Then why haven't they found him, I'm asking again?"

"We think they're moving him around. We're doing the best we can right now. You just have to be patient."

"But time is running out. He, in fact could be dead by how. They said they would kill him by December. That was a month ago."

"I think he's still alive. We've had some chatter to that effect. And most usually when they kill a hostage, the body shows up somewhere."

"This is my son you're talking about. Jason, I want you to move to get the US military home. That will solve many of our problems; save American lives and maybe bring the release of Andrew. You have to know that the election is coming up this fall and Americans are turning against the Iraq war. Your party is going to take a beating in the house and the senate if you don't do something to speak to the will of the American people. I know, I've been out there talking to them and they're going to vote your party out this fall. They're tired of your so called compassionate conservatism. They are tired of seeing you cut domestic spending and sending the money to Iraq."

Jason just looked at Carol, disbelieving what she was saying. "Carol, are you sure you want to run for this senate seat? It's going to get really dirty this year and you will not be immune just because you were the First Lady and your son is a hostage in Iraq."

"Don't change the subject, Jason. I want some action from you and I want it soon."

"I'm not changing the subject. This is all interrelated. What I'm trying to tell you is that, Washington is not for amateurs. You have to know the ropes or you will be consumed; eaten alive."

"Are you trying to frighten me into not running?" Carol looked him straight in the eye. "Because if you are, you're wasting your time. So called amateurs, as you call them, have been known to move mountains in Washington. They, like me aren't tied to all the special interests and work for the people. Remember the old saying, the government for the people and by the people? Wonder what happened to that standard? Well, I am bringing it back to Washington. In fact, you've just given me an idea. I am going to use that in my campaign."

"When you are caught up in the heat of the campaign and your opponent is nipping at your heels, just remember that I warned you." Jason got up from his desk and walked around to the middle of the room. He was clearly agitated now. "How's James doing? Have you talked with him recently?"

"Yes, I have. He's fine. I think he's enjoying his time in solitude. Being president is a tough job as you must know by now."

"Yes, yes… it is," Jason said as he sat down in the chair beside hers. "How does James feel about your running?"

"He wasn't for it. Said pretty much what you said. But you know, somebody needs to step forward and stand up for our country and it might as well be me. And if Andrew doesn't come home alive, my life isn't worth too much anyway."

They talked for awhile longer. Carol asked about the staff at the White House and about Diane, his wife. Jason said they were all fine and working hard. Diane had adopted a program to help foster children find homes and was spending every spare moment flying around the country talking with Child Protective Services and adoption agencies.

"You know Jason, if every child in this country were loved and wanted, we wouldn't have to worry about foster care. I know it is a lofty goal but we can work towards that end. And that means teaching sex education early on and I know drugs are a problem too. But rolling back Roe V Wade will not help."

With that said Carol rose from her chair and thanked Jason for his time. She asked again that he do everything he could to help Andrew. He promised Carol that he would, but Carol felt that they were empty words. But she had given it her best try.

*   *   *

It was dusk, and the shadows were long in Mohammed's room that had become a cell. At midday, they had taken him to an interrogation room again and he was concerned that they might torture him but they didn't. They asked him again what he knew about Amahl and where his compound was located. And then they told him that they were going tonight, to flush out the insurgents and they wanted Mohammed to go with them to show them the way. Mohammed was worried. He had seen how the Marines had handled operations like this before and knew it would be very dangerous. He told them again about his cousin Simone and asked that they take her out of there without harming her. He knew he had little control but he felt that if he were there he could try to insure that she would come out unscathed.

He heard footsteps in the hallway and then someone was unlocking his door. Two guards led him out of the room and down the long hallway to the main entrance and then out into the early evening air to the waiting convoy. One of the soldiers gave him a flack jacket and told him to put it on. They also gave him a pair of night vision glasses so that he could better guide them to the hideout.

"You're not going to take off on us are you?" asked the tall, dark haired sergeant who had interrogated him when he had first come to the base. He heard one of the other soldiers call him Sam.

"No, I just want to get Simone out safely. I am not going anywhere," Mohammed said as he wondered why he was a prisoner.

"Good, then we won't shackle you."

The sandy haired soldier, Matt was there along with about forty other soldiers, ready with M-16's casually slung over their shoulders. They too were wearing flack jackets and some had night vision goggles. They motioned him to get into a Humvee. As they were pulling out of the military base, there was sniper fire coming from somewhere and they stopped for awhile, responding with a MK-19 Automatic Grenade launcher, from the lead Humvee. The shooting stopped and they were on the road again. Mohammed glanced at the driver. He couldn't be much older than he was, nineteen or so and the sweat was beading on his forehead.

"Are you scared?" Mohammed asked, not expecting a straight answer.

"Hell, you bet I'm scared. We get this every day and some day I figure they're gonna get me." He shifted the gears on the Humvee. "If it ain't snipers it's the IED's and road side bombs or it's the suicide bombers. And you don't know who the fuck is your enemy. That's why we shoot first and ask questions later."

They drove along mostly in silence the rest of the way, with Mohammed periodically giving directions on where to go. It was getting very dark and there was no moon. They would need the night vision goggles tonight. Mohammed didn't know what to expect, but he knew it would be dangerous and he was frightened too although he wouldn't say so to the young driver. Two hours later they came to the road that led into the compound and pulled their vehicles off to the side, into some bushes. They would go on foot from here.

Silently they got out of the Humvees and gathered for instructions from the platoon sergeant. He told them to form two groups and march in from two directions, to surround the hideout and try to prevent anyone from escaping. With the element of surprise they might be able to break down the doors, catch them off guard and then capture them before they would have a chance to fight back. This would be hand to hand, soldier to insurgent fighting, combat of the most dangerous kind and Mohammed knew there would be killing tonight.

Mohammed led the men up the road where he had escaped many days ago and when they reached a place where they could see the buildings they stopped. There were lights on in the main building and it took on a life of its own looking like a monster ready to gobble them up. A dog barked. Mohammed pointed to the buildings and said this was the place. Sam had told them earlier not shoot if they didn't have to but to take as many prisoners as possible, hoping to get information out of them and Mohammed thought this was very good. There would then be a chance of information on where they were holding Andrew.

He let the infantry go first now, following along behind. The other unit came in from the other side and within minutes, they bashed in the door, machine guns and bayonets at the ready. There were three men in the main room, sitting around a table and the soldiers grabbed two of them when they jumped out of their chairs in surprise. As they grappled with the insurgents, they pulled their hands behind their backs, tying them with the plastic flex cuffs they always carried. The other guard slipped past them and was headed out the door when one of the soldiers fired shooting him in the back and he slumped over on the floor, his body convulsing until it was quiet. The shots brought out others, but they were ready for them. It was over in minutes and they had captured a dozen of Amahl's guards but where was Amahl? He wasn't among them. And where was Simone? Mohammed walked down the dimly lit hallway, opening doors, looking for Simone. He finally opened the last door and found her cowering under the bed.

"Simone, come on out. We came to get you. I am with the Americans."

Simone pulled herself out from under the bed and looked at Mohammed and went to his arms and cried.

"I didn't think you would ever get here. But I am so glad you did."

"It's all right now. We'll take you out of here. You are safe now."

Together they walked out of the bedroom and back to the main room where the soldiers were marshaling the prisoners out into the night to the waiting Humvees that had driven to the compound after the operation began.

Mohammed helped Simone into the back of one of the trucks where he could be near her. He looked at her carefully. She had lost weight, her clothes were soiled and her hair was unkempt. And she was still crying.

"Are you all right?" Mohammed asked.

"I will be. When we get out of here, I will be."

"Oh, Simone, I am so sorry."

"What are you sorry for? It was my idea."

He was glad that she still had some spunk. Yes, she would be all right.

Chapter 34

Politics as Usual

Snow fell on Washington DC, frosting trees and buildings like a Dickens Christmas Carol, giving a look of innocence to a city steeped in dishonesty and corruption. Carol was forced to spend another night in her $425 a night room much to her consternation. She hated spending the money and she despised being in this city where the all powerful politicians and lobbyists ruled. But soon, when she became a Senator, she would have to come back here and make Washington at least her part time residence and the thought was not pleasant. She would have to buy a small ranch outside Denver and use that as her retreat from the madness that was this city every day.

On Monday, the snow stopped and flight schedules were restored. As Carol was boarding her early morning flight, several people came up to greet her saying they had seen her on Meet the Press the day before and how they thought she would make a fine senator. It gladdened her that people were pulling for her. At least she thought they were until she arrived at the airport in Denver and picked up the Denver Post on the way home. After she had unpacked and listened to her thirty five messages on her machine, she poured a glass of wine and sat down to read the newspaper and there on page nine was an article with the headline, "Is Carol Walters Mentally Ill?" Reading further, the premise was that since she had been taken to a care facility two years ago for overdosing on sleeping pills that she was not mentally fit to run for the Senate. What utter nonsense, she thought. I'll just tell them the truth. I'll tell the whole country how the Secret Service broke into my bedroom that night, drugged me and took me away in an ambulance. The public needs to know how devious this government is.

Then, she thought, would they believe me? And she had promised the administration that she wouldn't say anything about this. What should she do now? She couldn't have people believing these lies.

Carol picked up the phone and called her campaign headquarters to find out what the impact of the article had had if any on her poll numbers. She was able to reach her campaign manager, Shirley Masterson.

"Shirley, have you seen today's paper?" Carol asked as she picked up the phone.

"Yes, Carol, it's all over town. But it's hard to know if this will have a negative influence on your poll numbers."

"What are the polls saying?"

"You're down about three points. But that isn't too bad because you had a four point boost from the Meet The Press appearance this weekend. I think we should just wait and see."

"I disagree, Shirley, I think we have to come back on the offense. We can't let them do this to us. I have to go to class this afternoon, but we'll have a meeting tomorrow morning to counter attack."

"You could be right. I'll see what dirt we can dig up on your opponent, Larry."

"No, I don't want to get down in the mud with Larry. We're going to go at this from a different angle. Honesty and integrity are what we are all about and when the people see this, they won't vote for Larry."

"I hope you're right, Carol. But you've seen the campaigns in the last four years and mudslinging is where it's at and if you don't do that you could get buried in Larry's mud and never dig your way out."

"You know, Shirley we need to find a way for Larry's mud to back slide and bury him."

Carol asked Shirley to schedule a meeting for the next day and then called the state Democratic headquarters to invite the Democratic chairperson, Charlotte McKenzie to attend. Charlotte was not optimistic when she called and Carol didn't spend much time talking with her. She then left her apartment and drove to the University for her two-hour class on Professional Responsibility. It fit right in to what was happening in her campaign. Ethics and truth telling; she had to maintain the highest standard, otherwise how could the people trust her. Even if sometimes the truth hurt, she vowed that she would be forthcoming and truthful to her constituents.

The class dragged on. She eyed the round white clock on the opposite wall. It was only three o'clock and there was another hour left. She had so much on her mind. But this course was going to be a breeze. Maybe she could cut these classes and read the summary of the text and pass the course anyway. Her schedule was so tight these days. A young male student sitting next to her asked if she had an extra sheet of paper to take notes and she handed him five sheets from her notebook. He smiled and mouthed the words thank you.

Finally the instructor gave a summary and instructed the class to prepare for a test next week. Carol bolted out of her chair along with fifty or so other students. Maybe she could get the guy who asked her for paper to take notes for her. That wasn't truly dishonest. She would still do the studying and take the tests. Something had to give in her life or she would be buried, and it wouldn't be from Larry's mud slinging.

Carol returned to her apartment an hour later. There were more messages, one from James asking if she was enjoying running for office now. He had seen the article too. She would give him a call later.

She wasn't hungry but she thought she had better eat something, so she grabbed a bowl of Thai noodles from her cupboard and poured another glass of wine. I had better cut out all drinking, she thought. It drags me down and makes me sleepy. But what else is there in life if you can't have a glass of wine now and then.

Taking the food into the living room, Carol looked out over the mountains to the west and wished she could go hiking or back packing; just get away from all of this. And it was just the beginning. She turned on the television to watch the news. The weather report came on; partly cloudy with a chance of showers and snow in the mountains. Then an ad appeared. In the ad two women were talking about Carol Walters when she was the First Lady.

"Shameful that Mrs. Walters was leaving her husband when he needed her most," the first woman, dressed in jeans and a sweat shirt said.

"I agree. President Walters was struggling with a war and the problems of the nation and his wife just ups and leaves him."

And the voice over said, "Mrs. Walters ran out on her husband. Will Mrs. Walters run out on you in your time of need?" There was a pause. "Vote for Larry Skelton if you want someone you can count on."

How low will they go, Carol wondered? Well, she should have expected this. It is all about money.

The phone rang and it was James.

"How are you liking this now?" James asked in his booming voice.

"I expected it. I don't quite know how to handle it though. We're meeting tomorrow. Any suggestions?"

"Do you have a good campaign manager?"

"I think so. But she wants to start digging up dirt on Larry and I don't' want to do that. I don't want to play his dirty political game."

"You know Carol, I think you are right about this. Stay above it. Don't get down to his level. Just keep pounding out your message about how you are honest and loyal and want to work for your constituents. Stay on message and keep talking about the issues. About what you're going to do when you're in office and what Larry won't do." James paused for a minute. "How's the money holding out? Are you getting enough contributions?"

"Yes, we've been doing really well. Those thousand-dollar-a-plate dinners have helped."

"Well, good. You know I'm pulling for you. I wasn't keen on you doing this but I will support you. I'm donating a few thousand dollars."

"You don't have to do that, you know. But I thank you."

"I still love you. You know that don't you?"

"That's sweet." Carol said.

"I know that a part of me will always be with you."

She studied for another hour and then took a book to bed with her. She was reading about the Pentagon and World War II and the dropping of the nuclear bombs on Hiroshima and Nagasaki. She read how hundreds of thousands of people were killed, mostly women and children and elderly people as the men were all away fighting the war. What a horrific event that was and she vowed she would do everything she could to try to get rid of nuclear arms around the world. War doesn't solve anything, she thought as she drifted off to sleep.

The next morning she drove to her headquarters for her meeting with the committee and her campaign manager. They were all in the room when she arrived.

"We have some good news and some bad news this week," Charlotte started out as she seated herself at the head of the table. "Meet the Press was a success, Carol. We need more of those interviews. But... Larry and team are coming out swinging as you all saw in the Post yesterday."

Jim Davies spoke up. "Carol I thought you answered Tim Russert's questions so well. And you looked great."

"It's going to take more than good looks, I'm afraid," said Carol. "We're going to have to come up with a strategy to counteract the negative ads and commercials. Did you all see the one last night saying that I abandoned James?"

"I've found out some interesting stuff about Larry that you all should know," Shirley piped up. "He's had some bad business deals with the American Trust Bank. Seems he ran out on some loans awhile back and for some reason they never went after him."

"How far back, Shirley?" Carol asked impatiently.

"Fifteen years. The question is did he pay someone off in the DA's office. The dollar figure was in the millions."

"That's pretty far back and I don't want to go there," said Carol. "I want to keep this campaign clean and I will not stoop to his level. We can run on honesty and integrity and I know the people will vote for me. I need to get on the local television talk shows, and to put some of our own ads out there, telling people what we are going to do for them. They won't care about this other stuff if they think I will change the way government works. I'm going to work on getting the corruption out of Washington."

"That's a tall order," said Peter.

"I know, but I'm committed to this. And to creating a more transparent government where the people are informed as to what we're doing. After all, it is the taxpayer's dollars and they are paying us to work for them. There is going to be a new day in Washington when I arrive on the scene."

"Did you know that your ex-husband, the former president donated to your campaign?" said Charlotte.

Carol's eyes widened. "He said he would. Well let's put it to good use. Shirley, we need an agent to get the TV appearances. I want to go on all of the local news shows and then the morning shows. And I am going to call in to all of the talk radio shows in the area and start the dialog going. We're not going to trash our opponent. This is a new campaign strategy and I know it'll work."

"I'm skeptical. This has never been successful in the past. Why do you think it will work this time around?" asked Phil Jackson.

"Because people are fed up with dirty politics. Trust me, we will succeed," said Carol looking at the eight people sitting around the conference table. Just as Carol spoke a thunder cloud formed over the capitol area not far from where they were meeting and a lightening bolt hit the spire on the State Capitol building. The immediate thunder that followed was deafening and Phil and Marion jumped in their chairs.

"Carol has spoken. You know I think you might have something there," said Sharon Johnson. "I think people are tired of dirty politics. But what about corporate interests? How can we neutralize the influence that they have with the media and the business community? They have the money and that means they also have the clout."

"That's what is wrong with our government. The corporate community, for the most part does not have the best interest of the people in mind. They are all about the bottom line and making money short term for their shareholders. If we don't take money from the corporations, we are not beholden to them and we have an excellent grass roots movement and plenty of money coming in from our constituents. If we can show the people that we will work for them and make laws that will help the workers of this country, they will vote for us. And that means getting the word out and then getting the vote out," said Carol.

"Carol, I think you are right on. And after that bolt of lightening...."

And they all laughed, applauding Carol.

"Thank you. Yes, I do have special powers and I am going to use them in this election year and become the next Democratic Senator from the state of Colorado."

"I believe you will," said Charlotte.

Chapter 35

The Campaign Trail Again

Carol tried to stay on message when she appeared on two local talk shows, but she was bombarded with questions about her relationship with her ex-husband and the state of her mental health. She couldn't seem to get around this. Would she have to issue a public statement saying that yes, she had left her husband but she didn't think of it as abandoning him. She left him because they didn't have the same values anymore and she said outright that she couldn't support him in the war effort. And that she wasn't mentally ill in any way.

She decided to call Marshal to see what advice he might have for her. And of course he invited her to dinner and she accepted telling him she would meet him at the restaurant the following evening after a speaking engagement with the Denver Press Club.

Arriving early at the Hyatt Regency Hotel, she was shown to the main ball room where she would be giving her speech that evening. Others had already arrived and Carol circulated around the room greeting people, shaking hands and introducing herself to those who might not know who she was. This was an important night as she wanted to have a positive rapport with the press; they held her future in their hands. And yet she didn't want to control the press. She had always subscribed to the idea that a free press is one of the essential elements in a free society and she would always adhere to that principle.

"Yes, Mrs. Walters, I know who you are. Everyone knows who you are," said Marge, a middle aged woman who was the editor of the North Valley News, one of the smaller local newspapers. "I admire you tremendously. I think it took great courage to do what you did and I am sure other first ladies have wanted to do the same but were afraid."

"Thank you, Marge. Now if everyone saw it that way, I would have no problem. I thought long and hard before I decided to divorce James. And, you know, he isn't a bad person. He just changed when he got into office and we were strangers in our marriage," said Carol as she sipped her soft drink.

"I'll write an op-ed and send it to other newspapers because I think you are being greatly maligned by Larry's campaign."

"Thank you again." And Carol was off to greeting other members and then it was time for her to speak. She approached the podium and sat next to the chairman of the club, a portly, gray haired man in his late sixties dressed in a gray pin striped suit, who stood to introduce her.

"Ladies and gentlemen, I am pleased to introduce our speaker for this evening, a woman whom we all know, our former First lady, Carol Walters. Carol is no stranger to adversity and has shown that she has the mettle to overcome whatever is thrown at her. When she goes to Washington, this experience will serve her well. She is bright and articulate, knowledgeable and will shake up Washington when she gets there. We welcome you Carol."

The audience clapped as Carol stood at the podium, dressed in a bright red suit, looking younger than her fifty five years. She raised her hands to quell the applause.

"I am honored to be invited to speak to this prestigious group; thank you for having me." And then Carol paused and looked around the room at the 300 some people sitting in front of her. "This senator's race is about the health of this state, and our nation. It is about whether we spend your tax dollars on war or on education, health care and other greatly needed domestic programs. It is about whether we protect our environment for our children and our grandchildren and it is about developing alternative fuels to get off the Middle Eastern oil stream. It is also about creating jobs, good jobs for Americans so they can support their families and live a decent life. Now, we don't want big business to lose out on all of this, but we don't want our workers to lose either. And so I am proposing that the oil companies retool and channel some of their profits into research and development of renewable fuel sources. This will, in turn create jobs, maybe even create an industry where we could export the technology and the products. And I am proposing that the defense companies do the same. Can you imagine a time when

America is exporting solar technology instead of war and guns. Believe me, the world will be a better place."

The audience once more applauded

"For the past five years our country has been on the wrong track and now it is time for a change and time to get this country back to where it was when this current administration took office. I intend to be a part of that. I intend to work for the people who elect me, the people who pay my salary."

Carol continued to talk about environmental issues in Colorado. She reminded them of earlier days in Colorado when the mining industry had done irreparable damage to pristine mountain landscapes and polluted the water ways and if they weren't careful, this could happen again. The price of precious metals and copper was going up, creating a demand for more mining. She also talked about how the oil industry was drilling in Wyoming and Montana, installing oil and gas rigs across the landscape.

"Is this the legacy we want to leave our heirs? Think of skiing down the mountain and looking over a horde of oil rigs."

Carol then summarized by reiterating that she was going to Washington to make a change in the way Congress does business. Instead of working for big business and the rich, she would be an advocate for the working people of America to bring jobs back to America along with peace and prosperity.

"Again, I thank you for having me. I will take questions if you have any."

Twenty or so people raised their hands.

"Yes, the gentleman in the third row, you have a question?"

"I do. And no doubt you are expecting this question. What can you say about the talk about you having mental disorders? Because until you lay this to rest, the public will be asking."

Carol took a deep breath. "I am going to tell you that it isn't true. That I have never overdosed on sleeping pills and my mental health has never been better. I am very grounded and determined to win this election and go to Washington so that I can serve this state of Colorado and the nation." Carol paused. "And, yes, the woman in the fifth row, your question."

"Where do you stand on health care? Do you see a universal health care plan like Canada, or more something like President Martin's plan for individual accounts?"

"I see something in between. I think we can use Canada's plan as a model, but I think too that we can improve on it. People want to have their own physician who knows their health care concerns and those of their family. And there shouldn't be a wait for services, surgery and such. But then I am going to ask that people take more responsibility for their own health in taking better care for themselves, improving their diets, exercising. " She looked around the room to see the reaction. "Another question, yes you in the back with the dark blue shirt."

"Carol Walters, did you abandon your husband?"

There was a titter from the audience. "No, I don't think so. I couldn't live a lie and I could not support what the administration was doing, particularly in going to war and many other issues. But it is personal. Every woman who has divorced understands that she does not do this without first thinking of the implications. In my case, though, I would not have dreamed that I would experience the odyssey that I have had in the year that I spent abroad. But I am a better person for it."

She acknowledged a woman on the side, half back in the room.

"Yes, Mrs. Walters and what is your position on the Iraq war. Would you bring the military home immediately?"

"I would recommend that they be phased out of Iraq as soon as possible, allowing the Iraqi people to take full control of their government. To pull all of them out all at once could create more havoc with security. But we do need to get out of that area. We had no business going there in the first place and to stay is just a thorn in their sides. They don't want us there, period."

The younger man stood and asked, "Have you thought about going back to your husband, now that he is out of government?"

"No. I have to move forward. James is now a part of my past and you the people of Colorado are my future." Carol than said, "I thank you all. I have enjoyed this time with you and I hope you will all support me in my bid for the senate."

There was a standing ovation. They do like me, Carol thought. I hope I can keep their respect and support.

Carol left the stage, shaking hands on the way out of the banquet room, heading out of the hotel and into the garage to fetch her car. As she drove out of the garage, she felt very positive about her speech.

The traffic was heavy and as she looked at her watch she saw that she would be late for her dinner engagement with Marshal. After parking behind the restaurant, Carol hurried into the steak house and asked for Marshal. The maitre de said that he had arrived some time ago and was waiting at the table.

"I will take you there, Mrs. Walters," the maitre de said as he motioned for her to follow.

"I'm late, I know. Have you ordered yet?" Carol said as she sat next to Marshal.

"No, I was waiting for you. I ordered some wine though."

Carol looked at the menu in front of her.

"How did your speech go tonight?"

"I think it went very well. When I finished, they all stood and clapped for a long time. I think they are on my side."

"Well, that can change in a day, so don't take anything for granted."

"I'm not. I am still getting questions about my mental health and my loyalty to my former husband. I don't know how to overcome this. Do you have any ideas?"

"I think this will just blow over. The public has a short memory and if you keep getting the good message out there on how you are working for them, I think they'll focus on that."

"That's my take on it. But some of the time when I'm speaking, I can't get to my message for all of the questions on my character. Why is this happening?"

"The opposition has to find something to discredit you and this is what they are using at the moment. They really don't have anything else to tear you down with. Frankly, I think Larry is running scared. Not just of you but of the Democrats in general. People are fed up with this administration. They haven't been forthright with the American people. And that can be your strategy, just being up front and honest, unlike the current administration and you don't even have to name any names. It is perfect. Let them hang themselves."

"Marshal, I like that strategy. And it is the truth."

The waiter brought the wine and they ordered dinner. Halfway through the meal, Carol looked over at Marshal and told him how glad she was to have him for a friend and on her team.

"I wish I could be more than your friend, you know that don't you?"

"Yes, I do. But I'm going solo for now. I am very happy being single at the moment."

"Sure you are. And all of your men are chasing you."

"All of my men?' Carol looked at Marshal incredulously. "Explain please."

"Well, James is still in love with you and then that Frenchman...."

"Why, Marshal, I do believe you are jealous," Carol laughed. "But I am an independent woman and I intend to stay that way for now."

Chapter 36

Simone Goes Home

When Mohammed and Simone were brought back to the base in the early morning hours after that fateful night, they were treated very differently than when Mohammad had first arrived there. They were assigned to rooms that were much like a budget motel room, austere but with the necessary amenities, a bath with a shower, a comfortable bed with clean white sheets, an easy chair in the corner and even a small desk. A female soldier gave Simone army issue night clothes and fatigues to wear during the day, with heavy army boots. These new duds were nothing like the feminine clothes she was used to wearing, but she was glad to have them as she had been wearing the same soiled clothes for many days. And then she asked if Simone would go to see the doctor on the base as a precaution and have an examination and Simone readily agreed.

When she returned to her room it was four AM, and even though it was a very early hour of the morning, Simone's first order of business was to take a long, hot shower. She peeled off the filthy robes that she had been wearing and turned on the water in the shower to as hot a temperature as her body could stand and she stayed there for maybe half an hour, scrubbing and rinsing and scrubbing again, washing away the dirt of Amahl, although she knew it would be years before she would be thoroughly cleansed of him and his abuse of her body. She then lay down on her bed and with her hands smoothed body lotion all over her body, drinking in the subtle scent of lavender. She was beginning to be whole again.

Then crawling under the army issue tan cotton blanket, she lay her head on the pillow, her long black hair fanning out around her face and closed her eyes, hoping to close out forever the horrors of the last two weeks. She slept a deep sleep that she hadn't known in many days.

Mohammed was relieved to be back as well. His worst fears that he or Simone would be harmed that night never materialized, and now he was back in a safety zone with hopes of returning back to his family. He had asked to call his father to let him know that he was alive and reasonably well and that he and Simone would be home, hopefully the next day. That was what they had told him when they returned to the base. Why the special treatment, he wondered? Two days ago he was a prisoner in a cell eating bread and water and now he was being treated like a special guest. There were no locks on the doors and an orderly had brought him a delectable breakfast of ham and eggs to his room. Had the word gotten back to Washington? They knew about Simone's quest at the base, had this also filtered back to the States? He wouldn't question the motives. He would enjoy and look forward to going home. Although his father sounded almost angry when he talked to him, but no matter, he would get over it and he would be glad to see them he was sure.

Later that afternoon, Simone awoke to the sound of shelling and bombs falling in the distance. Where was she? Still at Amahl's compound? Then she realized that she was at the army base and she was safe for now. She heard a knock on the door and she grabbed a robe and opened it. An orderly was there asking if she wanted anything to eat or drink and was there anything he could do for her? This was like going from the dungeon to the castle in one day. No, she just wanted to get back to Mohammed's house and then catch a flight back to Paris as soon as possible. But some fruit and cheese did sound appealing. After the orderly left, she dressed in her desert camouflage pants and shirt with a vest to match. She pulled on the wool socks and the heavy sand colored boots and when she walked out of the room her feet clunked with every step.

She was asked to meet with the sergeant and some other official and when she entered the room, Mohammed was there also.

"Come in, Miss Hashim. We would like to ask you a few questions before we take you back to Baghdad."

Simone nodded and looked over at Mohammed who was dressed in similar attire as hers. She smiled and he winked knowingly at her. They were going home.

"Are you sure you have given us all the names of your acquaintances in Paris who connected you with Amahl?"

"Yes, I can't think of anyone else." She paused and then asked, "Do you have a lead on where Andrew is?"

"Not yet, but we're working on it. We have the intelligence community working day and night on this and we should find him soon. I think they are moving him to put us off the trail. But capturing these guys last night is a major break through, not only for finding Andrew, but for rooting out more of the insurgents. So you two have been a big help. And I am confident that we will find Andrew soon" said the sergeant.

"So you think he is still alive?" asked Simone.

"We're hoping so. Haven't heard anything to the contrary."

Another soldier entered the room. "The truck is ready sir."

We're taking you back to Baghdad this afternoon. Are you two ready to go?" asked the sergeant.

They both nodded enthusiastically and then followed the soldier out to the waiting Humvee, parked in front of the office with its motor running. They climbed into the back of the cab while the driver and another Marine sat in front.

Neither spoke for several miles, taking in the scenery of the countryside with burned out vehicles along the roadside. Traffic was heavy and the air was filled with dust, magnifying the setting sun that looked like a giant orange beach ball on the horizon. The truck lurched as they tried to avoid a crater in the road.

"How long are you guys here for?" Mohammed asked, breaking the silence.

"We were supposed to go home last month but they extended our duty. So we'll be here until September is that right Charley?" the driver answered. He was young, maybe twenty years old.

"Yeah, September it is. Can't wait to get out of this hell hole," the other Marine said in anger.

"It ain't so bad Charley. If we don't have to go out on raids, it ain't bad."

"The heat; I can't stand this heat. I'm from Washington State where it's cool and rains all the time. I never want to see desert again after this duty."

263

"That's if we live to get outa here. Ya just never know. Ya could die tomorrow and that's the truth."

As Charley was talking, an RPG zoomed over their heads and hit the truck behind them. They stopped and Charley and the other Marine named Dan, got out of the truck and walked back to the mangled vehicle, smoke rising from the cab. The driver was alive and walking around to the rear of the truck, looking inside.

"They got us again. Don't know where that came from."

"Is everybody okay?" asked Charley.

"No, two dead and one wounded. I've radioed for a medic to take Tom out. He's pretty bad though, don't know if he'll make it back to the hospital," the soldier said as he put his hand to his forehead. "You guys get out of here. We'll handle this. And you've got precious cargo"

Charley and Dan came back to the truck, shaking their heads. They got back into the truck and continued to drive on in silence and Mohammed thought better of saying anything the rest of the trip. He thought about the thousands of Iraqis that had died in this bogus war and now seeing the Americans being killed made him feel very sad because he knew they had families back home as well.

When they arrived at Mohammed's house, his family was waiting for him and threw open the door and ran out to greet them, both parents enveloping them in their arms with tears falling.

"We're so glad you're safe. We thought you might not come back to us," said Jabar as he embraced his son, all anger of the night before forgotten.

And the family ushered them inside with many questions as to what had happened to them in the weeks that they had been missing. Mohammed told his family about Simone searching for Andrew and the meeting with Amahl and then being taken to the compound and all of the horrific events that followed.

"We knew something terrible had happened to you when the police found my car in a back alley six kilometers from our house," Jabar said. "We were afraid to call the police at first, but your mother said that we must and she was right."

"We feared the worst, that you two had been kidnapped and killed," said his mother. "But we never got a ransom note and when your bodies didn't show up in the desert, we hoped that you were still alive."

"We are so happy that you are both back safe and alive. Simone, your father and mother have been frantic. I called last night to tell them that you were coming home safe and they were so relieved," said Jabar.

"How soon can I get a plane ticket to Paris?" asked Simone.

"I made a reservation for you for tomorrow afternoon. Will that be soon enough?"

"I've enjoyed the visit, up until the last few weeks, but I do want to get back to Paris."

"We understand," said Thana.

And then the family sat down to a celebration feast, with lamb and rice, fresh vegetables and breads with red and white wine. Thana had made special cakes for desert and they ate until they could eat no more. After talking late into the night, they retired to their bedrooms and Simone lay awake long after thinking of the nightmare she had just been through and how fortunate she was to be alive and going home. She heard explosions somewhere in the city and closed her eyes and dreamt of her home, Paris.

Chapter 37

Election Day

As the mid term election drew near, the pace picked up and Carol found that one day ran into another. She felt like a race horse in a perpetual race going round and round the track with no end in sight. Her day ended at twelve or sometimes after and she was up at five every morning planning her new day and bracing for the barrage of press bombarding her with questions and people crushing her, smothering her with handshakes. She tried to tell herself this would soon be over, but then as she lay down on her bed at night and tried to soothe her injured hands, she felt as she had when she was campaigning with James in his bid for president. At times she thought she couldn't go on for another day.

And then there was the worry about money. Because she had refused to take special interest money, they were always behind the other candidates and that required more fundraisers, more rubbery, stomach churning chicken dinners and more handshaking. One evening as she was being surrounded by the crowd, her mind flashed back to the day on the beach in Spain when the agents, in trying to capture her, had tackled her and brought her to the ground. She shook her head and then came back to the moment. The end is near, the end is in sight; she had to remember why she was here. If she is elected, she thought, she would try to bring peace to her country once more. She would try to protect the environment, promote alternative fuels, and bring good jobs back to America. This was her pledge to the people of America.

And as the election drew even closer, Larry, her opponent, tried to portray Carol not only as mentally ill, but also as an incompetent person, not qualified for the job. There were TV ads every day asking the question of what Carol would do once she was in Washington. How could Carol, a former school teacher, take on a job she knew nothing about? And Carol's campaign came back with television ads saying that she knew as much and maybe more than Larry about being a senator after having had a view from the top, the White House for four years. She had been a Washington insider, as the saying goes. She knew people in high places and she knew how things were done inside the beltway.

It would be close. Carol and her campaign manager watched the polls daily now and they showed Carol with a two percent lead for several weeks and then she was trailing by three percent up until the week before the election.

November seventh rolled in with a vengeance; a dust storm followed by a thunderstorm and then snow all in one day in Denver. The local weathermen said they had never seen anything like this before. But Carol saw this as a good omen. She was going to win, go to Washington, shake up the status quo and bring change for her state and the nation.

Carol voted at her precinct early in the morning, seven AM, followed by the press lurking behind her as she emerged from the voting booth and handed her ballot to one of the election officials. As she left the high school, her thoughts went back to the days when she was a teacher so very long ago, in another lifetime. She walked out into the parking lot toward her car thinking it was finally over and either she would win or not and there was no more that she could say or do at this point in time. What to do now? She decided to go back to her apartment and spend the day cleaning up paper work and then later head down to her campaign headquarters to await the results. She suddenly felt very alone. Larry undoubtedly would be surrounded by friends and family, his wife and three children. Carol's family, her only son was somewhere in the Middle East. And she had no husband, nor any real prospects for having one unless she counted Marshal or Claude. She had very few real friends and had no time to cultivate new ones in the year she had been back in the country. And she didn't see that changing anytime soon. What loomed ahead for her would be more of the same; a kind of isolation, yet surrounded by people wanting something from her. You could not form friendships and play politics at the same time. And she couldn't see herself marrying at a time like this. She would have no time to devote to a new husband.

Driving into her apartment garage, she erased her negative thoughts and started thinking of the new adventure she was going to have in Washington. Yes, that would be her approach. This was going to be the adventure of her life. She went to her apartment, opened the door and saw the light blinking on her answering machine. There were numerous messages, as always, one from her campaign manager telling her to be at campaign headquarters, which had been moved to the downtown Hyatt Regency, early to watch the returns.

"We're going to have the party to end all parties," said Charlotte in one message. But Carol wasn't interested in parties. There was another from her best friend Karen wishing her luck, a message from James, one from Marshal and another from Claude. She decided to call Claude.

His phone rang five times before he answered.

"Allo," he said with his deep voice.

"Claude, I got your message, thought I'd give you a call back."

"Oh, Carol. I am so glad to talk with you. How are you? How is the election going? Are the results in yet? Well, no they couldn't be could they, it's only 8:00 a.m. your time."

"No, it will be hours before we know anything. We may not even know tonight with the race being so close."

"Carol, I had a call from Simone. She's back in Paris you know."

"No, I didn't know. I've been consumed with the election. How is she?"

"She said she was fine but she had a harrowing experience. They kidnapped her and raped her …. it was a most horrific experience for her. But she is one brave lady, let me tell you."

"I am so sorry to hear that. Did she have any news of Andrew?"

"Well, she said that the men who kidnapped her might know where Andrew is. And the Americans captured those men and have them in custody and they are interrogating them to try to get more information. I wouldn't be too hopeful though. Andrew is their wild card. They will use him as a bargaining tool to persuade the Americans to pull out of their country."

"I think you're right about that. But maybe that also insures his life. If he is a bargaining tool, they will want to keep him alive. He is no good to them if he is dead."

"I hope that is true," said Claude. There was silence for a minute or two. Then Claude spoke again. "Carol, I wish you luck today. But part of me does not want you to win. I feel that if you win, I will lose you forever."

"Don't say that, Claude. No matter what, we will always be friends."

"I want to be more than friends. Can you come over again, maybe for the holiday?'

"I can't promise anything right now. Let's see how it all plays out and I'll tell you more."

"I love you Carol."

"I love you too, Claude."

Carol hung up the phone and felt even more alone than she had before. She had an urge to call James and ask him to come to her apartment and spend the day but that thought passed just as quickly as it had come. She threw down her jacket, rolled up her sleeves and went into her office. The piles of paper were everywhere. School papers, campaign notices, and insurance papers. Fortunately she had the sense to put her bills in one corner so they wouldn't be buried and lost under this snowstorm of paper.

She thought about how funny it was when personal computers became popular and everyone was saying that soon we would have a paperless society. If anything, PCs just generated more paper faster than before.

She started by gathering piles of papers to file and got through two of them by noon time. She then decided to turn on the news to see if there was any word on the election. The weather had finally settled down although there was a dusting of white on the eastern slope. A reporter stood outside one of the polling stations saying the turnout was very heavy. That was good, she thought.

Carol went into the kitchen and fixed a sandwich and poured a glass of wine. Was she celebrating early? She took the sandwich into the dining room and ate while she looked out at the view of the mountains with dark clouds hanging above them. More snow tonight, she thought.

The skiers would be happy. She looked at the diamond ring on her right hand that Claude had given her. She didn't wear it often but she wore it today thinking it might bring her luck.

She then went back into her office to try to finish the boring job of organizing and cleaning. She wanted to finish this and have it done.

Carol looked at her watch; it was four o'clock. Where had the time gone? She yawned and thought a nap was in order. She might be up very late tonight. She went to her bedroom and pulled down the comforter, took off her shoes and crawled onto her queen sized bed and buried her head in the pillow and in no time was asleep.

When she awoke, it was dark outside. She looked at the clock beside her bed; it was six o'clock. She had slept a good two hours. Must have been the wine she thought. She climbed out of bed and went into the bathroom and as she was combing her hair, the phone rang. She ran to answer it and it was James.

"Carol, do you want me to be with you tonight?" he said in his booming voice.

"No, that's sweet of you James, but I don't think that's a good idea. I have to do this by myself."

"Well, I am pulling for you. Have you watched the news? They've had the largest turnout of voters since the eighties."

"That's encouraging. But we'll see tonight."

"I'll be watching the returns. Hope you win Carol. I know you want this."

"Thanks James. Thanks for your support. I'll talk to you soon."

Carol made some soup for supper and then went into the bedroom and selected a burgundy suit from the closet. She showered and then dressed. She combed her hair and put on her makeup with great care. She would be on camera tonight to be sure whether she won or lost.

By eight o'clock she felt it was time to head for the hotel, as much as she was now enjoying the quiet and solitude. When she arrived half an hour later, chaos met her at the door. There were people everywhere; taking phone calls, talking to the press, just talking to each other and when she entered the room, a cheer went up and the people, mostly volunteers, chanted, "Carol is a winner, Carol is a winner". Carol blushed and smiled at the same time. There was a enormous plasma television screen on the back wall and the returns were coming in fast with fifty percent of the precincts reporting in and Carol was ahead by 1034 votes.

Carol went to the podium, shaking hands with people on the way and stood in front of the microphone as the lights shone on her salt and pepper hair and the cameras started to run.

"Thank you all. We haven't won yet, but it is looking brighter every moment and I think we have a good chance." Everyone cheered. "I just want to take this moment and give my heartfelt thanks to all of you for your hard work. You are the people who made this happen. I couldn't have done this without you and I am grateful. It has been a tough campaign as you well know, but I don't think any one of you wavered, even when I did and that's what it takes to win. You all have it in you to stay on track and keep on going even when the going gets tough. I am indebted to you. Thank you again."

Carol stepped down and the music played. The room was feverish with activity and a party atmosphere prevailed. An hour later, with more returns, Carol had a 2300 point lead and at midnight, more than 3500. Everyone was anxiously awaiting a concession speech from Larry and they weren't disappointed. At fifteen past midnight, Larry spoke from his home in North Denver. He talked for only ten minutes conceding that he had lost the race and wished Carol good luck. And then the partying began in earnest. And Carol after making a brief statement to the press, deftly slipped away to go home and rest. She had won, but what had she won, she wondered as she was driving home on the deserted streets of Denver. Would she be up to the job that the people of the state of Denver had overwhelmingly bestowed on her? She would do her best. That was all she could do.

Chapter 38

Junior Senator

Carol arrived in Washington DC two weeks before the 110th Congress was to convene. She needed to find an apartment and set up her office, located in the Hart Senate Office building on Constitution Avenue and Second Street. Setting up the office was the easy part, although, because she was the Junior Senator from Colorado, she was assigned a small dingy area on the third floor in the back of the building with only one small window and a miniscule outer office for her secretary. But the size of her office was unimportant; she would be spending very little time there. She had hired Susan Carlson, one of the young women who had worked diligently on her senatorial campaign, to come to Washington and work as her office manager. Susan had not arrived as yet, but many of Carol's boxes of papers were stacked in the outer office, waiting to be organized and filed in the empty file cabinets.

Finding an apartment was a different matter. If Carol wanted to live close to the Capitol, the rents were out of sight, starting at 1500 a month for a studio, no less and going up to 4400 for a two bedroom in the Chevy Chase area. After spending three days looking in the high rent districts of Georgetown, DuPont Circle and Foggy Bottom, all very near the capitol, she decided to go across the Potomac to Alexandria and it was there that she found a small, furnished studio in the back of a very historic home on E. Maple Street with a deli and a grocery store within walking distance. There was bus service to the Capitol a block away and if sessions ran late into the night, Carol thought she could crash on the couch in her office.

There were photo ops and parties to attend leading up to the swearing in ceremonies on January 4th. As they were taking the traditional photo of the new junior senators on the step of the Capitol, Carol finally realized she had arrived; she was indeed the new Senator from Colorado.

The day of the swearing in ceremony started with a clear cold blue sky. It had snowed again the night before and the new snow was dazzling in the bright sun. The ceremony was held in the Senate chambers at noon. When her turn came, Carol walked to the podium, raising her right hand and placing her left hand on the bible, declared that she would uphold the Constitution of the United States of America, with a government for the people, by the people and in her heart she pledged to work for her state of Colorado, but more importantly, the people of America. As she finished reciting the oath of office, a tear slipped down her cheek. Her thoughts were with Andrew. He should be here with me, she thought. But he would be; she was determined to make that happen. She was in a more powerful place now, a place where laws of the land were made, where important decisions were pondered, debated and decided and she was a part of this.

Senate business started in earnest the day after the ceremony. For the first time in six years, the Democrats held a majority in the both the House and the Senate and they were not wasting any time addressing the issues for their constituents, the people of America. The Iraq war was at the top of the list and after that, special interest lobby reform, campaign finance reform, raising the minimum wage and immigration. Environment and global warming were also rising to the top of the agenda. These were issues that had been pushed aside and dismissed by the majority Patriots Congress in the past six years but now there would be legislation coming out of the house and bills sent to the president for his signature. And therein lay the problem. To write and pass a bill that would satisfy the needs of the Patriots and the American people, and one the president of the opposing party would sign, was the trick of the day. Carol now began to see the complexity of politics on the Hill. But she had known this before, had seen it when James was president. She wondered that any legislation was passed at all.

Jane Harkins, Representative from California became the new House Majority leader and Jane presented her agenda for the first 100 days of the new session and it was aggressive. The House, with 435 members, represents each state proportionately by its population, with California being the most populous, having fifty-three members. The House has the power to initiate revenue bills and the majority party in power sets the agenda deciding which bills will be brought to the floor for consideration and voted on and then sent to the Senate to be amended and voted on again becoming law if the president then signs the bill and does not veto. Representatives in the House serve a two-year term and may be reelected an unlimited number of times, while members of congress serve six- year terms.

And so, with a backlog of bills waiting for consideration, coming across from the House to the Senate, the pace continued at break neck speed and Carol found herself spending more nights crashing on her couch in her office than she had wanted, in order to be on the floor when it was time to vote. Reading each bill, so that she had an understanding of what she was voting for, became another immense hurdle for her as it was for every senator. Some of the bills were hundreds and sometimes thousands of pages in length and this is where Carol had to depend on her aids and others in her office to assist in sorting through the legalese and verbiage only a lawyer could understand and get to the meat of the matter of what these bills were all about. And then Carol soon found that, often times buried within the bill were earmarks appropriating and allocating money for special projects designated by members for their constituents. She found many of these earmarks to be innocuous, but there were some that were outrageously frivolous in wasting tax dollars. The decision then to vote for the bill would become extremely difficult. Should she vote for a bill that provided health care for children of the working poor, which also contained directives in allocating money to replenish sand for beach front homes of the wealthy in North Carolina after hurricane season had washed them away? It was heart wrenching.

Carol had a solution however, to try and get on the Appropriations committee where the decisions on the spending bills were made and ear marks were tacked on and scrutinized. But then she changed her mind. Was this the most important committee for her to be on? Wasn't she in Washington to help end the war in Iraq and prevent subsequent wars in the future? She then asked to be on the Armed Services Committee, a much more relevant committee for her purposes and was surprised when she was told that she had been accepted. Committee appointments are made according to seniority, but also in proportion to majority party. Carol decided that she was beginning her senatorial career in a position of power, even though she was the junior Senator from Colorado.

Chapter 39

Carol Goes to Iraq

Carol was relentless in her desire to present a bill before the house and the Senate to bring United States troops home from the Iraq battlefield. It could be said and was probably true that she had a selfish reason for doing so; to bring her imprisoned son home safely, but in her heart this was an altruistic gesture as well. She was getting reports and seeing first hand the ravages of war. She visited the wounded at Walter Reed hospital and saw men and women without legs or arms, sometimes both, their lives changed forever. For the most part these courageous men and women put up a brave front and tried to overcome the loss of limb, wanting to get on with their lives. But there was no doubt; their lives would be different from this day forward. And then there were the families whose son, daughter, husband, wife or sibling came home in a flag draped coffin. Carol contacted some of these families and went to funerals to pay her respect to the sacrifice these people had made for their country and government. But for what purpose, she always wondered? In her mind this war was, like most, an unnecessary war for power and greed. It was a geopolitical war to make money for the oil companies, war profiteers and contracting companies now in Iraq. These were the companies that benefited from the war. In her research she was proven right time and again. She had read about contracts given out early in the war to US firms with no contest, when Iraqis had made lower bids for the same contract. What was that all about, if not greed and avarice? And she saw how the conglomerate oil companies were making obscene profits from the inflation of crude oil from twenty five dollars a barrel before the war to over 100 dollars a barrel two years after the war began, driving up the cost at the pump to well over three dollars a gallon. And she discovered that many in congress had ties to these companies and would make obscene profits from the war as well. Was that why so many voted for the war when it was brought before congress? And is this what young men and women were giving up their lives for? It certainly wasn't Saddam's weapons; there were none. It wasn't to bring democracy to Iraq and the Middle East; Iraq was in the midst of a civil war and its government, like the war itself was failing and there was no way of knowing what form of government would emerge from the chaos at hand. Saddam had held the country, made up of many tribes, together with an iron fist policy. But now, the Shiites, who were the majority in Iraq, were gaining control and they were allies with Iran.

But just reading about the war and doing research was not enough for Carol. She needed to go to Iraq to see for herself. As a member of the Senate and of the Armed Services committee, she was now authorized to travel to Baghdad and could make her own assessment from personal observation. And she could then talk to the Generals in command and implore them to find her son and get him released. A bipartisan group of four Senators would be leaving next week for Baghdad and Carol would be among the four. She had little time to be excited about the trip in her preparation. She called her peace activist friend Debra Johanson the night before she was to leave to let her know that she would be traveling to Iraq some time soon. She couldn't tell Debra the exact date; all trips by congressional members to the Middle East were top secret. "Oh, what an opportunity" Debra said. "Now you can see the effects of this war firsthand and report to the American people."

"I don't expect to see much outside the Green Zone, it is very dangerous. But I will be able to talk with General Markham and urge him to bring an end to this horrific war and to find Andrew so we can bring him home as well."

"Still, you will see how Baghdad has been battered and the Iraqi people there are so much worse off now after the US attacked. I have heard that millions of people have fled the country and are now living in Syria and other countries. And those who stay have to face death and uncertainty every day. It's a travesty."

"Yes, I know, I agree with you. I'll call you when I get back. And then I would like to come back to Denver and talk to your Peace group again. I like the idea of renaming the movement to Peace Activist instead of Anti War. It is so much more positive and I hope we win this," said Carol. And she hung up the phone.

It was 4:00 a.m. before she could get to sleep. Oh, well, I'll sleep on the airplane, she thought. She had packed a small duffle bag with only essentials; a large t-shirt for sleeping, one change of clothing, a few cosmetics and a notebook to keep a log of her experiences for the next three days. It was to be in and out in that amount of time to minimize the risk of going to a very dangerous war zone. Their trip had not been advertised, not even the military brass in Iraq knew they were coming.

Dressing in khaki pants, a blue shirt layered over a white short sleeved t-shirt and walking shoes, Carol considered herself ready for this latest adventure. Fortunately the weather would be cooler in February. Summertime temperatures often reached 120 degrees in Iraq and the heat would have been unbearable for her. She thought how brutal it must be for the soldiers day after day in that heat wearing army fatigues and flak jackets.

When she reached Andrews Airforce Base, she realized that sleeping would likely not be an option. They would fly in an Airforce military transport aircraft, a C-141 Star lifter 4. This aircraft was configured somewhat like a commercial airliner in that there were seats with seat belts, but it was bare bones and Carol soon found as they were airborne that the noise and vibration of the aircraft would preclude any notion of sleep. She had brought a book to read but she started making notes. Later in the day, it would be an eleven-hour flight to Baghdad, she talked to several of the other people, including some of the contractors going to Iraq to work. In addition to herself, the congressional members included two Patriot Senators, Paul Morton from Minnesota and Mary Sanchez from Texas. The other Democratic Senator, Philip Bly, was from California. It wasn't long before they were involved in a heated debate of the Iraq war, both the negative and positive aspects and the time went by quickly. Paul and Mary were hopeful that Iraq would become a model for democracy in the region and a catalyst for other

Middle Eastern nations to follow suit. They also were adamant in their belief that removing Saddam had been beneficial for the country. And of course, Carol and Philip said while, Saddam was not a benevolent dictator, the cost in lives and money was not worth it and the idea that democracy could thrive, even survive in a region that had been controlled by many tribes for thousands of years was not realistic.

Before Carol knew it they were being warned of the imminent landing at the now infamous Baghdad International Airport and what to expect during the approach. They were told that the aircraft would remain at as high an altitude as possible until the last five miles when they would be dropping rapidly to the ground in order to avoid the risk of being hit with RPGs or missiles. It would be something like landing in Salt Lake City, avoiding the surrounding mountains, only there were no mountains here; it was bullets they were avoiding.

The aircraft banked and took a dive and Carol's stomach did the same. But then in minutes they were taxiing on the ground and Carol looked out the window and saw pot holes in the runway where other bombs had hit. Their aircraft was the only one landing and they soon taxied up to the barbed wire fence. An official looking military person took over the aircraft's PA system and told everyone that they would be given flak jackets to wear and that those special visitors should stay with their group at all times; that it was very dangerous to do otherwise. Carol believed him.

After deplaning, her group of congressmen and women were herded like a gaggle of geese towards a convoy of white SUVs and vans waiting to take them to the green zone. Carol climbed into the back seat of one of the portentous looking vehicles and soon they were driving away from the airport heading towards Baghdad. Carol tried to peer out the window to see what the surrounding countryside looked like and all she could see were burned vehicles, huge holes in the ground and the debris of war everywhere. They approached a checkpoint but were waved on.

She saw very few people in the countryside but as they approached Baghdad, more people appeared on the streets, apparently trying to carry on with their daily activities even though their city and country were being ravaged by many military factions every day.

The convoy speedily moved through the city, likely due to the high danger of being attacked, and before long Carol could see the "T-Walls" (reinforced and blast-proof concrete slabs) and barricades of the Green Zone. They passed through three checkpoints punctuated with coils of razor wire and chain link fences, and soon were inside the walls of the very plush, albeit heavily guarded compound, formerly the palace of Saddam Hussein, presently being occupied by American military and contracting personnel. It was like stepping into another world, a city within a city; lush lawns, towering date palms, koi ponds and beautiful flowering shrubs everywhere. Be it not for the occasional sound of bombs in the distance, one would never know there was a war going on here.

They were escorted into a building in the center of the complex, where a sumptuous lunch of pita sandwiches and fresh fruit was served to them and then they were taken to a lovely villa, probably once used by Saddam's family and friends. The Sergeant riding with the driver, told them this was where they would be staying for the next three days and to settle in, and rest up and a military "taxi" would be picking them up at 7:00 p.m for dinner where they would be addressed by the top military commander in Iraq, General Lawrence Markham. Carol was looking forward to hearing him speak, hoping to know more about the war and the direction it would be taking in the months ahead. But she was also anxious to meet with him and plead with him to take action in finding and releasing her son.

Carol awoke to the sound of bombs exploding very near her villa. What time was it? She looked at her watch; 9:00 a.m. Baghdad time. She heard the loud knock on her door and when she opened it there was a young soldier standing there holding an automatic rifle.

"Ma'am, you'd better go with me to the shelter. They're bombing us again and we can't guarantee your safety if you stay here."

"Yes, let me put on my jeans and I'll be right there," Carol said.

The soldier took her across the yard and into a bunker filled with about twenty or so other people from the compound, some of them her traveling companions. Most everyone had an anxious look on their face, like they were about to be hit by a tornado and didn't know what the outcome would be. Carol turned to a young man in a military uniform sitting next to her and asked if this was a regular occurrence.

"We've been getting a lot more of this lately. They're becoming more emboldened for some reason," he said.

"And who are they?" Carol asked

"We're not really sure. Could be insurgents, the Shiites, the Sunnis, or it could be al Qaeda. I don't think any of these people want us here anymore."

"If we pull our troops out now what will happen to this country?" Carol asked. She was beginning to have a different picture of Iraq than she had before she came there.

"Well, that's one of the problems we're facing here. We can't just leave them in this mess. We have to get them somewhat back on their feet so they can take care of themselves. We're the target but it's the civilians that take the brunt of this war."

They waited twenty minutes and there were no more bombs. The same young soldier told them they could leave and go back to their rooms or go about their business. Carol walked back to her villa. She had a meeting with General Markham in one hour and she wanted to prepare.

In another part of Iraq, the morning sun was rising on another kind of compound, one of mud walls, bars on windows and steel doors. Andrew lay in his cot thinking about his life and wondering when the US military would be rescuing him. He thought about this every day and conjured up the Hollywood scenarios of Special Forces storming the prison, going from cell to cell looking for him. Sometimes he thought he heard them yelling in the hall outside his cell and he thought, oh this is good. They've come for me and I'm going to be freed. But no one came and the days dragged on.

He wasn't being mistreated; they weren't torturing him. But being caged like an animal in a zoo, in this small room day after day with little or no human contact was torture enough. Every couple of weeks they took him to a room where they would video tape him shackled to a chair with guns at his head or a knife to his throat; a propaganda video that his captors hoped would bring around the US officials in Washington to bow to their demands of pulling out of Iraq. But to no avail.

And little did Andrew know that as he lay there, his mother was but several hundred miles from his prison, speaking on his behalf to the Commander of the Army to find him and get him released. And so he fantasized, hoping every day his dream would come true. There wasn't much else he could do.

Carol sat in a wooden chair outside Commander Markham's office. A male secretary sat at a desk outside the office, typing furiously on his computer keyboard and when the phone rang he motioned to Carol and showed her into the Commander's oversized office with a large pained window overlooking a tropical garden of palm trees and ferns. Maps of Baghdad, Basra, Karbala, and Fallujah covered the wall opposite the window and a large map of Iraq and the region hung behind his desk. Carol recognized many of these names only because they had been in the news in the past several years. Ten years ago she would not have known these cities.

"Mrs. Walters. What an honor. Please sit down." General Markham shook her hand and motioned towards a chair in front of his outsized oak desk covered with papers. He was an imposing person exuding the archetype of military commanders with his stature, a full head of graying hair, pressed uniform and spit polished shoes, shiny as a mirror.

"Thank you, Commander Markham. I am pleased to meet you and I appreciate your making the time to see me."

"Please call me Larry. And I am pleased to meet the wife of our former Commander in Chief, your husband James."

"I come here not as the wife of a former president, but as a congresswoman speaking for my constituents," Carol said thinking how patronizing his words were, however she also felt she was able to have this meeting with him because she was a former first lady.

"Ah, yes of course. Why else would you be here then."

"General...uh, Larry," Carol was having difficulty calling this six foot four, distinguished looking person by his first name, "I came here representing the people, Americans who are calling for the military to withdraw from Iraq. But, even though I have been here only two days, I see what a problem that would be for the Iraqi people."

"I understand what you're saying. You know, I was against this war when we came in here. And I am still against it. It was unnecessary and many of my colleagues felt the same as I did. But we are here now and we have to get these people back on their feet, get the Iraqi government stable and the security working to protect the civilian Iraqis. Too many innocent people have lost their lives already. When this happens, and I hope it will be soon, we can bring our men and women home."

"I am really glad to hear you say this," Carol said, surprised at his candor, warming up to the general a bit more. "But I'm also here as a mother. As you know, my son Andrew was abducted several months ago and I and others believe he is being held in Iraq somewhere. What are you doing to try to find him?"

The general turned in his swivel chair to gaze momentarily out the window and then he turned back to face Carol. "I know how you must feel, knowing the danger your son is in. We have people working on it, but they haven't come up with anything yet. I think it's going to take some time. To be honest with you, I haven't been following this. I have priorities and those are the boots on the ground and the military skirmishes we're dealing with every day."

Carol felt dejected. How could she convince him to take a more active role on behalf of her son?

"Larry, I understand the pressure you're under. But this is a matter of national security. The faction who took him is dangerous and could conceivably kidnap others, even our military personnel. I would think it would behoove you to find out who they are and where Andrew is being held."

"When you put it that way, you could be right. I'll see to it that we allocate more resources. There are kidnappings in Baghdad and all over Iraq every day. This place has become lawless and we have to change that and soon."

"Thank you, Larry. I trust you to be true to your word," Carol said as she looked squarely into his eyes. "Thanks for taking the time to see me. As you must know, these past few months have been so frustrating for me. I am a woman of action, but there was nothing that I could do about this, but hope others would take the initiative and find my son. And now, I'm confidant that will happen."

They continued talking for another few minutes about the war and what was going on in the States and then Carol rose to leave. She shook the General's hand and turned to walk out the door, but just as she was about to leave, she turned around and said, "General, Larry, I think you are truly a good person. I think you really care for people, our people and the Iraqis and I like that."

The General blushed.

The next day Carol and the other senators were taken to Camp Falcon southeast of Baghdad to mingle and talk with the troops. This base was part of an 800 million dollar project to build half dozen camps for the incoming 1st Calvary Division called Enduring camps, built with the purpose of providing improved living quarters for the soldiers, to be returned to the emerging government within the next five to ten years. This base of five thousand soldiers was deemed to be the safest one for them to visit.

Riding in the van, Carol was able to get a better view of the city and the countryside as they traveled the eleven kilometers from the Green Zone to the base and what she saw was appalling. The ravages of war were everywhere to be seen. The streets that had reverted to mud were pocked by bombs and skeletons of vehicles lay strewn across the landscape here and there. Some buildings and houses were still intact but many were half standing with walls missing or some with huge holes in the walls. Carol thought this might compare to the London Blitz, Arab style. They arrived at the base and drove through more concrete barriers and then came to a guard gate in the surrounding wall, stopped to be identified and were escorted on into the compound.

"Stay with the group at all times," their young escorting officer named Mark barked at them as the got out of the vehicle. "I'm taking you to the mess hall and we'll have lunch with the division. There aren't that many here today, most are out on patrol. But you should get a good idea of what life is like for these desert warriors in Iraq."

Carol looked around at the base and it looked well organized, neat and clean, albeit dusty from the dirt roads winding through the complex. They entered the enormous mess hall where probably 200 or more soldiers were eating at long tables.

"Ladies and gentlemen, I have a treat for you today. We have some special visitors from home, Congressman Paul Morton from Minnesota, Congresswoman Carol Walters from Colorado..." Mark introduced them all and told the men they would spend an hour or two talking to them. Then Mark turned to the senators and told them to get into the cafeteria line, get some food and find a table. Carol did just that.

Looking at the food, she was amazed at the many selections from salads to entrees of chicken, steak, fish with vegetables and potatoes or rice and it looked to be well prepared. And then the deserts, cakes and pies with several flavors of Dreyers ice cream. At least we are feeding them well, she thought and that was good.

She gathered her food, chicken breast with broccoli and mashed potatoes, picked up some chocolate cake with vanilla ice cream and found a table. There were fifteen or twenty men and women sitting at her table and they warmly welcomed her.

"What's the news from home?" one young woman asked.

"How're the Denver Nuggets doing these days," another male soldier asked.

Carol was happy to answer their many questions. Then she said, "I'm here to find out how you are all doing. It looks like you're eating well."

They laughed. "Yes, we are, ma'am," an older male soldier with a dark complexion named Melvin said. "We're doing as well as we can."

"It must be tough going out there on patrol every day. Do you think it is getting any better?" Carol asked.

"No, I think it's getting worse," said Melvin. "But we have a job to do and we just do the best we can every day. We are here to protect the Iraqi people and try to bring order to the region."

"Is the Iraqi army taking over more of this responsibility?" Carol asked.

"Somewhat," another younger man named Peter answered. "We've been training them but mostly they're not soldier material and they're not committed to the job. And then some of them go back to the insurgents after we train them."

"That must be disheartening."

"It is but we're prepared for anything out here, so we shrug it off and keep on trudging."

"I want to commend all of you. You are doing an extraordinary job here and the people at home think so as well."

"I've heard Americans are really down on this war," a young woman named Susan said.

"It's true. But we are supporting you here. We know you're here now and the job has to be done before you can come home," said

Carol. She hesitated for a moment and then said, "I just want to ask all of you, what is bothering you most about this war?"

"I think the fact that we are deployed for an extended time now, fifteen months. Then we can be redeployed again after we've been home only a few months. We don't have time with our families anymore. I'm missing seeing my little boy grow up and my little girl is already in high school and I hardly know her anymore," said Melvin, his eyes moistening.

"Do you all feel this way? Carol asked and they nodded. "I understand and I will report this back to the committee and we'll try to change this. No doubt this is due to a lack of people available for the military these days. As you well know you guys and gals are part of an all volunteer army. Not like in the days of Viet Nam when we had the draft. What do you think about having a draft?"

Peter spoke first. "If we are going to be fighting wars like this on an ongoing basis, I think we need a draft."

"And it evens things out. Everyone has to participate, even those from wealthy families," said Peter.

"You know how that goes, though. The wealthy always find loopholes and get out of it," Susan said.

"As it stands now I don't think we'll be reinstating the draft, but we need to find a better way of deploying you guys so you can rest up and be with your families more," Carol said. "And I will tell them this when I get back to Washington."

Susan then asked if Carol had any word on her son and how sorry she was that he had been kidnapped. Carol told her there was no word on his whereabouts but that she had talked with the commander who said he would do what he could to find Andrew.

Carol finished her lunch, chatting more with the group about families and home. She was so glad that she had this chance to talk to the soldiers first hand although she knew they were not saying all that was on their minds. They couldn't.

"Again, I am so pleased to meet all of you and I know the people at home are so proud of you as well," Carol said as she was leaving. They all shook her hand and said they were honored to meet the former first lady turned senator. It warmed her heart, but now she had to go home and make it right for them and she hoped she could. She was only a junior senator.

*   *   *

Arriving back from her whirlwind tour of Iraq, Carol was caught up in the day to day, back biting issues of Washington. After seeing the conditions in Iraq and talking to many people, both civilian and military, she had changed her position on immediately bringing the troops home and now her main emphasis was trying to pass legislation that would at least limit the presence of US troops in Iraq and reduce the deployment time for them. She held a press conference, reporting to the American people that from her observation, Iraq was a non winnable war militarily and even if we stay there 100 years, the many Arab factions would continue to fight among themselves. Saddam had held them together with an iron fist when he was in power. Was that the role we wanted to play?

"What then is the solution for Iraq?" asked Brian Johnson, senior correspondent with Associated Press International, conducting a television interview of Senator Walters upon her return.

"Education and jobs," answered Carol. "The people of Iraq are no different than you and me in many ways. They are raising families and they need to support those families. If they can get the education to be able to have decent jobs to support their families, there will be little unrest and young men and women won't join the extremists. The people of Iraq want law and order, in fact are demanding it."

"But it can't be that simple," said Brian.

"It is and it isn't. But we also need to look at what is not working in the region and that is our military going house to house breaking down doors killing people whom they think are insurgents, later to find out they were ordinary civilians. But then, if you think about it, at this point every Iraqi could be considered an insurgent in this civil war. And we do need to find a way to help the different factions work together for the good of the country. Maybe that means splitting the country into different zones. You know when Saddam was in power, he had a unified country of sorts, even though he governed in an unorthodox way. But the people had relative freedom to work and move about as they pleased if they towed the line. And women were much freer; they could hold jobs and go to school. Now they can't go out of their homes without a male family escort. This is not progress."

The Patriots and hawks in Washington were outraged at her speaking out in this manner. How dare she raise questions about the validity of going to war? How dare she say that a military solution wasn't going to work? Senator Kenmore of South Carolina said that she didn't know what she was talking about and Senator Worland of Connecticut, a Democrat who voted more often than not with the Patriots, said the Junior Senator from Colorado wanted to cut and run and leave the Iraqi people in limbo.

The bill, H.R.123 proposed in the house came out of committee and passed in the house. It stated that we would give the Iraqi people six months to tighten up security and get their government working in passing legislation to share the wealth of the oil revenues with all factions, Sunni, Shiite and Kurds, for the rebuilding of Iraq. It also stated that after six months the US would remain in Iraq on a consulting basis only, to help rebuild the infrastructure, utilities, roadways and water to insure that they could move forward as a country and to help build schools for the young people coming up to gain skills they could use to earn a living wage.

This bill then went on to the senate with an amendment stating that funding for military action in Iraq would end after six months. The thought being that if there is no funding, the American forces would have to be brought home and military action in Iraq would come to a halt. It failed by a narrow margin, with voting along partisan lines and some Democrats crossing over to vote against it.

But then something miraculous happened. On the night of September 22, a prisoner from southern Iraq, emaciated and battered, was delivered to Camp Freedom in Mosul, home of Stryker Brigade 101. And that prisoner was Andrew Walters. The news spread fast, with the news agencies in Iraq first reporting it and then the foreign news bureaus, BBC, the Guardian and even Al Jazeera. The US news bureaus picked it up soon after.

Carol often times watched the BBC news early in the morning and as she was getting ready for work, she heard the report. "Andrew Walters, son of the former president of the United States has been released. He was brought to Camp Freedom in the middle of the night and ...."

Carol couldn't believe what she was hearing. Was it true or was she dreaming. But no, Andrew was safe and alive and he would be coming home soon. There were no pictures, and they said he was somewhat battered and undernourished, but yes, he was alive.

Carol immediately called the Pentagon and asked to talk with Major General Craig Wellington, now top commander of all US forces in Iraq. His secretary put her through immediately.

"Is it true? Has Andrew been released?"

"Yes, Mrs. …ah, I mean Senator Walters. He should be coming into Andrews Airforce base tomorrow afternoon. I'm sure you will want to be there to welcome him home."

Carol was so ecstatic she hardly knew what to do with herself. She called James and talked with him, telling him the news he already knew. She then called her parents and Marshal and even her friend Karen. She just couldn't go to work today; she would never be able to concentrate on anything. So she called her office and of course they had all heard the good news. She told them she would not be in for a couple of days, but to call her immediately if there was anything urgent, which she didn't think there would be, and then spent the rest of the day organizing her office at home, which she never had time to do and reading and watching the TV for any other news of Andrew. She looked around at her small studio apartment and wondered where she would put Andrew. Then she thought, he would take her bed of course and she would sleep on the hide a bed in the great room. But she would have to get a larger place soon, although he would most likely need to be hospitalized for awhile until he got his strength back.

The day passed more quickly than she thought and in no time it was the next morning and she was preparing to go to Andrews to meet her son and bring him home.

At 3:00 p.m. Carol was on the tarmac at Andrews waiting for his plane to come in. And then in another half hour she saw it in the sky, gliding in with her precious cargo. After landing, the plane taxied close to the hanger where she was waiting. The press was there as well, only in limited numbers as they were required to have a special pass to get into Andrews. Carol watched intently as she saw a line of military and civilian people walk down the ramp of the aircraft and then she saw a young, skeleton like, man limping down the ramp. Was that Andrew?

She barely recognized him. But yes, it had to be. She ran over to him and wrapped her arms around him, holding him and never wanting to let him go. Then she looked into his eyes.

"Andy, you're home. I'm so relieved you're finally home."

"Yes, Mom, I am. A bit worse for wear but I'm here," Andrew said optimistically.

A military medic approached and said that Andrew would be taken to Walter Reed Hospital for observation and rehabilitation and Carol said no, she would take him to her private doctor. But then the medic, who was a sergeant, reiterated that he had orders from above for Andrew to go to Walter Reed and something about a debriefing. Carol decided not to put up a fight. Her son was home, he was alive and that was what mattered now. She kissed him and let him go with the medical corp.

"I'll follow you," she said. "And I'll be there at the hospital when you get there." Carol did not want to let her son out of sight.

Andrew looked at her with hollow eyes, he smiled slightly, showing the missing front teeth and acknowledged her words with a shake of his head.

After they had whisked Andrew away, the press surrounded Carol.

"Why do you think they let him go, Senator Walters?" a reporter from UPI asked.

"I don't really know. I would hope it was due to our concerted efforts to communicate to the insurgents that we are willing to drawdown our troops."

"But that would be bowing to their demands. Is that what we did?" asked another from CNBC news. "Or did money change hands in this deal?"

"It could be that my meeting with General Markham encouraged him to take matters in his own hands and do the impossible, find my son, I'm not sure, and we may never know. All I know is he's alive and he is home and now I'm going to Walter Reed to make sure they take proper care of him. Goodbye gentlemen." And with that last statement, Carol turned and left the area, leaving the press to speculate among themselves.

Chapter 40

Carol for President

The headlines were everywhere for the next week and a half; news items, editorials, political pundits and journalists talking about the former president's son's release from Iraq, all speculating on how this had come about. And then, the rumors started, that it had to have been Carol's recent visit to Iraq and her meeting with Commander Markham. If she had accomplished the release of her son, when others had failed, she was indeed a powerful woman and they started saying that she should run for the office of president. Carol would have none of this. When interviewed by the press she repeatedly told them she had no knowledge that she had been responsible for the release of her son, that it was a combined effort of intelligence services and our government intervening and she was definitely not running for president.

Andrew remained hospitalized for the next month, regaining his strength through physical therapy and good wholesome food. He was beginning to look like the Andrew she once knew. His teeth were repaired, new implants replacing the ones that had been knocked out, and his smiles were becoming more frequent. He was finally released from the hospital and came to live with Carol in her small studio in Alexandria.

Of course James was right there with her forming the family unit once more. He wanted Andrew to come back to Colorado with him, but Carol would not allow it and so he helped Carol find a larger townhouse so that she and Andrew would be more comfortable.

"Are you going to take back the presidency?" Carol asked one day when James was visiting.

"No, I have other endeavors that I want to pursue," James said emphatically. "And are you going to make a run for the presidency? Rumors are that you will."

"Don't be silly James. Me, the president? I can't see it. Not in my lifetime."

"I can. I think you would make a great president."

Carol looked at James as if he were daft. "Why on this earth would I want to subject myself to something as difficult and humiliating as running for the office of the president of the United States?"

"Because you care about this country and the people who live here, that's why. I see things so differently now. When I was approached by the power brokers to enter into the war with Iraq after the Trade Center had been obliterated and three thousand of our citizens had been killed, like many people, I wanted revenge and they talked a good talk saying that we needed to position ourselves geopolitically in the Middle East so we would be able to control the oil. They tried to convince me that it was in the best interest of our country to do this and I bought it along with many other people. But it was wrong. We haven't accomplished anything. Oil prices are sky high, inflating the prices of almost everything. Thousands of lives have been lost and thousands of families will never be same again, both American and Iraqi. This was not the right thing to do for the country. Yes, the defense and oil companies are thriving, but our country is in trouble. And you were trying to tell me that when I was in office."

"I know, James. I know," Carol said with an "I told you so" attitude. "But if I became president I would be fodder for those same power brokers, the lobbyists, the congress, and my political enemies. I wouldn't be able to survive six months. It's money and greed that are in control of our government now."

"And that's why we need someone like you. You wouldn't have gone to war. You would have tried for a diplomatic solution."

"I think that's true. I think war should only happen as a last resort, after everything else has been tried and only then if our country is attacked first. And the 9-11 Trade Center doesn't count; it was not the Iraqis who attacked us. In fact it is very murky as to who was responsible for 9-11; we've never had a thorough investigation into the

Trade Center crime. But, you know as well I, there is no money to be made with diplomacy."

After having this conversation with James, Carol began to think differently about what he said. Would she make a good president? Could she bring about change to our government and find a balance between the working people and corporations? Could she bring back decent jobs to America, so that more people could share the wealth? Looking back in history, it was the post World War II era that brought tremendous prosperity to the United States. Men and women were coming back from the war attending college on the GI bill, graduating and getting good jobs that allowed them to buy a house and raise a family in a new and growing middle class society. The public schools were doing a good job of providing an education in the lower grades for everyone that wanted one. The companies rewarded long term employees with good pensions, and if a person faltered, there were safety nets with unemployment insurance put in place by congress with the Social Security act in 1935. In those days, parents could foresee a better future for their children than they had had. That was no longer true today. With companies reneging on pensions, sending jobs overseas, and now this administration wanting to privatize and ultimately eradicate Social Security, removing the safety nets people needed and deserved, leaving them without an income to support themselves in their later years. Carol wondered, if there were no Social Security, would families step up and take care of grandma and grandpa. Some would but many more would leave the elderly homeless and starving.

But the obstacles to running would be many. Raising enough money was the first hurdle that she thought of. Carol hated the long primary season and she felt that the amount of money candidates spent during this time was obscene. In America, you want to believe that in our democratic, egalitarian society, anyone can achieve the highest office of the land. But, for the most part, that was a myth. You had to be rich and she was not rich, not rich enough anyway. Or you had to get backing from those with money and that is where the special interests, the corporations, came into the game. When a candidate allows for campaign contributions from wealthy individuals or corporations, they expect payback. This has been a problem dating back to the 1800's in our country and it has yet to be thoroughly resolved. There have been numerous campaign finance reform bills, one recently passed in 2004, limiting the amounts that special interests can donate, but as with many of our laws, people find a way around them.

So if Carol wouldn't accept money from special interests, where would her funding come from? It would have to be from the people, a grass roots campaign. Would that be enough for her to win, competing with a candidate who had millions more dollars in their war chest than she?

And then she thought of all of the problems that would be passed along to her from this last administration. The wars and unrest in the world, the economy and jobs, the environment and global warming, developing alternative fuels, education, health care, Social Security, the list was endless. Would she be up to the task of taking on these mountainous issues for the people of her once great nation? Did she have the will? Did she have the vision for the country to fight for what she believed in? Then she began to look at all of these obstacles as opportunity; opportunity to bring massive changes to government that would help all of the people of America and the country as a whole for many years to come, and this was very appealing to her.

* * *

In another part of Washington, seven members of the National Democratic Party were meeting. The national election for the next president of the United States was two years away, but it was not too soon to start planning and selecting potential candidates for office, which they vowed they would win this next time around. And Carol's name came up.

"Have you been hearing the scuttlebutt lately, that Carol Walters could make a run for the White House," said Roy Blanchard, the committee chairman.

"She's so inexperienced," said Travis Wilson. "She's new to the senate this year, just a junior senator."

"And she's a woman. Is America ready for a female president?" asked Daniel Roberts.

"She is all of that, but the country loves her and they would follow her lead and I think she has a vision of where this country needs to go in order to remain a great nation," said Roy Blanchard.

And they argued on into the late evening, not coming to a consensus on whether Carol was a qualified, bona fide candidate.

*   *   *

And so it was on a chilly morning in March, that Carol called a press conference on the National Mall, below the steps of the Lincoln Memorial looking towards the Washington Monument, to officially announce her candidacy for the office of the President of the United States of America. Thousands of people filled the Mall in addition to all of the press corps, Associated Press, UPI, TV and cable network news agencies.

"I have called you all here today to tell you that I have made the momentous decision to run for the highest office in this land, the President of the United States and I am asking all of you for your support in the months ahead. I have a vision for this nation to again become the great country that it once was and to move ahead into the twenty first century with new ideas, new technologies, bringing jobs and prosperity once more to all in America. I see our nation as a leader once more, developing alternative fuels for use at home and abroad and curbing global warming. I see our nation with a health care system, serving the needs of everyone in America. I see our public education system as the best in the world, where everyone in our country can have the chance to achieve any dream possible. And I see the United States as a diplomatic leader in world, helping other nations to work together for the common good, peacefully solving problems in the Middle East, and other regions where there is conflict. In the next decades we will see challenges in the world of the like that we have never thought possible, climate change with droughts and severe storms, famine and starvation and if we don't take action now, we could all feel the affects of these devastating events. We are citizens of the world. We will start here at home; helping our nation and our people to be stronger, which will in turn insure our safety, providing better lives for everyone in America in the future."

There was applause from the crowd; cameras were flashing and video cams rolling. This was an historic moment and the debate had begun; can a woman become the president of the United States of America? The next two years would be the test for Carol and all women in America.

For not liking politics, I certainly get involved a lot, Carol thought as she was on her way to a political rally prior to the Wisconsin primary, probably her 500th rally since the campaign had started less than a year ago at this time. It was now February, just months before the end of the presidential election primary season and seven months before the Democratic Convention to be held in San Francisco this time around. As the noise had gotten louder day by day, Democrats and thousands of other people were clamoring for Carol to enter the race, and she had given in once more, although she had many misgivings about putting herself out there again. Firstly, she was a woman and the United States had never had a woman leader and she felt that many, especially those in the conservative states and many men, would not vote for a woman. There would be many women who would not vote for her because of her gender as well. And then there was the question of her competency; did she have the experience? Being only a junior senator, she had much to learn about the workings of Washington politics. But she had accomplished a great deal in her short time in the senate, working with the Armed Services committee, getting better health care for the veterans coming home from the war in Iraq, and many people saw that. And the majority in the country truly loved this former first lady and believed that she had shown her mettle, and would be a strong leader.

There was also something elemental in the people supporting her candidacy; as if many thought she was the last hope for the country to become whole again after being ravaged by the current administration, taking the country to war, spending through the federal surplus and creating a deficit that would take many years to pay off. Everything needed fixing, education, jobs, infrastructure, health care, the environment. With the starve the beast policy of her former husband's administration, agencies had been gutted, the FDA, FEMA, SEC causing career professionals to leave these agencies to be replaced by sycophants to the administration, people who did not have the knowledge and expertise to run the agencies, causing them to fail. These agencies would have to be brought back to former standards in order to again work for the public.

Workers needed new and better jobs and Carol was hopeful that creating alternative fuels would provide those new jobs as well as a product to export to other countries. And mending fences abroad, bringing our country back into the community of world nations after a go it alone foreign policy that failed miserably on many fronts would be a primary objective of her administration.

These were just some of the tasks Carol would have to address when she became president and there were moments when she herself wondered whether she could handle the job. Much of it, of course, depended on the makeup of the congress whether she would be able to accomplish her goals for the country and the political landscape was looking brighter every day. Twenty five Patriots and Republicans from the senate and the house were stepping down this year. She guessed they knew they would not survive the election with the approval rating for the Patriots being at an all time low. The tide was turning from ultra conservative politics, which in this administration had not really been conservative at all, as government had grown more than twelve per cent in the last seven years with most of this growth in wasteful military spending, to a more center left politics. There had also been an attempt to privatize federal agencies, making them for profit entities, which only drove up the cost to the American public while providing little oversight in their management.

And so it was on this cold Tuesday morning, as the primaries progressed, Carol was ahead in all of the polls, her only opponent at this point a young southern lawyer, male, and a populist who had union support. However, it was a very close race. Robert Calhoun, a former senator, bright, good looking and charismatic, had done very well in most states, including the Southern states. But Carol had swept California and New York and other states with large delegate counts. Being that the race was so close, it could come down to a decision by the super delegates and she was not sure how that would play out for her.

Carol was aware that the super delegates, formally called unelected party leaders, are selected, having tremendous clout in the Democratic Party. They comprise one fifth of the total party delegates, made up of senators, and other past and present office holders of the party. They are an independent bunch and it would be difficult to predict which way they would lean. Carol hoped that in the last remaining months of the campaign she could command a measurable lead, making it clear to the party that they should get behind her as the Democratic candidate for the president. She was doing everything in her power to do this and she had the money flowing in from grass roots supporters to fund the events, although she was taking some corporate money to pay for the expensive television ads that were so critical to any political campaign. Carol didn't agree with this kind of politics, but she had to go along with it at this point. She would try to change things after she got into office.

The race had already been decided on the other side. If she won the nomination for her party, she would be running against Douglas Heron, a senior senator from Indiana, a Viet Nam war veteran and a Patriot. This was his second try for the presidency. He was a military hawk, a proponent for the Iraq war and talked about starting another war with Iran. He had tried to woo the Religious Right, however, since he was not necessarily a religious person himself, he had not been that convincing so far. But since the field of candidates had been very disappointing for the opposition this year, Douglas came out on top every time, as the person most likely to beat the Democratic candidate. The challengers were running scared.

Now, if Carol had been exhausted before the campaign, with her duties as senator, continuing to take two classes in law school on line, and administering to her son, she was ten times more tired now. The days blurred into nights like an abstract watercolor. She always had her public face on, seemingly twenty four hours a day. Her hands were raw from shaking the hands of constituents, her voice ragged from yelling over the crowds voices and her stomach churning from the greasy food served at most of the events. If she got four hours of sleep a night, she considered herself fortunate.

But her campaign raised enough money to lease a jet, a Boeing 737-800 with *Carol Walters for President* painted along the fuselage, and this would save time and money for the campaign, allowing her and her team to visit more states in a shorter amount of time. And she had now been assigned Secret Service Agents, as was the custom when it became apparent that the field of candidates was narrowing. The first day they arrived at her home to escort her to airport, she couldn't help but think how these men had hounded her when she was first lady. But it was time to put that in the past.

James had offered to help with her campaign, but she declined his offer, thinking she didn't want anyone who had been associated with the current administration to be a part of her campaign. She was bringing in a new day for America, a change in policy across the board.

Andrew was feeling well enough, after weeks of therapy, and he accompanied her most of the time. Often Carol watched him as he spoke to the cheering crowds, thinking how lucky she was to have him back again. Her opponents on the other side accused her of using her son just to get votes, but no one was really buying that. They loved Andrew and he was an asset for the campaign. She thought that when she became president she would find a job for him in her cabinet. Wouldn't that be a unique combination; mother and son governing together?

It was time now for Carol to start thinking of a running mate. There were so many young, qualified people coming up in the party, that she was having a difficult time deciding on who the right person would be. Several people caught her eye, one being Paul Nelson, Governor of Minnesota. He had bucked the trend of the conservatives and had gotten legislature to reduce fuel emissions in the state's power plants, and for automobiles. She thought that was huge and would set the tone for what the rest of the country had to do to stem global warming. He was very personable and extremely bright. Another was Senator Alan Dwyer from North Carolina, again a proponent of new energy development and in addition a former military man and a member of the Armed Services committee with extensive experience in foreign policy. Alan had that charisma with the people as well as the ability to carry votes in the Deep South. She would make her final decision just prior to the convention in August, but it was not too soon to vet these people and get to know them to see if they would work well on her team. And the office of vice president was of most importance because this person was next in line to take over the presidency should anything happen to the president.

There was one downside to her decision to run for the highest office of the land. And that was Claude. When her decision was final she had called him before she had told anyone else and it was one of the most difficult phone calls she had ever had to make. She loved Claude and had even, at one time, imagined herself living out her life peacefully in the vineyard in Bordeaux as Claude's partner and helpmate, but in the big picture, it didn't hold up for her. She had a mission and until that mission was fulfilled, she couldn't be with Claude. And she also knew she couldn't ask him to wait.

His final words that night when she called to tell him were "*Avoir*, my love. You will always be on my mind. I will never forget the beautiful lady from America, sitting alone in the French café". And as she said goodbye, the tears were flowing freely. She said she wanted to send the ring back to him, but he wouldn't have it. "It is a keepsake from me to you, so you never forget me," Claude had said. And so he was gone from her life.

Later that night as Carol was tossing in her sleep, dreaming about Claude, she heard a deathlike cry. Was she still dreaming? She opened her eyes and she heard it again. It was coming from Andrew's room. She ran into his room and sitting down on the side of the bed, she wrapped her arms around him, and held him and rocked him, just as she had when he was a small child when he had the flu.

"It's okay," she said. "You're safe now. No one is going to harm you ever again."

Andrew was sobbing. "I have this same dream over and over again. I can't get it out of my head."

She continued to hold him. "It'll take time, but it will get better. That is what the doctor said. It just takes time."

Andrew was shivering and sweating at the same time. "I keep seeing the guards coming for me." He stopped and looked at his mother. "I never knew when they were going to lop off my head. When my life would be over."

They sat there for a time, holding each other. "You know Andrew how I love you and I will do everything I can to help you with this."

"I know, Mom. I know you do." And Andrew laid his head back on his pillow and closed his eyes.

Chapter 41

Another Convention

"Change is coming soon," chanted the multitudes packing Moscone Center in the heart of the financial district of San Francisco, California. Another convention. Carol remembered the last one she had attended in Chicago when James was nominated for his first term as president and this was much like that one seemingly so many years ago now, except, Carol was the candidate this time around. Douglas had conceded the night before as the delegates had reported in with their votes. It was the delegation from Minnesota that put her over the top.

And in the end it was the people's vote that won the nomination for her, not the super delegates and she was grateful for that. She had chosen her running mate, Alan Dwyer, senator from North Carolina with foreign policy experience who would carry the all important southern vote. In years past, prior to the civil rights movement, the south had almost always voted Democratic, but after President Johnson sold them out, or so they thought, in passing civil rights legislation guaranteeing equal rights under the law for blacks in the United States, the South moved to the right and joined the Republican party. Alan would bring balance to the ticket. Prior to becoming a senator, he had practiced law, fighting large cases against big business and HMO's.

This was the last night of the convention and the night Carol, along with her presumptive vice president, was to make an appearance before her adoring crowd and speak to them. It was eight thirty and Carol was late. Outside the convention center, crowds had gathered, some protestors, as is to be expected at these events. Carol's entourage arrived in a Lincoln Navigator with two Secret Service men, followed by another with Carol and Andrew and then a third car carrying Alan and his wife, Ellen. They drove into the underground garage, but Carol could see the crowds of people and the protestor's signs. What were they protesting, she wondered? She wanted to know; she wanted to know what the people thought, what they wanted from their government.

Exiting from the shiny, jet black car, closely shielded by the Secret Service, she and Andrew made their way into the convention center and onto the monstrous podium in front of the large hall filled with throngs of screaming, animated people waving signs, throwing confetti. Carol, dressed in a tomato red suit and Andrew in a dark navy Armani suit with a blue shirt and red tie, stepped onto the podium. The cheer went up from the crowd, with music blasting in the background. Carol's eyes adjusted to spotlights focused on her. She took Andrew's hand and then reached for Alan's and together raised them over their heads in victory. The crowd kept cheering; balloons were released from the ceiling to add to the mayhem. This went on for maybe ten minutes, all being televised in HD TV across the country. Then Carol and her team lowered their hands and she called for the crowd to quiet down so she could speak.

"I come before you tonight humbled that you have chosen me to be your candidate. I am confidant that I can win in November and together we can take our country back and make it whole again."

Cheers again went up from the crowd. And Carol again raised her hands to quiet them.

"We have much work to do, you and I. We need to get the jobs back for people so they can take care of their families, like they used to. I have a plan."

More applause and cheering.

"We need to get a Universal health care system, like they have in the senate, so that people can go to the doctor or the hospital and not bankrupt themselves in the process. I have a plan."

Again the cheers went up.

"We need to get alternative fuels in this country, and this by the way will bring the new high paying jobs, and give us a product we can export to the world. I have a plan."

"We need to provide for more environmental protection so that we have a healthy planet to pass down to our children. When we get the alternative fuels, we won't need to drill for oil and gas and we can protect our old growth forests and mountain areas. I have a plan for that too."

"And,' Carol looked at Andrew, "we need to bring our young men and women home from Iraq and Afghanistan and start using diplomacy instead of guns, to help those people solve their complex societal problems. But when we get alternative fuels, we won't need to be in the Middle East vying for oil any longer. I have a plan."

"And, lastly, we need to fix this sick economy and make it work for the majority of the people. At the present time, the wealthy in this country are just fine; they don't notice the jump in prices, five dollars for a gallon of milk and a loaf of bread, but I know you do. And I have a plan for that as well. Can you see where we are going here? All that I have talked about is interrelated. The alternative fuels will give us jobs and help to fix the economy and the environment and make people healthier. And bringing our soldiers home will save lives, first of all and reduces the amount we are spending on weapons of war and that will help in balancing the federal budget and help the economy. It is all tied together and I am going to ask one more thing of you. I want you all to be my partners in these endeavors and then, and only then can we make our country great again."

Carol stopped talking, but the crowd would not stop clapping and cheering and waving banners and flags.

She felt powerful. She felt confident. She was doing the right thing. She would be the catalyst that would turn America around. She was sure of that.

Carol flew directly to Ohio after the convention to keep the momentum going and to take advantage of the huge bounce from the national coverage of the convention. Ohio, traditionally conservative, had been a key state in the past two presidential elections, and it undoubtedly would remain so in this next election. An industrial state, having lost thousands of manufacturing jobs in the last six years, Ohio's unemployment rate was twice that of the rest of the nation, and Carol's plan was to persuade conservatives to vote Democratic this time around. Her thinking was that jobs were as important, or even more so to working people than security, which the opposition was touting as the major issue in the country. Certainly security was important, but if you don't have a decent paying job to provide for your family, what good is security? And she pointed out to them that pouring money into the war in Iraq was not bringing security to America; where the borders, shipping ports and chemical plants were still wide open with no money to secure them. And with our military stretched to its limits with wars on two fronts, if there was an attack at home, we would be unable to defend ourselves.

Douglas, on the other hand was touting his expertise in military defense and that the most important issue in our country today was keeping America strong militarily. He was a proponent of the current administration's foreign policy of striking a potential foe first and asking questions later, pre-emptive war, a policy that had been unthinkable in the years leading up to this time. In the past, war had more often than not, been a tactic of last resort.

Carol was out to debunk this theory that keeping the country militarily strong was the only way to keep America safe. In her mind, it would be jobs that would strengthen America again, putting money into people's pockets that would be spent for essentials and hence, more money circulating into the economy. This would grow companies, making them robust, so they would again hire more people and make capitol investments. The so called trickle down economic policies hadn't worked in the past and they weren't working now. Giving tax breaks to corporations, especially since two thirds of them paid little or no taxes anyway in locating their headquarters offshore, put more money into their pockets, but had they then hired more people? No. They had sent more jobs over seas; over four million jobs had left America since the current administration had been in office. She could never understand how that would help America grow strong. It was like giving large companies desert first and hoping they would eat the main course, and that never happened. They ate the desert and forgot about the pot roast. Especially when they paid out billions in bonuses to CEO's and top executives.

And as Carol had said in her speech at the convention, she did have a plan. Her plan was to provide incentives to develop alternate fuels, solar, wind power and to research others and then manufacture them. There were factories in Ohio standing empty that could be retrofitted for new industry. This would provide jobs for engineers, information technology, manufacturing, distribution and marketing. It would provide America with another means of heating and cooling homes and fuel for automobiles. She had another plan to retrofit buildings in large cities to become green, with solar and new insulation. This would make green collar jobs available to thousands of workers and grow the economy, making us less dependant on fossil fuel. And it would possibly give the United States a technology to export to other countries. Everyone would win.

At first people were skeptical, especially conservatives. But as she explained over and over again, putting money into these projects would, in the long run bring America back from the brink of bankruptcy, they started to believe that what she was saying was true.

Her next stop was Michigan, where the automobile industry was sinking fast due to the disappearing market for gas guzzling SUV's. When she spoke about alternative fuels and retooling to build cars to be more fuel efficient, the workers were on board. Management was slow to comprehend, however, but then the CEO's were only after one thing, short term profits for the shareholders and bonuses in their pockets. She pointed out to them that if, after Pearl Harbor manufacturing plants could be retrofitted in a year's time to build tanks, airplanes, and arms, this could be done today to build more fuel efficient automobiles for America.

It was then time to head west, stopping in the Midwestern states, the breadbasket of the nation. With so much of America's produce coming from foreign countries, Carol talked about the benefits of preserving and bringing back the family farm and locally grown, organic produce. She promised to help the more eco friendly small farmer, putting a cap on farm subsidies that had in the last thirty years primarily been going to the large factory farms making over a million dollars a year.

"In Europe, the family farmer is revered and helped to stay solvent. We need to do that in America," said Carol, when speaking to a group of farmers in Lincoln, Nebraska. This was risky talk for her; the larger, wealthy factory farms had more money and more clout. However, Carol and her team were telling the small farmer to organize and that together they could have the influence to compete in the marketplace.

Heading further west, the issues were different again, where people were concerned about logging, mining and drilling for gas and oil in the Rockies, Wyoming and Montana. There was an unusual coalition forming among ranchers and conservationists against big businesses that were trying to drill gas and oil wells in rancher's back yards. One rancher put it bluntly, "I don't want my land polluted and these wells are a blight on what was once a beautiful landscape. Is this the legacy we are leaving our children?"

Although the concerns were very diverse in every part of the country, there was a common thread among the people. Would they have jobs next year, would they have enough money to buy the essentials, food, clothing, gas for the car, pay the rent or mortgage and utilities and have enough to educate their children. And would they and their children have the chance to better themselves in the future; have a chance to earn more money, move up the ladder away from living day to day, worrying about where the next dollars would be coming from? And health care, how were they going to pay for health care? These were basics, not luxuries. Parents wanted to make sure that their children would be better off than they were and that was not possible in today's economy. The future had dimmed in the past eight years and did not look promising for the middle class.

After a month long tour of the country, getting a maximum of four hours of sleep every night, Carol was exhausted. But in another way she was exhilarated by the possibility that she could make a difference in the lives of Americans. If only they would see this and vote for her instead of her opponent who would continue with the same policies of tax breaks for the wealthy and perpetual war. Her message, however, was always the same throughout; Carol wasn't going to do it for them. They had to be partners in this and demand reform. Demand the soldiers be brought home so that, what had been billions of dollars going to Iraq and Afghanistan, would be brought home to pay for education, health care, renewed infrastructure and renewable energy resources at home.

It was turning out to be a tough race, not the slam dunk that her strategists had said it would be even though the Patriots were much in disfavor at the present time. The thinking was that in a year where the economy was in trouble, the wars in Iraq and Afghanistan were not going well with other troubles breaking out anew in Pakistan and Israel, education was failing, the housing problems, and so many without healthcare, that Americans would want something different. But the other party continued to play on fear, that another attack could happen at any time and we should be prepared and continue to build our military strength around the world.

And then the gender factor came into play along with the question of whether Carol had enough experience to run the country. Douglas was a veteran campaigner and they were pulling out all the stops, running ads saying that Carol had run out on her husband, would she run out on the country when the times were tough. They had done some digging and discovered her relationship with Claude in Paris. "Do you want a woman in the White House who has had an affair with a French national while she was still married to the President?" one of the attack ads said. Carol was put on the defensive. She immediately issued a statement to the press saying that she had not been disloyal to James, and that her friend, Claude was just that, only a friend. But there were leaks to the press that Carol had indeed gone to Paris and slept with her "friend".

This was all very disturbing to Carol. She knew she had done nothing wrong, but the distressing part was that she couldn't get her message out. Every time she tried to talk about real issues, the questions were flying about her affair with a French man. Were they holding her to a higher standard than all of the candidates that had gone before her? She felt there was indeed a double standard; if she were male, the media would likely have not brought it up. She called a press conference, hoping to put this issue to rest for good.

"When I was in Paris, I did meet a man there who became a very dear friend," Carol said with about thirty reporters gathered around and millions watching the televised news conference. "He was a very kind person and provided me with a safe haven when I needed it." Carol paused, trying to hide the tears that were beginning to well in her eyes. She cleared her throat and continued. "After I was divorced I went back to Paris to see Claude. He asked me marry him and I told him that I couldn't do that as I had unfinished business at home. Andrew was still in Iraq or a place unknown at the time and my first commitment was to him. Did we have an affair? Yes, I guess you could call it that. I did sleep with him as I loved him very much. It was not a decision taken lightly; I was not married at the time and I am an adult woman," Carol said, thinking how politics intrudes into your personal life. These things were really none of anyone's business but hers. But that is what American politics had become of late.

"Are you still thinking of marrying him?" a young male reporter in the third row back asked.

"No, I called him when I first decided to run for this office, and told him that I would be running for president and should I win the presidency could not possibly marry him for at least four years. And since he is no longer a young man, and looking for a partner, that he should find someone else. It made me very sad but I had to make a choice and I am staying with that choice."

"Then who would be our First Lady, uh, I mean First Man if you are elected? Who will take on the social duties of the White House?" asked a young woman in the back row.

"I will have a team to do that; my secretary and whomever she hires as her team," Carol shot back. "Now I want to put this kind of talk to bed... oh, poor choice of words...." There was laughter from the audience. "to rest, I meant, and get on with the important issues concerning the people of this country; the economy, the wars, housing, education and healthcare to name a few."

The press conference was a success, Carol had leveled with the press and the country, told the truth and the question seldom came up again. Of course the ongoing question was her competence to run the country, being only a junior senator, having not yet finished law school, but Carol went back in history and pointed out other presidents who had less experience then she had, who had then been very successful after they were elected. "How can someone possibly train for this job?" she implored one afternoon at one of her rallies. "You can't. But if a person is first of all smart, honest, hard working, can work with all kinds of people in difficult situations, and cares about the country, those are just some of the qualifications. And above all else that person needs to be a leader, have a vision, showing the way for her people to go and helping them to get there. I have all of those qualifications and I have the vision."

The gap was narrowing by September. Polls across the country showed Carol ahead by three percent. She still had work to do.

Chapter 42

Information Highway

If the election were held today and only eighteen to thirty-five year olds were voting, Carol would win in a landslide. This was partly due to her presence on the Information Highway, the World Wide Web. The Internet was another tool for raising money for Carol's campaign, posting events and bolstering her cause. Not that older, over thirty-five year olds didn't Google and access the Internet, but it was the younger people that spent hours on MySpace, YouTube, and the blogs.

Andrew was the mastermind in getting this network organized for his mother. He had contacted a friend from Colorado University who was a professional web designer, and this very talented person created the Carol Walters for President web site. Carol's campaign team, many in their twenties, were excited about using these online venues and confident that it would give her an edge and it had. She had a presence in all of these Internet places twenty-four by seven. Every speech, every town hall meeting was recorded on DVD and downloaded to YouTube within hours, even minutes of the event and some of the events were live via pod cast as the event was happening. She had a question and answer forum on MySpace and volunteers working the blogs and message boards, blogging her talking points and touting her ideas throughout cyberspace.

Traditional media, newspapers, television and radio were fast becoming obsolete; by the time a major event happened, and hours before it was reported on network news, it had been seen on the Internet. Carol wanted to take advantage of this powerful scene. As yet, her opponent hadn't understood the value of the Internet. And, although they had a web site, it was nowhere near the same quality and presence as Carol's.

There was another interesting phenomenon happening among young Evangelicals and the religious right; they were, in large numbers abandoning the support of the wedge issues their parents had supported, issues like gay marriage and abortion and were embracing poverty in America and environmental issues. They saw the disconnect, of forcing poor women to bring babies into the world and not being able to feed and clothe those children. And they could not see how same sex marriage was a threat to the traditional marriage.

Labor Day was fast approaching. Carol and her team were in the air more than on the ground, literally hopping from city to city, holding town hall meetings, breakfasts, lunches with potential voters and fund raising dinners. It was all beginning to become one big blurred event to Carol and she often thought to herself as she was shuttled from airport to airport, city to city and another downtown Hilton, that she would be glad when this was all over, regardless of the outcome. She sometimes didn't even know what city she was in. And she often thought about how hectic it was going to be if she won. Taking on the responsibility of the whole country, and in some instances the world, was definitely a huge job in anyone's imagination. It was no wonder that a young president would age twenty years in an eight-year term. She hoped it would not be like that for her. She intended to surround herself with the most competent people she could find and delegate. She would lead and it would be her policies that she would try to promote, but she would have others doing the majority of the work.

The Gallup Poll was showing that she and her running mate were running even with Heron. "I can't understand this," she said to Andrew one evening as they were getting off the plane in Columbus. "But it has to be my gender and perceived lack of experience."

"I think you're probably right. But I don't think the people really know you yet and when they do, they'll find out that you have their best interest at heart. And that isn't true of Douglas Heron. He represents only a small segment of America, mainly the wealthy."

On the day after Labor Day, Carol and Alan were in flight on their way to the battleground state of Ohio. Andrew had "crashed" in the first three seats in the front of the airplane and five team members were eating donuts and drinking coffee while busily finalizing plans for the town hall meeting that was to be held at the convention center in downtown Columbus, when they heard snippets of the morning news of a shooting in California.

Alan walked to the back of the plane where Carol was sitting to tell her what he knew. "Heron has been shot. It happened at the airport."

Carol looked up at him in disbelief. "Well, is he... is he okay?"

She opened up her laptop and immediately went to the CNBC news site. And there it was. "Douglas Heron, Patriot presidential candidate, was shot twice in the arm around nine this morning at the Los Angeles Airport as he was walking from his plane to his SUV, parked on the tarmac nearby. Secret Service sprawled over him, knocking him to the ground, but they may have saved his life. He was taken to a local Los Angeles hospital for treatment. No one else was hurt in the incident. "

"I hope he's okay. This is not good. Did they catch the shooter?" Carol looked up at Alan in a concerned way. The threat of assassination was always in the back of every candidate's mind as well as the president's. Carol knew throughout American history, four presidents had been killed while in office; Abraham Lincoln in 1865, James Garfield in 1881, William McKinley in 1901 and John F. Kennedy in 1963. And she was aware of the numerous assassination attempts on many presidents, one coming very close to killing President Reagan in 1981 and of course the very tragic assassination of Bobby Kennedy when he was running for the presidency in 1968. Since then, every major candidate is assigned Secret Service detail, usually 120 days before the election, to ensure their safety.

"Did they catch the shooter?" Carol was still surfing the web on her laptop trying to find information. "Oh, look here, they did." At the very bottom of the article, she read that they had determined where the shots came from and had the Secret Service on it in minutes; they found the sniper and shot him dead. "No more information about the shooter at this time, not even a name. This is tragic. But it sounds like Heron wasn't too badly wounded and that is good."

"I agree, having your opponent die is not a good thing. You don't want to win by default," said Alan as he sat down beside Carol. "Now are you up for this next town hall meeting? This is enemy territory. These people are long time Republicans and now favor the Patriot party and trying to convince them that they've been voting against their own self interest all these years is going to be a challenge."

"Yes, maybe. But working people are really hurting right now. When you have to make a choice between putting gas in your car and buying groceries, new ideas should resonate." The strategy from the beginning of the campaign was to go after the Red states as they felt reasonably confident the Blue states would continue to support them and that seemed to be holding true. So, even though they had teams in every state, they had more of a concentration in the battle ground states of the South East, the upper Mid West and the heartland states. They needed 270 electoral votes to win. The east and west coast states were sewn up and if they could win in Ohio and Indiana, they would be in good shape to reach their goal. Colorado was a given being that was Carol's home state.

Alan and Carol were back stage at the convention center where they were scheduled to speak, when Harry Stone, one of the Ohio liaisons approached.

"Have you heard the news recently?" he asked.

"No, what is it now?" Carol looked at him incredulously.

"They found out that the guy that shot Heron had ties to one of our campaign managers."

"That can't be," said Alan. "We vet our people very carefully, especially our managers."

"It's all over the news. So when you go out there be prepared to answer questions about this. These people are not exactly our friends. I'm just warning you."

"Who was it in our campaign that he had ties to?" asked Carol.

"Don Baker, our man in Washington D.C.," said Harry.

"I don't believe this. I've known Don for years. And I know his family; none of them would ever do this. He worked on Walter's re-election team. This has to be a mistake." She looked around the room searching for someone and then she saw the person she was looking for. "Marv, please come over here," she called.

Marv, tall with red hair in his mid thirties, approached. "What do you need Mrs. Walters?"

She and Alan told him what they had heard. "I want you to dig deeper into this story. I think there is something very wrong here. I think the Patriots are up to more dirty tricks. We need to expose them in this dishonesty," said Carol.

Alan looked at her admiringly. "Spoken like a true politician. I think you will make it yet."

"You had your doubts, Alan?" Carol retorted.

"No, Carol, you are one of the strongest women I've ever known and I know that no matter what happens, you will prevail."

They walked out together onto the stage and into the bright lights. There was polite applause. Then she heard a chanting rise up, "We need jobs, we need jobs" being repeated over and over again. These people were in a world of hurt and they were crying out for help.

Carol raised her hands and asked them quiet down. "Well, that is why we are here. You do need jobs, you can't feed your families on minimum wages, I know that and that is exactly what we intend to fix." The roar went up from the crowd. And Carol laid out for them her plan to rebuild the country's infrastructure, the crumbling bridges and roads, and told them how that would keep jobs in the United States, good jobs. She told them about developing alt fuels and the many benefits, including not having to wage wars any longer in the Middle East. She told them how making the public and corporate buildings in cities green would bring even more jobs to the country.

"They can't outsource these jobs," she shouted. "These will be your jobs and you will be whole again."

"Not one question about the shooter," Alan said as they were leaving.

"You know, I think some of the people are on to the tricks being played," Carol said. "But we'll see what the polls have to say about this."

It later came out that the shooter had once been briefly married to a third cousin of Don Baker's wife, certainly not a close relative by any means and that he had a history of mental illness. This was reported by the press, but quickly became a back page story. And the people had moved on. Carol was confronted with a couple of questions about the shooter at every campaign stop, but they seemed to be at ease with her answers, having more trust in her. But Carol would always wonder; was this guy recruited by the Patriots? Or did he act on his own. She would most likely never know.

Chapter 43

The End is in Sight

Andrew was tiring of the twenty-four by seven campaign schedule. After his return from Iraq, he had spent six weeks in the hospital recuperating and rebuilding his strength and he was just now beginning to feel like the old Andrew before the horrific experience he had had while being held captive. And he was becoming more cynical and questioned his mother's sincerity in wanting to help turn the country around or had she now become power hungry like his dad when he had been president. In his mind it was like being a rock star and getting drunk on the crowds. It was compelling having people cheering and grabbing at you and thinking you are god-like and can do anything, almost messianic in nature. But that was the character of American politics, and politics around the world for that matter. He saw, however, as he had known for a long time, that in America, it wasn't the people who chose their leaders, it was the corporations, providing the funds and promoting the candidate they thought would be in their corner, passing favorable legislation for them along with tort reform. Even with campaign finance reform, large corporations had found loopholes to funnel money to the candidates that would favor their companies. Corporations are only beholden to shareholders and the bottom line and could care less about Americans as a whole. That was how the country had gotten to be in such terrible trouble in the past eight years. And big business didn't like his mother, so that did confirm one thing to him, that she did, after all have some sincerity in wanting to represent the people of the country.

He also had been wondering how Simone was doing. He had heard about what she had done to try to help him get released and about her horrendous ordeal and he would be forever grateful to her. He hadn't known when they were together, how much she really cared for him.

It was the end of a busy October day in Washington. They had returned to his mother's townhouse in Alexandria; he had yet to find his own place, not being sure what he was going to do for the next few years. He thought he might call Simone and thank her for her heroic efforts. He tried calling their old apartment and of course the number had been disconnected. Then he tried calling her parents home and a woman, most likely her mother, answered the phone. When he asked for Simone, she asked who was calling and he told her. "Just a minute," she said coldly.

"Yes, this is Simone. Andrew, is that you? Are you well?"

"Yes, I am, thanks to you and the many others who were looking for me. I'm so deeply sorry for what happened to you. You are the most courageous woman. I want to thank you for everything that you did."

There was a silence, neither Andrew nor Simone knowing what to say next.

"When are you coming to Paris, for god's sake?" asked Simone.

"Do you really want to see me after all of this?"

"Yes, I think about you every day. And I'd love to see you. And then, who knows…"

"Well, okay then. I will. I'll be there next month. And like you say, who knows. I still think about you as well, every day."

November rolled in with a vengeance. Early snows blanketed Washington and the New England states while tornadoes ripped across Indiana into Oklahoma. In the West, unusually high winds were downing thousands of trees along the coastal areas while record snowfalls closed roads and ski areas in the Tahoe area of California.

The election was days away and Carol and her people were making a last ditch effort, hopping across the nation, visiting two and three states a day. The polls showed this to be a very close race; one day she was ahead by five points and the next behind by as many. It appeared that different polls showed different results, and so the question remained of how accurate these polls actually were. And Carol worried. She worried that she had not done enough campaigning, that she had not gotten her message across to enough people.

She was concerned about another problem and that was the voting system and her people shared that concern. It varied from state to state. There were new systems in place in Ohio and Florida, a touch screen computerized system that, according to two prior elections had not been reliable. This same system had been purchased and then thrown out in California, due to the system not working correctly. There was the nagging problem with computer systems in general; they could be hacked and they had no paper trail. Potentially a programmer, if they knew the system, could change the votes with one line of code. It was too late now to worry about such things, but she vowed that if she was elected she would push for a uniform system that was easy to use and had a paper trail to allow for accurate recounts. There were several states across the country that had such systems in place.

Arriving back home in Colorado, a day before the election, Carol and Andrew began to wind down and relax. There was nothing more to do at this point but to watch and wait. Many of the votes in the country had already been cast with mail-in ballots, absentee ballots, those who were in the armed services overseas, expatriates living abroad, in Mexico, South and Central America and elsewhere in the world.

Election Day was here. Carol had slept for a full eight hours the night before. She was ebullient and felt confident they would win this; she was about to become the first woman president of the United Sates of America.

The returns started to come in early. And they were predictable on the East Coast. She was winning in New York, New Jersey, Massachusetts, Vermont, and Delaware. The Southern States were a different story however, with the Carolinas going to her opponent as well as Florida. But later in the evening there were some surprises. Ohio, Indiana and Michigan voters were voting for her. But then as the votes were being counted across the Midwestern states, Carol's lead began to diminish.

Carol and Andrew had arrived at the Hilton Garden Inn in downtown Denver at about ten o'clock that evening. A loud and boisterous cheer rang through the main ballroom as they entered. "Speech", they chanted in unison. "Victory is ours," they yelled. Carol walked up to the podium and spoke to her supporters. "I am hopeful that we will have a victory tonight. But clearly it is too soon to tell. It was predictable that we would prevail in the Eastern Seaboard states and we are running close in the Midwestern states. I do think when the tallies come in from California, Oregon and Washington State that this should give us a boost in electoral votes. So at this point, even though I would like to declare victory, we will have to wait and see. Just keep those positive thoughts and hopefully later tonight, we will be the clear winners." Her supporters chanted "Change is coming, Change is coming" as she left the podium.

By 1:00 a.m., the race was so close that it could go either way. Most exit polls showed her winning in Minnesota, Wisconsin and Iowa, but as the tally of votes came back in, she was behind by a small percentage in every one of those states and in some running neck and neck with Douglas Heron. Carol and Andrew left the hotel to go back to her apartment where they could watch the returns coming in from the West Coast and hopefully get some rest.

Andrew looked over at his mom as they were riding through the streets of Denver. "I know how you must feel. But even if you lose, you've fought a valiant battle."

"I know what you're going to say, Andy, it's not whether you win or lose …. But I don't buy that in this case. This nation is in need of an overhaul and if Heron gets in, it will be business as usual on K Street and the little guy will most certainly lose."

There was silence between them for the rest of the ride. Then when they were back in the apartment, Andrew told his mother of his plans.

"I'm going back to Paris after the election," Andrew blurted.

"You're going back to see Simone?"

"Yes." Andrew looked at the TV then back at his mother. "I could be staying there with her and marrying her."

Carol felt a stab in her stomach, but she didn't want to let on to her son. "I know how you must feel about her. Simone was a courageous woman in trying to help you."

"But what? You were going to say But…" Andrew said looking squarely at his mother. "I do think I love her and isn't that what's important?"

"Yes, Andrew that is what counts in a marriage." She did not want to say, but you are leaving me all alone, I have no one else now and I need you more than ever. No, that wouldn't be fair to Andrew, but she thought it.

The results would not be in tonight. They both dragged off to their beds hoping to hear good news in the morning.

Carol awoke the next morning to the phone ringing and turned on the TV. The news told her what she was waiting to hear. She had won in the majority of states in the West, even Arizona.

"Andrew, we did it. We won. I am the new president elect of the greatest nation in the world."

Andrew poked his head out of his bedroom door. "I know, Mom."

Her opponent conceded later that morning. She had done it. She and her team. And now the work was just beginning. Would she be able to live up to the standards she had set forth? Would she be able to put the country back on track again and make it the country it had been and that the forefathers had foreseen? A place where everyone had a chance, where people counted. Yes, the work had just begun.

Chapter 44

The Lady is President

With the world watching and her son at her side, Carol raised her hand and repeated the words read to her by Chief Justice Rutledge. "I Carol Walters do solemnly swear that I will faithfully execute the office of the President of the United States, and will, to the best of my ability, preserve, protect and defend the Constitution of the United States."

Her eyes again moistened with tears as she recalled another inauguration, when she was standing beside her husband as he proclaimed those very words eight long years ago. She remembered the excitement and the hope but also the trepidation and foreboding she felt that day and now, here she was standing on these same steps, saying the same words.

Carol looked out over the throngs of people cheering and raising their hands above their heads in victory, people who believed in her to lead them back from the brink and into prosperous and peaceful times once again. It was now up to her to repair the devastating damage that had been done to the country in the last eight years. It would take a monumental effort and a part of her wondered if it was even possible. The last administration had started two wars, Afghanistan and Iraq and gutted most social programs to pay for these wars. With jobs leaving the country, middle-income workers could no longer count on supporting their families in a time when housing costs had risen seventy-five percent in the last four years alone and inflation on the rise. And the environment had been violated in the worst ways, with mercury levels rising in ground water due to unfettered emissions from power plants, running to oceans making fish unfit to eat. New roads were snaking through National Parks, with old laws relaxed allowing the cutting of old growth forests and drilling and mining, laying waste to the land in the name of corporate greed.

But Carol had a plan and with the support of congress and the American people, she hoped to make this country great again. Her first official proclamation was to cancel the expensive Inaugural balls and donate the money that would have been spent to the Federal School Lunch Program for the poor, another program that had been gutted by her husband's administration. She decided that a simple reception in the rotunda of the White House would be fitting, with the public invited, as many as could be allowed in a day's time, bringing back the government by the people for the people.

Carol turned to her son and kissed and held him for a moment, then stepped up to the podium to talk to the people of the country and the world. She felt a shiver for a moment and it was not from the temperature. The day was uncannily warm for this time of the year, the sun shining brightly out of the clear blue sky, an omen she thought. Her once dark brown hair turned gray, peaked out from under her royal blue hat, and she looked presidential in her matching worsted suit.

"This is an historic moment and I am honored that you have selected me to lead our great country out of the past and into the new century. "

Carol paused, took a deep breath, taking in the magnanimity of the moment.

"We have been on a journey in this country for the past 200 years, but recently we seemed to have lost our way. We have been floundering in the wilderness and it is time to get back to the path that we, as a great nation, had started on so long ago. It is time to fulfill the vision of our forefathers; the vision George Washington fought for in liberating our country from the dominance of the British so that we could be free to pursue our own destiny in the way we saw fit. The vision of Thomas Jefferson in creating the Declaration of Independence, the vision Abraham Lincoln had in preserving our country and the abolition of slavery and the vision that Lyndon Johnson carried further in invoking civil rights laws many years later, declaring that we are all equal under the law no matter what the color of our skin or our gender. I stand here before you, the forty fourth president, humbled by all that these men and others have achieved. It is time now to find the right path for everyone, not just the few and return to the journey that our forefathers had envisioned when they formed this great nation so many years ago."

The applause was deafening. Carol looked over the sea of faces before her and acknowledged their exuberant support. She raised her hand to quiet them and went on with her speech.

"A nation formed by people looking for opportunity in a great country with untold resources and a promise of wealth for anyone willing to work hard enough to get it. A nation formed by people looking for freedom to live their lives as they saw fit, to worship as they pleased without government dictating to them, a nation where the rule of law is paramount to the core principles, protecting everyone from tyranny and lawlessness. We are going to make this a country where quality public education, the cornerstone of democracy is available to all and this includes higher education and a country where everyone has the chance to realize their dreams. A country where corporations serve the people and bring well paying jobs back to this country so that people can afford to buy the products they are manufacturing. "

Carol paused again and waited for the applause.

"We are getting back on the path of planning for the future, for our children and our grandchildren and preserving what was once perceived as unlimited and bountiful, but is indeed finite. We are getting back on the path of fiscal responsibility so that our children and grandchildren will not have to pay our bills. And we are going to get back on the path to social responsibility. Survival of the fittest is an archaic way for people of a civilized country to behave. We can provide if need be, in this wealthy nation, the basics for everyone; housing, enough food to eat and health care for all."

There was silence but Carol went on.

"This all costs money and how are we going to pay for this, you might ask? We will be going on a fast track program to develop alternative fuels, wind and solar, and in doing so will create new, good jobs in America. We will no longer have to depend on foreign fossil fuels from the Middle East and elsewhere. And we will bring our troops home from Iraq and Afghanistan as soon as it is feasibly possible to do so without doing more damage to those regions."

The crowd roared with enthusiasm and waved miniature American flags.

"Once we are back on that path, we can begin to heal a very sick nation and I want you to be partners in this effort. Let us work together to get back on the path to prosperity and peace for all throughout the land."

"Thank you. I will not let you down."

Later that day Carol and Andrew were sitting in the family quarters of the White House talking about events of the day and about what the future might bring. Carol was hopeful, with the competent team she had been assembling over the last several months, that during this next four and hopefully eight years, she would be able to carry out her programs and the country would have a very different landscape by 2012 and beyond. She knew that those who opposed her and her policies would be continuously trying to knock her down, but, she thought when the economy starts turning around and people have jobs again so they can afford to pay for shelter and food and other essentials, she would have their support and they would then help her thwart these attacks from her foes.

"Well, Mom, you did it. You have reached the pinnacle, a place that no other woman has been in America. I was doubtful at first that you could, but I am blown away by it," Andrew said, thinking of the election and all of the events leading up to it.

"No, I haven't yet. Not until the people of this country are in a place where all have the opportunity to better themselves, and I accomplish all or most of my goals will I feel that I have done it."

There was a silence for a time.

"And, Andy, you can call me any time from Paris," said Carol. "And if you want to come back and help out I wouldn't be unhappy about that. And bring Simone with you."